JD KIRK

A DEATH MOST MONUMENTAL

CANELOCRIME

Penguin
Random
House

First published in the United Kingdom in 2020 by Zertex Crime

This edition published in the United Kingdom in 2024 by

Canelo Crime, an imprint of
DK Publishing, a division of Penguin Random House LLC
1745 Broadway, 20th Floor, New York, NY 10019

The authorized representative in the EEA is Dorling Kindersley Verlag GmbH.
Arnulfstr. 124, 80636 Munich, Germany

ISBN 9798217261277

Cover design by Tom Sanderson

Cover images © Shutterstock

Look for more great books at
www.canelo.co | www.dk.com

‒

154078558

A Death Most Monumental

JD Kirk is the author of the multi-million bestselling DCI Logan series, set in the Highland s of Scotland . He also d oes not exist. Instead , JD is the pen name of former child ren's author and screenwriter, Barry Hutchison, who was born and raised in Fort William. He still lives in the Highland s with his wife and child ren. He has no id ea what the JD stand s for.

Also by JD Kirk

DCI Logan Crime Thrillers

A Litter of Bones
Thicker than Water
The Killing Code
Blood and Treachery
The Last Bloody Straw
A Whisper of Sorrows
The Big Man Upstairs
A Death Most Monumental
A Snowball's Chance in Hell
Ahead of the Game
An Isolated Incident
Colder than the Grave
Come Hell or High Water
City of Scars
Here Lie the Dead
One For the Ages
In Service of Death
A Dead Man Walking
Where the Pieces Lie
A Killer of Influence

Chapter 1

Ian Hill was going to spot a black-throated loon tod ay, even if it fucking killed him.

He'd been coming to this spot before the crack of d awn all week, making the twenty-mile d rive from Fort William with his camera gear and waterproofs, convinced each time that tod ay would be the d ay. Tod ay, he would clap eyes on one of the bird s, and snap a photograph or two to prove it.

Every d ay so far, he'd been wrong. Every d ay so far, they'd elud ed him.

Now, time was running out. On Frid ay, he was d ue to return home to Kent, back to his wife and child ren, back to the office and the d aily grind . Tod ay was Wed nesd ay, which meant he had tod ay and tomorrow to get his photograph. Less than forty-eight hours to make the trip and the expense all worthwhile.

It was early—need lessly early, some would argue. It was head ing into late September, so the first fingers of light would n't creep across the sky until just before seven. Even if he heard the loon's d istinctive croak, or the panicky 'uweek' if it sensed d anger, he would n't be able to see it. But it would give him somewhere to aim the camera, in the hope he was pointing it in the right d irection when the sun eventually d ecid ed to rise.

Besid es, while he had n't managed to get a photo of a black-throated loon so far, he'd filled a whole memory card with pictures of the d awn breaking over Loch Shiel. As consolation prizes went, they weren't too shabby.

He wasn't really into land scapes, as a rule, but he mad e an exception for this place. From his vantage point by the Glen-finnan Monument, he could see right along the loch as the sun rose on the left, d appling first the mountains and hills on the right, then the water itself with d ancing strand s of gold en light.

Assuming, of course, that it wasn't pissing d own.

Ian cast his gaze skyward s and saw the faint twinkling of d istant stars. That bod ed well for a rain-free morning, although if the last week had taught him anything it was that even now, at the tail end of summer, some form of precipitation was never far away.

Now that his camera was all set up and read y to go, he unscrewed the lid of his flask, brought it to his nose, and inhaled d eeply as he carefully popped the plastic top off.

Coffee. Black and hot. Was there anything better on a morning like this?

He took a sip, and immed iately felt a little jolt of energy, getting a psychological boost from the caffeine before the actual physical one had time to hit. It would kick in soon, though, firing him up for what was likely to be another long d ay of stand ing around .

It wasn't even that the black-throated loon—or black-throated d iver, as the few locals he'd met who'd d emonstrated even a passing interest in the subject referred to it—was a partic-ularly interesting bird .

Certainly, they weren't the most visually striking. Not in an area where gold en eagles, white-tailed eagles, peregrine falcons, and more could all be spotted . From a purely eye-catching perspective, even the red -throated loon was more noteworthy, although a far more common sighting across much of the northern hemisphere.

The black-throated loon's population was in d ecline, but not so sharply that anyone was all that fussed about them. Although Loch Shiel had been d esignated a Special Protection Area, d ue to its importance as a breed ing ground for the bird s, so evid ently someone somewhere was concerned enough to fill out the required paperwork to make that happen.

All in all, though, there was nothing spectacular about the bird . And yet, Ian had found himself d rawn to the black-throated loon for some time now. He knew why, of course.

How long had it been since his d ad had brought him up here? Since they'd hud d led sid e by sid e, eating meat paste sand wiches, and watching two of the bird s swimming together on these very same waters? Thirty years? Thirty-five?

Ian had mad e the d ecision at the funeral. He would come back. He'd bring his own child ren. He'd relive the experience with them that he'd had with his old man. It would be a great bond ing moment. A memory of a shared experience, passed d own through the generations, from his father to him, and from him to them.

They had n't been interested , of course. They were too old , they said . Too busy. Too wrapped up in pubs and girls and God knew what else.

Jasmine, his wife, had n't been keen on the id ea, either. She'd offered fewer excuses, but had mad e up for that with a brutal honesty that had once been ad orable, but which these d ays stabbed at him like a knife in the back.

'Not really my cup of tea,' she'd said . Then, when he'd pushed her on it, 'Come off it, Ian, it sound s boring as fuck.'

And so, he'd come alone. Him, his camera, and his memories, d etermined to catch sight of the bird s, even if they seemed equally d etermined to stay out of sight.

Soon they'd be clearing off for the winter, feet pattering across the surface of the water before they launched themselves southward , far beyond the reach of his lens.

They'd be back next year, but he would n't. Jasmine had almost talked him out of coming this time, but had eventually told him to go and get it out of his system. Any talk of him returning the following breed ing season would only lead to arguments, and he'd had enough of those to last him a lifetime.

No. This was it. This, here, now, was his one and only chance.

He took another sip of his coffee and clicked on his pocket torch, using the beam to double-check the camera's settings. He had a variety of lenses lined up in a case at the base of the tripod, ready to whip on and off depending on where the bird might show.

Because they would show today. He could feel it. Today would not be like the other days. Today would be different. Today he'd get what he came for, then tomorrow he'd have a long lie, take a wander through Fort William, and treat himself to something nice to eat. Haggis, maybe. He'd never tried haggis. Surely one of the local restaurants did haggis? Missing a trick, if not.

A croaky groan rang out through the darkness. Ian instinctively pointed his torch straight down at the ground, but otherwise didn't move.

He listened, breath held, for the sound to come again, desperately trying to force his eyes to read just to the gloom.

Moving slowly, he reached for the tripod and found the handle. If the sound came again, he'd be ready. He could pinpoint it, aim the lens, be ready for the first suggestion of sunlight. He could do this. He was going to do this.

The sound came again. A creak. Not what he'd been expecting, nor where he'd been expecting.

It was behind him, over by the monument, somewhere up high.

Shuffling around in a half-circle, Ian raised his torch, and the misshapen oval of light went speeding across the sand and the scrub of the shore until it found the base of the towering stone column.

His eyes darted ahead of it, racing the light, finding an unexpected bulge protruding from the top of the monument's wall.

The torchlight caught up half a second later, turning the shapeless bulge into something all-too recognisable.

Something all too awful.

Thoughts of the black-throated loon took to the air and left him as, standing alone in the shadow of the Glenfinnan Monument, with the waters of Loch Shiel lapping at the land behind him, Ian Hill opened his mouth and screamed.

Chapter 2

Detective Chief Inspector Jack Logan of the Police Scotland Major Investigations Team ran through the streets of Inverness, sweat slicking his skin, his legs and chest competing to see which could most feel like they were on fire.

The particular street he was running on this morning was Sir Walter Scott Drive, out on the east sid e of the city. And a long, flat, featureless bastard of a thing it was, too.

Nose-to-tail early morning traffic snarled its way toward s the city centre, each vehicle creeping incrementally forward whenever the lights changed at the big Raigmore round about d own at the end of the road .

To the frustrated observers sitting in those cars, saying Logan was 'running' might have seemed generous. It was more like 'accelerated plod d ing', the d etective's gaze fixed on the pavement a couple of metres ahead of him, his big feet pound ing the ground in his cartoonishly large trainers.

He was not built for running. That's what he had told everyone who asked how his new fitness regime was going. It should 've been obvious, he thought, just by looking at him, that a man of his height and build was not d esigned to move at speed . He was much more 'immovable object' than 'unstoppable force', and this thrice-weekly running regime was like something from a blood y nightmare.

Granted , it was probably necessary. He'd barely passed the bleep test that had been set for him by Detective Superintend ent Mitchell a few weeks earlier. In fact, he had n't passed it the first time at all, after one of his laces had come und one and he'd shed a trainer halfway through the third sprint, much to the amusement of the rest of the MIT.

He'd been allowed to repeat it half an hour later, this time with the trainers d ouble-knotted . It had been a close call, but he'd mad e the required number of bleeps before head ing back insid e the station and projectile vomiting in the visitor's toilet.

That was then. This was now.

Things had improved slightly in those few weeks, but not much.

He'd mad e the mistake a few minutes ago of thinking about how he was breathing. Until then, air had been entering and leaving his lungs without any real d ifficulty. Now, though, merely by thinking about the process, he'd turned it into a panicky, chest-tightening ord eal that was likely to end in either hyperventilation or no ventilation at all. It was impossible at the moment to say which.

A jogger approached him in the opposite d irection, all springy feet and swishy ponytail. He momentarily forced his legs to pick up speed —or at least to carry him in something resembling a straight line—and hoped to Christ he wasn't crying.

'Morning,' the young woman chirped , all perky and bright.

Given his current struggle to remember how to breathe, replying was completely out of the question. He tried to smile at her instead . Although, given the look of mild horror on her face as she passed , he guessed whatever expression he pulled fell some way off the mark.

They continued in opposite d irections, her bound ing on, him letting out a pained whimper as those few second s of increased speed took their toll on his bod y.

How long had he been running? He could n't say. The app-thing that Shona Maguire had mad e him install on his phone clearly wasn't working, because it was supposed to have beeped long before now to tell him to go back to walking.

Maybe it was his fault, he reasoned , as the smell of the McDonald 's breakfast menu wafted tantalisingly over to him from the Inshes Retail Park. Maybe he had n't pressed the start button. Maybe he should knock it on the head tod ay, and try again tomorrow. No point putting himself through all this if the app wasn't even on.

The bastard ing thing beeped in his ear just before he could stop.

'Walk now,' it announced in a robotic voice so cheerfully upbeat he instinctively wanted to punch it in its non-existent face. 'One minute until next five-minute run. You are on run two of five.'

'Christ!' Logan ejected , startling another approaching jogger and causing them to cross to the other sid e of the road .

He tried to limit the d amage with another smile, then remembered how well the last one had gone d own, and d ecid ed not to bother.

Instead , he spent the next fifty-od d second s frantically gulping air into his aching chest. Then, without warning, the app chimed in his ear again and a voice he'd never tire of kicking ord ered him to resume running.

'Oh, fuck off!' he told it, d rawing looks from the closest cars.

But, d espite his protest, he d id as he was told . He accelerated his plod d ing.

He'd never hear the end of it if he d id n't.

–

Detective Inspector Ben Ford e chewed thoughtfully on the last of his Crunchy Nut Cornflakes and regard ed the crossword page of the newspaper currently spread out on his kitchen worktop. He'd almost finished the puzzle now, although he had n't bothered to write any of the answers in.

Someone had once told him that mentally d oing a crossword puzzle was a good way of training the memory. He forgot who.

'Three d own. *Not suitable for the role*,' he read aloud . 'Five letters.'

His spoon rattled in his bowl as he scooped up the last of the milk and the few soggy crumbs left floating in it. He slurped it d own, his gaze still fixed on the page.

With his other hand , he fid d led with the thin chain he'd taken to wearing around his neck some months previously. The improvised pend ants on the end of it brushed against his chest beneath his shirt.

'Not suitable for the role,' he said again, putting a slightly d ifferent emphasis on it this time, which he found sometimes helped . 'Five letters. Not suitable for the role.'

Ben stared ahead at the kitchen wall, his tongue id ly sweeping his breakfast off his teeth. 'What blood y role?' he wond ered , before checking the intersecting clues to see if he had alread y figured out any of the letters in the word .

He had n't.

Or not that he could remember, anyway.

'Not suitable,' he said , breaking the clue d own into sections. He found this sometimes helped , too. 'For the role.'

Before he could d well on it much longer, the kitchen d oor flew open, and a bear in a tracksuit came stumbling in, all wheezing and sweaty.

Ben looked d own at the crossword and took out his mental pen. 'Unfit,' he said .

Logan closed the d oor with an unintentional bang, leaned against it in raspy-breathed silence for several second s, then somehow found the energy to nod his head . 'All right, Benjamin,' he gasped , clinging to the d oor like it was the only thing stopping him becoming a pud d le on the floor. 'No need to blood y rub it in.'

'I was about to phone you,' Ben said . 'You want the good news or the bad news?'

Logan groaned . He d id n't really want any news right at that particular moment. Or conversation. Or even company. What he wanted —what he would really love, more than anything— was a comfortable chair and a blast of oxygen. And , id eally, something for his blisters.

He'd settle for the chair, though.

'I only remembered to put the immerser on twenty minutes ago. The shower won't be very hot,' Ben said . He smiled apologetically. 'Sorry.'

'It's fine,' Logan said . His bod y felt like it had been d ipped in lava, and the careful application of some tepid water, while unlikely to be pleasant, would be bearable. 'What's the good news?'

'That is the good news. That I remembered to put it on at all,' Ben said .

Logan would 've frowned , but his face had been fixed in a permanent scowl for the past forty-five minutes, and those muscles were as knackered as the rest of them.

'Christ, what's the bad news, then?' he asked .

Ben's expression became solemn. 'We've had a shout,' he said . 'Teenage lassie. Glenfinnan.'

'Shite. Have you—?'

'Rallied the troops? Aye. They'll meet us at the station so we can pick up what we need to take d own the road . Mitchell's suggested Dave David son for Exhibits again. He's fine to relocate to Fort William for as long as we need him.'

Logan managed to grunt something vaguely positive-sound ing, then peeled himself off the back d oor. 'You should 've called me as soon as you heard ,' he said .

'I had it all und er control,' Ben said . He looked his old friend up and d own, a smile tugging at the corners of his mouth. 'Besid es, you might have shifted a few pound s—'

'Over a blood y stone, I'll have you know!' Logan objected .

'But you've still a way to go until you're fighting fit,' Ben conclud ed . He flicked his gaze up to the ceiling above them. 'Now, go get showered and d ressed , and I might be nice to you and cut up your grapefruit.'

Logan shot a forlorn look in the d irection of the frid ge and tried not to think about the smell of those Bacon and Egg McMuffins.

'Great,' he muttered , ignoring his rumbling stomach and forcing his legs to carry him in the d irection of the hall. 'I can hard ly blood y wait.'

Chapter 3

Logan untangled his legs from beneath the steering wheel of his Ford Fiesta and wrangled himself out of a car that had been carefully chosen for him for its entirely inappropriate size.

Burnett Road Police Station stood at the edge of the Longman Industrial Estate, glass glinting in the uncharacteristic Inverness sunshine.

This late in the summer, the sun rarely made more than a fleeting guest appearance, but it was up and about this morning in a rare display of keenness, and there was barely a cloud in the sky.

Unfortunately, none of this was reflected in Logan's mood, and he paid the warm caress of the sunshine precisely zero heed as he slammed the Fiesta's door closed with enough force to make both of the car's axles sharply squeal their objections.

He didn't bother locking it. There was nothing in there worth taking, and he'd consider it a massive stroke of good fortune if someone came along and nicked the car itself. He was tempted some days to leave the keys in the ignition and a 'Free to a Good Home' note on the wind screen. The only thing that stopped him was the thought of what vehicle Detective Superintendent Mitchell might saddle him with as punishment.

An electric scooter or a skateboard, maybe.

Or, God forbid, another Ford Fiesta.

DCs Tyler Neish and Sinead Bell were already in the Incident Room when he arrived, packing laptops and iPads into bags, and assembling everything else they'd need to take down to the Fort William station with them.

That station was fully equipped, of course, but being surrounded by the familiar generally helped them get settled in more quickly. Besides, Sinead had spent too long tracking down the red wool she used for the Big Board just to leave it in her desk drawer.

Sinead greeted the DCI with a smile and a little wave, while Tyler opted for his usual, 'All right, boss?' in a voice just a little too loud and a smidgeon too irritating.

Of the two, Tyler had been in plainclothes a good bit longer, although Sinead was rapidly proving herself to be just as competent in the role.

Actually, that was doing her a disservice. Even now, she was arguably better.

It wasn't that Tyler was bad at his job. He was generally solid, with the odd glaring mistake balanced by the occasional flash of brilliance that Logan purposefully never gave him enough credit for.

It was the only way the bugger was going to learn.

As the DCs were in a romantic relationship, there had been a real fight to get them both on the same team. DI Forde had spent whole days in discussions with the shadowy figures he referred to as 'the high heid yins,' and, when he'd finally convinced them to let the officers serve together, he'd made damn well sure that Tyler was aware all three of their necks were on the line if it went wrong.

To his credit, the lad had pulled his socks up there and then. He and Sinead were in the office earlier than the rest of the team most days, and if the couple had fallen out at any point in the last few months, neither one had shown it at work.

'Aye, no' bad,' Logan said, not bothering to shrug off his coat.

'Been running, sir?' Sinead asked. She had an uncanny ability to know when he'd been exercising, even when there were no outward signs of any recent exertion.

'Aye. Kind of,' Logan said, which he felt was a pretty accurate description.

'You're looking good . Weight's fairly shifting,' Sinead told him, tossing two balls of red wool and a packet of push pins into a box on her d esk.

Logan subtly sucked his gut in, ad d ing to the effect. He was pleased by the comment, but mad e every possible attempt not to show it. 'I should blood y hope so. I'm going to turn into a bastard ing grapefruit at this rate.'

Tyler's eyes narrowed in something like suspicion. He paused with a laptop halfway insid e a pad d ed case. 'How d oes running turn you into a grapefruit, boss?'

Logan regard ed him impassively for several second s, then gave a shake of his head . 'Doesn't matter. What's the latest from d own the road ?'

'Local CID and Uniform are on the scene, sir,' Sinead replied . 'Scene of Crime team is en route, and the Pathologist is head ing d own shortly.'

'I can give Dr Maguire a lift,' Logan suggested .

'You could , but she's not going, sir,' Sinead told him. 'Dr Rickett is on d uty this morning.'

Logan tried to hid e his d isappointment but mad e a pretty poor show of it. Although he'd d ealt almost exclusively with Shona Maguire on all his cases so far, he'd occasionally crossed paths with her colleague, Albert Rickett.

Albert was old er than Shona. In fact, he was consid erably old er than DI Ford e, which was saying something. Most of the polis and some of the hospital staff referred to him as 'Ricketts' for obvious, if not particularly kind , reasons.

Technically, he had retired a d ecad e ago, but it had been d ifficult to find a replacement, so he still worked part-time at Raigmore, keeping his hand in with the od d post-mortem. His sutures weren't as straight as they used to be, and much of the more mod ern technology involved in testing and analysis went some way over his head , but he was solid enough on the less complex cases.

Quite how he'd cope at a crime scene, though, was anyone's guess.

Ricketts was a crotchety old bastard , and so Logan d ecid ed to go ahead and assume that he alread y had transport arranged , and kept his mouth firmly shut on the subject.

'Morning, all,' said DI Ford e, strolling into the Incid ent Room with his waterproof jacket zipped up to the neck.

Logan shot a glance at the wind ow to make sure the sun was still blazing outsid e. 'What's with the jacket?' he asked .

'Fort Augustus Weather Nexus,' Ben replied . This meant nothing whatsoever to Logan and , jud ging by their faces, it d id n't make a whole lot more sense to Tyler or Sinead .

'Eh?'

Ben beamed , like he'd been d esperate for someone to ask. 'Fort Augustus Weather Nexus. Alice came up with it. She and I used to joke about it whenever we d rove that road . If you're head ing to Fort William and it's sunny in Inverness, it'll start pishing d oon from Fort Augustus. And vice versa. Sunny d own the road , wet by Fort Augustus. We called it the Weather Nexus.' He shrugged . 'I mean, neither of us knew what a "nexus" was, but it sound ed good .'

Something flickered behind his eyes, momentarily glazing them over. For months, Ben had been unable to say Alice's name, to allow himself to think too much about all their years together.

That had changed a few weeks back, but this new phase of grief had brought its own challenges.

'Daft, really,' he said .

'Aye, sound s like a load of blood y nonsense,' Logan said . He looked over at Sinead and Tyler. 'But better grab jackets and pack a brolly. I'm buggered if I'm letting Alice Ford e have the last laugh.'

Ben chuckled at that. 'Christ, can you imagine? She'd never let you hear the end of it.'

'I can just hear her now,' Logan said . *Fort Augustus Weather Nexus. You can't say you weren't warned.*'

'Uncanny,' Ben said . A look passed between them. A smile. A nod .

'Right, let's get our fingers out of our arses and get a shifty on,' Logan told the room. 'Where's Hamza?'

'Meeting us down there, boss,' Tyler said, zipping up the last laptop case. 'Already on the way.'

He picked up his mug from his desk, pulled a slightly horrified face when he looked inside, and then set it back down again. The mug had been a present from his mum, and had originally said, 'World's Greatest Detective' on the front.

Now, thanks to some careful application of Sharpie by an as-yet-unnamed fellow officer, it read *This Man is Not the* World's Greatest Detective,' and then had an arrow pointing upwards to where DC Neish's mouth would generally go.

If anything, it had just made Tyler love it all the more. Given what was growing at the bottom of it, though, he elected to leave it behind.

'Right, think that's us, sir,' Sinead said, folding over the top of the cardboard box she'd been packing.

'Good,' Logan began, before a thought occurred to him. 'What about Harris?'

Since the accident that had claimed the lives of their parents, Sinead had been responsible for her younger brother. He was a cracking wee lad, in Logan's experience, although no doubt he had his moments. Given everything he'd been through, though—including being taken hostage (twice)—he appeared to be a surprisingly balanced young man.

The DCI's question prompted Sinead to take her phone out of her pocket and check the screen. 'I'm hoping Auntie Val can get time off work to look after him,' she replied. 'He's getting a lift to school with a friend, but I need Val to pick him up.'

'No word from her?' Logan asked, reading the look on the Detective Constable's face.

'Nothing yet, no.'

Logan took the box from the desk in front of her and tucked it under one arm. 'Right, you two hang back here, then. Get Harris sorted, then hold off for the post-mortem. Head down the road once you've done that.'

'Post-mortem, boss?' DC Neish asked , his sculpted eyebrows d ipping in concern. 'You want us to go to the PM?'

'Aye,' Logan confirmed , eyes flitting briefly to Tyler, then back to Sinead . 'You haven't d one one yet, have you?'

'No, sir,' Sinead confirmed . 'Not yet. Be good to see what it's all about.'

'Aye, well, you can go in and I'll wait outsid e,' Tyler told her.

Logan clapped the younger man on the upper arm. 'Nonsense, son. I need your keen analytical mind in there,' he said . 'And , on a personal note, the thought of it'll amuse me all the way d own the road .'

Tyler groaned but gave a d ouble thumbs-up. 'Glad to be of assistance, boss.'

'Good lad . Right then, Benjamin. Wagons roll,' Logan announced . 'But this box is going in your car, because there's no way it's fitting in my boot.'

-

They almost mad e it to the lifts before the voice rang out behind them.

'DCI Logan? A word .'

Logan sighed , but quietly, so as not to let the woman behind him hear. Without a word , Ben took the box, hand ed Logan the three laptop bags he was carrying, and continued toward s the elevator with a whispered , 'Good luck.'

'Detective Superintend ent Mitchell,' Logan said , spinning a one-eighty on his heels.

The new DSup was physically far less imposing than her pred ecessor had been. She was shorter, slighter, and her d ark skin wasn't prone to the same blood rush bursts of tantrum-red that had so often coloured Hoon's face.

She d id n't share his booming voice, or his flair for creative bad language, either. And yet, Detective Superintend ent Chuki Mitchell could d o with one eyebrow what it had taken Bob

Hoon a clattering of furniture, a snarl, and a bellowed *Khob-jocking fucktards,*' to achieve.

The eyebrow was raised now, and Logan felt a momentary instinct to hoof it after Ben and jump into the lift before Mitchell could stop him.

But that would 've meant running, and his legs were in no mood for any more of that nonsense.

'What can I d o for you?' he asked , ad d ing, 'We were just on the way to a shout,' in the hope that it hurried things along.

It d id n't.

'I'm aware of that, Jack,' Mitchell said . She stepped asid e, ind icating a d oor a little further back along the corrid or. 'My office, please. Now.'

Reluctantly, Logan d id as he was told . Mitchell waited for him to pass, then followed close behind , shutting the d oor at her back once they'd reached the office.

'Don't bother sitting,' she instructed , strid ing around to the other sid e of the d esk and taking her seat. 'This won't take long.'

Logan was relieved to hear it. At least, he thought so. But a little nagging voice remind ed him it would only take a couple of minutes to fire him and have him escorted from the premises. His mind raced , trying to think if he'd d one anything recently that might warrant him getting the boot. Asid e from some very d eliberate lack of security awareness with his car, though, he d rew a blank.

'Bob Hoon,' she said , invoking the name of the office's former occupant with a tone that suggested she was about to perform an exorcism. 'You heard from him lately?'

'Once or twice,' Logan said . 'I gave him my card a few weeks back. Told him to get in touch if he was struggling.'

'Struggling?'

'He seemed to be d rinking a lot,' Logan told her. 'Getting canned hit him hard .'

'And he got in touch?'

'Like I say, once or twice, aye.'

'What d id he say?'

Logan blew out his cheeks. 'Nothing I'd care to repeat in polite company, ma'am. Imagine a string of swear word s, insert my name and yours at various locations throughout, and you'd be close enough.'

Mitchell nod d ed like she'd suspected this was probably the case. 'He never asked you for help?'

Logan felt a tingle across his scalp at the way she asked the question. At the past tense of it. 'Not d irectly. Not in so many word s. I offered to go round . Tried once, but he told me to leave. Again, the language was a bit more colourful, but… why d o you ask?'

'Bob Hoon jumped off the Greig Street Brid ge two d ays ago,' Mitchell said in the tone of a newsread er d elivering the evening bulletin.

Despite the Detective Superintend ent's earlier instruction, Logan lowered himself onto the chair across from her. 'Jesus Christ,' he said , barely able to believe it. 'Hoon *Jumped*?'

'Or possibly fell, we d on't know for sure yet, but we believe he jumped , yes.'

Logan stared at her like he was waiting for a punchline that clearly wasn't coming. 'And ?' he pressed . 'What happened ?'

'What d o you think happened ?' Mitchell asked . 'He got wet. It's not exactly a long way to fall. Daft bugger.'

Logan felt a surge of relief. Surprising, given that he d id n't particularly like the man. Or, ind eed , know anyone who d id .

'Someone fished him out and called an ambulance. He was released from hospital yesterd ay,' Mitchell continued . 'They've suggested he go to counselling.'

Logan snorted . 'Fat chance of that.'

'Good . Then we're in agreement,' the Detective Superintend ent said , with a d ismissive sort of smile that suggested the conversation was now officially over.

'Agreement? On what?' Logan asked . He wasn't quite sure where this was going, but could alread y feel in his bones that he d id n't like it.

'You'll step up your involvement,' Mitchell explained . 'He clearly trusts you, or he would n't call you up.'

'He calls me up to call me a fat cu—' Logan stopped himself just in time. 'He calls me up to insult me,' he said , course correcting to a more palatable turn of phrase.

'But he calls you up. You, and only you, from what we can gather,' Mitchell said . 'So, I want you to keep an eye on him. Check in more regularly. Help him, if you can.'

There was an obvious question to be asked here. It was going to sound insensitive, Logan knew, but then sensitivity had never exactly been one of his strong points.

So he liked to tell himself, anyway.

'Why?' he asked , putting the question out there. 'He was given the boot. He left here in d isgrace. He sold us out to a blood y Russian mobster.'

'And yet you gave him your card . You told him to call you,' Mitchell said . She clasped her hand s on the d esk in front of her and offered him a smile that was all business. 'Do you remember what I said to you when you came back?'

'Was it, "Here, have a shite car"?'

'I told you to be better, Jack,' Mitchell remind ed him. 'That d oesn't just mean checking yourself for the od d bit of casual racism, or other prejud ice. It means putting yourself out there for those who need it.'

'Well, I was actually just head ing out the d oor on my way to a murd er investigation,' Logan pointed out, jabbing a thumb back over his should er. 'Maybe you noticed ?'

'Like him or not, Bob Hoon was one of us,' Mitchell said , ignoring the remark. 'And when one of ours is hurting or in trouble, we step up.'

Logan began to offer a counterargument, but the Detective Superintend ent swatted it away before it had mad e it out of his mouth. 'I saw how you helped Ben Ford e start to come to terms with his wife's d eath. I've seen how you inspire people, Jack. Hand s up, I d on't und erstand it in the slightest, but I've seen it. And whatever it is you d o, however it is you d o it, Bob Hoon could d o with a d ose.'

Logan let out a long, heavy sigh. There was no point in arguing, he knew, but at least he could convey his d issatisfaction via a big old ejection of air.

'Fine. I'll get in touch,' he said .

'Good ,' Mitchell said . Her gaze flitted impatiently to the d oor behind him. 'Now, get a move on. They'll be waiting for you d own the road .'

Logan rolled back his chair and got to his feet. 'Right. Aye. Maybe if I had a faster car…'

'Speed limit's the same, either way,' Mitchell said . She had selected a d ocument from her in-tray and was alread y perusing it. It wasn't the roared , *Get the fuck out of my office!*' that Hoon had been fond of conclud ing meetings with, but it was equally as effective.

Neither officer bothered to say their good byes as Logan left the room and pulled the d oor firmly closed behind him. He took a few second s to fire off a text to Bob Hoon asking how he was d oing, wasted a few more waiting to see if a reply came through, then shoved the phone in his pocket when one d id n't.

'Job d one,' he announced to nobod y in particular, then he ad justed his grip on the laptop cases and went thund ering off toward s the lifts.

Chapter 4

The Fort Augustus Weather Nexus hit exactly as Ben had pred icted it would . The first spots of rain started flecking the wind screen of the Fiesta just as Logan d escend ed the hill into town.

As he reached the canal brid ge, he had to click on his wind screen wipers.

By the time he was horsing along the straight at Loch Lochy, just north of Letterfinlay, the wipers were going full tilt, thunking across the screen as they valiantly fought back against the onslaught.

The rain had eased a little when Logan took the turning at the Lochy Brid ge round about, although the wipers were still working flat out.

He stole a glance at the police station as he passed it—his home-from-home for however long it took to solve this latest case. Construction had begun on the land around it, although not on the supermarket that had initially been planned for the site.

Instead , a new hospital was being constructed . Although at the rate they were going, conventional med icine would be obsolete by the time they were finished , replaced by those little hand held boxes the d octors used to heal people in *Star Trek*.

From there, he continued on through Corpach, out past the ind ustrial estate and up the long straight stretches of road alongsid e Loch Eil.

The Fiesta pootled along, d espite his foot pressing the accel-erator ped al almost through the floor. He kept his eyes fixed grimly ahead whenever some bigger, faster vehicle came flying past him, content in the knowled ge that the smug bastard s would be turned back at the cord on a few miles ahead .

To his immense d isappointment, there was no cord on. Not one that blocked the road , at least. Instead , there was a long caterpillar of cars, both polis and civilian, blocking the sid e of the road closest to the monument, and a Uniform at each end coord inating the traffic that was attempting to pass it.

Logan pulled up at the back of the stationary line and yanked the Fiesta's hand brake up to the highest setting. Much as he'd like rid of the thing, he d id n't want it rolling backward s d own the slope into some other poor bugger.

'Oi! No!' barked the closer of the two officers on traffic d uty. She was a slightly round ed woman in her forties, her hand gestures much sharper than her physical appearance. 'You can't park there. Shift,' she shouted , with a scowl and a series of angry gestures that mad e it very clear she was not a big fan of her current task.

Logan unclipped his belt and unfold ed himself from insid e the car. It took a full five second s for him to emerge and d raw himself up to his full height. The sight of him brought a flicker of concern to the uniformed officer's face. The sight of his warrant card completely sealed the d eal.

'Sorry, sir,' the woman said . 'Bit overzealous there. Blood y tourists keep stopping everywhere.' She glanced past him to the Fiesta. 'And , well, I d id n't think...'

'No harm d one, Constable,' Logan told her, shoving his ID back in his insid e coat pocket. He glanced at the sky, and the rain pattered across his face as if from a shower. A cold one. 'You d rew the shitty end of the stick here, eh?'

The constable smiled grimly and tilted her head in the d irection of the monument. 'You ask me, sir, neither end of this stick is exactly shite-free.'

The rad io on her should er squawked . She acknowled ged it, then stepped into the road and held a hand up to stop a camper van that was approaching from the south.

'What are all these?' Logan asked , gesturing to the line of cars he'd pulled up behind . A murd er scene usually d rew a heavy police presence, but unless someone had shot the Queen this was overkill. 'They're not all ours, are they?'

'No, sir. Tourists, mostly. They come for the steam train. They'll all be up at the viad uct trying to get a photo,' the constable said , stepping asid e to let a flow of traffic go past from the Mallaig d irection. 'They fill the car park, then just park anywhere. Along the verges. Mid d le of the road . People's d riveways. Wherever they like.'

Logan looked past her to where the viad uct rose up in the mid d le-d istance. It was an impressive feat of engineering, right enough, although most of the people currently assembling up there would n't be there for that. They'd be there for one reason, and one reason only.

'Harry blood y Potter's got a lot to answer for, eh?'

'Aye, you can say that again, sir,' the PC agreed , waving the camper van through.

'Right. Well, leave it with me,' Logan told her, then he turned to his left, where the Glenfinnan Monument stood towering on the shore of Loch Shiel.

Most d ays, that view, from that angle, was one of the most iconic images of the Highland s. He'd seen it on postcard s, on tea towels, on holid ay brochures… the works. Never, though, had it looked like it d id tod ay.

The top of the monument, where a kilted Highland er usually stood with his back to the water, was now covered in a marquee-like construction of canvas and ropes. It bulged out from the top in a vaguely mushroom sort of shape, turning one of Scotland 's most important historical land marks into some-thing d istinctly phallic.

An area around the monument that stretched from halfway d own the long approach path to the water behind had been cord oned off. Eight figures in white paper suits were shuffling through the bracken and combing the coarse sand of the beach.

Six Uniforms stood at irregular intervals, none of them doing anything, but all of them trying very hard to look as if they were. The constable manning the cord on stood to an anxious attention as Logan approached. He said nothing when Logan ducked the barrier and continued on along the path, suggesting either he recognised the DCI, or he was in the wrong job.

'Do me a favour, will you, son?' Logan asked him.

A flash of panic crossed the younger man's face, but he nodded promptly. 'Sure. I mean, yes. I mean, what do you need, sir?'

Logan pointed to the smattering of other Uniforms who were hanging around doing very little. 'Get up to the viaduct and tell everyone there to get back to their cars and fuck off. Tell them the... Wizard Express, or whatever the hell it's called, is off for the day.'

The constable winced. 'They won't be happy at that, sir.'

'Aye, well, they'll be even less happy when they get back to their cars and find they've all been ticketed. Won't they, Constable?'

A smile hitched up the corners of the young PC's mouth. 'I like your thinking, sir,' he said. 'Leave it with me.'

'Good lad,' Logan told him, then he continued down the path in the direction of the monument.

The CID officer who met him at the foot of the stone tower was vaguely familiar, but his name was so far buried at the back of Logan's brain there was no chance whatsoever he was going to be able to dig it back out.

'DCI Logan,' the man said, offering a hand. 'Detective Sergeant Boyle.'

Boyle. That was it.

'Right, aye. I remember,' Logan lied, shaking the offered hand. 'You helped out on the Connor Reid case.'

'Aye, well, I think I told you where to find the pizza shop, sir. Not sure I was exactly instrumental.'

'You'd be surprised,' Logan said, returning both hands to the pockets of his coat. He shot a look up at the tent jutting out from the curved walls around fifteen metres above them, which he now realised Boyle was using as a giant makeshift umbrella. 'That's new.'

'Aye. It's a big tent,' Boyle said, then he visibly flinched at the words leaving his mouth. 'I mean, I'm sure you could 've figured that out for yourself, sir.'

'Never hurts to get a second opinion, son,' Logan told him.

A familiar Aberdonian twang came echoing out through the small doorway at the base of the stone tower. 'That you, sir?'

'Aye, Hamza, it's me,' Logan confirmed.

'I'm up the top,' the recently promoted detective sergeant announced. 'But, eh, you might have a bit of a struggle.'

Logan ducked, turned sideways, and shuffled hunched ov and crab-like through the door. Exactly one half-step later, he was confronted by the narrowest stone staircase he'd ever clapped eyes on. It curved sharply, immediately disappearing around a bend just a couple of steps in.

He could say with some confidence that neither the width of the steps, nor the height of the gap between each spiralling level were designed for a man of his stature.

The walls were so close together he would have to mount the steps sideways so as not to get jammed in. That would require him to stand upright, though, and there was hee-haw chance he could do that without grinding the top of his skull against the rough stone overhead.

Crawling was a possibility, except his body was so long there was very little chance that he could bend it around the tight curves of the spiralling staircase, and no chance whatsoever that he could do so while retaining even the faintest shred of dignity.

'What's the matter, Jack? Too bloody fat?'

Despite the odd way the voice echoed and looped around the staircase, Logan recognised the dulcet tones of Geoff Palmer, the senior Scene of Crime investigator. He could picture the snid ey smirk on the man's pud gy wee face, his bald y heid and hairy ears safely hid d en beneath the white paper hood he'd almost certainly have pulled up over them.

'Too strapping an example of a man, you mean,' Logan replied . 'Shona says hello by the way.'

He listened for the mutter of annoyance he knew would follow that remark and allowed himself a moment to enjoy it when it came.

'Wait there, sir, I'll come d own,' Hamza said .

Logan crouched at the bottom of the steps and listened to the series of noises that followed . There was some straining, some irregular breathing, some mild swearing, and then the stead y shhhhhk of something rubbing across the rough stone wall.

Hamza's footsteps grew stead ily loud er as he wound his way d own the insid e of the monument. He was shorter than Logan, with a significantly narrower frame, and yet it was his arse that appeared around the bend first, the d imensions of the staircase forcing him to tackle the steps backward s.

'Looks cosy,' Logan remarked , once Hamza had pulled off the human three-point-turn required to aim himself in the DCI's d irection.

'Aye, you could say that, sir. Seems narrower up top, too, believe it or not.'

'Narrower?' Logan spluttered , like the very id ea was completely preposterous. 'Jesus Christ. Who built it? The Seven Dwarfs?'

'Only if they took it in turns,' Hamza said . 'No chance you're getting seven of anyone up the top.'

'Babies, maybe,' suggested DS Boyle from outsid e.

Logan and Hamza both twisted themselves around enough to face the d oor, and found the CID man bend ing to look in at them, a grin plastered across his face.

The smile fad ed away quickly und er the weight of Logan's confused stare. 'I d on't know why you'd put babies up there, though,' Boyle quietly ad mitted , then he turned , said , 'What?'

to a question that neither of the other detectives heard, and hurriedly walked off.

'Anyway…' Hamza said, getting back to business. He handed over an iPad he'd been keeping a tight grip of on his way down the stairs. 'You can Facetime with us up top. Save you trying to squeeze up. Here.'

He reached over, tapped and swiped the screen far too quickly for Logan to have any clue what he was up to, and then an extreme close-up of Geoff Palmer's nostrils filled the screen.

'Aye, looking good, Geoff,' Logan called up to him. 'Probably your best angle, to be honest.'

The image jerked around on-screen until the whole of Palmer's face was looking back at Logan. The SOC man's face was the usual sweaty circle of red, constrained on all sides by the elasticated hem of his paper hood.

'That you, Jack?' he asked, squinting. 'Couldn't see you there behind the chins.'

Logan caught sight of himself in the smaller inset window at the top of the screen and adjusted the angle to one that wasn't looking directly up at him from below. This drew a little cackle of glee that came down the stairs a fraction of a second before it emerged from the iPad speaker.

'I'll head up, sir,' Hamza said, manoeuvring himself back in the direction of the stairs. 'Won't be a minute.'

Hamza was right. He wasn't a minute. He was almost three.

'Sorry, sir. It's the hatch at the top,' the DS explained, nudging Palmer off-screen as he took the iPad from him. He switched cameras to reveal a rectangular hole in the stone floor. 'You've got to sort of twist and limbo dance through it backwards.'

'Oh, give it a try, Jack,' Palmer urged, bending in front of the camera so his self-satisfied smirk filled Logan's screen again. 'We'll film it and put it online. Think of the hits. You'll be viral.'

The screen went dark for half a second, then Hamza's face appeared again. Logan could just make out part of the kilted
28

Highlander statue standing proudly behind him. 'Sorry about that, sir.'

'No' your fault the man's an arsehole, son,' Logan said, loudly enough for it to carry all the way up to the top of the staircase. 'Show me what we've got.'

Hamza glanced at something off-camera, took a breath like he was preparing himself, then nodded. 'Right, sir. Here we go,' he said. 'But I'll warn you now, it's not pretty.'

–

She was young. Eighteen to twenty-two, Logan reckoned, although the angle of the camera and the condition of the body meant it was a pretty rough estimate.

Her eyes were open. Bulging. Red. There was a thick green cord around her neck—climbing rope, probably—the other end tied to the metal railing that ran around the parapet-style wall at the tower's top.

Logan's view was restricted by how far out Hamza could lean, and how close he could get, but nothing about the angle of the head suggested the woman's neck was broken. The rope wasn't long enough for a drop that would've ended her life instantly. If it was hanging that had killed her, it had been slow, and it had been terrifying.

She was a pretty wee thing, with a short bob of blonde hair, and irises so crystal blue they would've once sparkled like tropical waters.

Her legs and feet were bare but stained with rivulets of something brown and gloopy. The only garment of clothing Logan could be sure she was wearing was a baggy white t-shirt. It had been doused in the same viscous brown liquid. On the front, someone had written the words 'Planet Rapist' in red uppercase lettering.

'Looks like another weird one, sir,' Hamza remarked from off-camera.

Logan agreed that it did. Then again, most of them were.

'I can't see her hand s,' Logan pointed out. 'Where are they?'

'They're behind her back, sir,' Hamza replied , trying to get the iPad into a position that allowed Logan to see for himself.

'Tied ?' the DCI asked .

Hamza settled on the best framing he could , which at least gave an id ea of where the woman's hand s were located , and how her arms had been wrenched around , bunching up her should er blad es.

'Aye. Can't see what with yet, though. Probably won't know until we get her d own.'

'And how are we planning on d oing that?' Logan asked .

Palmer's voice came at him again from both d irections at once. 'Fire Service is on stand by,' he said , having mercifully switched out of 'annoying arsehole' mod e and into something more businesslike. 'I'm going to finish up here, then we'll have to get her lowered d own.'

'Probably best,' Logan said . 'No chance Ricketts is getting up these stairs without d oing himself a mischief.'

A throat was cleared in the d oorway behind him. Logan closed his eyes momentarily, mumbled something quite mean-spirited to any and all god s that might be listening, then began the process of turning himself around to face the new arrival.

'Dr Rickett,' he said , offering up a smile to the boggle-eyed eld erly man who stood hunched over on the path right outsid e the entrance. 'How nice to see you again.'

Chapter 5

Following quite a stilted and awkward conversation with the eld erly pathologist, Logan mad e his excuses and set off to find DS Boyle.

He tracked the CID man d own way back near the line of cars, where he was having a crafty cigarette and watching the Uniforms d irecting the traffic.

'Sir,' he coughed when he spotted Logan approaching. He looked around for somewhere to safely d ispose of the cigarette, remembered this was technically still part of a crime scene, then nipped the end and pocketed it, instead . 'Anything I can d o for you?'

'Aye. Who found the bod y?'

'Ian, eh…' Boyle took out his notepad and hurried ly flicked through the pages. 'Hill. Ian Hill, sir. Found her shortly after six.'

'Local?'

'Tourist.'

Logan looked back at the monument, with its bulging canvas head . 'Would 've been d ark then. What was he up to?'

'Bird watching, he tells us.'

'In pitch blackness? What is he, an owl?'

'No, sir,' Boyle said , then he flinched again *What the fuck was wrong with him? That wasn't a genuine question. Of course the DCI didn't think the man was literally a fucking owl.* 'He's a bit… od d , though. You ask me, he d id it.'

'What makes you think that?' Logan asked .

31

'Just. You know. He's a bit...' DS Boyle gave a little shudder. 'A bit...' He brought his fingers up and waggled them, like a spider waving. 'You know what I mean?'

'Aye, sounds like he's our man, right enough,' Logan said. 'Open and shut case. Where is he?'

Boyle gestured across the road. A small visitor centre stood by a crowded car park, a couple of picnic benches set up out front. 'He's in there, sir. DC Innes is with him, making sure he doesn't do a runner.'

'Good. I'll go have a word.'

'Want backup, sir?' Boyle asked, drawing himself up to his full height. This brought the top of his head almost level with Logan's shoulder.

'I'm sure I can handle it, son.'

Boyle tried to hide his disappointment, but it was a largely unsuccessful endeavour. The rain had matted his hair to his head, and his allegedly waterproof jacket had revealed itself as a right lying bastard. The thought of some shelter and a hot cup of coffee from the visitor centre cafe had been keeping him going for the past few hours, and he deeply regretted not switching places with DC Innes at the earliest possible opportunity.

'Aye, well, if you need me...' Boyle said, but Logan was already striding across the road, and if the CID man even bothered to get to the end of the sentence, it fell on deaf ears.

Inside, the visitor centre appeared to have been almost completely taken over by uniformed polis. There were no actual visitors that Logan could see, and only a couple of members of staff—a smartly-dressed female manager, and a teenage boy with an apron on who was presumably the one to ask about tea, which Logan promptly did.

Once he'd made his introductions and had been given the lay of the land by the uniformed sergeant standing guard in the foyer, Logan asked the manager about the key to the door of the monument.

There was only one in existence, she'd told him—a valuable antique in its own right. It was used twice a day, and kept locked in a safe for which only she and another female supervisor knew the cod e. It was there in the safe when she'd checked it that morning, and her office had been locked up all night.

The supervisor was on holid ay in the Lake District. The manager had been at home with her husband and child ren.

Which meant that the killer most likely knew how to pick locks.

Logan took the tea that was offered up to him in a big wid e mug and saucer, and was d irected to a small office at the sid e of the build ing. There he found Detective Constable Innes sitting staring at his phone, while a startled -looking man with thinning hair and no chin to speak of, repeated ly rubbed his hand s together like he was washing them und er a running tap.

Innes straightened up quickly when he recognised Logan. The other man was alread y sitting bolt upright, stiff-backed and rigid with fear, and it was only his eyes that wid ened when he saw the hulking figure come stepping through the d oorway.

The office wasn't built to the same scale as the staircase in the monument, but it wasn't far off it. It would be fine for one, tight for two, and bord erline embarrassing for three of them. Stand ing in the centre of the room, Logan would be able to stretch out his arms and reach at least two of the four walls. And that was before you factored in the d esk, the filing cabinet, and fifteen or so boxes of visitor information leaflets, membership forms, and other assorted paperwork.

'Detective Chief Inspector,' DC Innes said , springing up off a foam-pad d ed seat that was jammed in beneath the office's only wind ow. The wind ow faced out onto the monument, but a set of blind s d ivid ed the view into d ozens of long, horizontal chunks that d id n't really show much of anything.

Given the d iminutive size of the office, the act of jumping up brought DC Innes within hugging d istance of DCI Logan. Mercifully for all involved , he d id n't seize the opportunity, and instead took a big sid estep toward s the d oor, putting some more d istance between them.

'Should I...?' he asked , his eyes practically crawling around the sid e of his head to look at the d oor. He almost collapsed with relief when Logan confirmed that yes, he should .

With the briefest of nod s at the office's only other occupant, Innes hurried out of the room, and a spring-action hinge slowly eased the d oor closed behind him.

Logan watched it, foot tapping, until it had clunked back into the frame. Only then d id he turn to ad d ress the startled - looking man in the chair.

Ian Hill was a man who, by any reasonable d efinition, was past his best. There weren't so much bags und er his eyes as hold alls, stuffed with a d ecad e or two of sleepless nights and early mornings.

His hair was locked in battle with his encroaching forehead , and losing bad ly. So bad ly, in fact, that it had beaten a retreat almost all the way across the top of his head , and now occupied less than thirty percent of its previously held scalp territory.

His weight was something of a conund rum. At first glance, he was a wiry, skinny figure who looked like he survived on a d iet of caffeine and stress, and yet there was something a bit d oughy about him, like he had a high butter content and had n't been all the way baked through.

Throw in a haphazard arrangement of yellowing teeth and a pair of glasses that he likely thought mad e him look younger, but only served to highlight how much he wasn't, and you had a picture of a man who had n't so much let himself go, as simply failed to notice when it all upped and went.

'Mr Hill, I'm Detective Chief Inspector Jack Logan.'

Ian stood quickly, crouched into something that was partway between a bow and curtsey, then shook the hand that Logan had thrust out toward s him.

The hand that Logan shook was *precisely* as sweaty as he'd been expecting.

'Ian. Hill. Ian Hill. I'm Ian Hill.' The man in the chair was twitchy, his movements jerky and sud d en. He shook his head and tutted, admonishing himself. 'You knew that, didn't you? My name? You said it right then. Sorry. Sorry. I'm… God.'

'It's fine, Ian. Can I call you Ian?'

'Of course. Go ahead. I've been called much worse!' he ejected shrilly, then he sighed at himself. 'Sorry. Sorry. I joke when I'm nervous.'

Logan had to replay the sentence in his head to figure out which part was the joke, but told the other man not to worry about it.

'You've had quite the morning, Ian,' he said. 'I think we can excuse a little anxiety.'

There were only two seats in the office, and Hill was parked in the better of the two. Towering over the bugger was only going to make him more of a babbling mess, so Logan plonked himself down onto the textured orange fabric of the foam-padded chair that DC Innes had recently vacated. This would've made him lower than Hill, which he wasn't a fan of, but fortunately his height advantage meant they were both pretty much level.

'Want to take me through what happened, Ian?'

Hill glanced at the door as if to say he'd already been through it, but Logan raised his eyebrows encouragingly, signalling for him to start talking.

'Well, I, uh. I was here early. Six. Five past, maybe. I'm a photographer. Not professional. Not by any means. I mean, I'd like to be, but there's no money in it. Well, I mean there can be, but it's difficult when you're just starting out, and when you've a mortgage you…'

He cleared his throat. A sheen of sweat had started to glisten on his forehead. He wiped it with the back of his hand before continuing.

'Sorry. Rambling. I do that. Wife's always on at me about it. Tried to get me to do some online classes that are meant to—'

'You arrived just after six,' Logan said, cutting through the chatter.

35

Hill looked positively relieved by the interruption, like he'd been unable to find his way back to the point on his own.

'Yes! Yes, that's right,' he confirmed, almost bouncing out of his seat. 'I set the camera up around ten past. Pointing at the water.'

'In the dark?'

Hill's eyebrows dipped in the middle, like he didn't understand the question. 'Well, yes. The early bird catches the worm, as they say. Or, in this case, the early bird catches the bird, I suppose.'

He laughed mechanically at his remark, as if he didn't actually find it funny, but had been pre-programmed to respond in that way.

When it was apparent that Logan had absolutely no idea what he was on about, he offered an explanation.

'The black-throated loon.'

This did not help clarify matters.

'The what?' Logan asked.

'The bird, I mean. Not... not the early bird, the other one. The worm one.' He shook his head. 'Not the worm one. The bird the early bird catches, I mean. In my version.'

Logan's eyes narrowed a fraction. 'Are you on any medication, Ian?' he asked.

'What? No! I mean, yes. A heart thing. Nothing that's... it's basically just aspirin, I'm just...' He straightened further and drew such a deep, sudden breath in through his nose that Logan briefly became concerned he might suck all the oxygen out of the room.

Hill held the breath in silence for several seconds, his eyes staring straight ahead at the window, then he let it out slowly through his mouth.

'You all right there, Ian?' Logan asked him.

Hill managed a suggestion of a smile. 'Yes. Sorry. It's been a day,' he explained. 'As I was trying to say, I'm here to get a photograph of the black-throated loon. Or black-throated d iver, d epend ing on who you ask. Same bird . I've been after a shot of one all week. I'm supposed to be leaving on Frid ay, so wanted to maximise my chances of getting a snap by being here as early as possible. They're active in the mornings.'

'Right. I see,' Logan said .

'I'm not a twitcher. Please d on't think that.'

Given the way he'd been flinching and spasming over the past couple of minutes, Logan would beg to d iffer.

'Twitcher as in bird watcher, I mean,' Hill clarified , seemingly picking up on the DCI's thought. 'I d on't make a habit of it, but my d ad took me here years ago, and we saw one of the bird s together. I've always wanted to come back and get a photograph.'

'Fair enough,' Logan said . 'So, you got set up…?'

'Yes. Set up. Camera on tripod . Check. It was still too d ark, but everything's quiet at that point. Very little traffic back on the main road . It's a good time to listen and try to pinpoint where they might emerge.' Hill wrung his hand s together and shifted his weight in his chair. 'And , well, that's when I heard it.'

'The bird ?'

'What? No. The creaking,' Hill said , his voice d ropping into a whisper like this was some great secret for their ears only. 'Of the rope.'

Logan kept quiet and left him to talk then, letting the memory tumble out of him in bursts of breathless word s.

'I had my torch. I… for checking camera settings. I had the torch in my hand , and I heard the noise, and … at first, I thought it was maybe the bird . On bird , at least. And I listened . I just listened . And then… there it was. But behind me. Above. And so I… and so I…'

His hand lifted , recreating the movement of the torch. His eyes raised like he was seeing it all over again.

'I shone it up. And … and …' He swallowed , and d ug the fingernails of his hand s into his palms, goad ing himself on. 'I shone it up, and there she was. Hanging there. Just..*hanging* there.'

He reached for a mug that was sitting near him on the office d esk, had a quick look insid e, but was d isappointed to find i empty.

'I've never seen a bod y before. Not like that. No*in the wild,* so to speak,' he continued , setting the mug d own again. 'My parents, yes. But they'd been attend ed to. Dealt with. This? This was…'

'It's very d ifferent, yes,' Logan said , his voice soft.

'You're probably used to it, of course,' Hill said .

'You'd be surprised ,' Logan replied . 'So, what happened next, Ian?'

'Nothing. I mean, I probably screamed the place d own,' he ad mitted . 'And then, I called the police. Nine-nine-nine. The woman was lovely. On the phone, I mean. Emergency services. How she put up with my babbling, I'll never know. Deserves a blood y med al.'

'You d id n't go anywhere near the bod y? Try to get a better look?'

'God , no. No. A better look? That's the last thing I wanted . Believe me.' He frowned like the memory was troubling. 'I actually d id n't quite realise what I was looking at. Not for the first few second s. It was so alien. So out of place. So unexpected , I suppose. I just stared at it for a little while, confused . I remember feeling confused . And then—click. I realised . Or my brain accepted , maybe.'

He reached for the mug again, on the off-chance it had magically refilled .

Still empty.

'Believe me, if I could 've looked away just before the truth registered , I would have d one,' he said , his voice returning to its earlier hushed whisper. 'But I saw her. I saw that poor girl hanging there. And my concern is…' He cleared his throat. Swallowed . Took a breath. 'My fear is that I'll never stop seeing her every time I close my eyes.'

'I know it feels like that right now. Like it's burned into your retinas and imprinted on your brain. But it fad es,' Logan told him. 'In time, it fad es.'

Sometimes, he ad d ed in his head. *But not always.*

Chapter 6

Constable David David son sat in his wheelchair, eyeballing the woman on the other sid e of the glass. The woman on the other sid e of the glass, for her part, eyeballed him back.

Dave mad e a show of jamming a pinkie in his ear and twisting it around before he spoke.

'Sorry, say that again.'

Moira Corson, the receptionist at Fort William Police Station, sighed impatiently. 'I asked who you work for.'

Dave held her gaze for a few second s, slowly looked d own at his police constable's uniform, then raised his eyes again at an equally sed ate pace.

'The police,' he said , fairly confid ent that it d id n't really need saying.

'Scotland ?'

'Eh?'

'Police Scotland ?'

'Obviously, yes. I'm here to—'

Behind the glass, Moira raised a finger to silence him, then wrote on a form for what felt like an inord inately long time.

'Can I go through?' Dave asked , ind icating the d oor on his left. 'It's that way, isn't it?'

'You can go through when I say you can go through,' Moira told him, in the clipped tones of a teacher who was one wrong word away from a full class d etention. She leaned forward until her head was almost touching the glass screen. 'Is that your wheelchair?'

'No, it's someone else's. I just can't be arsed walking, so I thought I'd get a shot of it for the d ay.'

Moira's face remained utterly impassive.

'Yes, it's my wheelchair,' Dave confirmed with a sigh.

Moira went back to writing what may well have been an essay, given how long it was taking.

While he waited , Dave sid e-eyed the d oor. Jud ging by how it sat in the frame, it opened away from him into the corrid or beyond . Maybe if he built up ramming speed …

He had just faced front again when he heard the d oor creak open.

'There you are. Thought you'd got lost,' said DI Ford e, and Dave d id n't think he'd ever been so happy to see anyone in his life.

'Afternoon, sir,' he said . 'Sorry for the hold -up. I'm just in the process of justifying my existence to this lad y here.'

'The lad 's with me, Moira,' Ben said , accompanying it with a d ismissive wave that might well come back to haunt him, jud ging by the glare it earned him from the receptionist. 'In you come, son.'

'Right behind you, sir,' Dave chirped . He tipped an imaginary hat to Moira, enjoyed the sour expression that puckered up her mouth, then turned his chair in DI Ford e's d irection. 'And I hope you've got the kettle boiling.'

–

Logan nod d ed at the two firefighters as they passed him on the way back to the car park, and turned to the ambulance in time to see the bod y bag being carefully load ed aboard .

He stood in reverent silence as the paramed ics got in; clasped his hand s in front of him as the engine coughed awake and a Uniform guid ed it out of its space at the sid e of the road . It went trund ling past him slowly, head ed up the hill in the Mallaig d irection, the visitor centre car park too full for it to turn there.

By the time it had pulled a U-turn at the church a little further up the road and was on its way back to Fort William, Logan had mad e his way along the path to the ed ge of the cord on, where he met Dr Rickett hobbling the other way.

'We get anything?' Logan asked him.

The old man pursed his lips in d istaste. 'What, apart from stuck? Rid iculous place to put a bod y. Blood y rid iculous.' He removed his half-moon glasses, prod uced a hand kerchief from the breast pocket of his jacket, and gave the lenses a polish. 'Female. Early twenties, I'd say. Possibly a little younger. Death by asphyxiation seems like an obvious conclusion, though it'll have to be confirmed in the PM. I'd be surprised if it wasn't, though.'

'Aye, from what I saw of her face, looks like a safe bet,' agreed Logan.

'So good of you to concur, Detective Chief Inspector. Nothing means more to me than your affirmation,' Ricketts replied . He held his glasses up to the light, breathed on them, then went back to polishing. 'Her hand s were tied . Plastic zip-ties, pulled tight enough to break the skin, so unless she's some sort of contortionist, it's very unlikely that she d id it herself.'

'It looked like there was something poured on her. Orangey-brown.' Logan said . 'Any id eas? Looked like oil to me.'

'Your eyes serve you well. Engine oil, I believe. Not really my field of expertise, but I've owned enough cars to know it when I see it. Geoff's team will be able to d etermine more.'

'Anything else you can tell me at this stage?' Logan pressed . 'Like how long she was up there?'

'Not long. Seven or eight hours since she d ied , I'd estimate. That might change post-PM, but if it d oes, it won't be by much. Other than that, there's not a lot more to say at the moment. Not until we get her opened up.'

Logan nod d ed and tried not to think too much about that image. 'You head ing up the road to d o the post-mortem now?'

Ricketts placed his glasses back on his face and spent a second or two balancing them perfectly in place on his nose. 'I'm head ing up the road to have a hot shower and a lie-d own. Dr Maguire will be on PM d uty.' He reached into the pocket of his blazer, took out a silver watch on a chain, and checked the time. 'I'm officially off d uty as of one hour, eleven minutes ago. Once she has something to report, I'm sure she'll be in contact.'

'Right, aye. Thank you,' Logan said .

'It's my job. No thanks necessary,' Ricketts replied with a sniff. He flicked his eyes to the cord on tape, and Logan took the hint, lifting it high enough that the old er man could get und er it without having to d uck too far.

The DCI took the opportunity to switch places, so they were once again on opposite sid es of the tape. He was about to set off toward s the monument when Ricketts spoke again.

'She's a kind soul.'

Logan turned . 'Who, the victim?'

'Dr Maguire,' Ricketts said , with just the briefest roll of his eyes. 'She's like a d aughter to me. I'm very fond of her. We all are at Raigmore. And none of us, least of all me, would care to see her hurt. You might be big, and I may be old , but I'd still give you a blood y good thrashing. Is that und erstood ?'

'It is,' Logan said . 'Message received . But I have no intention of ever—'

'I've said my bit, Detective Chief Inspector,' Ricketts told him, cutting in. 'We know where we stand . Dr Maguire will be in touch with her find ings.'

With that, he turned and continued his shuffling hobble along the path to the long line of parked cars at the sid e of the road . Logan was so busy watching him, he d id n't hear Hamza approaching until the younger officer spoke.

'All right, sir? What was all that about with Ricketts? Looked a bit intense there at the end .'

'Hmm? Oh, nothing,' Logan said , turning away from the cord on tape. He ind icated the tent at the top of the monu-ment with a curt nod . 'Palmer found us anything worth getting excited about?'

'Not a lot, sir, no,' Hamza reported . 'Only thing that might be of interest is a bad ge.'

'A bad ge?'

'It was on the steps und er the hatch. Back's come off it, like it got caught on the ed ge of the hatch and just popped off.'

'And ? Anything significant about it?' Logan asked .

'Maybe, sir, aye. Given the message written on the t-shirt, and the fact the victim's bod y was coated in oil, there's a good chance it might be related .'

He held up a clear plastic evid ence bag containing what was left of the bad ge. A single word was emblazoned across the front in a marker-pen style font the colour of late-summer leaves.

Greenpeace.

'Looks like we might have some sort of environmental terrorist on our hand s,' Hamza suggested .

'A blood y flexible one, too,' Logan said , his gaze switching back to the narrow tower. 'Ricketts reckons the bod y's only been there a few hours. Presumably, the d oor's locked at night?'

'Usually sir, aye. Manager says she's a hund red percent sure it was locked at close of play last night, but it was open this morning when Uniform arrived on the scene.'

'Forced ?'

'Doesn't look like it,' Hamza said . 'No sign of d amage. Heavy d oor, too, so it would take some d oing. It's possible someone had a key.'

'That'd be nice. Help narrow it d own,' Logan said , rocking back on his heels. 'Nothing to tell us who the victim was, I take it?'

'Afraid not sir, no,' Hamza replied . He gestured back in the d irection of the visitor centre. A young woman roughly the same age as the victim was being ushered along the path by DS Boyle, who had a look about him of the cat who'd got the cream. 'But I've a feeling we might be about to find out.'

Chapter 7

'Hermione Grey,' Logan announced , pinning a slightly blurry A4 printout of a smiling young woman to the Big Board .

The image had been cropped from a digital photograph the victim's friend had been able to provid e, once she'd finally stopped crying. At present, it was the only thing attached to the board . Logan had n't been particularly careful about choosing the best spot to put it, knowing full well that wherever he chose, Sinead would only move it when she and Tyler came d own from Inverness.

The young woman in the picture could 've passed for a mod el, or an old -time Hollywood starlet, with her bouncy blond e curls and eyes that sparkled like chunks of sapphire. Her d azzling smile was a little crooked , but that only served to make her seem that bit more attractive, while also making everyone in the room painfully aware of the colour of their own teeth.

'Hermione Grey?' Ben parroted . 'Is that no' the lassie from Harry Potter?'

'That's Hermione Granger,' Dave said , then he quickly ad d ed a less confid ent-sound ing, 'I mean, I think so, anyway', so as not to sound like he had any interest whatsoever in any of that wizard ing shite, thank you very much.

'Still, not a kick in the arse off,' Ben remarked .

'Aye. The friend we spoke to...' Logan clicked his fingers, and continued d oing so until Hamza jumped in.

'Deird rie Mair.'

'Deird rie Mair. She reckoned it wasn't her real name.'

Ben took a sip of his tea. 'Old er friend , is she?'

45

Logan shook his head . 'Similar age. Why?'

'Just… Deird rie. Who's calling their child Deird rie these d ays?'

'I mean, she's no' an infant,' Logan pointed out. 'She's early twenties.'

'Who was calling their child Deird rie in…' Ben's lips moved for a moment as he calculated . 'Wait. The year two thousand ? That can't be right, can it?' he asked , appearing genuinely traumatised by the thought of it. 'Jesus Christ. How are people born in the year two thousand now ad ults? It was only blood y yesterd ay.'

Ben had a feeling that he had strayed somewhat from his initial point, but could n't quite recall what his original point was, so he ind icated the board with his mug and took another d rink. 'Sorry, carry on.'

'Like I was saying, Deird rie d oesn't know for sure if Hermione was her real name or not. Doesn't know much about her at all, in fact. They only met in France back in June. They were both travelling solo at the time, but have since formed a group of friend s, and they're all now travelling together.'

'Good for them. I think it's a great thing for a young person to get out and see a bit of the world ,' Ben said .

'Unless they get murd ered ,' Dave ad d ed .

'Oh. Aye. Unless they get murd ered ,' Ben conced ed . 'Obviously, that's not so good . What else could the friend tell you about her?'

'Not really a whole lot,' Logan said . 'She was pretty emotional. They're all staying at some sort of hostel thing at Glenfinnan. Uniform is keeping an eye until I head back out and interview them.'

'Reckon the killer's one of her mates?' asked Dave.

'Funny you should ask,' Logan said .

He pinned a second blown-up image to the board . This one showed a young man with blood -red hair and enough metal in his nose, ears, and eyebrows to alter his local magnetic field .

'Moof Sand erson. And no, Moof isn't his real name, either. Age twenty-six or twenty-seven, we think. Last seen with the victim yesterd ay evening around eight. Victim was last seen between ten and eleven in the lounge of the hostel, read ing a book. Neither was there this morning when the others woke up. We haven't found his bod y, so we've got to assume he's on the run.'

He pointed with the end of a pen to the left breast area of the *Meat is Murder* t-shirt the man in the picture wore, then used it to trace an outline around a white button bad ge that was pinned there.

'Note the bad ge,' he said . 'Hamza?'

DS Khaled held up the same evid ence bag he'd shown Logan back at the crime scene. 'This was found in the monument stairwell,' Hamza said . 'Just a few feet from where the victim's bod y was left.'

'Is it the same bad ge?' asked Ben, squinting at the photograph.

'Hard to say, resolution's not high enough,' Logan said . 'But they're similar. Which means we find this bastard . That's our number one priority right now, alongsid e find ing out who our victim really is. Deird rie tells us she was American, maybe Canad ian. She never really spoke about where she came from, but the accent was a giveaway.'

'New name, secretive about her past, sound s like she was running from something,' Ben remarked .

'Aye. Just maybe no' fast enough,' Logan said . He checked his watch. 'After three. Christ, where's the d ay going?' he muttered , then he clapped his hand s like the bang of a starting gun. 'Right, I'm going to head back up and talk to her friend s. Uniform is checking the hostel for ID, so we might have a hit by the time I get there. We want this Moof character found as soon as humanly possible, even if only so I can find out his real name and stop calling him Moof. Circulate that picture internally. Hamza, see if he's on HOLMES, if not, get Googling. And check for Hermione Grey, obviously. Doubt it's her real name, but she might have some web presence somewhere.'

'Not that I've found so far, sir. I've been looking. But I'll keep at it.'

'Any word from Tyler or Sinead?' Logan asked.

'They're heading to Raigmore for the post-mortem just after five, then Tyler's going to drive down here,' Ben said. 'Sinead's having some trouble getting care sorted for Harris, so she might have to follow tomorrow.'

'Fair enough. Can't be helped,' Logan said, pulling his coat on.

'Also, worth a mention—we've no' got anywhere to stay sorted yet. Hotels are chock-a-block,' Ben said. 'Admin here is trying to get us sorted out, but they've warned it might be a struggle.'

'You never know, we might not need it,' Logan said. He rapped a knuckle on the picture of the red-haired man on the board. 'If we find this bastard quickly, we could all be back home and sleeping in our own beds tonight.'

'Or my bed, in your case,' Ben said.

The others stopped what they were doing.

'Aye aye,' Dave remarked, raising a single salacious eyebrow.

Ben quietly cleared his throat. 'In the bed in my spare bedroom, I mean. No' my actual bed.'

Logan clapped him on the shoulder as he passed on the way to the door. 'Aye. Well. Play your cards right, Detective Inspector, and you never know your luck.'

—

The roads were noticeably quieter when Logan returned to Glenfinnan. The cars that had lined the grass verge around the visitor centre and monument were mostly gone. The car park was all but empty of civilian vehicles, although there was still a heavy police presence, and the tent that had been cobbled together at the top of the monument was still in place.

Logan continued past the visitor centre and floored the accelerator. The Fiesta whined shrilly in protest as it climbed the hill that led past one of the most picture-postcard churches the DCI had ever seen.

He had plenty of time to admire it, too, as the Fiesta crawled past, engine screaming like it was the victim in an old horror serial, and his right foot was the monster of the week.

The car calmed down as the road levelled off, then almost blew a gasket when he hung a right onto the steep driveway that led up to Glenfinnan railway station.

Pulling into a narrow space between two polis vans outside the station, Logan turned the key and the Fiesta gasped with relief, then fell silent, save for the faint ticks of the cooling engine.

With some difficulty, Logan clambered out from the driver's seat, squeezed between the car and the neighbouring van, then adjusted his coat so he didn't look like he'd just been pulled through a hedge backwards.

That done, he stood there in the fine Highland drizzle and spent a moment taking in his surroundings.

The station was a working one, with trains running regularly along the West Highland Line from Mallaig through to Fort William, then onwards to Glasgow. The route had been voted one of the most picturesque railway journeys in the world, and that, combined with the draw of the Glenfinnan Viaduct—or 'Harry Potter Bridge' as certain demographics of visitors and locals alike insisted on calling it—meant a steady supply of tourists all year round, with a veritable explosion of the bastards in the summer months.

The station had been converted to take full advantage of all that tourist money, although it had steered clear of going down the rabbit hole of cheap plastic wands and spellbooks.

Instead, the station building itself now housed a small, but lovingly curated museum that brought the history of the West Highland Line to life. On a siding off the main track were two old carriages—a d ining car, which was now a working cafe, and a sleeping car that had been converted into hostel accommod ation.

It had been a while since Logan had eaten, and while the former car was the one that by far appealed most, it was the second one he head ed for.

The female officer who had been d irecting traffic when he first arrived moved to block him at the foot of the stairs that led up to the sleeping car, then her mouth formed a little circle of surprise when she recognised him.

'Sorry, sir. Rain in my eyes,' she explained . 'Did n't see it was you for a second .'

'No bother. You all right out here?'

She'd clearly been stand ing out there for a while now, and the relentless precipitation had d ampened everything but her enthusiasm.

'Fine, sir. Just keeping an eye. Alan—Constable Brown, I mean—he's insid e, making sure there's no funny business.'

Logan looked past her, up to the d oor at the top of the stairs. 'Are they being kept apart?'

'Yes, sir. Everyone's in d ifferent rooms. There's not enough for all of them—most of them share rooms—but there are a couple in the d ining car.'

Logan glanced in the d irection of the other carriage. The wind ows were a little steamed up, but he could make out a Uniform sitting in the mid d le, and two other figures hunched over tables at each end .

'Right. Good ,' he said , then he gestured over at the main station build ing. 'Away you go and get insid e for a bit. No one's going to be trying a runner with two of us insid e.'

The officer sagged with relief. 'Thanks, sir. I'll see if they've got a towel, then be right back.'

She scurried off through the rain, and vanished insid e the build ing as quickly as her d ripping-wet legs and squelching feet would carry her.

The steep set of wood en steps that led up to the sleeping car entrance groaned ominously und er Logan's weight as he mad e his way up them, but held together long enough for him to open the narrow d oor and d uck insid e.

He found himself in a surprisingly spacious lounge area that felt like it had been surgically removed from the 1950s and transplanted here to the present d ay. The seating was arranged like a stand ard railway car of the era, allowing groups of four to hud d le together around tables that were fixed to the wall beneath the wind ows.

The d ecor was a throwback to the same period in time, with a lot of wood on d isplay, and a careful arrangement of old railway posters ad orning the walls.

Ever the pessimist, Logan had been bracing himself for a cramped , squalid shithole of a place, but the reality could n't be further from it.

A narrow d oor at the end of the short aisle led through into an equally surprising kitchen that wasn't much smaller than the one in his last flat. It was currently a bit of a mess, with pots of jam, bags of red uced -price fruit and veg, and an assortment of d irty d ishes all lying scattered across the crumb-strewn surfaces, but the fittings and fixtures themselves looked to be in good nick.

Before he could scope the place out any further, a male constable in his thirties popped his head into the kitchen from the narrow corrid or that presumably led to the sleeping area.

'Eh… hello?' the Uniform said , looking the new arrival up and d own and sizing up his chances if it came to a fight. *Not great* would be the only conclusion he could feasibly d raw, which explained the sigh of relief when Logan prod uced his warrant card and introd uced himself.

'They all through there?' the DCI asked .

'They are, sir, yes. I've kept them apart. Did n't want them d iscussing things between themselves until you'd had a chance to talk to them.'

'Good stuff,' Logan said . 'Scene of Crime gathered up her belongings?'

'They have, sir, yes. Been and gone.'

'Any ID found , d o you know?'

The Uniform puffed out his cheeks. 'You're asking the wrong man there, sir. They d id n't tell me anything.'

Logan nod d ed sympathetically. Dealing with Palmer's team was never a particularly pleasant experience. Most of them were professional enough, and none of them came close to the sheer *arseholery* of Palmer himself, but they could be an officious bunch if they wanted to be.

He approached the start of the corrid or and immed i-ately spotted a problem. 'Jesus Christ, what are they, blood y Hobbits?'

The corrid or could best be d escribed as 'cramped ', provid e the person d oing the d escribing had a flair for wild exaggera-tion. It stretched along the rest of the length of the carriage, but was so narrow that even if Logan turned sid eways and somehow sucked in everything from his thighs to his forehead , he'd struggle to fit along it.

It must've been a nightmare when it was busy, he thought. Trying to move several people into their d ifferent rooms would be like some sort of logic puzzle.

'Aye, you can forget that,' Logan told the uniformed officer. 'You bring them out one by one, I'll interview them out in the lounge bit.'

'Right you are, sir,' the constable said . 'Any particular ord er?'

'No, just as they come,' Logan said . He started to turn, but something caught his eye. 'Oh, and Constable?'

'Sir?'

Logan pointed to one of the kitchen countertops. 'Is that a kettle I see?'

Chapter 8

Anastasia Pelletier sounded French, looked Chinese, and dressed like a Raja from the Indian subcontinent. She came sweeping into the dining car lounge in a sunshine yellow sari made of silk and chiffon, and a similarly coloured hat with a peacock feather stitched onto the front.

Logan barely managed to contain an 'Oh, for fuck's sake' when the young woman appeared, and he hurriedly glugged down a gulp of tea to make sure the words didn't force their way out.

'May I?' she asked, gesturing to the chair across from him with a forced theatricality that, just three seconds after first clapping eyes on her, was already making his teeth itch.

'Please,' he said, setting down his mug and reaching for his notebook. 'Anastasia, isn't it?'

'Anastasia Pelletier,' she said grandly. 'That is correct.'

She tucked and folded various parts of the complicated garment she was wearing until she had enough of it bundled together to allow her to sit down.

Once she had finished making a meal of that simple task, she carefully spread the fabric out around her and smoothed it all into place with a few strokes from her gloved hands.

'Charmed,' she said, holding out a hand like she was the Pope offering up the Fisherman's Ring for him to kiss. He clasped the hand firmly, gave it a single curt shake, then let it go.

'Aye. Good,' he said, picking up his pen. 'Let's start with the basics. Can you tell me your real name?'

'My name? Why, it's Anastasia Pelletier,' she replied with a roll of her eyes and a wave of a gloved hand . 'I suggest you pay closer attention, good man.'

Logan regard ed her for a moment, then very d eliberately set his pen d own again. He interlocked his fingers on the table between them and d id something with his mouth that wasn't really a smile, but d id show quite a lot of teeth.

'Before we get off on the wrong foot here, miss—if it's no' too late for that alread y—I'm going to remind you that another young woman has been murd ered . A young woman who, I'm led to believe, you've been spend ing a lot of time with. A friend of yours, even.'

The chair beneath him creaked as he shifted his weight forward on it. The woman in the sari leaned back the same number of inches.

'My job is to find whoever is responsible and put them in prison,' Logan continued . 'Your job—your only job—is to answer my questions fully and honestly, and no' to piss me off. So far, I'm sorry to say, you are failing on both counts.'

He unclasped his hand s, picked up his pen, and held the nib against the paper of his pad .

'So, are you going to grow the fuck up, stop all... whatever this nonsense is, and help me figure out who killed your friend ? Or are we going to continue this conversation in a more formal capacity back at the station, only minus the blood y peacock feather?'

He gave her a few second s to consid er her options, then pressed on again with his questioning.

'Name?'

'It's... it is actually Anastasia Pelletier,' she replied , still in the same French accent, but with notably less pomp and attitud e this time. She fished in her sari and prod uced a small burgund y book. 'My passport. See?'

Logan took the passport from her, flicked to the page with her d etails, and scanned the French text. Sure enough, she was telling the truth about the name. He scribbled it d own, along with her d ate of birth.

'That makes you... what? Twenty-three?'

'Twenty-two. Twenty-three in one week.'

'Right, aye,' said Logan, flicking through the passport. Most of the pages were stamped , pred ominantly by other EU Member States. 'Been travelling a while?'

'Almost ten months,' Anastasia replied . 'Mostly Europe. Thailand for one month. We went to see the Taj Mahal.'

'In Thailand ? That's some trick.'

She stared blankly at him, like she either had n't und erstood his accent or could n't figure out what the word s meant.

'I assume you went to Ind ia, too?' he said , to clarify.

'Oh. Yes. We d id . Where we saw the Taj Mahal.'

'We?' he asked . 'The same group you're with now?'

'Some. Not all. We... mix-up. Meet new people as we move around . Some stay, some move on. Some for a few d ays, some for much longer.'

'What can you tell me about...' He hesitated , his mouth reluctant to form the word s. 'Hermione Grey? I'm assuming that isn't her real name?'

Across the table, Anastasia shrugged just one should er, raising it so high she was briefly resting a cheek against it. 'I d o not know for sure. It is what she always wished to be called , and I—we, all of us—were... how d o you say? We were respectful of her wishes.'

Great. That was no help, then.

'Bit d angerous to be travelling around with people if you d on't even know their names, isn't it?' Logan asked .

Anastasia pulled her half-shrug again. 'She d id not seem d angerous. And we all look out for one another.' Her eyes blurred , and she wiped them on the arm of her sari. 'At least, that is what I thought. But now... oh, poor, sweet Hermione.' She placed the back of her hand against her forehead . 'It is so cruel. I cannot bear it. I just cannot bear the thought of it.'

There was a real d anger that the girl was about to slid e back into character again, Logan thought, so he ad d ed a touch of urgency to his voice in the hope it d ragged her back to reality.

'Had she been arguing with anyone in the group?' Logan urged , but the girl just shook her head . 'What about this...' Another hesitation. '...*Moof* character?'

'Corey?'

Oh, thank Christ for that, Logan thought, jotting the name d own on his pad . 'Corey? That's his name? Corey Sand erson?'

'Yes, that is correct. We all call him Moof.' She frowned , like she was recalling a joke she'd never quite grasped . 'Because he talks a lot. That is how he got nickname. From school, I think. His accent is hard for me, sometimes. Like yours.'

'He's Scottish?' Logan asked , trying not to take offence at that remark.

'Yes. From Scotland , yes. Uh... Scotland east?'

'The east coast?'

'Yes. Yes, I think that is correct. East.'

'Thanks. You're being very helpful Miss...' He stole a quick peek at his pad . '...Pelletier. You're d oing very well.'

It took a second or two for this to filter through the language barrier, then she smiled , pleased with herself. 'I can go?'

'Not quite yet, I'm afraid , no,' Logan told her. 'I've still got a few questions to ask about Hermione.' He watched her closely, stud ying the lines of her face for anything that might contrad ict the next word s out of her mouth. 'The main one being, why would anyone want to kill her?'

–

DC Tyler Neish stood frozen in place, his heart thumping so fast it was one constant hum, his stomach twisting around itself as it fought to hold onto its contents.

He could feel the heat of his breath on his face, trapped as it was behind the protective face mask. It was d ragging up the temperature of the rest of his bod y, too, so his shirt was now sticking to his back, and he was quietly confid ent his feet would squelch when he walked .

'You all right, Detective Constable?'

Tyler tore his eyes from the ceiling and met the gaze of Dr Shona Maguire. She stood up near the head area of an operating trolley, while he stood d own at the opposite end , trying very hard not to look at the sheet between them.

The shape und er the sheet was technically the third occupant of the room, although, only if you d id n't get too bogged d own in semantics. Because, while two of the room's occupants were upright, breathing, and otherwise alive, the third was none of these things.

'Aye. Good . Fine,' he lied , swallowing back a tasteless mouthful of saliva.

'You look uncomfortable,' Shona said .

'Me? Nah!' Tyler replied with false conviction. 'I'm grand . I'm just… another officer was meant to be here with me, but she could n't make it, so…' He wiped his brow on his shirt sleeve and blew upward s, trying to expel the warm air through the top of his mask. 'It's hot in here, isn't it? Is it hot in here? Or is it just me?'

'I'm not really feeling it,' Shona said . She ind icated the shape between them. 'If it's easier, I can just type everything up. You d on't have to go through all this.'

Tyler straightened his back and should ers, clenched his fists into tight balls, then relaxed them again and tried forcing some levity back in his voice.

'It's no problem. I can cope with pretty much— *Oh God, what the fuck is that?!*'

Shona followed his outstretched finger until she found a compact black mass that closely resembled the lower half of a human stomach. It was sitting in a small bowl on a set of scales just to the right of the trolley.

'Oh. That? That's a trichobezoar,' Shona explained .

Tyler stared at her, his face still contorted into a scowl of horrified confusion. 'A tricho…?'

'Bezoar.'

'Is that not a kind of d inosaur?'

'I'm afraid not, fun as that would be,' Shona said , her eyes suggesting a smile behind her mask. 'It's a hairball. Took it from the victim's stomach. I reckon she's been eating her hair since she was… ooh. Eight or nine, at least? It gathers in the stomach, can't be d igested , and so forms these packed clumps. They're not that unusual, although hers is bigger than most I've seen.'

'She ate her own hair?' Tyler asked , his voice rising in inflection, like this was worse than any murd er. 'Why would she eat her own hair?'

'Not on a plate with a knife and fork. Chewed on it. Habit, probably, although the amount she'd packed away in there suggests she most likely had an anxiety d isord er of some kind .'

'Blood y Nora,' remarked Tyler, who felt like he was on the brink of forming an anxiety d isord er of his own.

Shona took the ed ge of the sheet. 'Right, you read y for this?'

Tyler swallowed , flexed his fingers, then nod d ed . 'Read y.'

Shona pulled back the sheet, revealing the bod y below.

'Fuck. No. Not read y, not read y,' Tyler said .

Shona covered the bod y again.

She gave him a moment.

'Right. OK. Read y,' Tyler said .

The sheet was pulled back again. He flinched , but held his nerve.

'There. Not so bad , is it?' Shona said .

If the bod y wasn't bad , Tyler would hate to see one that was. Hermione Grey—or whatever her name was—would 've been an absolute stunner just twenty-four hours ago. A perfect ten.

Now, she was like something out of a horror film, all sutures, and bruising, and mottled grey skin.

'Fine,' Tyler said , keeping his throat tight in the hope it would hold back anything that might try to escape his stomach. 'What d id you find ? And , eh, I'm pretty new at this bit. Can you keep it quite basic?'

58

'Basic. Right.' Shona thought for a moment. 'Well, she's dead, for starters.'

Despite the sights and the smells doing their best to stop him, Tyler smiled behind his mask. 'Maybe not *quite* that basic.'

'Right. You might want to take notes,' Shona suggested, and Tyler fumbled in his pockets with his gloved hands until he found his pad and pencil. 'I put her age at around eighteen to twenty. She's in good health—or she was, anyway, not so much now—and preliminary tests show no signs of alcohol in the blood, although there are some elevated levels that might suggest drugs. Toxicology report will tell us more, but it'll take a few days to a week.'

'Cause of death?' Tyler asked, because he was pretty sure that was a thing that detectives were meant to ask in this situation. They did on telly, anyway.

'Basically what you'd expect from someone left dangling from a rope.' She noted that Tyler wasn't writing. 'Asphyxiation.'

Tyler's pencil began to move across his pad. His brow furrowed a few letters in and he regarded what he'd written in confusion.

'YXI,' Shona said, and the DC blushed just a little as he carried on writing.

'Thanks.'

'No problem,' Shona told him. 'You're doing fine. You'll want to write this bit down, though.'

She leaned forward and indicated the victim's throat. It was, unsurprisingly, wrapped in a scarf of bruises and rope burns.

'It wasn't the rope that cut off her air supply. See here? These marks were made by hands. Partially collapsed the oesophagus.'

Tyler rubbed his throat in sympathy. 'Meaning?'

'Meaning, I think someone strangled her *then* tied the rope around her neck, probably after she was already dead.'

'Why would someone do that?' Tyler wondered.

Shona shrugged. 'You tell me.'

Tyler stared back at her like a rabbit in car head lights. 'Um...'

'I d on't mean you have to tell me right now,' Shona said . 'It's not a test. I mean, it's not really for me to figure out, is it? That's your lot's d epartment.'

'Oh!' Tyler ejected , visibly relieved . 'Right, aye. No bother. We'll figure that bit out.'

'Well, here's another piece to the puzzle for you,' Shona said , walking around the table and stopping level with the victim's waist.

Leaning forward , she ind icated the backs of the young woman's forearms. 'Take a look at this.'

Tyler hesitated . He felt like he was pretty much as close to the corpse as he wanted to be. Much closer than he wanted to be, in fact. He had no urge to bring any part of himself closer, least of all his face.

'She's not going to bite,' Shona urged .

This was true, but she *was* going to smell. Then again, the od our of the place was firmly jammed up both nostrils now, and had most likely alread y permeated every pore of his bod y, so one more whiff probably would n't hurt.

With just the faintest suggestion of a whimper, Tyler leaned d own and followed Shona's finger.

'What's that? Are those scrapes?' he asked , spotting some pretty extensive surface d amage to the area between the victim's elbow and wrist.

'They are. Several layers of skin rubbed away. Rubbed away completely in some spots. Sid es of the hand s, too.'

She straightened up again. This could 've been Tyler's cue to d o the same, but instead he squatted d own, giving himself a better view of the und ersid e of the victim's arms. Shona stood back and watched him, her smirk hid d en by her mask.

'What was she scraped on? Stone, maybe? I've seen stone d o that. Have to be pretty rough, though.' He pointed to the arm closest to him. 'Can I...?'

'Knock yourself out,' the pathologist urged .

Tyler pinched the arm between one gloved finger and thumb, and eased it up off the table, giving himself a better view of the d amage.

'Aye, that's pretty nasty,' he remarked .

'I've seen similar on d rag victims in the past, although it's usually much worse.'

Tyler looked back and up over his should er, his face awash with confusion. 'Drag victims? What, as in the guys that d ress up as—'

'As in people who are d ragged behind moving vehicles,' Shona said , saving him the ind ignity of finishing that question.

That mad e much more sense, Tyler conced ed , then he returned the arm to the slab more or less where he'd found it. 'Any more anywhere else?'

'There's some on her calves and the back of the heels. Little bit on the back of the thighs. Mostly, it's her arms, though.'

Tyler leaned sid eways to get a look at the und ersid e of the legs, then he had a moment of clarity about what he was d oing and he sprang back upright like his legs were powered by pistons.

'Right. That's… that's all very interesting,' he said , hurried ly swallowing again.

'Theories?' Shona asked .

Tyler took on that same startled rabbit look as before. 'About…?' He pointed to the bod y.

Shona could 've come back with at least three or four d evastatingly sarcastic replies, but to her cred it chose not to. 'Yes. About the bod y. Specifically, the scrapes.'

Tyler glanced d own at his notepad like the answer might be written there somewhere. To his immense d isappointment, it wasn't.

But there was something, though. Not on the pad , but pulling itself together in his brain somewhere. He could feel thoughts shifting around in there. Drawing together. Organising themselves.

'She was wearing a t-shirt, right? When she was found ?'

'That's right.'

Tyler slipped his notepad and pencil into his shirt pocket, then placed his hand s behind him, wrists together. 'Right, so. Hand s tied like this. T-shirt covers her bod y and the top of her arms, protects those parts from the worst of it. Legs and feet are bare, so they get it, but the arms take the brunt.'

He picked up a leg by the ankle and checked the back of the heel. 'It's pretty minor. Would 've hurt, aye, but no worse than coming off a bike.'

'So...?' Shona said , nud ging him toward s a conclusion.

'It's like she was d ragged , but lightly, somehow,' Tyler said , setting the leg d own again. 'If she was pulled along a road , or whatever, for any length of time, it'd be way worse on the heels. State of the arms suggests she was d ragged for a while, though.'

'Meaning...?'

'Meaning... what?' Tyler muttered , his eyes flitting in all d irections like he was seeing a myriad of possibilities before him, but not settling on any.

Finally, when he had looked through all of them, he threw his arms into the air and sighed . 'Meaning, I d on't know. Unless she was on the moon, where gravity wasn't...'

He stopped , then half-choked on an unexpected , 'Fuck!' when the puzzle revealed itself, the truth of it sud d enly becoming clear, like the 3D image in a Magic Eye picture you've been staring at for blood y hours.

'Gravity. She wasn't pulled along the ground . She was pulled upward s. They d id n't hang her from the top of the tower, they hoisted her up from the bottom!'

'God . Yes. That makes total sense,' Shona said , neglecting to mention that she'd come to the same conclusion an hour ago. 'Well d one.'

Tyler was pleased he was wearing the mask because he could n't keep the grin off his face, and he'd hate to appear too cocky.

'Well, it's just a theory,' he said . It was important to be humble at times like these. Nobod y liked a braggart, even if it was *completely* justified .

'Jack will be impressed ,' Shona told him. 'He speaks very highly of you.'

Tyler's eyes wid ened in shock. 'Does he?'

Shona smirked . 'Nah, not really,' she ad mitted . 'But I would n't take it too personally.'

'Oh. Haha. Right, aye.'

Shona groaned . She could n't d o it to him.

'He told me to say that. To wind you up,' she revealed . 'Truth is, he might not speak highly of you—he might go out of his way *not* to speak highly of you, in fact—but he clearly thinks it.'

Tyler brightened again. 'You reckon?'

'I d o,' Shona confirmed .

She interlocked her fingers and pushed them outward s, cracking her knuckles so loud ly that it mad e Tyler d raw a breath in through his teeth.

'Now, then,' she began, ind icating the bod y with a flick of her eyes. 'Want to get into the good stuff? Because I've found something that I think might turn out to be *very* significant ind eed ...'

Chapter 9

DCI Logan was d etecting a running theme among Hermione Grey's travelling companions.

They were a shower of blood y weird oes.

He'd spoken to most of them now, and a bigger group of misfits he d id n't think he'd ever seen. Given the organisation he worked for, and the colleagues he'd had over the years, that was really blood y saying something.

The brightly coloured theatricality of Anastasia Pelletier had given way to the whimsicality of a space cad et that tried to introd uce herself as 'Trixie Fae' before Logan knocked that on the head with a scowl and a 'Try again'.

Her real name was the marked ly less interesting Jane Smith. Trixie Fae was her Elven name, she'd explained , with absolutely no prompting from Logan who frankly could n't care less. She thought it mad e her sound like 'one of the fairy-folk.'

Logan, on the other hand , thought it mad e her sound like a New York prostitute from the 1980s.

She d id not look impressed when he told her.

Trixie had just turned nineteen, came from Bath in England , and had set off travelling with Deird rie Mair five months ago. She had loved Italy and France, been less keen on Spain, and hated Germany. That was where they'd met Hermione, which she insisted was 'the only moment of brightness in an otherwise d reary nation', although Logan thought he picked up a sugges-tion of regret about the meeting. He mad e a note to pursue it further at a later time, listened to her waffling on about fairy magic for as long as he could stand it—roughly six second s—then sent her packing back to her room.

Next in was a surly-looking lad with blue hair, matching lipstick, and what Logan was going to go ahead and assume was a lifelong battle with obesity. His name was Kenny Murphy, and Logan heard him before he saw him, his bulky frame squeaking along both corrid or walls as he battled his way through it.

He was from the far south of the Republic of Ireland — County Wexford —but was sorely lacking in the famous Irish charm, spend ing most of the interview staring at the table and mumbling out answers of just one or two word s.

He'd been travelling solo for most of the last year, although he had n't yet mad e it beyond the UK. The rest of Europe was d efinitely on the card s at some point, he insisted , but he'd lost a lot of money after getting mugged in Lond on, and had been scraping by d oing the od d bit of work here and there ever since.

'Why d id n't you just go home?' Logan asked , but from the flash of panic and the way the lad shrank back into the chair, it was clear that going home wasn't an option, for whatever reason.

Not so much travelling, then, as homeless and on the move.

The next lad in, Hayd en Howard , came as something of a relief. To begin with, at least. He was a little old er than the others—twenty-six, it transpired —and was apparently the first of the group not to get the memo to come in some form of fancy d ress.

Instead , he wand ered in wearing Bermud a shorts, flip-flops, and an unpressed short sleeve shirt unbuttoned far enough to show off the top of a six-pack. He slid onto the seat across from Logan, all bronzed skin and surfer hair, his mouth constantly moving as he chewed on a wad of gum.

He hailed from New Zealand and had been travelling for about six months now. Originally, he was supposed to be going with a mate, 'only, he went and got his bird knocked up, see? Daft bugger. But I thought, nah, fuck it. Screw staying home, I'm going, anyway.'

Whereas getting information from Kenny Murphy had been like trying to extract AB Positive from the proverbial rock, Hayden Howard would n't shut up. Logan pretty much knew the lad 's whole life story after asking just one question.

He was an only child. He'd done badly at school. He'd bounced from one job to another, then decided to go travelling a year ago, primarily so he could sleep with as many different women from as many different cultures as possible.

'All about broadening the horizons, brah,' he'd said, and then Logan had forcibly steered him back to the matter at hand.

He'd been travelling with Hermione for a couple of months, though he'd actually crossed paths with her back in New Zealand when he was still getting organised. They'd swapped numbers, and had made plans to meet up somewhere down the road. Down the road had become Thailand, and they'd been knocking around together ever since.

'I never tapped that, though,' he insisted, anticipating Logan's question before he'd asked it. 'I mean, she was hot. Smoking hot. But she wasn't into guys.'

'She was gay?'

'Christ, yeah. All lezzed up with Deeds.'

'Deeds?'

'Deirdrie. Her girlfriend.' Hayden looked back in the direction of the kitchen. 'She's through back. Pretty cut up about it all.'

'Aye, we met down by the monument,' Logan said.

Hayden shot another, more furtive glance at the doorway leading through to the rest of the sleeping car. 'You know about Moof?'

'I know of him,' Logan confirmed.

'Know where he is?'

'Do you?'

Hayden shook his head. 'Nah. But…'

He twitched and bit his lip as if battling some compulsion to say the next few words.

'But what, son?'

The younger man d ropped his voice to a whisper. 'Moof reckoned he and Hermione were pretty tight. Like *tight* tight. Know what I'm saying?'

He mad e a circle with a finger and thumb, then slid the ind ex finger of the other hand in and out of the hole in the mid d le.

'They were having sex?'

Hayd en flinched . 'Keep it d own, brah. Deed s has no id ea.'

'How d o you know he was telling the truth?'

'I d on't,' Hayd en ad mitted . 'I mean, I asked Hermione about it one night—reckoned if he could have a crack at her, there was nothing stopping me from firing one up her.'

'And they say romance is d ead ,' Logan remarked .

'She d enied it,' Hayd en said . 'Called bullshit. Told me Moof was lying. Next thing I know, they go off for a walk together. Just the two of them. She comes back all puffy-eyed like she's been crying. He rocks up an hour later, and won't say a word to me. Won't even look at me, like he knows I know he was talking shit. You know?'

'When was this?' Logan asked .

'Few d ays back. Second night here, so… what? Sund ay?' He turned to the d oor and raised his voice to a shout. 'Trix? When d id we get here?'

There was a tiny pause before the reply came. 'Saturd ay, I think.'

'That is correct. It was Saturd ay,' confirmed a familiar French accent.

Hayd en turned in his chair to face the d etective again. 'Yeah, so it would 've been Sund ay when they went off together.'

'And how were they after that?' Logan asked . 'Around each other, I mean.'

'Don't think they spoke much. It was all a bit fucking awkward , to be honest. A bit fucking uncomfortable. Everyone picked up on it, not just me.'

Logan mad e a note in his pad . 'And d id you mention it to anyone else? What Corey had told you?'

Hayd en's forehead creased into lines of confusion. Logan sighed .

'Moof. What Moof told you?'

'Oh. Shit. Yeah, sorry,' Hayd en said , the penny d ropping. 'No. Not a word . Hermione asked me not to.' He stopped chewing his gum long enough to flash the d etective a toothy grin. 'And , believe it or not for a big-mouthed jackass like me, I'm actually pretty good at keeping secrets.'

-

Hamza clicked the hand set of his d esk phone back into the crad le, and finished scribbling his notes on the big A4 d esk pad .

DCI Logan had called back to the station between interviews to give them Moof Sand erson's real name, and Hamza had quickly collated an extensive amount of information on the young man. Just, sad ly, not his whereabouts.

'He's not with his parents, then?' Ben asked .

Hamza shook his head . 'No, sir. They haven't seen him in months. Haven't heard from him at all since mid -August. They follow what he's up to on Instagram. I'm going to circulate the link to the team for reference. I've had a quick gand er and it's mostly scenic stuff. He only appears in a few.'

'It'll help build up a picture of where he's been, though.'

'Aye, be hand y for that, right enough,' Hamza confirmed . 'They gave us a couple of d ifferent mobile numbers for him. One's going to voicemail, the other one's cut off. I'm going to get onto the network and hand it over to the tech bod s to see if we can get a location from the phone.'

'Have we checked with the bus and the train?' Ben asked . 'If he's no' knocking around town somewhere, he must've taken transport.'

'Or hitched ,' Dave suggested from his d esk. SOC had started d elivering bags of evid ence, and he was carefully cataloguing it and labelling it up. 'When I went travelling after I left school, I hitched . Cheaper than public transport.'

'You went travelling?' asked Hamza, sound ing impressed . 'Where d id you go?'

'Well, the plan was to d o a big round the world jaunt. Proper ad venture stuff,' Dave said . 'Start off in Inverness and circumnavigate the globe.'

'Nice one. How far d id you get?'

'Greenock.'

'*Greenock?*'

'Aye. Went into a pub there, blew the whole bud get in twelve hours, and hitched north again four d ays later after I woke up,' Dave said . A wistful smile played across his face as he recalled the experience. 'Worst hangover I've ever had .'

'Christ, watch out, Michael Palin, eh?' Ben remarked , then he turned his attention back to Hamza. 'Check with Uniform where the most likely hitchhiking spots are. Have them d rive by. Never know, he might still be around .'

Hamza reckoned that was unlikely, but nod d ed and reached for his phone again. 'Any id ea when Tyler's coming d own? Be hand y to have an extra pair of hand s,' he said , prod d ing at the number pad .

'Still waiting to hear back from him after the PM,' Ben said . 'If Sinead 's coming d own in the morning, he might as well wait until then. Still no word of us getting anywhere to stay, so no point ad d ing to the problem.'

'True,' Hamza agreed , then he pressed the hand set to his ear and turned to face his screen as he waited for someone from Uniform to pick up.

Ben shunted himself up out of his seat with a groan and a creaking of bones, then mad e his way across to Dave at the Exhibits d esk. At first glance, it looked as if all the clear plastic evid ence bags had been d ropped onto the d esk from a height. Look more closely, though, and it was possible to make out a suggestion of some kind of system. A method to the mad ness.

'Anything juicy come in?' the detective inspector asked.

'Bits and pieces, aye,' Dave said.

Without him really looking, his hand reached for one of a few larger bags in a pile, and he set it on top of all the others. A coil of climbing rope lay curled up inside, like a snake held frozen in stasis.

'This was the rope she was strung up with,' he explained. 'It's climbing rope, but pretty cheap stuff. Not sure I'd trust putting my weight on the end of it.'

Ben picked up the bag and turned it over in his hands, studying the contents. The rope was maybe seven or eight feet long. Factor in the noose that would 've been at the end, and the victim would n't have had far to fall before it went tight around her neck.

'I suppose the rope breaking on you is less of a worry if someone's using it to hang you with.'

'Depends where they're hanging you,' Dave countered. 'I would n't fancy falling off that monument.'

'Least you'd have a chance,' Ben muttered. 'The fall's onto grass. It might not kill you.'

'Aye, if you're lucky it might just shove your arse out through the top of your head,' Dave agreed.

He reached for another bag. This one contained the t-shirt the victim had been wearing. The scrawled message was clearly visible through the plastic.

'*Planet rapist*,' Ben read.

'They id entified the stuff poured over her, too. Motor oil. And somewhere...' He raised both hands in front of him for a moment, as if seeking spiritual guid ance, then reached straight for another bag. 'There's the bottle it came in.'

Ben took the offered bag and turned the bottle over. It was Esso brand car engine oil. Two litres. Now completely empty.

'They get any prints off it?'

'It's clean, unfortunately,' Dave replied. 'No prints off anything.'

'Not even the badge?'

'Not even the badge. Guess he was wearing gloves or wiped everything down.'

'Bit odd that,' Ben mused. 'Wiping your own badge clean that you've accidentally left at the scene.'

He set both evidence packages down on the desk. Both were immediately moved to other areas of the pile.

'We'll get hold of the local Esso station, see if anyone there remembers anything.'

'Pretty sure people buy oil there most days,' Dave reasoned.

'Aye, but you never know. Maybe something jumped out at someone.'

'Could get a lucky break, I suppose.'

Ben nodded. 'Lucky breaks are what solve half the cases we investigate. Always worth pursuing.'

Both men turned when Hamza joined them at the desk. 'How did it go?' asked Ben.

'Tech team are getting onto the phone network to see what's what,' the DS replied. Something on the desk caught his eye, and he frowned for a moment, then shook it off. 'Uniform's going to check out the most common hitching spots now. I spoke to Tyler quickly, too. He was just coming out of the post-mortem.'

'God, I'd have liked to have seen that,' Ben remarked. 'And?'

'I didn't get a lot out of him yet, think he was trying not to throw up. But based on what he told me...' Hamza picked up the bag that had caught his eye and turned it over, studying the coil of blue cord inside. 'I'd say we're missing some rope.'

Chapter 10

Logan stood   on the shore looking out at Loch Shiel, the monument towering above him at his back, the tarpaulin tent crackling as it shifted   on the breeze.

It was after seven now, and   the d ay was close to calling it a night, the sun d rooping behind   the mountains like a fruit left to hang too long on its tree.

As he watched , three bird s went flying across the surface of the loch, croaking loud ly through their black throats as they skimmed   above the water in a tight formation.

He was relieved   to have finished   the interviews with Hermione's travelling companions, although the information he'd   gleaned   from them had n't amounted   to anything particularly useful.

She'd   insisted   on going by Hermione Grey at all times, and most of her friend s either assumed   it was her real name, or had been so respectful of her wishes that they'd   never thought to ask what name her parents had   given her.

Only Deird rie Mair could   offer any help whatsoever on that front. She'd   heard   a passport control officer ad d ress Hermione by her real first name once, but it had   been noisy in the airport, and   she'd   been tired , and   so had n't really been paying all that much attention.

Alice, she thought. Possibly Alex. Feasibly, something else entirely.

As Hayd en had   warned , Deird rie was more cut-up than the rest of Hermione's travelling companions. They'd   hit it off from the moment they'd met in Germany, ended up in a drunken embrace back at the hostel, and had been a couple ever since.

Neither of them had been in a gay relationship before then. 'But it felt right,' Deirdrie had told Logan, the words strained through a mesh of tears. 'Me and her together, we fit. We worked. It just felt right.'

From the way she described it, their relationship had been intense from the get-go. They did most things together after that. Shared rooms—and often beds—in whatever hostels they ended up at, huddled side-by-side on buses and trains, and to⦁ the same temporary jobs wherever they could.

They ate together, danced together, laughed together.

'And now she's gone,' Deirdrie had sobbed, her head on the table, arms wrapped around it. 'And she's not coming back.'

She was cut-up. That bit was real, no doubt about it.

But something about the rest of it…

Logan couldn't pinpoint what bothered him about her statement, exactly. Maybe it was the insistence that everything was so relentlessly rosy. They'd never argued, she'd said. Never kept secrets. It was the perfect relationship.

Maybe it was his personal bias talking, but Logan knew there was no such thing.

The four others he'd spoken to didn't really know the rest of the group very well. They were all girls, all at the tail end of their teens, and they'd been on the road together since leaving Ontario two months earlier.

They'd been in Glenfinnan for a week now, and had only met Hermione's group for the first time when they had come swarming into the sleeping car on Saturday.

Since then, two of the women had engaged in sex with Hayden Howard. Neither of them was aware that the other one had.

They'd confirmed that Deirdrie and Hermione had seemed close, although two of the four—the two who hadn't fallen victim to Hayden Howard's charms—reckoned Deirdrie was far more invested in the relationship than Hermione had been.

'Deed s just seemed ... clingy,' one of them had remarked. 'And sometimes Hermione would have this look, like she just wanted to be left alone.'

Logan had felt vind icated by that. *Perfect relationship, my arse.*

A squelching of a foot sinking into a pud d le of mud snapped him back to the here and now. He turned to see Geoff Palmer hopping clumsily through the bracken, muttering below his breath as runny brown slud ge d ripped from his shoe.

He'd changed out of his coveralls now, and the small army of Scene of Crime operatives had packed most of the equipment away in their vans. The tent would stay for a few d ays to protect the scene, in case there was anything that need ed to be d ouble-checked .

'Watch where you're stepping there, Geoff,' Logan warned . 'Bit mud d y.'

'Aye? You d on't blood y say,' Palmer spat. He kicked his foot around , trying to fling off the worst of the mud , then sighed and planted it back on the ground . 'That's us packing up.'

'So I see,' Logan said .

'We've d elivered what we found to your man at Fort William. Taken samples of anything that might tell us more.'

'I can hear a "but" coming.'

'*But* whether you'll need it or not is another matter. We'll process it all for the prosecution, obviously, but from what I hear you've alread y got your man.'

'Have we? And who's that?'

'The fella CID was talking about. Boof, or Moof, or Poof, or whatever he's called . Did a runner the night she d ied ? Telltale sign, if ever I saw one.'

Logan nod d ed slowly, then looked back out across the water. One of the bird s he'd seen earlier was now running across the surface, its webbed feet spread ing ripples on the otherwise motionless loch.

'How's Shona?' Geoff asked , and Logan could n't miss the resentment in his voice.

'Aye, she's good. We'd planned dinner this weekend. Just the two of us, you know? Nice meal out somewhere,' Logan said, rubbing it in.

It was true. They had planned dinner. Of course, now that he was seventy miles away dealing with the murder of a young woman, and she was preoccupied with the corpse of the young woman in question, the chances of the plan actually coming to fruition were slim.

This, it seemed, was the story of their relationship. So many close calls. So many not-quite-dates. So many chances to get to know each other cut short by death, or kidnapping, or—in one recent instance—the teenage daughter of a Russian mobster.

Their entire relationship was one big 'almost'.

Not that he was going to give Geoff Palmer the satisfaction of knowing that.

'I got into a relationship recently myself,' Palmer said. He yawned and stretched, an exaggerated attempt to make this sound like it was no big deal.

'Good for you, Geoff,' Logan told him. 'Blind, is she?'

'What? No!'

'Masochist?'

'No! She's very nice, actually. Fit. Proper fit,' he said, waggling his eyebrows. He licked his lips then pursed them in a way that was 50 per cent creepy, and 50 per cent even bloody more so. 'Right little goer, she is. Twenty-eight. So, you know, young enough to still have everything in the right place, old enough to know what she's doing.'

Logan watched the bird running across the water, and idly wondered if he could do the same. If he put some welly into it, he could be halfway across the loch before Palmer knew what was happening.

'I'm very happy for you, Geoff. What's her name?' he asked, steering the conversation onto less nauseating ground.

The hesitation was only a split-second, but it was enough to tell Logan everything.

'Rihanna,' Palmer said . His mouth clamped shut as soon as the word was out, like it was trying to swallow it back down.

Logan turned to look at him. 'Rihanna?'

Geoff swallowed , then nod d ed , d oubling d own. 'Tha right.'

'Rihanna what?'

Another hesitation. A fraction longer this time.

'Smith.'

'Rihanna Smith?'

'She lives in Aberd een,' Palmer said . 'She's... a nurse. Aye. Likes to wear the uniform when we meet up. If you get my meaning?'

Had Logan not alread y d oubted the existence of Ms Rihanna Smith that last remark would 've set alarm bells ringing. He'd known plenty of nurses over the years, and not one of them had ever felt attractive in their work gear.

There was very little they consid ered less sexy than a thread - bare NHS tabard flecked with blood , piss, and whatever other bod ily fluid s happened to be flying around the place on that particular d ay. Most of them could n't get the blood y thing off quickly enough—and not for any funny business.

Logan resisted the urge to call bullshit, and left Geoff with the microscopic shred s of d ignity that he clung to like the last of his hair.

'Well, good luck to the pair of you,' Logan said . 'I'll be expecting an invite to the wed d ing.'

Palmer interlocked his fingers and placed them behind his head like he was lounging on a d eckchair in the sun.

'Christ, no. There'll be no wed d ing for me, Jack. Last thing I want is to be tied d own to one woman. No, it's the free-agent life for yours truly. Sasha and me are just all about the passion.'

'Who's Sasha?' Logan asked .

Palmer froze, panic etched across his face. 'That's my pet name for Rihanna,' he said , unconvincingly. Then he turned to look back at the vans and cupped a hand to one ear, straining to hear a shout that had never come. 'Eh? Aye. I'll be right there.'

He faced Logan again, rolled his eyes and smiled . 'Boss's work's never d one,' he said . 'I'd best shoot off. We'll get the preliminary report sent out to you. Probably tomorrow now.'

'Fine. We'll be here,' Logan said .

Palmer turned and set off in the d irection of the vans. He turned back a few steps later. 'About Shona,' he said , and Logan felt himself bristle in anticipation of what was going to come next.

'Aye? What about her?'

'She's a good one. Make sure you treat her right.'

Logan blinked , surprised by the sincerity of the comment. 'I will,' he said .

Without another word , both men turned their backs, and Logan allowed himself a grin when he heard a squelch, a schlop, and a muttered 'not my other fucking shoe' from behind him.

—

Ben Ford e broke the news as soon as Logan had battled his way past Moira in reception and mad e it back to the Incid ent Room. The enormity of it almost put him on his arse, and he had to perch on the ed ge of a d esk while he consid ered the ramifications.

'*Pregnant?*' he said , just in case he'd somehow misheard . 'She was pregnant?'

'About six weeks along,' Ben confirmed . 'She would n't have been showing outward ly. It's possible she d id n't even know herself.'

'If she d id , I d on't think she'd mentioned it to anyone,' Logan said , mentally running back over everything the gaggle of od d balls she'd been travelling with had said . There was nothing in there that suggested any of them had suspected anything like this. 'Pregnant,' he said again. 'Jesus blood y Christ. So much for her being gay.'

77

'Not uncommon for lesbians to have babies, though,' Dave remarked . 'My mate's sister's gay, and she and her missus have two kid s. I think they got some fella they knew to fire it up her and —'

Logan stopped him there. 'Aye, not unusual for gay couples to have kid s. But there's no way this was planned . She's nineteen or twenty. She's backpacking around the world . She's no' going to stop off for a quick skoosh of artificial insemination along the way.' He shook his head . 'No. It had to be an accid ent. She must've hooked up with some lad somewhere.'

'Or some lad hooked up with her without her knowled ge,' Hamza suggested . 'Happens quite a bit with youngsters in hostels. Too much to d rink, maybe slipped something. Next thing they know, they're waking up without their und erwear.'

Hamza was right, of course. That sort of thing happened far too regularly, and often the women involved had no clue what had been d one to them while they slept.

Logan checked his watch, then stood up. 'Get onto Uniform, will you? Reiterate that no one is to leave that hostel until I say so. I'm going to want to talk to them all again, as d epressing a thought as that is. We'll bring them in tomorrow, put the wind up them a bit in here, see what comes out of them.'

'Will d o, sir,' Hamza confirmed , reaching for his phone. 'Rest of the pathology report's in the shared inbox.'

Ben prod uced a printed single-page summary and passed it over to the DCI. 'Based on what the report tells us, our current theory is that the bod y was hoisted up from below. Strangled by hand , possibly at the bottom of the monument, then a rope was lowered d own from above, looped around the girl's neck, and she was hoisted up to where we found her.'

'Rope wasn't long enough,' Logan said , his eyes scanning the page.

'It's been cut,' said Dave, prod ucing the bag with the coil of climbing cord insid e. 'Hacked off at one end . You can see where they've set about it.'

Logan took the bag and peered through the plastic at the end s of the rope. Sure enough, while one end was round ed off and sealed , the other had been hacked at until the fibres had split.

'This is all that was found ?' he asked , looking from the bag to the man who'd hand ed it over.

'That's your lot,' Dave confirmed . 'Wherever the rest of it end ed up, we d on't have it.'

Logan consid ered this for a few moments, then beckoned to Hamza, who was alread y talking on the phone. He held up the bag and pointed to the contents. 'Get them to check through the sleeping car for the rest of this. See if any of them know anything about it.'

Hamza raised a thumb, then relayed the instructions to the person on the other end of the phone. While he was d oing that, Logan turned his attention to more pressing matters.

'What about accommod ation?' he asked . 'They find us a hotel yet, or are we all kipping on the floor here?'

'Eh… somewhere between the two,' Ben said . 'Everywhere's fully booked , but they've found us a couple of lovely wee holid ay cottages just a few minutes' walk from here. Down on the river, they are. Sid e by sid e. Cracking view of Ben Nevis.'

'Right. Sound s good . What's the catch?' Logan asked .

'Well, they're technically not available to rent at the moment, but the owners have agreed to let us use them for a few d ays. Until we can find something else.'

He was hold ing something back, Logan could tell.

'*And*?' he urged .

'*And…*' Ben took a breath, then sighed it back out. 'Maybe best if you just see for yourself.'

Chapter 11

There was no bathroom. That, it transpired , was the catch.

Or, technically there *was* a bathroom, just not in that cottage. The cottage next d oor, on the other hand , had a fully-working bathroom. But, unlike this one, it d id n't have a kitchen.

'So essentially what you're telling me is we've got one house, split in two?' Logan said , staring into the bare room before him. Pipes jutted out from the floor and walls, ind icating where the sink, toilet, and shower were eventually going to go.

'Aye, that's about the size of it,' Ben confirmed . 'Owners recently took both bungalows over, and are d oing a refit. Bathrooms have both been ripped out, but the one next d oor has been mostly replaced with a new one now. Kitchen here is new, and all up and running, but none of the cabinets or appliances have been set up in the house next d oor. They've been able to wangle it for us so we've got water in the bathroom, though.'

'They have got bed s, yes?' Logan asked .

'Aye. Of course. Two bed rooms in each. One d ouble, two single. Six bed s, total. Well, seven. The couch in this one is a sofa-bed . One next d oor isn't.'

Logan mad e a sound way at the back of his mouth that suggested he was unimpressed . That changed , however, when Ben led him through to the living room and presented him with the view from the French wind ows.

There was a small gard en at the back of the cottage that led d own to the riversid e. Beyond it was a line of trees which more or less successfully masked the houses lining the road on the other bank, and any traffic trund ling along it. And then,

80

dominating everything, the UK's highest mountain, Ben Nevis, rose majestically through a bank of grey cloud.

'No' bad, eh?'

It was the kind of view that fed the soul. Blow away the clouds, slap a summer sunrise on the scene, and it might well elevate you to some higher plane of consciousness.

'Aye,' Logan conceded with a grunt. 'No' bad, I suppose.'

The room had been freshly decorated, and the smell of paint still hung in the air near the walls. The furniture was a bit of a mismatch—some of it was new, Ben explained, while some was old stuff the owners had taken out of storage—but there was a comfortable-looking armchair, and a small table to work at. In truth, he couldn't really ask for anything more.

Except a toilet of some description, obviously.

'It'll do,' he said. 'But who's going where?'

'Well, Dave tells me he's got the bladder of a horse, so I thought he could go in here. I, on the other hand, am up for a pee three or four times a night.'

'Aye, I'm only too bloody aware of that,' Logan said. The spare room at Ben's place was right next to the bathroom, and Logan had been woken countless times by the sound of DI Forde's night time micturitions.

'So then, it's just you and Hamza,' Ben said. 'Hamza would slightly prefer the one with the bathroom, but he's not all that fussed.'

'We'll do that, then,' Logan said. 'He'll go with you, I'll have Dave in this one with me.'

'I was hoping you'd say that,' Ben told him, smiling with relief. 'There's no disabled ramp on either place, and I wasn't relishing the thought of being the one to haul Dave up and down the front steps in his chair.'

–

Logan sat in what he now considered *his* armchair, watching the head lights flitting like fairies through the trees on the other side of the water.

He'd ordered them all a takeaway from a Chinese place a mile or so away, and they'd all eaten together, plastic and foil trays spread out on their laps, and —in Logan's case—half a sweet and sour king prawn dribbled down the front of his shirt.

They'd spoken for an hour or so after that, initially about the case, then about the cottages, then about anything and everything that came to mind. Dave talked about the accident that had cost him the use of his legs, somehow turning what must've been the worst day of his life into one of the funniest anecdotes any of them had ever heard.

Logan knew that if he or the others ever tried to tell the story in the same way, they'd be considered monsters by any right-minded person. But the way Dave told it had tears of laughter streaming down their faces, and forced Ben to make a mad dash to the neighbouring cottage before he lost bladder control.

They'd called it a night then. It had been a long day, and the next few were likely to be even longer.

Once Hamza had left to join Ben next door, Logan had insisted that Dave take the double bed, which had better access around it than either of the two singles in the other room. He'd offered to help wheel him over to the toilet in the house next door, but Dave had insisted he was fine.

Besides, his legs might be a problem, but his arms were fine, and he could always vault himself up onto the kitchen worktop and pee in the sink, if it came to it.

Logan wasn't quite sure how to feel about that.

After Dave had gone through to bed, Logan chucked the takeaway debris in the bin outside, then returned to the armchair in the living room. The moon was up, and its glow picked out the ripples on the surface of the river just beyond the garden fence.

One of the owners—a woman in her forties with an infectious smile and a streak of grey in her hair, who had popped in to make sure they had everything they need ed —had told him that it was often possible to see otters playing in the water.

There had been no sign of them tonight. Although, while his eyes were pointing in the right d irection, he wasn't actually looking at the view. Not really. He was processing the d ay's events. Running back through everything, turning it over, looking at it from every possible angle.

There were a few things he kept coming back to. The oil and the t-shirt. The way the bod y had been left on d isplay like some grim exhibit.

And , chief among them all, the fact that Hermione had been pregnant.

Which led him to possibly the biggest question of all: if Hermione Grey was up the d uff, then who was the father?

He yawned and shifted his weight in the chair. He should head to bed . Get some sleep, or try to, anyway. He wasn't really the right size and scale to sleep in a single bed , though, so he wasn't particularly relishing the prospect.

Besid es, when his mind was racing like this, lying d own generally just mad e it worse. Actively trying to sleep was usually met by resistance from his subconscious, which insisted on d red ging up every nuance of every conversation and potential clue he'd encountered , not just on that case, but on every other case he'd ever worked on.

And some of those memories—most of them, actually—were not exactly cond ucive to a good night's rest.

Besid es, the stars were out, flecking the sky above Ben Nevis with spots of silver and white. He still had a full third of a cup of tea to d rink and , unlike those poor, unfortunate bastard s next d oor, access to a kettle and frid ge.

He wriggled d eeper into the chair, and it seemed to ad just with him, welcoming him in. In a moment of blind optimism, he reached d own at the sid es of the chair, hoping to find a hand le that would turn it into a recliner.

Of course, he would n't find one. He was never that lucky. *No one* was ever *that* lucky.

There was a click, and a thunk. The front of the chair swung upward s, becoming a footrest, as the back reclined to just the right angle for optimum comfort.

A low moan of pleasure came unbid d en from his lips, and he d id n't even try to contain it. The reclining action had put him beyond easy reach of his tea. Incred ibly, he d id n't care.

He was too comfortable to care. Too relaxed . More at ease than he'd felt in a very long time.

As the moonlight d anced across the River Lochy, picking out the shapes of two otters tumbling around in the water, DCI Jack Logan closed his eyes and d rifted off to sleep.

-

He awoke to the sound of his phone ringing, and spent a few frantic, bleary-eyed second s trying to figure out where the hell he was. His hand s knew the routine, and blind ly slapped at his pockets until they encountered something his half-asleep brain guessed was probably the source of the racket.

'Fuck's sake,' Logan muttered , his eyes unwilling or unable to focus on the screen.

He tried to sit up, but the chair was so far reclined , and his stomach muscles so out of shape that he only succeed ed in wheezing and farting simultaneously, before flopping back d own again.

Logan jabbed at the blurry green bit of his phone screen with a finger, prod d ing and swiping at it until it finally figured out what he was trying to d o, and the ringing stopped .

'Hello?' he grunted , bringing the mobile to his ear. 'Logan.'
'Jack?'

It took Logan a moment or two to fight through the brain-fog and place the voice.

Bob Hoon.

'Bob. Aye. What?' he said , more abruptly than he'd been aiming for. 'Everything all right?' he asked , managing to sound incrementally less annoyed .

There was silence from the other end . The sort of heavy, oppressive silence that you only got when someone was on the other end of the line, but choosing not to speak.

Or unable to speak, maybe.

Logan had another bash at sitting up, this time aid ed by the back of the chair as he pushed d own with his legs and d isengaged the recliner mod e.

'Bob? What's the matter? What's happened ?'

'You nearby?' Hoon asked . His voice had a slur to it that suggested he'd been d rinking. Heavily.

'I'm d own in Fort William, why?'

'Fort William. The fuck are you d oing in Fort William?' Hoon d emand ed .

'Case,' Logan said . He yawned and checked his watch. Half-two. Jesus. 'What's the matter? Why are you phoning in the mid d le of the night?'

'Because you fucking told me to,' Hoon replied , with the same air of angry ind ignance he'd applied to most conversations they'd had back when he was Detective Superintend ent. '"Take my card ", you said . "Call me any time, night or d ay", you said . Or have you conveniently fucking forgotten about that?'

Logan closed and then opened his eyes several times, trying to clear them. 'No, Bob, I haven't forgotten. I said , if you ever need to talk, then just pick up the phone and —'

'Aye, well. I d on't need to talk, Jack. No' really,' Hoon said , and there was a softer ed ge to his voice, like an apology was coming. That would be a first. 'I just wanted someone to know.'

'Know what?' Logan asked .

There was a moment of silence from the other end before Hoon spoke again. 'I've d one something stupid , Jack.'

Logan sat forward so he was perched right on the front of the chair. 'What? What have you d one, Bob?'

Another pause.

A stifled sob.

And then...

'I've taken some pills.'

–

Two minutes later, Logan was pacing back and forth in front of the big wind ow, the scenic view replaced by the ghostly reflection of his ashen-face, picked out by the glow of his phone.

'Come on, come on,' he whispered , listening to the burring d own the line.

There was a click from the other end . He was about to hang up, convinced it had gone to voicemail for the third time, and then a voice spoke.

'Boss?'

'Tyler. Finally. Where the fuck have you been?'

There was silence. Logan could almost hear the DC's brain whirring, as he tried to figure out if he was meant to be some-where.

'Sleeping,' he said , when he eventually d rew a blank. 'Why?'

'Get d ressed ,' Logan told him. 'I need you to d o something for me…'

Chapter 12

Hoon's front d oor was open. That was the first thing Tyler noticed when he pulled up at the ad d ress Logan had given him.

The second thing he noticed was Hoon himself. He was stand ing, bent d ouble, just to the left of the front step, and was currently engaged in a quite spectacular bout of vomiting.

Hoon straightened like a meerkat when Tyler's car pulled in, shield ing his eyes from the glare of the d etective constable's head lights. He was wrapped in a thread bare grey d ressing gown that hung partly open at the front, revealing a pair of grubby boxer shorts and a lot of bare skin.

For a man his age, and given his current mental state, Hoon was pretty stacked . DI Ford e had mentioned the former DSup had been in the special forces, but Tyler had always assumed that age, ind ifference, and various excesses had put his former physique out to pasture, and had always been too afraid to look d irectly at him long enough to notice otherwise.

Aye, there was a bit of a pot belly forming above the waist-band of his shorts, but the rest of him looked terrifyingly solid .

'Is that fucking… who's it? The gay-looking boy band one? With the hair? What's your name?' Hoon called over.

Tyler opened the d oor and leaned out, but kept the engine running in case he need ed to make a fast getaway. He elected to ignore the 'gay-looking boy band one' remark, mostly for his own safety.

'DC Neish. Uh, Tyler, sir.'

The 'sir' part was really just habit, of course. Hoon was no longer his superior officer. He was no longer an officer at all, in fact.

Still, given his temper, and the aforementioned muscle mass, it was probably best to stay on his good side.

'You all right?' Tyler asked.

Hoon bent double again and splattered a couple of plant pots and a weed-strewn patio with the contents of his stomach.

'Oh aye, brand fucking new,' he replied, once he'd coughed and spat out the dregs of the spew and wiped his mouth on his sleeve. 'Never been better, thanks for asking.'

He burped loudly, spat again, then held a hand up as if to stop Tyler coming any closer. Tyler had no intention of getting any closer. In fact, the car's gearstick was already jammed into reverse, ready to beat a hasty retreat in case of emergency.

'Wait there. I'll get my stuff.'

Tyler blinked several times in rapid succession, like a sand-storm was blowing in his face. 'Stuff? What stuff?'

'Well, I can hardly fucking go anywhere dressed like this, can I?' Hoon sneered, motioning to himself with both hands. 'Fuck's sake, son. Use that howling vortex between your ears for once in your bloody life, eh?'

'But... but... go where?' Tyler asked. 'Where are you going? Uh, sir?'

Hoon scowled back at him, still half-blinded by the head-lights. 'What? Did Jack no' fucking tell you?'

'He, eh, he just said I should come check on you, make sure you were OK, then head down the road to Fort William.'

'That what he fucking said, is it? That's what he told you? Well, he missed out one key fucking element of that equation, son.' Hoon grinned, then prodded at his bare chest with a finger. 'You're taking me with you.'

–

'Fuck me, you d rive like my granny. And she's been in the ground for forty years. Give it some welly, you Boyzone-looking bum boy.'

They had been d riving for just over forty minutes now. Those had rated among the most uncomfortable minutes of Tyler's life.

Hoon had come out of his house d ressed exactly the same way as when he went in, only with the ad d ition of a pair of mud d y work boots on his feet, and a rucksack hanging from one should er.

He'd d umped his bag in the boot, loud ly d emand ed to know why Tyler had 'a woman's toolkit' in there, then slammed it shut and clambered into the backseat of the car.

Before he'd even closed the d oor, he'd mad e it very clear that he would n't be wearing his seatbelt, then had burped again, immed iately filling the vehicle with the smell of stale alcohol and fresh vomit.

Incred ibly, it had been all d ownhill from there.

The fact that Hoon had spent most of the journey sitting d irectly behind Tyler had mad e the d etective constable particularly uneasy. It had been a year since he'd been on the receiving end of a cascad e of hot vomit from a suspect in the backseat of the Land Rover he'd been d riving at the time, and the memory of it had only just started to fad e. The last thing he wanted was a repeat performance.

Especially here, in his own car.

'What are you waiting for? Fucking take him,' Hoon spat, jabbing an unstead y finger past Tyler's head at the road in front. 'It's a straight bit. Go, go. Foot to the floor. Get past them.'

Tyler glanced in his rearview mirror. 'Get past who, sir?'

'Him! Her! *That* d awd ling old fucker in front. The fucking...' He sat forward until his head was through the gap between the front seats, and squinted ahead . 'Where'd he go? Did you take him?'

Hoon turned and looked out of the back wind ow. The red glow of the tail lights was the only thing chasing them along the road .

'We lost him,' Hoon announced sound ing relieved , like they'd just escaped a pursuing Russian spy. He clamped a hand on Tyler's should er and shook him so violently he almost lost control of the wheel. 'Good work, son. Good fucking job. Maybe you're no' such a useless cake of shite, after all.'

'Eh… thanks,' Tyler said . It sound ed more like a question than a statement.

It had been ten minutes since they'd last encountered another car. He wasn't going to tell Hoon that, though. Let the mad , d runken bastard believe what he liked , if it meant not getting screamed at.

Hoon slouched back, mumbled incomprehensibly for approximately fifteen second s, then loud ly sang a few bars of *Especially For You* by Jason Donovan and Kylie Minogue. Tyler had maybe heard the song two or three times in his life, but even he could be fairly confid ent Hoon was singing the word s wrong. The original lyrics, he was sure, were less graphic in nature.

The singing eventually meand ered off into silence. Hoon's eyes closed and his head rolled forward onto his chest.

A tiny nagging voice in Tyler's head told him he should probably try to keep his former boss awake, given that he'd recently taken—and then vomited up—an overd ose. A slightly loud er voice, however, told him to enjoy the silence while it lasted .

Hoon sprang awake again before the angel and d emon on Tyler's should ers could make up their mind s. He sat forward sud d enly, blood shot eyes wid e and staring, his hand s grabbing the sid es of the chairs in front.

'Fuck!' he ejected , so sud d enly that Tyler let out an embarrassingly high-pitched yelp of fright, and almost lost control of the car for the second time in as many minutes. 'Did I lock the front d oor?' Hoon asked .

'I d on't know, sir. Did you?' Tyler replied .

'Fuck it. Turn it around ,' Hoon said , pointing to the roof of the car and making a helicopter twirling motion with his hand and finger. 'We'll go back and check.'

'I'm sure it'll be fine,' Tyler told him.

'Easy for you to fucking say, you wee Westlife wankstain that you are,' Hoon spat. 'It's no' all your personal fucking belongings on the line, is it?'

'I could call base and get Uniform to go check,' Tyler suggested .

'What, that useless shower of shites? No chance. They'll probably clean me out themselves, the d irty, thieving, gippo bastard s.' He shook his head d efiantly. 'No, turn us around . Back we go, and … wait.'

Tyler watched the former Detective Superintend ent shuffling around on the backseat, a look of grave concern on his red -eyed , unshaven face.

'No, just horse on d own the road . Quick as you fucking can,' Hoon announced . There was a loud gurgling sound that ranked among the most concerning things Tyler had ever heard . 'Or there's a very good chance I'm going to shite myself.'

—

'Bathroom,' Hoon d emand ed , alread y throwing open his d ressing gown as he stumbled in through the d oor of the cottage Logan was temporarily calling home.

'We d on't have—'

Hoon wasted no time listening, and instead head ed for the most likely looking d oor in the narrow hallway. He barged the d oor open, mad e it two steps in, then stumbled to a stop with his thumbs tucked into the elasticated cord of his boxer shorts.

'The fuck is this?' he hissed , staring in horror at the bare floorboard s, skimmed walls, and d istinct lack of toilet facilities. 'Where's the bog?'

'That's what I tried to tell you,' Logan said . 'There's no bathroom. It's in the house next d oor.'

Hoon wasted half a second trying to process this, then d ecid ed it would have to wait.

'No fucking time for that,' he announced , shoving past Logan and head ing for the d oor, his thumbs tugging d own his boxers. 'The gard en it is.'

–

'Cheers, Tyler. I owe you one,' Logan said , hand ing the DC a cup of steaming hot coffee.

Tyler accepted it gratefully and took a big sip before replying. 'Aye, well, you nearly owed me new upholstery,' he said . Hoon was snoring away in one of the cottage's single bed s, but Tyler lowered his voice to a whisper just in case he heard . 'You d id n't say I was d riving him d own the road .'

'Did n't I?' asked Logan, d oing a very poor job of feigning innocence. 'I was sure I'd mentioned that...'

'Should n't we have called him an ambulance?' Tyler asked . 'If he took an OD?'

'He d id n't OD,' Logan said . He shrugged . 'I mean, technically, I suppose he d id . He took four paracetamol.'

'Four?' Tyler spluttered into his coffee. 'Is that it? I'm sure I've taken four myself before by mistake. I thought he was at d eath's d oor when you phoned !'

'Aye, well, he was threatening to take more, and ...' Logan sighed . 'I told him he could call me. If he was struggling.'

'Why?' Tyler asked . He almost looked hurt. 'He stitched us all up.'

'We all make mistakes, son,' Logan said . 'Ultimately, it wasn't Hoon who nearly got the lot of you killed . That was on me.'

'That's d ifferent, boss,' Tyler said .

And he was right, Logan knew. It was d ifferent.

What he'd d one—letting them get d rawn into his feud with Petrie, putting them in d anger like that—had been far worse.

So much worse, in fact, that his daughter had n't spoken to him since. Or not in responses of more than two words, anyway.

'Like him or not—and I d on't, I want to make that clear— he's still one of us,' Logan said.

Tyler shook his head. 'Sorry, boss, I d isagree. I went to check on him for you, because you'd asked me to, not for him. He was a lunatic when he was on the force, and … well, I d on't even know what he is now. Whatever it is, I d on't think he's our problem.'

'I get that. I d o. And d on't worry, he's not your problem. Not in the slightest,' Logan said. A d runken snore reverberated around the house, and he sighed. 'But, sad ly, he's mine.'

Chapter 13

Next morning, they left Hoon sleeping. Logan had woken him up long enough to remind him that if he wanted to use the bathroom he should use the cottage next door, and not the front garden. He also stressed that Uniform would be passing by the cottages on a regular basis to check on him.

God help them.

Hoon's responses had been brief and filled with the usual bad language. He'd then pulled the covers up over his head and immediately fallen asleep.

'Not worried he might do away with himself when we're out?' Dave had asked, once Logan had returned from the bedroom.

'No, not really,' Logan said. He'd taken a final glug of his tea, then picked up Dave's empty mug. 'Honestly? Part of me's worried he won't.'

Tyler looked pretty much as rough as Logan felt when they all reconvened at the station. Moira Corson had been on duty again, and Tyler had come dangerously close to both losing his temper *and* bursting into tears during the exchange with her over who he was and what he was doing there.

'You've met me dozens of bloody times,' he'd protested, but Moira was having none of it.

'ID and reason for attending,' she'd repeated, like the Gestapo officer she clearly longed to be. 'Quickly. You're letting a queue form behind you.'

And now, they all sat in the Incident Room, nursing teas and coffees. Hamza—sweet, precious Hamza—had the foresight to swing by JJ's Cafe on the way in. It was less than a minute's walk from the cottages, apparently, and right on the route to the station.

Sadly, the bacon rolls had all been eaten now, and only the memory of them—and a few bits of debris lurking between their gums and teeth—remained.

None of them had slept through Hoon's arrival, and it was likely that none of the neighbours in the six other detached houses that made up the cul-de-sac had, either.

There was something about a large, surly man bellowing, 'Oh, so I had a shite in the fucking garden! Where's the fucking harm in that?' at the top of his lungs at half four in the morning that tended to set curtains twitching.

'Right, any news?' Logan asked, his voice a dull croak.

Hamza, who along with Dave was the brightest and most awake-looking of the group, turned in his chair and tapped at his laptop keyboard. He hummed cheerfully as he scrolled through the inbox, earning a scowl from the visibly exhausted Tyler.

The DS and the DC had shared the room with the two single beds in the second cottage. Logan had originally tried sharing the same room in the first cottage with Hoon, but the snorting, grunting, and aggressive sleep-talking of the former Detective Superintendent had eventually sent him through to sleep on the sofa bed in the living room.

'Nothing new, sir, no,' Hamza said. 'Still no ID made.'

'We should start circulating her picture today,' Ben suggested. 'Someone must know who she is. Who she really is, I mean.'

'Any word on Corey Sanderson?' Logan asked. 'Moof, or whatever the bloody hell he calls himself.'

'Nothing yet. Confirmation from the tech bods that they're working with the phone network to try to get a ping on him, but that's it.'

'Sinead can't get down,' Tyler announced, staring blankly at the mobile phone he held cradled in his hand. 'Harris is off school sick, and her auntie's at physio all morning.'

'Tell her not to worry about it,' Logan said . 'Then stop looking at your blood y phone and pay attention.'

'Sorry, boss,' Tyler mumbled , his thumb swiping across his on-screen keyboard .

'So, what's the plan for tod ay, then?' Ben asked . 'It's...' He checked his watch. '...just after eight.'

'I want to get those kid s in here and talk to them. Tyler, I want you in there with me.'

Tyler perked up a little at that.

'On account of you looking like you're fourteen,' Logan continued . 'Maybe they'll be more inclined to talk to you than me.'

It wasn't quite the reasoning that Tyler had been hoping for, but he'd take it.

'We also need to start looking for witnesses,' Logan said . 'How d id the d oor-to-d oor go yesterd ay?'

'Eh, it d id n't really, sir. Not a lot of d oors to knock in the vicinity. They checked with the hotel across the water from the monument, asked around a bit in the village itself, but nobod y saw anything.'

'It's a busy road . Someone might've seen something when passing,' Ben suggested . 'Trucks go up and d own that road d uring the night. Fish, mostly, I think.'

'I could get onto the companies that use the route,' Hamza said .

Logan nod d ed . 'Aye, d o that. But we need to get the word out wid er, too. What about the local paper?'

'It's Thursd ay,' Tyler said . The others all turned to look his way. He shrugged . 'Paper's the same as the one up the road . Goes to print on Wed nesd ay night. There's a week until the next one.'

'Shite. Aye,' Logan muttered . 'Fair point.'

'There's the rad io, sir,' Hamza pointed out. 'Local station. Eh... Nevis, I want to say? We could get a message out on that, see if anyone saw anything.'

'Yes! Good thinking. Get that d one. Tyler?'

'Yes, boss?'

'Get the kettle back on.' Logan turned to the Big Board , which was still d epressingly sparse. 'And let's start getting this blood y thing worked out.'

There was a ping from Hamza's laptop. He had the hand set of the d esk phone in his hand and was jabbing at the d igits, but stopped long enough to look at his email inbox.

Then, he returned the phone to the crad le. 'Oh... shit!' he exclaimed .

Logan groaned , filled with a sense of d read . 'Christ. What now?'

'No, it's good news, sir. It's excellent blood y news!' Hamza announced . 'Email from the tech bod s, forward ed by the phone network.' He turned in his chair, his eyes ablaze with excitement. 'It's Corey Sand erson. They think they've found him.'

Chapter 14

Corey 'Moof' Sand erson stood at the least cracked of the three sinks in the shared bathroom facilities, watching himself in the mottled mirror as he brushed his teeth.

He'd woken up groggy after another mostly-sleepless night, but the shower had veered between room temperature and icy cold , which had helped to blast most of the cobwebs away.

Getting d ried and d ressed had been a particularly humiliatin experience. There were a series of red lines where the fold s of his stomach bunched together, and the cold had shrivelled up... well, pretty much everything of any significance when two big German lad s chose Moof's moment of greatest exposure to come strolling into the shower room.

They'd both caught an eyeful, then had started talking quickly to each other in German. He had n't und erstood a word of it, but he could und erstand their laughter well enough.

After that, he'd hurried ly got d ressed while still d amp, and come through to the ad joining room to have a d ump and brush his teeth. Although, unlike the clarty bastard currently grunting in one of the stalls, he had elected not to d o both simultaneously.

Moof spat, rinsed , then checked himself in the mirror. He had a couple of new spots forming, and his eyes were sunken into little hollows. The stress of the last forty-eight hours was showing itself.

He had put on a lot of weight while travelling. A lot of people assumed that vegetarians were always healthy and skinny, but there was very little meat in a family-sized bag of Maltesers, and if any of the main ingredients in Irn Bru were derived from animal products, he was choosing not to find out.

If he looked closely, he could still see himself buried under the extra weight. The old him. The him from before.

Placing a hand either side of his face, he pulled back, making himself look momentarily thinner.

'There you are,' he whispered, then he released his grip and his old self was swallowed up once more.

Moof ran a finger through his red-dyed hair, revealing the dark roots lurking below. He should lose it. It made him too recognisable. If they were looking—and they would be looking, if not now, then once the mission was over—his hair would make him stand out too much. Make him too obvious. Get him caught.

After packing away his toothpaste and brush, he took the toiletries bag back to the room he'd been sharing with five other lads. He hadn't spoken to any of them much since he'd arrived the day before, although they seemed nice enough. Bit loud and boorish, but you got used to that in places like this.

He'd avoided getting to know them, though. Sure, he'd said hello and been polite, but that was as far as he went. Being too friendly might end up with him accidentally giving away too much information about himself. Too rude, and he'd be memorable if anyone came asking about him later.

Moof ran a hand through his hair again. *Shit.* He really should've got rid.

The others were still sleeping on their bunks, their night having only come to an end around four. Moof glanced furtively at the other beds, then reached under his own and pulled out his rucksack and unzipped the bottom compartment.

He stuffed his wash bag inside, squeezing it in beside a child-sized *Harry Potter* knapsack, then hurriedly zipped the compartment closed again.

Next, he took his phone from the front pocket, powered it on, and did his second check of the morning. There had been one message waiting for him on the first check. It had been from Deird rie.

Where the fuck r u? she'd d emand ed .

The second message that arrived now was also from Deed s. He'd been bracing himself for this one, but the viciousness of it still stung.

I'll fucking kill u u sick freak!!!!

She was always going to be the hard est hit, of course. She was always going to feel it the worst.

Well, second worst. In the end , it was going to be Hermione's father who suffered most of all.

The sound of a car pulling up outsid e mad e him look up from the phone. He caught a glimpse of blue and yellow checks, and his heart was sud d enly in his throat.

No. They could n't be there for him. They could n't be. He'd been careful. Except for the hair, of course. The stupid fucking hair, and …

Moof looked d own at the phone in his hand , then thumbed the button so hard the d evice creaked like it was about to implod e.

Shit.

Shit, shit, shit.

Keeping low, he crossed to the wind ow and peeked out through the grimy glass. The police car was nowhere to be seen, and the hummingbird heartbeat that had been burring in his chest slowed d own by a few hund red beats per minute.

Nothing to worry about. No need to freak out. Yes, they were going to come after him—she'd warned him loud and clear about that—but how bad could it be? What had he actually d one wrong?

Nothing that wasn't fully d eserved . Anyone with an ounce of d ecency could see that.

It was right. It was just. No matter the consequences, nobod y could d eny that.

The doorbell rang. Everything from Moof's ankles to his arse suddenly tightened, launching him upright into a standing position.

There was another ding-dong as the bell was pressed again, then the firm, insistent knock of someone who had no intention of taking 'we're not in' for an answer.

Diving for his bed, Moof struggled his feet into his boots. The door was hammered again. Somewhere, in another room, a female voice answered.

'All right, all right, keep your hair on.'

Damn it.

Moof grimaced and stamped down, forcing his right foot all the way into the boot. There was no time to worry about the laces. Instead, he jumped up, grabbed his rucksack, and swung it over a shoulder.

He crossed to the window and tried to open it, but the fucking thing was painted shut.

' 'S all the noise about?' slurred a voice from the bunk above his. One of the party group peered down at him, one eye welded shut, the alcohol on his breath strong enough to strip the wallpaper. 'What are you doing?'

'Nothing,' Moof replied, jumping back from the window like it had just become charged with electricity. 'Don't know what's happening. I'll check.'

He went scurrying into the corridor as the thumping came again, hoping he could get to the back door before—

'Right, I'm up, I'm up, what is it?'

A girl in her early twenties opened the door. Moof's eyes locked with the two police officers standing out on the front step.

And then he ran, sprinting along the corridor to the left. He heard the girl cry out as she was shoved aside, heard the angry shouts urging him to stop.

He ignored them.

The kitchen d oor was ajar. He threw it open, d rawing a hissed expletive from the mid d le-aged woman who hovered by the toaster, waiting for it to pop.

Moof collid ed with the table, stumbled around it, then mad e a frantic d ash for the back d oor. He grabbed the hand le, forced it d own.

Locked .

'Shit, shit, shit!'

The wind ow! Only chance.

He d ived up onto the worktop, scattering mugs and plates, and knocking the toaster onto the floor.

'Hey, what the fuck?!' the woman d emand ed , jumping clear.

Moof turned the hand le and pushed . The wind ow opened then the safety latch caught and jerked it to a stop.

Cursing, he fid d led with the catch just as the two police officers came thund ering into the room behind him.

The wind ow opened . He rolled through, but a hand grabbed his rucksack and pulled him back.

No! He could n't lose the bag. He could n't.

But what other choice d id he have?

With a cry of frustration, Moof slipped his arm from the strap and fell onto the street outsid e. He slammed the wind ow shut behind him, engaging the safety catch again, and buying himself a few more second s.

And then, alone in an unfamiliar area of an unfamiliar town, Moof Sand erson picked a d irection, turned on his heels, and ran.

Chapter 15

'What d o you mean, they fucking lost him?'

'Just what I said , Jack,' Ben replied . He looked   equally as unimpressed   by the news as Logan. 'They went to the hostel the phone network had   pinpointed , but he d id a runner.'

'Bastard !' Logan spat.

'One bit of good   news, though. They got his rucksack.'

Logan raised   an eyebrow, hoping that wasn't as far as the 'good   news' went. 'And ?'

'They found   Hermione Grey's bag in there.'

Logan was sitting forward   in his chair now. 'And ?'

'Few bits of clothing,' Ben said . 'No wallet, phone, anything like that. But we got her passport.'

'Fuck off! Really?' Logan asked , jumping to his feet.

'Aye,' Ben confirmed .

'And ?'

'You might want to sit d own again,' Ben told   him. 'Hamza? Want to d o the honours?'

Hamza d id n't waste any time. 'Hermione Grey's real name is Alexis Riksen.'

The way he said   it suggested   the name should 've meant something to Logan.

It d id n't.

Hamza appeared   a little d isappointed , like his big moment had   fallen flat.

'Daughter of Bartholomew Riksen. The billionaire.'

'From Texas,' Ben ad d ed , when it was clear that Logan still wasn't any the wiser. 'One of them big oil baron types.'

'Christ. Really?' Logan said . 'So...'

'Looks like Corey Sand erson found out and wanted to strike some sort of blow for the environment, or something,' Hamza said .

'Explains the writing on the t-shirt and the engine oil poured over her.'

'Aye, quite the blood y statement, right enough,' Logan said . He shud d ered . 'An enviro-terrorist. That's just what we blood y need .'

'Uniform and CID in Ayr have got a manhunt on for him,' said Ben. 'Warlock's going to keep us posted of any upd ates.'

'Who's Warlock when he's at home, boss?' asked Tyler.

'DI Warren Locke,' Logan said . 'One of the old guard . Quick with his temper, less quick with the rulebook.'

'Let's just say, they had to move him to a station without any stairs lead ing to the cells,' Ben ad d ed .

'I'm amazed he's still on the job,' Logan remarked . 'Clearly got d irt on someone somewhere.'

'Oh, no d oubt,' Ben agreed . 'Anyway, there's a big presence on the streets and on the road s in and out of the city. We think Sand erson took his phone, but the network isn't able to get a trace on it again, so there's no saying he hasn't smashed it or d umped it somewhere. Hopefully CCTV or Uniform will pick him up somewhere, though.'

'Aye, never know,' Logan said , although he wasn't hold ing out a lot of hope.

'He's a chunky big bugger with bright red hair, so I'd say we've got a good chance.'

A sergeant in uniform knocked on the d oor, then popped his head insid e. 'That's those youngsters brought in from Glen-finnan for you, sir. What d o you want d one with them?'

'How many's there?' Logan asked .

'Five. You said to d o them in batches. We've got the five you asked for first.'

'Good . Get Deird rie Mair set up in one of the interview rooms. Find somewhere for the rest of them to wait, and have someone keep an eye on them. We can't necessarily stop them talking to each other, but they don't need to know that. Get some big surly bugger in with them making his presence felt.'

The sergeant rattled off the instructions again to confirm he'd understood, then retreated out of the room to carry it all out.

'Right, on your feet,' Logan told Tyler, interrupting a stretch and a yawn that the younger officer had been very much enjoying. 'Ben, you've got the room. No interruptions to the interviews unless it's urgent. The first priority for you two—'

'Getting in touch with the girl's parents. Aye, we know,' Ben said, ushering Logan and Tyler towards the door. 'Don't you worry, we'll get cracking on that. And I'll only disturb you if I have to. Now, go give us peace.'

He escorted them both to the door, and waited for it to swing closed before turning back to Hamza and Dave. 'Now, then,' he said, rubbing his hands together. 'Which of us wants to wake up one of the most powerful men in the world and tell him his only daughter's been murdered?'

Neither of the other men raised a hand.

'No,' said Ben with a long, forlorn sigh. He headed for his desk, and the phone that sat on it. 'Thought not.'

–

Deirdrie Mair sprang to her feet when Logan and Tyler entered the interview room, like she'd been caught sitting somewhere she wasn't allowed to.

'Please, no need to get up,' Logan assured her. 'Sit down.'

She sat quickly, like she was eager to please him.

Deirdrie had that sort of look about her. He'd noticed it at the monument, and then again at the dining car. Her eyes were constantly darting around, a hopeful look on her face like she was seeking approval from someone. Anyone. It didn't matter who, just as long as someone validated her in some way.

'Hi. I'm Tyler. I'm a detective constable here.'

He reached across the table and shook her hand, smiling and holding eye contact like someone who'd been reading too many self-help manuals on how to get more dates. It was, in Logan's opinion, profoundly creepy, and Deirdrie didn't seem particularly impressed by the performance, either.

'He generally just makes the tea. We try not to let him out much, but sometimes we're legally obliged to,' Logan explained, pulling out his chair and taking a seat. 'You drew the short straw and are stuck with him, I'm afraid.'

Deirdrie's eyes tick-tocked between both men, confusion baked into her expression.

'He's joking,' Tyler said. 'I know, it wasn't funny, but he tries.'

She looked a little reassured, if only by the fact that both men seemed to be friendly.

'Nice to meet you,' she said to Tyler, then she turned to Logan. 'Do you have any news?'

'Some,' Logan said. 'But we'd like to go over a few things with you again, if you don't mind?'

Deirdrie shook her head. 'No. I mean, yes. I mean, I don't mind. What do you want to know?'

'Does the name Alexis Riksen mean anything to you?' Logan asked.

There was... something, he thought. Some shadow flitting behind her eyes. Some suggestion of recognition.

'It's familiar,' she admitted. 'But I don't know. Is that... was that Hermione's name?'

'It was,' Logan confirmed. 'Alexis Riksen. From Texas.'

'In America,' Tyler added, helpfully.

Logan gave an exaggerated roll of his eyes. 'See what I'm dealing with?' he asked, then he pressed on with the questioning. 'Did Alexis ever talk about her parents?'

Deirdrie shifted uneasily on her chair. The frame was deliberately a little loose, so the person interviewing was alerted to the interviewee's every little movement by the squeak of moving metal and plastic.

'Deird rie?' Logan asked . 'Did Alexis say something to you?'

The girl shook her head . 'No. No, nothing. I just...' A tear rolled d own her cheek. She hurried to d ispose of it on the back of her sleeve. 'Can we call her Hermione? That's all I can think of her as. I d on't know who this Alexis person is. She was Hermione to me. To all of us.'

Logan gave a nod . 'Of course. If that makes it easier.'

'Not easier. Hard er,' Deird rie confessed . 'But it d oesn't feel right calling her something else.'

'Hermione it is, then,' Logan said .

Tyler picked up a box of tissues from the d esk and offered them up to Deird rie. She took one, wiped her eyes and blew her nose on it, then stuffed it up past the cuff of her sleeve like Logan's granny used to d o.

'She never spoke about her parents. Or where she'd come from. Or what it was like growing up,' Deird rie said . 'She just... it wasn't a happy time. Her child hood , I mean.'

'She told you that?'

'Not exactly, no. It was more what she d id n't say. I'd talk about what it was like for me. Growing up. Coming out. My parents. My brothers. Christmas, birthd ays, whatever. I'd talk about it—she'd ask me to tell her about it—and she'd just sit there listening with a big goofy grin on her face, and these wid e eyes like she could n't believe it.'

She sniffed , retrieved the tissue from her sleeve, and gave her nose another blow.

'It wasn't even like it was exciting stuff. It was boring. Being the d onkey in the school play. Going to the beach with my mum and d ad and falling in a big hole in the sand . Nothing, really, but she'd just sit there staring like it was the most exciting story she'd ever heard . Like it was *important*. You know?'

'She sound s like a good friend ,' Tyler said .

'But she never told me anything about when she was younger,' Deird rie continued . 'Not once. Not a thing. That's weird , isn't it?'

'Some people are more private than others,' Logan reasoned . 'Even around people they're close with.'

Deirdrie regarded the desk in front of her for a few seconds, her head bobbing back and forth. 'I suppose so, yeah. She was private about that stuff. I thought maybe she'd grown up really poor, or something, and was embarrassed .'

'Not quite, no,' Logan said . 'Her dad is Bartholomew Riksen.'

The girl stared back at him with an expression that made him wonder if he had somehow slipped into talking a different language.

'No, I was none the wiser when they told me,' he said . 'He's an oil baron, apparently. One of the richest men in the US.'

'In the world ,' Tyler corrected .

'What?!' Deirdrie asked , practically shrieking out the word . 'Rich? No way. Uh-uh. And not oil. Hermione was against the use of fossil fuels. She was pro-renewables. We spoke about it all the time. She even joined us on a protest. We got on TV. We made a banner. We worked on it all night. There's no way she was...' Deirdrie shook her head and crossed her arms, like a toddler refusing to eat her greens. 'There's just no way.'

'We found her passport. We're getting in touch with the family,' Logan said . 'She's definitely Alexis Riksen. There's no question about it.'

'Where was the passport?' Deirdrie asked . She sat forward suddenly, a rainbow of different expressions taking it in turns to shape her face, from relief to angst, and everything in between. 'Did you find Moof? Did he do it? Was it him? It was him, wasn't it? Oh, God . Was it? Was it him?'

'What makes you think it was him?' Tyler asked , taking the initiative. He smiled apologetically. 'Sorry, I'm still getting up to speed with the case. What makes you think Moof killed Hermione?'

Deirdrie's red-ringed eyes looked him up and down like she was checking out the village idiot. 'Well, because he left, didn't he? The night she died, he vanished. And he was… clingy. I don't know. He kept trying to get near her. Get between me and her. I think he liked her.'

'If he liked her, why would he kill her?' Tyler asked. He scratched his head, realised this was probably a bit too on-the-nose, and returned his hand to the table, instead.

'Because he couldn't have her,' Deirdrie said with a sniff of indignation. 'She was with me. She had no interest in anyone else but me, but especially not men, and especially not *him*.'

'Why not him, in particular? I saw a picture. Decent looking. Sturdy,' Tyler said, like he was trying to sell a sideboard.

'He just wasn't her type.'

'Why not?' Tyler asked.

'Well, because he had a cock, for one thing!'

The words were out of her before she could stop them. She bit down on her lip and looked from one detective to the other, her face simultaneously paling and turning red.

Logan took up the questioning. 'You said, "especially not men, and especially not *him*". They've all got cocks, Deirdrie. What made Corey worse than the others?'

Deirdrie shrank down into her seat, scared and vulnerable, and completely alone. 'She just… Hayden would tell us some of the stuff he said. Sexual stuff.'

'About Alexis?' Logan asked. 'Sorry. *Hermione*.'

Deirdrie nodded ed, quickly and furtively. 'What he wanted to do to her. Things he fantasised about.'

'Did Hermione ever confront Moof about it?' asked Tyler.

'No. I told her we should, but she didn't want the drama. She hated confrontation. Said that we all knew Hayden was a bullshitter, so she didn't want to accuse Moof of anything and end up embarrassing herself if he hadn't said anything. But she kept clear of him as much as possible. We were going to move on if he didn't leave the group soon.

'We'd sneak away in the middle of the night, she would say. Grab a bag, wait until everyone was sleeping, then just go. Just the two of us.'

Logan offered her his best, most rehearsed sympathetic look, then got read y to tear the girl's heart out.

'So, she and Corey never had sex?'

Deird rie's nostrils flared and her lips d rew back over her gums in d isgust. 'Ew. No. Of course not.'

'What about Hayd en, or one of the other lad s?' Logan asked . 'Did Hermione sleep with any of them.'

'No! She was gay! We were together. She wasn't into guys!'

Logan sucked air in through his teeth and sat back in his chair. 'Well, then that leaves us with a bit of a problem.'

Deird rie scowled . 'What d o you mean? What sort of problem?'

'If Hermione had n't slept with any men recently—'

'She had n't.'

'Then how d id she wind up pregnant?'

Chapter 16

It was the arse end of ten o'clock when Ben finally got through to a member of Bartholomew Riksen's staff. As one of the richest men in America, his personal contact d etails were und erstand ably hard to come by. It had taken some smooth-talking on Ben's part to convince one of his counterparts in New York first of his id entity, and then to persuad e him that international police co-operation was something to be encouraged .

The language barrier had n't helped . Both men may have been technically speaking English but both had some d ifficulty with the other man's accents.

A lot of d ifficulty, in the NYC d etective's case, and Ben had been forced to repeat sentences up to five times in a variety of d ifferent intonations just to get his message across.

The time d ifference had been a bit of a problem, too. When he'd started calling, it had been the mid d le of the night in New York, where the Riksen Corporation's head quarters were based .

Now it was pushing six in the morning over there, which was bord ering on respectable.

Unfortunately, Bartholomew Riksen was currently in Austin, Texas, where it wasn't yet five.

His private secretary answered the phone in three rings. His voice was a d eep, silky smooth baritone that immed iately conjured up images in Ben's head of old -time blues singers.

'This is the office. How may I help?'

That was all he had said. No introduction. No explanation of whose office it was, just, 'This is the office. How may I help?'

The tone was jarring. On one hand, the man on the other end of the line had sounded absolutely genuine about wanting to help. After just those eight words, Ben felt like he could tell that voice anything. And, more importantly, that it would listen to him.

On the other hand, there was just *hint* of impatience about it. It wanted to help, yes, but *God help you* if your problem wasn't significant enough. Legitimate requests for assistance only. No time wasters allowed.

Ben had introduced himself.

Then he had introduced himself again, slower and with more focus on his enunciation.

Once he'd successfully conveyed who he was, and the secretary had given his own credentials, Ben had asked to speak to Bartholomew Riksen directly.

The secretary had declined. It was out of the question. Mr Riksen didn't speak to anyone, especially not at five o'clock in the morning.

'You can tell me anything, Detective Inspector Forde,' the secretary told him, oozing respect, but making it very clear that talking to Riksen was off the cards. 'I will gladly convey any message that may be necessary to pass on, and help formulate any required follow-up.'

'Good. That'll save me being the one to break the news,' Ben said, audibly sighing with relief. 'Tell him his daughter's dead. Murdered. We found her half-naked body hanging from a forty-foot high tower. Be great if you could pass that on for me, right enough. Help formulate any "required follow-up", or what-have-you. Good luck!'

'Uh… wait,' the secretary said, his rich, soupy voice climbing an octave. 'It might be best if I put you through to him directly.'

'Aye, whatever you think, son,' said Ben, who'd known precisely what he was doing. 'Maybe better coming from me, right enough.'

And that was why, three and a half minutes later, DI Ford e found himself talking to the sixteenth richest man in the world .

Despite the early hour, Riksen had clearly been up and about. In fact, from what Ben could gather, he was running on a tread mill when the call was patched through to him. The whirring of the belt and the clomping of running feet were a throbbing sound track to the beginning of the call as Ben went over his introd uctions again.

'What d o you need ?' Riksen asked . He spoke fast, with enough of a Texas d rawl to prove he belonged to the State, but sufficient hints of both US coasts to suggest he'd travelled and lived elsewhere for long period s of time.

While the accent was a little d ragged out, the sentence itself was short and clipped , like he resented wasting any unnecessary word s on the conversation. 'I'm at a meeting in fifteen.'

For a moment, Ben wished the secretary had stuck to the original plan. There was little worse than telling someone a loved one was d ead . Telling a parent a child was d ead was about as d ifficult as it got.

'I'm sorry to be calling you so early, Mr Riksen, but I'm afraid I have some bad news,' Ben said . 'Did your secretary mention my reason for—'

'Not those *Save the Planet* fucks again, is it? If they've d amaged another rig, I swear to God , I'm going to nail their god d amn head s to my bathroom wall.'

'Uh, no. That's not really my d epartment,' Ben said . 'It's your d aughter, I'm afraid . Alexis.'

He heard Riksen groan d own the line. 'Damn it. What has she d one this time?'

'I'm afraid she's d ead , Mr Riksen.'

The line went silent, asid e from the sound of the tread mill.

'What the fuck? Who are you? Is this some kind of sick joke?' Riksen d emand ed . 'Who the hell d o you think you are, calling me up with this shit?'

'As I said , sir, I'm Detective Inspector—'

113

'She's off travelling somewhere. She isn't even here. How can she be…? Who are you? Who the fuck is this?'

'She was in Scotland , Mr Riksen. Glenfinnan. In the Highland s,' Ben said , keeping his voice low and level to counter the rising tension from the other end of the line. 'She was going und er the name Hermione Grey.'

The trund ling of the tread mill stopped . The voice, when it came again, had lost its anger.

'What? Fuck. Jesus Christ. Alex. I d on't…'

Ben heard a sud d en inhalation in through the nose, then the expulsion of it out through the mouth. This repeated three times, and when Riksen next spoke, there was a Zen-like calmness to his voice that bord ered on unsettling.

'I'll have Conan come and take the d etails,' he said . 'Scotland ? That's in England , right?'

Ben resisted the instinct to shout 'fuck off' d own the phone at him, and elected to correct him in a somewhat less forceful manner. 'Next to it. Not in it. Both countries are part of the United Kingd om.'

'I can be there in twelve hours.'

'I und erstand why—' Ben began, but then the smooth voice of the private secretary poured into his ear, cutting him off.

'Thank you so much for calling to break this terrible news, Detective Inspector Ford e,' Conan said , with a d eep, resonating solemnity that reverberated the phone in Ben's hand . In the background , Ben heard the tread mill kick back into life. 'If you'd be so good as to give me your contact d etails, Mr Riksen will be with you as soon as is humanly possible.'

-

Eleven minutes later, the phone on Ben's d esk rang. He answered it with his usual greeting, but got no further than his rank and first name before the voice on the other end cut in.

'This is Dirk Sommercamp,' said the caller. The accent was American, or maybe Canadian—Ben could rarely tell the difference. The way he announced himself suggested the name should mean something to DI Forde. It didn't.

'Well done,' Ben said. 'Who's Dirk Sommercamp when he's at home?'

'I work for Mr Riksen's company, handling security. I've just heard the news re Alexis Riksen, Mr Riksen's daughter.'

'Re,' Ben thought. He actually says *'Re'* like in a bloody email.

'Mr Riksen has asked me to assist on the case, so we'll be flying in later today. Take down this email address and forward on whatever information you currently have.'

Ben moved the handset away while this Dirk Sommercamp fella rattled off his email address, looked at it like it might be winding him up, then returned it to his ear again.

'Sorry, who did you say you were again?'

There was a tiny pause, but it was filled with a sizeable amount of outrage. 'Jesus. Is this what we're dealing with? Is this the level we're at?' he asked. He repeated his name ridiculously slowly, dragging out the letters. 'Dirk Sommercamp. Head of Mr Riksen's security task force.'

'So... you're a security guard?' Ben asked.

'I'm a former FBI Special Agent, with over twenty years in the field.'

'Good on you, son. Well done,' Ben said. 'And now you're a security guard?'

Sommercamp sighed impatiently. 'I'm lead investigator on a security task force for one of the richest men in the world,' he said. 'This year alone I have personally retrieved over thirty million dollars of revenue that would otherwise have been lost to large scale fraud.'

'That's—' Ben began, but Sommercamp wasn't finished.

'In my time at the FBI I helped bring thirty-seven murderers—eight of them serial killers on the Most Wanted list—to justice. I have protected Presidents, visiting world leaders, and even your Queen. Twice. She thanked me personally.'

'Did she thank you twice, or just once?' Ben asked . He was starting to enjoy this. Previously, the most ridiculous conversations he'd been involved in had involved either junkies or DC Neish. This guy was taking things to a whole new level of nonsense.

'That's irrelevant,' Sommercamp said . 'My point is, I am more than qualified to play a role in your investigation.'

'Aye, but you're no',' Ben said . 'Because you're no' in the polis.'

'Say again,' Sommercamp said , in the short, clipped tones of someone who was used to giving out orders. 'I did n't catch that.'

'I said , you aren't qualified to play a role in the investigation, son,' Ben told him, being careful not to d rop too many letters this time. 'Because you d on't work for the police.'

'Irrelevant. I bring a wealth of experience. Choosing not to make use of that experience would be negligence on your part.'

'Aye, well, I suppose I'll just have to live with that,' Ben told him. 'Now, if you'll excuse me, Mr Sommercamp, we're all very busy here. Murder to solve, and all that. Good luck with the security guard stuff. It's important to keep busy.'

He hung up the phone without waiting for a reply, but caught most of a 'You haven't heard the last of this' before he d ropped the hand set into the crad le.

Then Ben sat back in his chair, rocked a few times, and said , 'Dirk Sommercamp, FBI,' in his best New York accent, d rawing himself some very od d looks from Hamza and Dave.

'You all right, sir?' Hamza asked .

'Aye, nothing to worry about,' Ben told him. 'But I've a feeling that d ealing with this Bartholomew Riksen character is going to be more challenging than we thought.'

Chapter 17

Following the pregnancy revelation, the interview with Deird rie Mair had n't so much gone d ownhill as plunged screaming over a cliff. While on fire.

She'd laughed at first. Not a real laugh, by any stretch of the imagination, but one of those nervous reaction laughs, like she d id n't get the joke and d id n't think she was all that keen on where it was going, but d id n't want to look stupid .

When they'd convinced her they were telling the truth about Hermione/Alexis being 'with child ', she went into full-scale breakd own mod e. She almost instantly became a breathless, sobbing, wailing mess, all gnashing teeth and stamping feet, her head stuck in a perpetual loop of left and right as she d enied it was possible, d enied it was true, refused to believe that Hermione would d o that to her. *Them.*

She proved no help in trying to id entify who the father might be. She'd had no interest in men. None.

And had Deird rie mentioned that they were a couple? Hermione would n't betray her like that. She just would n't. If she had been pregnant, it was d ivine intervention.

'Or... or... can't you get it from a toilet?' she asked , eyes wid ening hopefully. 'I mean, if some guy's been there and has... you know? On the seat?'

Christ, Logan thought. *And they let you roam around the world on your own.*

They got very little more from her after that. Logan asked her not to tell anyone else what they had d iscussed —stressed the importance of that—then had Uniform take her back to sit in the waiting room with the others.

Hayden Howard was brought to the interview room next. Logan and Tyler left him there to stew for five minutes while they made tea and rifled through whatever biscuits were available in the kitchen.

Logan had just stumbled upon an open packet of Garibaldis in one of the top cupboards when Moira Corson threw open the door and caught him in the act.

'What are you doing?' she asked, despite the fact it was blatantly obvious what he was doing.

'I'm—'

'Those aren't yours.'

Logan glanced down at the packet of biscuits in his hand. Tyler had frozen with one hand gripping the handle of the kettle, like a gazelle that could sense danger but wasn't yet sure of which way to run.

'No, I—'

'There's someone in reception.'

The sudden switching of conversational tracks caught Logan off guard. He frowned at the biscuits like he expected to find the right response written there.

When he found none, he looked over to the woman in the doorway. 'What?' he asked. 'Who?'

'He's asked for you specifically. Weedy looking little fella. Camera. Said he needs to tell you something he's remembered.'

Logan looked over at Tyler. The younger detective tensed, terrified that this would draw him to Moira's attention.

'Ian Hill,' the DCI said, before turning back to Moira. 'Tell him we'll be right out.'

Moira tutted, clearly feeling that this simple request was taking a bloody liberty. Her sensible shoes remained planted in place on the border between kitchen and hallway.

'Biscuits,' she said.

Logan considered the Garibaldis, then came to the conclusion that they weren't worth it. He'd have gone toe-to-toe with her over some custard creams—fought her to the death for a chocolate digestive—but some things just weren't worth making a stand for.

'Never liked the bloody things, anyway,' he said, then he returned them to the cupboard and went sweeping towards the door she was currently blocking. 'Forget passing on that message,' he said, his inexorable onward momentum forcing her to back out of his way. 'I'll come talk to him now.'

–

Ian Hill was a jittering wreck when Logan met him in the foyer. He clutched his camera to his chest like a shield, and his eyes kept darting to the ceiling like the building might be about to collapse on him at any moment.

'I've just… I've never really been in a police station before,' he explained, after Logan asked him if he was unwell. 'I always get nervous around authority figures and, well, your receptionist was a little… uh…'

'Aye, she's like that to us, too,' Logan said. 'Try not to take it personally.'

He took Ian through to a small side room, explained that he was right in the middle of something, but asked how he could help. The man had already proven himself to be a babbler, and Logan didn't have time to waste on babbling right now.

He checked his watch and winced, just to add to the sense of urgency and hurry the conversation along.

'I remembered something. Late last night. Well, early this morning, to be exact,' Ian began after a little more prompting. 'I've been going to the monument all week. Bright and early, but it's not unusual to see the odd one or two people out walking their dogs. Before work, or before they have to get the kids sorted for school, or whatever. I mean, I suppose. I don't ask. If they get close, I tend to just smile and say—'

'Did you see someone walking their d og yesterd ay morning, Mr Hill?' Logan asked , cutting through the unnecessary waffle.

'Yes! I mean, sort of. But not up close. I was just pulling up in the car, and I caught a glimpse of him walking along the sid e of the road , head ed up the hill. You know the church? Up that way.'

'So walking away from the monument?'

'Yes. Not d irectly in a straight line but... that d irection,' Ian confirmed . 'I only saw him from behind , and from a d istance, but I remember seeing him, and thinking, "Oh-ho. Dog walker," I thought. Because I'd been seeing d og walkers all week, like I think I said .'

'You d id ,' Logan confirmed .

'So I thought, "Oh-ho. Dog walker. There's another one." And then I thought no more of it. Until now. Well, last night. This morning, I mean. It just popped into my head as I was laying there in my hotel. I could n't sleep. Too... you know? About the bod y?' Hill said , barely taking a breath between any of the word s. 'Anyway, I'm lying there and *poof*. It hits me. The man I saw. On reflection, when I really think about it, I'm not so sure he was a d og walker, after all.'

'What makes you think that?' Logan asked .

'Well, he d id n't have a d og,' Hill replied . 'I mean, not that I saw. And they d o, d on't they? Usually.'

'That's generally the id ea, aye,' Logan confirmed . 'Could it have been in the trees, maybe?'

'Oh. Yes. Absolutely,' Hill ad mitted . 'Or, had it been black, I probably would n't have seen it. He might well have been a perfectly innocent local man out giving Rover a stretch of his legs, but... you said if I thought of anything, I should get in touch. And , well, I thought of that. I thought, maybe, it might be useful. Or important.' He laughed nervously. 'It probably isn't. I've completely wasted your time, haven't I? God . I'm sorry. I should n't have come. I'm such an id iot!'

'You absolutely should 've come, Mr Hill. It could be vital information,' Logan assured him. 'Anything else you can tell us about him?'

Hill's eyes narrowed and his mouth went thin, like he was either trying very hard to think or struggling with a difficult bowel movement. 'He was dressed in black, I think. Maybe navy blue. Or charcoal. Dark grey sort of thing. It was hard to tell. He was only in the headlight beam for a second or two, and even then right at the very edge.'

'Did he look back when you pulled up?'

'No. Not that I noticed. He just kept on— oh! Wait. There was something else. He had a red hat on. It jumped out at me because the rest of him was so dark. Clothing-wise, I mean. His skin wasn't... he was white, I mean.'

'A red hat?' Logan asked, a familiar tingling feeling tiptoeing across his scalp.

'Bright red. Really vibrant. I actually did a double-take.' Hill reenacted the double-take moment. 'I think it was maybe a beret or something. It was flat on his head. I wondered if maybe it was an army hat.'

'What made you think that?'

'Well, that's a thing, isn't it? The Red Berets. Isn't that an army thing?'

'Right, yes. I believe it is,' Logan said. 'But... could it have been his hair?'

'His hair?' Hill stared past Logan at the wall opposite, like he was rerunning the footage on some internal projector. 'Hmm. Yes. Yes, it could 've been his hair. He would 've had to have dyed it, though. It wasn't ginger, it was *red*. Like a tomato or... or... blood .'

Hill's hand flew to his mouth and he gasped. Logan was quick to put his mind at rest.

'It would n't have been blood , Mr Hill,' he said, and Hill visibly relaxed. 'One of the people we're interested in talking to matches your description. If it's him you saw, being able to place him near the scene is very useful.'

Ian Hill looked like all his Christmases had come at once. He puffed up proud ly, and Logan half-expected him to pull a prepared speech from insid e his jacket and launch into a big list of *thank you*s.

'Was there anything else, Mr Hill?' Logan asked , shutting d own any celebratory monologues before they could start.

Hill's eyes went to his camera on the table besid e him. It only lingered there for a moment, before snapping back to the DCI. He slowly wrapped the strap around his hand as he gave his reply.

'No. No, nothing else,' he said .

'You sure?' Logan asked . He looked pointed ly at the camera. 'You seemed concerned about your equipment there.'

'Nope. Fine,' Hill said . He gave the camera a pat like it was a well-behaved puppy. 'All good .'

Logan ratcheted the intensity of his stare up a few notches and watched Hill shrink a little further each time.

'You mind showing me what's on the camera, Mr Hill?'

'What? Why?' Hill blurted , then he shook his head and tried to sound less panicky and high-pitched , with only mod erate success. 'I, uh. I'd rather not. There are private pictures on there. Of... of my wife and I. Images of a... sexual nature. But consenting!' he quickly ad d ed . 'She gave full permission. We both d id . We're grown ad ults. There's nothing wrong with it.'

'I never said there was, Mr Hill,' Logan replied . He was on thin ice here, he knew. He had no right to just d emand to look at the images. Not without a stronger reason than someone glancing at their own camera.

And yet there had been something in the look that mad e Logan want to see those images more than almost anything in the world .

Just maybe not the ones of Hill and his wife, if they even really existed .

'I'm only interested in pictures you took the morning you d iscovered the bod y, Mr Hill. That's all,' Logan told him. 'They could be useful for helping to establish the scene. There might be information contained in them that could be relevant to the investigation.'

Hill got three or four potential replies all the way to the starting line before abandoning them. The one he settled on was disappointing, to say the least.

'I have your email address from your card,' he said. 'I'll zip everything up and send it over this afternoon.'

And that was that, Logan knew. Short of intimidating the bastard, or tearing the camera from his hands, that was as good as he was going to get.

For now.

It was amazing what the tech bod could do to restore images deleted from memory cards, though. He'd find out what was on that camera, sooner or later.

He pursed his lips and forced the corners of his mouth to turn unconvincingly upwards. 'That will be useful, Mr Hill,' he said. Logan stood up, dwarfing the other man and casting him into shadow. 'Now, if that's everything, allow me to see you out.'

Chapter 18

Moof d id n't like being so visible, but what other choice d id he have? He had n't eaten since lunchtime yesterd ay, and he'd barely been able to keep that d own because of the stress. He was ravenously hungry now.

Unfortunately, given that he had no money with him, he had been forced to resort to some pretty d esperate measures.

He had almost mad e it out. Almost got away with it.

Almost.

He had just reached the front d oor of the shop when it was nud ged open from the other sid e, and a woman with a three-wheeled pushchair began backing her way in. She was making a right blood y meal of it, too, wrestling with the oversized buggy like she was trying to haul in a great white shark on a single length of fishing line.

The front wheel caught on the outsid e step, and she muttered below her breath as she bounced the pushchair back out onto the street, before trying the same technique again.

Moof's weight rocked between the ball of each foot. The sand wich and packet of crisps he had stuffed up insid e his jumper felt huge and obvious. The jumper was shapeless and baggy, with room for another whole person to fit insid e, but it was d oing a pretty awful job of concealing the contraband he'd stuffed up insid e it.

He glanced back at the till. The Ind ian shopkeeper peered back at him from behind a counter cluttered with chocolate bars and vaping prod ucts, his eyes narrowed suspiciously.

Shite.

Moof faced front again. He'd picked this place because it was less likely to have CCTV, but now he was wishing he'd gone to Tesco a few dozen yards further along the street. Most of the staff didn't give a shit if you nicked from one of the larger supermarket chains. They weren't paid enough to get involved in the drama.

A place like this, though, with an on-site owner? Those guys cared. Those guys would hunt you to the ends of the bloody Earth, if they had to.

God. What had he been thinking?

Maybe he'd still get away with it. The man behind the counter must've been in his sixties. He'd be able to outrun him, no problem.

But he'd call the police. He'd give a description. They'd find him, and that would be that.

'Come on, come on,' Moof whispered below his breath, as he watched the woman continue to battle her buggy through the door.

The shopkeeper might not have noticed yet. He hadn't said anything. Moof was probably just being paranoid, that was all. He was worrying about nothing.

And then, as if picking up his cue, the shopkeeper called out to him, his Indian accent positively humming with indignation. 'Hey. You! What do you think you are doing?'

Moof froze, rooted to the spot, the stolen food becoming a lead weight beneath his jumper.

'Young man, I am talking to you,' the shopkeeper said, raising his voice further.

The stupid cow was still stuck in the door, blocking Moof's escape. The windows were encased in wire mesh. Even if he'd been able to break one—which was unlikely—he couldn't escape that way.

Slowly, with a sense of dawning dread, Moof turned his head. 'Who, me?'

'Yes, you!' the shopkeeper said, the upside-down letter U of his mouth a mirror image of the shape his eyebrows were making. 'What are you just stand ing there for? Can't you see the lad y need s help?'

Moof blinked .

Then stared .

Then blinked again.

'Oh. Right. Sorry, aye,' he said . He caught the d oor and prised it all the way open, which brought his reflection into sharp focus in the glass.

God , he looked like he was homeless. His face was pale, his eyes were d ark, and his roots seemed to be showing much worse than usual.

He'd run away in just the clothes he was wearing, and his jumper—alread y thread bare and full of holes—was d ripping wet from that last d ownpour.

Looking through his reflection, he saw the woman with the pushchair give him a grateful but somewhat exasperated smile.

'Thanks. Stupid blood y thing. Should 've gone for something smaller.'

'Tesco has automatic d oors,' Moof said on auto-pilot. He heard the 'tut' of the shopkeeper all the way from the till.

'Don't tell her that, for God 's sake. I've almost got her in the shop now.'

The buggy came through the d oor with a jolt, rocking the tod d ler who lay fast asleep in the seat. The girl murmured and her mother froze, breath held , a grimace of horror painted across her face.

And then, there was the sound of a d ummy being sooked , and the woman came alive again. 'Thank fuck for that,' she mouthed , before steering the pushchair around Moof and off into the shop's narrow aisles.

Moof stole a final glance at the shopkeeper, who was still watching him, then started for the freed om of the street outsid e.

'You forgot your d rink.'

He should 've run. He knew that. But the word s caught him off guard , and he found himself turning back to the man behind the till.

'Uh... sorry?'

'Meal d eal. Sand wich, crisps, bottle of juice.'

Moof followed the gesture the shopkeeper mad e and found himself staring into his own eyes again. This time, his scruffy, homeless-looking alter ego was reflected back at him from the mirrored trim of the d rinks frid ge that stood against the wall.

'If you're going to steal from me, young man, you might as well take the full set.'

There was no malice in the way the man spoke. He wasn't exactly d ancing a jig, either, mind you, but Moof d id n't reckon he was angry. From the look on his face, he was more sad than furious.

'But get yourself something hot to eat when you can, all right?' the shopkeeper instructed . 'Or you'll catch your blood y d eath.'

'Um... thank you,' Moof said . He regard ed the chiller cabinet like it might be a trap, then scurried over to it and grabbed a bottle of water. He fancied Coke, but thought that might be taking the piss.

To his amazement, no alarms rang when he picked up the bottle. A portcullis d id n't d escend over the d oor, and the man behind the counter failed to prod uce a shotgun from beneath the counter and take aim with it.

'Take care of yourself, young man,' the shopkeeper urged . 'But please, for both our sakes, d o me a favour and d on't come back.'

–

'Fuck's sake! *What*?'

The uniformed constable on the front step of the holid ay cottage almost jumped out of her skin when a semi-naked man hauled open the front d oor and scowled from behind what she initially thought was some sort of Halloween mask, but then realised was the man's actual face.

127

Her instructions from the MIT DCI had been to knock on the door around lunchtime, and to keep knocking until the person inside responded, regardless of how long that took.

She'd been on the brink of phoning the DCI to report that the occupant had either gone out or died, when the shape of something that might conceivably have been some sort of troll had appeared on the other side of the frosted glass.

'Well?!' the man demanded.

His eyes were a fiery shade of red, like he'd been rubbing sand into them, and the smell of body odour wafting from his hairy naked top half was threatening to do the same to the constable's.

Had she been a religious type, she might've feared that the Devil himself had come for her. As it was, she knew a hangover when she saw one.

'Mr... uh... Hoon?' she said, with a quick check of her notebook. Something troubling flitted across her face for a moment, then her eyes went wide. 'Wait. Hoon? As in?'

'As in none of your fucking business, princess,' Hoon told her. 'What do you want? Did that fat bastard put you up to this? What time is it?'

He looked at his wrist, realised he wasn't wearing a watch, checked the other one in case it was there, then reached over and grabbed the female constable's arm before she could stop him. Hoon grunted when he saw the time, then let the arm go.

'Bollocks, it's one o'clock,' he spat, refusing to accept the evidence of his own, admittedly blurry eyes. 'No way.'

'I'd ask you not to do that again, Mr Hoon,' she warned, brushing her sleeve where he'd caught it. 'And it's just after one, yes. DCI Logan asked me to check on you.'

She looked him up and down, accelerating her gaze quickly past his grubby boxer shorts in both directions. It was obvious, despite the impassive look she tried to plaster on her face, that she was far from impressed by anything she saw.

'Are you OK, sir?' she asked , conclud ing that she was clearly d ealing with someone suffering from at least one mental illness, and possibly several. 'Are you in a state of d istress?'

'Do I look like I'm fucking d istressed , hen?' Hoon asked , presenting himself with a wave of his hand . 'I was quite happy, out for the count, until you came poking your nose in, looking like a bulld og licking pish off a nettle.'

'There's no need for that sort of—'

'Oh, there is *every* fucking need , Constable,' Hoon inter- jected . 'There's every fucking need . Can a man no' get any peace? Eh? Is that out of the question, is it? What is this, Vene- fucking-zuela?'

The Uniform shook her head . She had n't agreed to this to be verbally abused . She'd checked he was alive, and she was reasonably confid ent that he was. Maybe not for long, given the state of him, but he was alive right now, and that was as far as her concerns stretched .

'Sorry to have bothered you, Mr Hoon,' she said , returning her notebook to the breast pocket of her jacket. 'I'll leave you to...' She gave him another once-over with her eyes. '...d o whatever it is you're d oing.'

'Aye, that's right. Off you fuck,' Hoon called after her. 'Run on back to the big boss man and get your pat on the head , you arse-licking, human fucking glove-puppet that you are.'

She rose above it, ignored the remarks, and closed the gate with a *bang* that shook the fence.

She was almost back at her car when the troll spoke again.

'Oh, one thing, Constable,' he called after her.

The Uniform stopped , sighed , then turned back in the d irection of the cottage. 'Yes? What?'

Hoon smiled sheepishly and scratched his arse through his boxer shorts.

'Don't suppose you know where I can get some grub round here, d o you? My stomach's eating my arse from the insid e out.'

Chapter 19

Once the last of the victim-formerly-known-as-Hermione's travelling companions had been led out of the interview room, Tyler finally let out the low whistle he'd been holding in for quite some time.

'Christ.'

'Aye,' Logan said.

'Right shower of weirdoes.'

'You can say that again.'

Tyler cupped his hands behind his neck, cradling his head, then gazed up at the ceiling, trying to process it all.

'So... did that lassie genuinely think she's a fairy?' he asked. 'I mean... properly, like?'

'Oh God. Beats me,' Logan said. 'I'd like to think not, but...'

'She seemed awfully bloody convinced,' Tyler finished.

He was right. Trixie Fae *did* seem to believe she was some sort of fairy, pixie, elf, or some such nonsense. Similarly, Anastasia Pelletier appeared to be labouring under the delusion that she was a French film star from the 50s, while the Irish lad, Kenny Murphy, was pretending to have zero personality whatsoever.

Actually, that last one might have been true.

During a short break between the first and second interviews, Tyler had made a suggestion on how he thought they should progress.

'What if we do good cop, bad cop, boss?' he'd said.

Logan had mulled it over for a few second s, then shaken his head . 'Let's stick to what we usually d o, son. Good cop, incompetent cop. I'll be the good cop.'

In truth, though, Tyler had proven himself useful several times d uring the interview process. Logan's hunch was right, and the interviewees—particularly the girls—respond ed far better to his questions than they d id to Logan's. Grad ually, d uring those d iscussions, Logan had stepped back and let the DC almost completely take over the interrogation.

'Thoughts?' Logan asked . 'Besid es, 'I hope I never see any of them again,' I mean.'

'Ach, they were all right, boss,' Tyler said , unhooking his hand s from behind his head and sitting forward again. 'Just young. Younger than their age, I mean. They've just stepped out of the real world for a while, haven't they?'

'Aye, well, all right for some,' Logan grunted . 'The rest of us are stuck here in the real world . So… thoughts?'

'Thoughts. Right,' Tyler said . He had the sud d en sense that he was being tested , and felt a cold clamminess start rad iating out from his lower back. 'I think Deird rie Mair knows a bit more than she's letting on. I reckon the waterworks over the pregnancy were real enough, but I think she either knows or has suspicions about who the father is.'

'She said she had no id ea.'

'Aye, but Trixie Fae said she could visit the astral plane, boss,' Tyler countered . 'Oh, and just for the record , I heard you mumbling "arsehole plane, more like" and I'm pretty sure she d id , too.'

'Good . She was meant to,' Logan said . 'I agree, by the way. On Deird rie having her suspicions on who the father is. Denial was too ad amant.'

Tyler felt like he'd been award ed a shiny gold star on his homework, and beamed happily, all puffed up and proud .

Logan wasn't d one with him yet, though.

'What else?'

'Uh… right. What else?' Tyler said , his mind racing. He looked d own at his notepad . 'I got some mixed messages about Hermione… sorry, Alexis's relationship with Moof.'

'Corey,' Logan corrected .

'Corey, right, aye. Sorry, boss. The French lassie was talking like Corey and Alexis were pretty close friend s. I got the impression she thought Deird rie might have been jealous.'

'Jealous enough to kill Alexis, you think?' Logan asked , gently guid ing the younger officer between the d ots.

Tyler stared into space for a few second s, then sucked in his top lip and spat it out again. 'Jealous enough, maybe, but not strong enough. No way she hauled her up on that rope.'

'What about Kenny Murphy?' Logan asked .

'Personality of a card board box. Trying to d isguise that fact by d yeing his hair and plastering on the makeup.'

'I mean could he have killed Alexis Riksen?'

Tyler spent less time consid ering that one. 'Can't see the motive, boss. And , at the risk of being accused of fat-shaming, he's fucking huge. From the photos I've seen of the monument stairs, the only way you're getting him to the top is with a helicopter and winch, so there's no way he was the one who hoisted the bod y up to the top.'

Logan had come to the same conclusions. The lad was d oing well.

'Hayd en Howard ?' he asked .

'For the killer?'

'Thoughts in general.'

That one took a bit more consid eration. Hayd en had been the second interview, just before a scrawny wee lad who looked like he should 've still been in primary school, and who had only known Hermione's group a few d ays.

Hayd en was marked ly more confid ent than the others, and had spoken to Tyler like they were old bud d ies, even going so far as to ask for hair prod uct recommend ations.

It was clear that he could 've easily been perceived as charming, but probably only by those younger than he was.

Tyler—and , most likely, anyone out of their teens—found him to be a bit full of himself. Logan felt the same, and had spent most of the interview resisting the urge to punch the smug bastard square in the coupon.

'He's a big fan of himself,' Tyler said , breaking d own his thoughts on the lad . 'He was quick to talk about Moof… sorry. About Corey and Alexis. I got the feeling he was maybe making more of their relationship than was necessarily there.'

'Or maybe he just knew more than the others,' Logan suggested . 'He said Corey spoke to him. Told him things.'

'True. But… I d on't know. He just seemed a bit eager to pass it all on. What d o we know about him?'

'Just what he told us. Nothing's been corroborated ,' Logan said . 'Should we look into him?'

Tyler glanced back over his should er, assuming Logan was talking to someone else who was stand ing there. It was only the snap of the DCI clicking his fingers that d ragged him back around to face front.

'Sorry, are you asking me, boss?'

'Yes, I'm asking you. Should we be looking further into Hayd en Howard ?'

This was all still part of the test, Tyler realised . 'Yes, boss,' he replied . 'And Deird rie Mair. Those are the two I'd be checking up on. I think the chances of any of the others being involved are slim.' He smiled weakly. 'But, eh, that's just my opinion. Whatever you think yourself. You're the boss.'

Logan fold ed his notebook closed and stood up. 'Right, then, Detective Constable,' he announced . 'Looks like you know what you need to be getting on with.'

Tyler practically floated out of his chair and onto his feet. 'Right, boss. No bother. I'll get right on it.' He hesitated , before continuing. 'But, eh, just to check, you d o mean you want me to look into Deird rie Mair and Hayd en Howard , yeah?'

'Yes. I want you to look into Deird rie Mair and Hayd en Howard .'

Tyler's smile wid ened . 'Got it. Thought so, boss, just thought I'd … aye. Got it. I'm on it. You can count on me.'

'First time for everything, son,' Logan said . 'When you've d one that, head up to the scene and talk to Deird rie.'

'Talk to her? About what? Did n't we just ask her everything?'

'She has her suspicions about the father of Alexis's wean,' said Logan. 'I want you to get her to open up.'

Tyler's look was as blank as the Arctic tund ra. 'How am I meant to d o that, boss?'

Logan shrugged . 'Fucked if I know. I'm sure you'll figure it out. Before you start any of that, though, I want us to reconvene at the Big Board to go over a few things.'

He glanced at his watch and let out a groan that seemed to expand to fill the entirety of the interview room.

'And then, I suppose I'd better go check in on our house-guest and see if those holid ay cottages are still stand ing.'

–

The Big Board was looking a little healthier now. Between them, the d etectives had ad d ed several key bits of information, although it was unclear how a lot of it currently fit together.

Ian Hill's red head ed d og-walker-without-a-d og was scribbled there on a Post-It Note. A second note below it read 'Corey Sand erson', with three question marks after it.

Hill had d ropped off his memory card soon after his conver-sation with Logan, on the und erstand ing that they sent it back to him when they were finished with it because they d id n't grow on trees.

Hamza had gone through the images and found nothing but uninteresting and uninspired scenic shots. They'd passed it over to the tech bod s for further checks, but there was nothing to ind icate it was hid ing any big secrets.

A vague timeline had been set out across the top of the board , with the estimated time of d eath written on an ind ex card and the time of the bod y's d iscovery on a second card that was pinned a few inches along to the right.

The last time Alexis Riksen had been seen alive was between ten and eleven o'clock on Tuesd ay evening, when she'd been sitting alone in the lounge of the sleeping car, read ing a book. Based on the post-mortem, she'd been killed at some point between half-two and half-four in the morning. Her movements between those two points in time were currently anyone's guess.

'We're getting Corey's and Alexis's bags sent up from d own the road , sir,' Hamza said .

Dave let out a little cheer and shook his clenched fists besid e his head in celebration. 'Something for me to check-in and catalogue. Wooo!'

'List of the contents is being emailed through,' Hamza continued . 'Should be here any time.'

'Nobod y show me,' Dave instructed . 'I want to keep it as a surprise.'

'Any sign of Sand erson himself?' Logan asked .

Ben shook his head . 'Nothing yet. It was in Ayr that they nearly nabbed him this morning, so they're focusing the search there. Checking other hostels, watching the bus stations, looking into any connections he might have in the area. They'll get him.'

That last part had sound ed less than convincing, but Logan tried to remain optimistic.

'Anything back from the rad io appeal or the haulage firms?' he asked .

'Nothing from the truck d rivers, no, sir,' Hamza replied . 'Nobod y saw anything. Got a few responses from the rad io appeal, though.'

Logan sat forward in his chair, an eyebrow raised . 'Aye?'

Hamza tabbed across to another wind ow on his computer, scrolled with the trackpad for a moment, then cleared his throat. 'Here we go,' he said , before starting to read from the screen.

'While investigating this murd er, might I suggest the police take some time to explain to visitors that parking on the road at Glenfinnan is d angerous for both d rivers and ped estrians alike? The increase in traffic at this time of year is an accid ent waiting to happen.'

'Who sent that?' Logan asked .

Hamza shrugged . 'Anonymous, via the rad io station's web contact form,' he said , then he scrolled to the next one. 'This one just says, "Never mind the murd er, what about all the fucking tourists"—tourists spelled with two Os—"who are pissing and shitting at the sid e of the road ? My d og nearly ate one." Spelled W-O-N. "It is fucking d isgusting." That's D-U-S-G-U-S-T-I-N. Also anonymous.'

'Nothing useful, then?' Logan asked , sitting back.

'Afraid not, sir, no.'

'That last one...' began Tyler, angling himself for a better look at Hamza's screen. 'Did the d og nearly eat a shite or a tourist?'

Hamza checked the email again. 'Not sure, it could go either way,' he ad mitted . 'Probably the shite, though.'

'How'd you get on with the security camera?' Ben asked the d etective sergeant.

Logan perked up at that. 'Security camera? What security camera?'

'I noticed there's one in the exhibition centre, sir,' Hamza replied . 'In the cafe bit. It's mostly looking d own at the till and part of the cafe, but going by the angle, I reckon it might just catch a bit of the main road . They're getting me the footage, and we'll see if I'm right, and if there's anything interesting on it.'

Logan stabbed a finger in Tyler's d irection. 'See that, son? That's proper polis work. What have you been d oing?'

Tyler's mouth d ropped open. 'I was d oing interviews with you, boss!' he protested .

Logan kept his finger raised for a few second s, then let it d rop. 'Aye, fair point,' he ad mitted , then he turned back to the Big Board and considered the information they had put together.

The more of a picture they were building on the board, the worse things were looking for Corey Sanderson.

He'd argued with the victim a few days before she'd died.

He'd been sitting in the hostel lounge with her a couple of hours before she was last seen alive.

His badge had been found at the scene.

Someone that matched his description had been spotted walking away from the scene shortly after the body had been found.

He'd done a runner, then been found with the victim's bag and personal belongings in his possession, including her passport.

Then he'd done a runner again, almost breaking his neck clambering out of a window.

Aye, it was looking pretty cut and dried. This could all be wrapped up by the end of the day. They just had to find the bugger.

Still, considering he was a big lump of a lad with a head of bright red hair, someone was bound to spot him.

Sooner or later.

–

Moof sat huddled between two large metal bins at the back of a chip shop just off Ayr Beach, his ears practically swivelling as he listened for danger.

He had just finished wolfing down the last few bites of his stolen sandwich and was now getting ripped into the crisps. Salt and vinegar Discos. Not normally his first choice—he was more of a cheese and onion man—but they had been the easiest to snaffle when the shopkeeper wasn't looking.

He felt bad for nicking from the guy. He'd seemed like a nice bloke, and letting him take the bottle of water had been a classy act.

If only the old man had known what he'd d one. Would he have been so generous then?

Almost certainly not.

Why had he turned the d amn phone on? The plan had all been worked out. He'd known what he had to d o, where he had to be. And yet, he'd turned on the blood y phone. He'd d rawn attention to himself.

Stupid , stupid , stupid .

Obviously, it had all gone wrong. He'd been connected with the... act.

The d eed .

He chastised himself. *Call it what it is, you bloody coward.*

He'd been connected with the *murder*.

A sob caught in his throat. He pretend ed not to notice.

'There,' he said in a croaky whisper. 'Wasn't so hard , was it?'

Forcing all thoughts of it from his mind , he quickly finished the crisps and washed it all d own with the last of the Highland Spring.

After d isposing of the wrappers in one of the bins, Moof stole a furtive glance out over the street and the kid s' playpark to where the water lapped at the sand y shore.

There were a few child ren running around in the park, and some old er kid s throwing Frisbees around on the beach. Disin-terested parents kept half an eye on them, while keeping the remaining one-and -a-half fixed firmly on their phone screens.

Moof briefly wond ered if he could make a run for it d own to the beach, then swim across to Northern Ireland . From there, he could hitchhike south to the Republic, stow away on a ferry across to France, and get lost in Europe.

It was a simple plan, but not without its flaws. For one thing, if he set out from the beach it would be the Isle of Arran he land ed on, not Northern Ireland .

Also, he could n't swim.

His stomach rumbled , d emand ing more food . He gave it a rub through his d irty jumper, and then reached around to the back of his trousers, where he'd stuffed the other item he'd stolen. This one was larger and much riskier to grab than the food had been. Ironically, he didn't think the shopkeeper had realised he had it.

Just as well, because it was probably the one thing that was going to help him avoid capture.

He'd been watching the public toilets just a few dozen yards away while he'd been eating. Nobody had gone into the disabled bathroom the whole time he'd been sitting there. Nobody seemed to be heading in that direction now, either.

Nobody but him.

Keeping his head down, Moof set off briskly towards the toilet block, reading the instructions on the box of hair dye as he walked.

Chapter 20

Logan heard the alarm and saw the smoke as he pulled up outsid e the holid ay cottage.

An outburst of panicky swearing accompanied him as he explod ed from the Fiesta like a cork from a bottle and went stumbling in through the front d oor of the bungalow.

He found Hoon stand ing over a frying pan of what might once have been bacon, but was now fire.

The former Detective Superintend ent seemed mesmerised by the d ancing flames, and he d id n't look up from the pan until Logan bellowed , 'Drop it in the blood y sink!' and turned on the cold tap.

This sud d en outburst cut through his hangover haze and Hoon tossed the flaming pan into the sink. There was an angry hissing and crackling as cold water met hot oil. The flames, to Logan's d ismay, d oubled in size, erupting upward s and outward as a brief, brilliant fireball forced him back and came d angerously close to setting the curtains on fire.

'Jesus Christ!' Logan hissed , whacking at the flames with a d ish towel until they were swallowed by the water in the sink. A few experimental prod s at the smoke alarm finally persuad ed it to knock it off with the blood y racket.

'So much for my fucking breakfast,' Hoon scowled , as if all this was somehow Logan's fault. 'That's one-ninety-nine you owe me for that bacon.'

'You nearly burnt the blood y place d own!' Logan barked back at him.

'My arse. It was all in hand . I was just crisping it up.'

Logan fished in the sink and prod uced a sliver of something that might have been charcoal. 'Into what, fucking d iamond s?'

'It's the stupid bastard hob. It's no' like my one,' Hoon said , slumping sullenly onto one of two chairs that stood besid e a small semi-circular table, against the back wall of the kitchen.

He was fully d ressed , which was unexpected . Granted , he was mostly wearing Logan's clothes, which the DCI wasn't exactly overjoyed about, but this was still a marked improve-ment on what he'd been bracing himself for.

'Where d id you get the bacon from, anyway?' Logan asked him, opening the wind ow further.

'Miss Piggy's arse cheeks,' Hoon retorted . 'The fucking shop round the corner, Jack. Where d o you think I got it from?'

'There's a cafe right next to it. J.J.'s. If you were hungry, why d id n't you just grab a bite to eat there?'

'Because I'm perfectly fucking capable of putting a couple of bits of bacon in a pan, Jack.'

Logan glanced at the sink. 'Aye, you've mastered that bit, I see. Still work to d o on the "taking it out again" part.'

Hoon mad e a noise somewhere in his respiratory system that might have been a grunt of annoyance, but could equally have been a snort of laughter.

'Aye. Well. It's not the same as my hob at home,' he reiter-ated , his voice losing some of its harshness.

He looked small sitting there on the kitchen chair. Every time Logan had seen him since coming back from his sabbatical in Orkney, Hoon—who had always loomed large like some sort of Biblical giant—seemed to have shrunk just an inch or two further.

Physically, he was still the same size. In every other aspect, though, there was very little left of him.

Logan lowered himself onto the chair on the other sid e of the table. As soon as he'd settled in place, Hoon asked him to put the kettle on.

With a sigh, Logan stood up again, mad e them tea in near-silence, then returned to his seat. They both sipped from their matching 'wild animals of Scotland ' mugs, neither one quite sure what to say, or how to start.

'Not a bad cup of tea,' Hoon said . From the way he said it, he grud ged every word .

'That's maybe the nicest thing you've ever said to me, Bob.'

Hoon tutted . 'Aye, well, it's probably the first compliment you've ever fucking d eserved .'

Logan took another swig of his tea. Hoon was right. It was a fine brew.

'Don't suppose you thought to buy biscuits when you were out, d id you?' he asked .

Hoon gave a shake of his head . It was slow, and sad , and lad en with regret. 'Did n't think,' he confessed . 'I was fucking looking right at them, too. Had load s. Caramel Wafers. Snowballs. Teacakes.'

'I was never a big fan of a teacake,' Logan said .

Hoon spluttered into his mug. 'Fucking take that back,' he warned . 'Or I'll throw this tea in your face.'

Logan chuckled . 'I mean, they're all right. It's the biscuit base I'm not keen on. Too soggy.'

'You've just gone right d own in my estimation, Jack. And believe you me, that's some fucking achievement.'

They slurped their tea, and Logan tried not to d well too much on how nice a snowball would be right now.

Instead , he turned to more serious matters.

'I heard about the brid ge, Bob.'

Hoon's face d id n't shift so much as an atom, but something in his eyes changed , like an incoming weather system had swept away everything that was previously there.

'Aye. Well,' he said . 'Stupid .'

'And last night?' Logan pressed . 'The pills. What was that about?'

Hoon shrugged , like a child who'd just been asked why he'd kicked a ball through a wind ow. Logan could see his throat moving, like there was a response waiting to come out, but it was stuck there, somehow, unable to escape.

'You need to talk to someone, Bob,' Logan told him. 'Someone professional who knows what they're d oing.'

'I d on't need a shrink,' Hoon said . It was flat and matter-of-fact, d evoid of his usual bile and venom. 'What would be the blood y point?'

'The point would be that you might not try and kill yourself every couple of d ays.'

'I wasn't trying to kill myself. No' really,' Hoon muttered , gazing into his cup. 'I just...' He shook his head like it was pointless to try to explain. 'Forget it.'

'You just what?' Logan asked , not letting him off that easily.

'It's all right for you. Fucking strid e in, cock of the walk, and they're all fucking jizzing themselves to welcome you back.' Hoon may have lost some of his bite, but the bark was returning to his voice now. 'I show my face, and they look at me like I've got a big d aud of shite smeared all over it.'

'As far as they know, you sold us all out to Bosco,' Logan pointed out.

'Aye, but we know fucking better, d on't we, Jack? We know I d id n't have a choice. We know I put my own bollocks on the chopping block to protect all those bastard s.' He prod d ed himself in the chest. 'My testimony put the fat Russian fuck behind bars. Mine!'

Logan consid ered pointing out that Bosco had been complicit in the kid napping of several police officers and civil-ians, all of whom testified against him in court, but d ecid ed it would be like kicking a d og when it was d own, so elected not to.

'And d on't think he's the end of it, either, by the way. No fucking way,' Hoon said . 'There'll be another Bosco now. He'll worm his way into the fucking d epartment somehow, if he hasn't alread y. You mark my word s, Jack, one of those hapless clusterfucks of boiled ham you call your colleagues will alread y have been compromised by the new player in town.'

Logan had n't yet heard about anyone stepping into Bosco's shoes, but knew that it was only a matter of time. His arrest had created a vacuum that was just waiting to be filled .

It was Bosco's flair for the theatrical that had first brought him to Logan's attention back in Glasgow all those years ago. If there was a new player on the scene, then they had the good sense to keep their head d own. That would potentially make them even more of a problem than Bosco had been.

But none of that was his problem. He'd had a personal connection with Bosco from back in the d ay, but his replacement would remain firmly in the hand s of CID.

'Aye, well. We'll see,' Logan said , steering the conversation back on topic. 'And yes, I know you had your reasons for what you d id . But it's over, Bob. You're off the force, and there's fuck all point in crying over spilt milk. You need to suck it up, d eal with it, and move on with the rest of your life.'

Hoon gave another grunt, and this time it d efinitely *was* a laugh. 'The rest of my life? I'm fifty-fucking…' He frowned , trying to calculate, then gave up. '…od d . What rest of my life?'

'Jesus Christ. Aye. You're fifty-od d . You might keep going until you're ninety-od d . You're hard ly knocking on d eath's d oor here. There's plenty of opportunities waiting out there.'

Hoon set his mug d own and crossed his arms. 'Oh aye? Name me fucking one.'

Logan tried not to flinch. He'd been hoping Hoon would n't ask him that. 'Well, like… security guard .'

Hoon stared at him in silence for several second s, then stood up. 'Does that petrol station across the road d o paracetamol in bulk, d o you know?'

'It's just one suggestion,' Logan said .

'Fucking *security guard*? Me? I was a fucking Detective Superintend ent, Jack! I ruled that fucking place with a fist of iron. And what…? You think I should be wand ering around some shopping mall or build ing site with a torch in one hand and my cock in the other?'

Logan blinked. 'Well, the torch, maybe…'

'No way, Jose. I'm the fucking organ grind er, Jack, no' the monkey.'

'Fine. Then start your own security company,' Logan said. 'Be the boss. Hire some retired ex-constables.'

'What, work with that shower of gelatinous shite-sacks again? I'd rather have rats eat my fucking eyes out.'

Logan threw his arms into the air, then let them fall back onto the table. 'God, well, I d on't know, Bob. Be a florist. Start a restaurant. Become a blood y astronaut. But find *something*. We all need something to get up for in the morning. Some reason to keep going.'

'Where'd you get that from, a Hallmark card?' Hoon asked, screwing his face up in d istaste. 'Jesus, it's like being lectured by Forrest fucking Gump. I had a reason to keep going, Jack. I had a purpose. I was making a d ifference to the world. Aye, maybe I d id n't follow the rules d own to the letter, but I was making a real fucking d ifference.'

Logan was staring at him now, stunned into silence.

'What?' Hoon d emand ed. 'What are you fucking gawping at?'

'Are you… are you crying, Bob?'

'Fuck off!' Hoon barked. He wiped his eyes on the back of his hand. 'It's the fucking smoke, ya jeb end! Got in my eyes, that's all. Course I'm not fucking crying! And you know how I know I'm not crying, Jack? Because I'm neither a woman nor a raging homosexual.' He shook his head and scowled in a d isplay of contempt and d isgust. 'Am I fucking *crying*? Jesus Christ.'

Logan began to respond, but Hoon wasn't d one yet. Far from it.

'I've been through shite that would turn your fucking hair white, Jack. I've watched good men—good fucking friend s—get their faces blown off by IEDs. I've had ten-year-old s point fucking assault rifles bigger than themselves at me, and I've had to d o whatever it took to keep me and the rest of my boys safe.

Whatever it fucking took. So, no, in answer to your inane little question, no, I'm no' crying.'

'Well, maybe you should . But sorry, my mistake,' Logan said , sensibly choosing not to press the matter further. He checked his watch, then stood up. 'Still, at least you know what you need to d o now.'

Hoon frowned . 'And what's that?'

'You said it yourself. Find a way to make a d ifference,' Logan conclud ed . He ind icated the sink, and the bit of bacon-scented charcoal currently bobbing around in the oily water. 'And you can start by cleaning up your blood y mess.'

Chapter 21

Tyler stood on the shore of Loch Shiel, his hand s in his pockets, gazing out across the water.

He had n't planned to come d own to the murd er scene, but the view had grabbed him by the eyeballs and more or less d ragged him all the way d own from where he'd parked the car.

It had never really been his cup of tea, scenery. Aye, he appreciated a nice mountain, or a sweeping glen, or whatever, but no more than the next man.

But this was d ifferent. It was early afternoon, so the sky wasn't d oing anything particularly d ramatic, but the light d anced joyfully across the surface of the water, turning it into a living, breathing thing.

It helped that it wasn't raining. It had been lashing d own earlier in the d ay, and it would almost certainly be lashing d own again later, but in the interlud e between them, the air smelled so crisp and clean and fresh that Tyler was convinced just breathing it in was making him a better man.

Ten minutes passed . Fifteen, maybe. Then, somewhere in the recesses of his mind , he heard Logan nagging at him to get his finger out.

We're no' paying you to admire the view, Detective Constable. There's work to be done.

He allowed himself another few second s to stare at the loch, wid e-eyed and unblinking, like the scene might imprint itself on his eyeballs.

Then he turned back toward s the path, and heard a panicky 'hwrook' from d own on the ground . A family of gull-sized , black-throated bird s all scattered away from him, bead y eyes shooting accusing looks in his d irection.

'Sorry! My fault,' he told them, then he crept past, keeping his d istance as much for his own sake as for theirs. He'd seen the film *The Birds*. He knew what happened if you got on their wrong sid e.

Once he was safely out of beak-strike reach, he d iverted toward s the base of the monument. The protective tent was still covering the top, but it was slouching away from the water, the wind roaring along the loch that morning having clearly taken its toll.

Tyler stepped over the cord on tape and approached the narrow d oor at the bottom of the column. It had been shut tight and fastened with a pad lock, preventing him from entering.

Still, if the size of the d oor was anything to go by, he'd mad e the right call on Kenny Murphy. There was no chance in hell he was getting through that entrance. Not without being pureed and poured through a funnel.

Stepping back over the cord on, he looked for the bird s, but found they were gone. A prickly sensation of d read crept up the back of his neck, and he spun on the spot, making sure the bastard s weren't sneaking up behind him.

His phone blared out from within his pocket, making him simultaneously jump and emit a noise he hoped he never emitted again. Fortunately, there was nobod y around to hear it, or he'd never have been allowed to live it d own.

Tyler took out the phone, saw the name on the front, and broke into a broad smile that he could n't have held back if he'd tried to.

'All right, gorgeous? You coming d own yet?'

'Hey!' Sinead replied , and there was enough in just that one word to tell Tyler that no, she wasn't. 'Can't get anything sorted for Harris until later this evening. He's going to stay with Auntie Val, but I can't d rop him off until about eight.'

'That's not bad . You can be d own here by, what? Ten?'

148

'Afraid not, no. Ben's asked me to meet someone at the airport at around nine-forty,' Sinead told him. 'Victim's father. Apparently, he's flying into Inverness. His, I d on't know, secretary or something just sent the station word .'

'Isn't the airport shut by then?' Tyler asked .

'Private jet,' Sinead said . 'He's paying to keep the place open for him.'

'Blood y hell! I mean, I heard he was minted but... blood y hell!'

He could hear the cringe in Sinead 's voice. 'Aye, tell me about it. And there's me going to pick him up in a Ford Focus. I'm blood y d read ing it. I mean, what d o you say? "Sorry your d aughter's been murd ered . I like your plane. I hope you haven't brought too much luggage, because the boot's not very big."'

'In America, they call it a "trunk",' Tyler said .

'That's not exactly the point I was trying to make. But great, now I'll sound like an id iot, too.'

'He's from Texas. Just stick on a Country and Western CD and pour some barbecue sauce into the air vents, and he'll feel right at home,' Tyler assured her. 'You're bringing him d own the road then?'

'Mortuary first to ID the bod y, and then d own the road , yeah. Me and him. Two hours in the car, after he's seen his d ead d aughter for the first time.'

It d id not, Tyler had to ad mit, seem like a fun time waiting to be had . 'You'll be fine, though. I have complete faith. And , eh, you're staying d own?'

'Aye, tomorrow and Saturd ay, at least.'

'Right. Good . That's great,' Tyler said , his big beaming grin returning. 'Has, eh, has Ben mentioned anything about the sleeping arrangements yet?'

'No. Why?'

'It's a bit... cramped , is all. Not sure who'll be sleeping where.'

He heard her smiling d own the phone. 'I'm sure we'll figure something out.'

'Aye. I'm sure we will,' Tyler said , then his phone chirped in his ear. 'Message. One sec.'

He checked the phone and found a text from Logan positively glaring out at him from the screen.

You spoken to her yet? If not, get a bloody move on and get back here!

Tyler sighed . 'Sorry,' he said . 'Duty calls.'

–

Hayd en Howard was sitting on the steps of the sleeping car when Tyler pulled up at Glenfinnan station. He was smoking a roll-up cigarette, which he promptly d isposed of into the bushes at the sight of the d etective's car, then spent the next several second s frantically flapping the air as he watched Tyler walking over.

'Hey, brah!' he said , jumping to his feet and rushing to close the gap. 'How's it going? Everything OK?'

Tyler sniffed , making it very clear he knew exactly what had been going on. 'Fine, thanks. You?'

'Uh, great, yeah. Just… having a cigarette. No smoking insid e.'

Tyler sniffed again. 'Imports, are they? Smell funny.'

Hayd en's eyes flitted between Tyler's, trying to figure out just how much the d etective knew.

'Yeah. Imports. All legal, though.'

'Glad to hear it,' Tyler said . He nod d ed in the d irection o the sleeping car. 'Is Deird rie in?'

'Deed s? Nah, brah. She went to watch the train, I think. Fucking… Harry Potter Express, or whatever it's called . Crossing the brid ge. She and Hermione used to d o it all the time. It was kind of their thing, or whatever.' He grinned . 'Well, that and all the hot lesbo sex, I guess. At it like rabbits, they were. But, you know, gay rabbits.'

Generally speaking, Tyler was never one to shy away from what might be d escribed as 'a bit of banter'. Particularly where lesbians were involved .

But sometimes, even he had to d raw the line.

When he looked back on the moment later, Tyler would conclud e that the word s that came out of his mouth were as much DCI Logan's as they were his own.

'One of the young women you're talking about is d ead . Show some blood y respect.'

Hayd en's face fell. He cleared his throat and nod d ed , looking suitably chastised . 'Yeah. Shit. Sorry. Out of line,' he said . 'It just… it d oesn't feel real, you know?'

'Not to you, maybe,' Tyler said .

Hayd en scratched id ly at a forearm and moved his weight from foot to foot. 'Yeah. I'm sorry, brah. Not on,' he said . 'Does her family know yet?'

Tyler nod d ed . 'Aye. Her d ad 's flying in.'

'Shit, really? Wow.' Hayd en stared past Tyler for several second s, like this was the most shocking aspect of the whole awful affair. 'That's crazy. When?'

'I d on't know. Tonight.'

'Tonight? Will we have to talk to him?'

'Not necessarily, no,' Tyler said , only half paying attention. 'But I'm sure he'd appreciate the chance to meet and talk to you all. Share your memories of her. Whatever.' He gestured vaguely up the hill behind the station. 'Is there a viewpoint or something?'

'Uh, yeah. But she d id n't head that way. Too many blood y tourists,' Hayd en said , without so much as a whiff of irony. 'She's gone along the tracks.'

'The tracks?' Tyler looked along the railway line to where it d isappeared into a thicket of trees. 'Is that not d angerous?'

'Nah. I mean, sure, yeah. A bit,' Hayd en replied . 'But there are places to stand if you know where to go.' He saw the unim-pressed expression on the d etective's face and smiled awkward ly. 'I mean, it's not like it's illegal.'

'Walking on a train line is completely illegal.'

'Shit. Is it? Right.' Hayden ran his tongue across the front of his teeth. 'Well, in that case, maybe don't tell her I told you where to find her? She looked pretty unhappy as it is. Don't want her losing the rag with me. She can be *fierce* when she wants to be.'

'Unhappy?' Tyler continued to look along the tracks. 'How unhappy are we talking?'

'Pretty miserable. I mean, hardly surprising, I suppose, given... you know.'

Shite.

Tyler checked his watch. 'How long until the train?'

'About ten minutes,' Hayden said, with enough uncertainty to make Tyler almost immediately discount it.

'Does it stop here?'

Hayden shook his head. 'Nah, brah. There's no station staff until the next regular train comes through later. Steam train just flies straight through. Backwards, too.'

'Backwards?'

'It can't get turned up at Mallaig. Drives up forward, then reverses back the whole way. It's pretty wild.'

Reversing. Poor visibility, then.

Double shite.

Turning, Tyler looked along the track in the opposite direction, then cocked his head and listened. The only sound was the chirping of birds and the rumble of cars passing on the road at the bottom of the hill.

He put a foot on the metal rail and held it there for a few moments, but felt nothing. If the train was coming, it was some way off yet.

'Right, I'm going to go get her,' he announced.

'She should be back in, like, fifteen minutes,' Hayden said, but the look the DC shot him made him reconsider. 'Shit. You don't think she's going to...?'

'No. Probably not. I don't know. Wait here. I'll go get her,' Tyler said. 'Go inside, tell the constable in there to try to stop the train here, if he can.'

Hayden gave a double thumbs up. 'Sure thing, brah,' he said.

When it was clear that Hayden wasn't about to move, Tyler tutted and ushered him in the direction of the sleeping car. 'Well, get a move on, then!'

'Oh! Right, yeah.'

Hayden scurried back towards the wooden steps that led up to the carriage's front door. Tyler didn't wait to make sure he went inside. There was no time.

Instead, he took another quick glance along the railway line to his left, and listened for the tell-tale chuff-chuff of the steam engine.

Once he was satisfied there was no immediate danger, he jumped down onto the track, muttered a few unpleasantries below his breath, and broke into a jog.

Chapter 22

Logan arrived back at the station to find one of the things he
d espised most in all the world waiting for him outsid e the front
d oors. The thing he hated more than murd erers, more than
d rug-d ealers, more than almost anything.

A med ia circus.

Cameras flashed furiously as he pulled into the car park, like
someone had spilled a pint on a nightclub lighting rig, send ing
it haywire.

He recognised a few of the faces as they ran alongsid e the
Fiesta, barking questions at him. Some bastard from *The Sun*.
Some twat from the *Daily Record*. Some clown from the *Daily
Mail,* most likely a Nazi.

It was always the same. The sight of them always sent his
blood pressure skyrocketing, and his ad renal gland s into over-
d rive. There was something primal at work d eep d own insid e
him. One sniff of a tabloid journalist and the caveman in him
pulled on his loincloth and reached for the first available club.

Logan slammed on the brakes, catching the journos off guard
and send ing them tumbling over one another as they all tried
to stop, and all failed spectacularly.

Crunching the gearstick into reverse, he backed into the
nearest empty space, quickly got out, and mad e sure to lock the
car behind him. They would n't nick it—unfortunately—but he
would n't put it past the parasitic bastard s to comb through it
when no one was watching. The car was bad enough without
the stench of *desperate paparazzo* festering away insid e it.

Fixing his gaze firmly on the front d oor, Logan went strid ing toward s it, d oing his best to pretend that he had n't noticed the d ozen or so microphone-toting specimens racing to intercept him, all of them practically foaming at the mouth to be the first to get their questions out.

'Time for a quick word , Mr Logan?'

'Detective Chief Inspector, is it true that Bartholomew Riksen's d aughter has been murd ered ?'

'Any comment for our read ers?'

'Is it true the girl had been raped ?'

'Have you got a suspect in custod y?'

He reached the d oor before they d id . He even managed to grab the hand le, and was almost home free when he caught sight of them all reflected in the glass like an oncoming zombie hord e.

He'd have preferred a zombie hord e, actually. Nobod y objected if you caved a zombie's head in. Although, why anyone would object if you d id the same to a tabloid journalist was beyond him.

Some of them were alread y muttering into record ing d evices, no d oubt making up statements he had n't given, attributing quotes that he'd never said . The usual bullshit.

With a sigh, he released his grip on the d oor hand le and turned to confront them.

'First of all, everyone fucking shut up,' he said , raising his voice above the chatter. 'I won't be answering any questions, but I'll give you a statement.'

Logan looked across their faces, his gaze sweeping over them very slowly and d eliberately.

'If any of you d eviate from that statement by one blood y word , I will find a way to put you in jail. I d on't care how long it takes, or what I have to d o, I will either find or d evise some means to have you locked up,' he warned . 'You record or write d own my statement. If you ad d or remove anything, or even if you spell a word wrong, I will hunt you to the end s of the Earth. Is that clear?'

The general murmuring of und erstand ing was quickly over-shad owed by some mouthy bastard at the back.

'Is Mr Riksen flying in from America?'

'Is there a part of "I won't be answering any questions" you failed to grasp, son?' Logan asked , glowering through the gaps in the crowd at an eager, bright-eyed youngster who had n't yet become the hollow, d ried -out husks the rest of them had long-ago turned into.

'Uh, no. I just—'

'Pens read y. Here comes my statement,' Logan said . 'And remember, one word wrong, and you're fucked . Your whole life. Just totally fucking ruined forever. OK?'

He waited until everyone was suitably silent, and he was sure they were paying attention.

'There will be no comment at this time,' he said , then he turned on his heels, pulled open the d oor, and more or less skipped into the station.

The interior d oor buzzed as he approached , without him even having to ask. He met the eye of Moira Corson behind the reception d esk, and she gave him a nod of approval.

'Nicely d one,' she said . 'Gaggle of bastard s, the lot of them.'

-

'Someone could 've warned me about the pack of blood sucking rod ents scurrying around out front,' Logan said , barging into the Incid ent Room. 'How the hell d id they get word so fast?'

'Who?' asked Ben, looking up from his notebook.

'The press. The blood y tabloid s. There's a whole gang of them out front.'

'Is there? Shite!'

Hamza's fingers d anced across his keyboard . The groan he let out d id nothing to lower Logan's blood pressure.

'What now?' the DCI asked .

'It's everywhere, sir,' Hamza said . 'Just d id a search, and it's all over Google News. BBC, STV, the *Record*, *The Sun*, they're all running it on their websites.'

'It's trend ing on Twitter, too,' said Dave, who had jumped onto the social med ia site on his phone. 'Also, I think Paul Daniels is d ead . The magician fella.'

'Paul Daniels d ied years ago, d id n't he?' Ben remarked . 'Or am I thinking of another one? The Great Soprend o, maybe?'

Dave tapped his screen. 'Ah, no. You're right. He d ied years back. Don't know why he's trend ing now.'

'Sex pest allegations, maybe?' Ben guessed . 'Always thought there was something a bit funny about him. Putting women in boxes and poking them with sword s. It's not normal.'

'Can we stop worrying about Paul blood y Daniels, and focus for a minute?' Logan barked . 'How d id the press get to hear about the victim's id entity? We've barely just figured it out ourselves. I swear to Christ, if we've got another leak I'll plug it by sticking my big toe up its arse.'

'Deird rie Mair tweeted it, sir,' Hamza said , scrolling on his laptop trackpad . 'Bit of a tweetstorm, actually. Six… seven. No, eight tweets. Nine. Photos of them together. Lots of stuff about feeling lied to and betrayed .'

'Oh aye. Just found it,' Dave said . 'Lot of retweets, too. Thousand s of them.'

Hamza rolled back his chair and stood up sud d enly. 'Shite!'

'What now?' Logan asked .

'Top Tweet, sir,' the DS said , picking up the laptop and turning it so Logan could see the screen. 'Sent fifteen minutes ago.'

Logan read the message Deird rie has sent out into the world . It was short but to the point. An excellent example of concise writing, as suicid e notes went.

'Shite!' he spat. 'Someone get on the phone, and get me blood y Tyler!'

Chapter 23

Christ, it was high.

DC Neish had seen the Glenfinnan Viaduct from the roadside in real life, and from above in photographs. He'd also seen it in one of the Harry Potter movies, but had n't been paying too much attention.

Besid es, he was d imly aware that a flying car had been involved , so he'd had some d oubts over the accuracy of the viad uct's d epiction.

Stand ing at the start of it, though, with a quarter of a mile of elevated track ahead and a one hund red foot d rop over th sid es into the River Finnan below, it felt like a much more epic feat of engineering than he'd been prepared for.

Deird rie stood near the centre of the viad uct, five or six hund red feet away, leaning on the small wall that ran along both sid es of the track, and peering d own into the river.

Tyler shouted to her. Called her name. But the wind had a roar to it at that height, and the word s were whipped away from him before they could start their journey.

He ad d ed a much quieter 'Bollocks' to the rest of his stolen utterances, then gingerly took a step onto the viad uct and prod d ed around with one foot, testing the stability of it.

Logically, he knew that if the structure could hold a massive train filled with people, it could hold his weight, too. And yet, heights had never been his strong point, and some d eep-seated survival instinct was going to make d amn well sure the thing was safe before letting him set off along it.

Once he had persuaded himself that he wasn't going to fall straight through the bottom of it and plunge screaming into the river below, he crouched down and put a hand on the rail, feeling for any vibrations.

To his relief, there were none.

He stood up and shouted Deirdrie's name again.

No response.

'Shite!' he said to nobody in particular, then he set off walking across the viaduct, being very careful not to look down over the sides. Or, for that matter, to his left or right.

His phone buzzed in his pocket when he was a dozen paces in. Mistaking it for the vibration of the train tracks, he let out what was his second panicky yelp of the day, which he reluctantly accepted might not be his last.

'Ham?' he said into the handset, once he'd figured it all out and calmed down enough to talk. 'What's up?'

'Where are you?' Hamza asked.

A bird flew past Tyler's head. It was a good five or six feet away, but he ducked, anyway.

'You don't want to know,' he muttered. 'Why?'

'It's Deirdrie Mair. She's going to kill herself.'

Tyler groaned, his gaze fixed like a laser targeting system on the young woman in question. She was still leaning on the barrier and hadn't yet noticed him.

'How do you know?' he asked.

'Because she tweeted "I'm going to kill myself" a little while ago,' Hamza told him. 'Are you still at Glenfinnan? Do you think you can find her?'

'I can see her from here,' Tyler said. He heard Hamza relay this news to Logan, and a relieved-sounding response from the DCI. 'Aye, let's not count our chickens yet,' Tyler said. 'She's halfway across the viaduct. Right in the middle. I'm on my way out to get her.'

Hamza relayed that message, too. The next voice Tyler heard was Logan's.

'Tyler? What's happening?'

'All right, boss? Just what I said to Hamza. She's parked herself halfway across the viad uct. Train's d ue in a few minutes, but I've hopefully managed to get that to stop at Glenfinnan.'

'Hopefully? What's hopefully?' Logan d emand ed . 'If it isn't stopped get the hell off there.'

'It'll stop, boss,' Tyler insisted , sound ing far more sure of that than he felt. 'And … I think she might jump, if I d on't go talk to her.'

'Aye, and you might both end up mashed to bits if it d oesn't stop!'

'I can't just leave her, boss.'

Logan exhaled so hard that Tyler swore he felt it against his cheek.

'Fine. But leave the phone on. Keep it in your pocket, if you have to. I want to know what's going on.'

'Will d o, boss,' Tyler said . He slipped the phone into his shirt pocket. 'Can you still hear me?'

He realised he could n't hear a response, so took the phone back out again and repeated the question.

'Could you still hear—?'

'Yes, we could still hear you,' Logan snapped . 'Now, if you're insisting on going out to her, get a blood y move on.'

Tyler stuffed the phone back in his shirt pocket and continued to make his way along the track, stepping from one sleeper to the next. As he walked , he called out to Deird rie again, but either she still could n't hear him, or she wasn't letting on. Either way, she continued to stare d own at the river crashing over the rocks a hund red feet d own.

The gap closed . A hund red feet. Eighty. Fifty. The wind was shoving at him now, jostling him around as if his being there was some sort of affront that could not go unpunished .

When he was around thirty feet away, Deird rie finally respond ed to her name. She looked up and stared vaguely ahead , all tears and snot and confusion.

Tyler closed in another ten feet or so before she figured out where the voice had come from, and spun to face him.

'What are you d oing?' she yelped , backing right up against the barrier at the ed ge of the track. 'Why are you here? Piss off! You should n't be here!'

Tyler opened his mouth to say the perfect combination of word s that would encourage the girl to get the hell off the viad uct as quickly and as safely as possible. The surgically selected platitud es and word s of wisd om that would make her realise this was silly, and that she still had everything to live for.

Unfortunately, he had n't quite thought that far ahead . He'd been so preoccupied with not tripping up and falling to his d eath that it had n't occurred to him to plan out what he was going to say should he arrive at Deird rie in one piece.

In the end , he settled on 'All right?' which probably wasn't going to win him any award s for quick-thinking.

Deird rie stared back at him, mouth slightly open, brow d eeply furrowed . 'What?'

'I mean... what are you d oing out here?' Tyler asked .

'What d o you think I'm d oing out here?'

Tyler shrugged . 'I mean, I'd like to say bird watching, but...'

'I'm going to fucking kill myself, all right?'

'Aye.' Tyler nod d ed . 'That was going to be my next guess. Except, see, it'd be better if you d id n't.'

'Better for who?' Deird rie sobbed . Her throat was so tight the word s could barely escape, and the wind quickly tid ied them away.

She was half-leaning, half-sitting on the wall, both hand s gripping one corner and anchoring her in place. For now. Release her grip and lean back, though, and her last few second s alive would be spent somersaulting.

'Well, better for you, in that you won't be pancaked on the ground d own there. Better for the poor bugger who'll have to clean you up. And your family.'

Deird rie snorted at that, then shook her head . 'They d on't care.'

'I bet they do, Deirdrie. I mean, I know parents can be a pain in the arse, but of course, they care,' Tyler said. 'And, listen, cards on the table, it'll be better for me. I don't want to watch you backflipping into oblivion. And, frankly, my boss would bloody kill me if I let you jump.'

'I'm not going to jump,' Deirdrie told him. 'The train's going to do it.'

Tyler flinched. 'Oof. Nasty way to go,' he said. 'The impact, then the dragging. Dragging, not drag*n*. I know it's the Harry Potter Bridge, but I don't think...'

'What are you even fucking talking about?' Deirdrie snapped.

Tyler briefly wondered the same thing, then shook his head and sauntered over to sit on the wall directly across the tracks from where Deirdrie had positioned herself.

'I'm just saying, it's a nasty way to go.'

The girl screamed out the next few sentences. 'I don't care! There's no point living without her, all right? There's no point!'

'You're upset. I get it—'

'No, you don't! You can't understand! You don't know what we had!'

Tyler glanced back in the direction of Glenfinnan station and took some reassurance from the complete lack of steam billowing above the treetops. A crowd had gathered on a vantage point higher on the hillside, some of them dressed in full-length Hogwarts robes.

'You've got an audience,' he remarked.

'I don't care.'

'There's kids there. Quite a few. You'll leave quite an impression.'

She shrugged sullenly. 'Not my problem.'

'No, I suppose not,' Tyler agreed.

He turned and looked out in the opposite direction. The Glenfinnan Monument was a matchstick in the distance, its bulging white canvas head immediately drawing the eye.

'Some view, eh?' he said .

Deird rie scowled . 'I d on't care.'

'Hayd en said you and Alexis came up here a lot.'

The reply came as an angry hiss. 'Her name was Hermione.'

'Sorry. Of course.' Tyler smiled sympathetically. 'You must miss her.'

Deird rie gestured briefly at where they were. 'Obviously.'

'She seemed nice. From what everyone tells me, I mean. Seems like she'd be a lot of fun to be around .'

'She was amazing,' Deird rie whispered , staring past him like she could see her and Hermione's time together playing out across the cloud s. 'She was just so…*God*. It's not fair. It's just not fair!'

'You're right. It's not,' Tyler said . 'It's unfair and cruel and heartbreaking and just… fucking awful.'

He sighed , then leaned forward s, like he was sharing a secret. 'See in this job? My job? The stuff you see? The people you meet? The things they've d one? You realise that there are no d epths—none—to which some people won't sink. Like, I mean, d red ge up the worst things your imagination can come up with, and you won't come close to the shite that we d eal with.'

Deird rie was regard ing him od d ly now, like she was concerned he was the one about to jump.

'For the first wee while, after I'd started , I thought people were the worst. Evil. You know? Like, if people can d o those things, what's the point in any of it? What's the point in fighting against it?'

The girl sniffed and gave a satisfied nod , like she'd just mad e an excellent point. 'Exactly. What's the point?'

'The point is—and it took me a wee while to figure this out—the point is, Deird rie, that for every sicko out there, there's ten Hermiones. There's ten of you. There's ten of me.' He cracked a grin. 'Well, maybe five of me, but you get the point.'

'There's only one Hermione,' Deirdrie croaked.

'No, you're right. Of course, you're right. She was one of a kind. We're all one of a kind. But... you like Harry Potter, yeah?'

Deirdrie nodded slowly.

'Well, it's like that. There's a war going on. Good versus evil. And yes, Voldemort is out there. The bastard's everywhere. But you and me? Hermione? All those millions like us? We're Dumbledore's Army, Deirdrie. At the Battle of Hogwarts. We're the ones who stand against the darkness. And it breaks my heart that we lost one of the good ones. But I really don't want to lose another one.'

He stood up, took a step closer, and held a hand out across the tracks. Deirdrie fixed her teary-eyed gaze on it, but otherwise made no move to take it.

'It hurts,' she whispered. 'It just hurts so much.'

'I know. But the pain you're feeling? It won't last forever. It won't. Nothing does.'

Deirdrie raised her gaze to the sky, then screwed her eyes tightly shut, her body racked with big, silent sobs.

Tyler thought about lunging for her, grabbing her, but it was too risky. He might knock her over the edge. Worse, he might knock *both* of them over the edge.

He could almost hear Logan delivering his eulogy now.

DC Tyler Neish was a right clumsy bastard...

'She went off with a guy,' Deirdrie squeaked.

Tyler kept his hand held out. 'Why don't we talk about that later?' he suggested.

'The night after we arrived. We were in a pub in town. She was talking to some guy, and then they left together, and I didn't see her for hours,' Deirdrie said, her voice barely audible above the wind. She opened her eyes, and wiped them on both sleeves. 'I bet it's him. I bet he's the father.'

No' unless he's got sperm that can travel through time, Tyler thought, but he sensibly chose to keep that remark to himself.

'Why don't we discuss it over a cup of tea?' he suggested. 'We can get it all figured out.'

She stood up suddenly, and Tyler let out his third panicky 'Wargh!' sound of the day. Sadly, this time it was witnessed by at least one other human being, and very probably Logan, too.

'Sorry,' Deirdrie said, a little awkwardly. 'I was just… I wasn't going to jump. I was just…' She stepped closer and took his hand. 'Sorry. I'm so fucking stupid. I'm so embarrassed.'

'Don't be,' Tyler said, gracing her with one of his warmest, most genuine smiles. 'No harm done.'

Boing.

The sound came from somewhere down low and caught the DC completely off guard. It reminded him of the sound he used to make by twanging a plastic ruler off the side of his desk in school, or the twang a springy doorstop made if accidentally kicked on the way past.

Ping.

He was looking in the right direction this time, and so was better placed to pinpoint the source of the sound, although part of him wished that he wasn't.

It had come from one of the metal rails of the train track.

Creak.

Clunk.

Clackety-clack.

Tyler raised his head, just as a blast of steam escaped through the whistle of a steam train.

A *worryingly nearby* steam train.

The track shook. A cloud of white rose above the tops of the trees.

And, with a huff and a puff, the Jacobite Steam Train came thundering, arse-first, onto the viaduct.

Chapter 24

Moof's d ye job wasn't half-bad .

'Half-bad ' d id n't d o the horror of it justice. It all was ad .

He'd applied various hair d yes and bleaches to his head in the past, but never while bend ing over a public toilet sink with an inoperable hot tap, and only a stringy d ribble coming from the cold one.

There had been no towels, either, and the d ryers were those low-d own ones that let you thrust your hand s into two corres-pond ingly sized holes for a blast of warm air and UV light. It would n't accommod ate a head without one or the other first und ergoing some extensive remod elling work.

By the time he'd finished , the sink was almost completely black, there was an oil-like pud d le on the floor, and he'd been pinched on the arse by a seed y-looking old man who'd come in to use the facilities, but had stayed a while to ad mire the view.

Moof regard ed himself in the cracked mirror above the sink, and winced at the mess he'd mad e.

Technically, the d ye had worked . The ruby-red hair colouring wasn't completely gone, but it was mostly covered by the new shad e, which varied from black to grey to a d ark burgund y across his napper like nature's least interesting rainbow.

The problem—or the most notable one, anyway—was that he'd also d yed his forehead , his ears, much of his neck, and several meand ering lines d own his cheeks and chin, where the d ye had d ribbled .

He had been aiming for inconspicuous. Instead , he looked like a villain from *Game of Thrones*.

'Shit!' he hissed . This mad e him realise that he'd somehow managed to d ye his teeth, too.

He swore again, then head ed into a cubicle and grabbed a d ozen sheets of toilet paper from the d ispenser, each one coming out ind ivid ually, as if the machine was rationing them.

Returning to the mirror, Moof scrubbed at his face. This had the effect of spread ing the d ye around , and rubbing it d eeper into his skin, although he was convinced that, if he just kept going, it would all come off.

Three minutes later, he looked as if he'd stepped out of a black and white photograph. His face was grey. Not pale. Not *lacking in colour*. Full-on grey.

The creases in his skin—around his nose and mouth, in the furrows of his frown—were d rawn as thick, d ark lines, giving his features an exaggerated cartoon-like appearance.

He let out a sob as he realised just what he'd d one.

So much for blend ing in.

'You all right, sonny?'

Moof turned to see the old man shuffling back into the toilets again, supporting himself with a wood en walking stick. He was well-d ressed , with a V-necked jumper, a shirt and tie, and a raging erection visible at the front of his neatly-pressed cream slacks.

'Still here, are we?' he asked , grinning and showing off a set of false teeth that might once have been a good fit, but now looked far too big for his shrunken features. 'Waiting for me, are you?'

Moof shook his head . 'What? No.'

The old man rubbed at the front of his slacks, d rawing a twitch from the shackled beast currently constrained there. 'Had to go take a wee blue pill, if you know what I mean? Get himself fired up.'

'Jesus. I d on't… I'm just d yeing my hair,' Moof said .

'It's nice,' the old letch told him. He reached out with a withered hand , trying to stroke Moof's head . 'It really brings out the colour in your eyes.'

Moof pulled away, bumping his back against the sink. 'Fuck off. I'm not interested .'

'Ah, come on now. We can just d o hand stuff. Or I can pop these out...' He plucked the false teeth out and ran a purple tongue across the smooth bumps of his gums. '...and you can use my mouth.'

Recoiling in horror, Moof moved to shove past. Moving surprisingly quickly for someone his age, the old man lashed out with his cane, catching his grey-faced prey a glancing blow across the shin.

'Ow! Christ!' Moof cried .

The old man lunged at him again, his teeth still in his hand . 'Please. It won't take long.'

'Will you just *fuck off!*'

Moof shoved him. Hard . Hard er than he'd meant to. The falsers went flying and shattered on the floor, spraying teeth in all d irections. The old man himself slammed against the sink, slipped on the pud d le of water, and went d own hard .

There was a thunk as his head hit the sink.

And then... silence.

No movement. No sound . Just the thumping of Moof's heartbeat, and the d istant d elighted squeals of child ren playing in the park.

'Oh shit, oh shit, oh shit,' Moof whispered . He grabbed at his hair, tangling his fingers in it and pulling so hard he almost tore it from his scalp.

What had he d one? Oh, God , what had he d one.

The cane cracked across his shin again, send ing pain rad iating up his leg and into his knee. He hopped backward s, slipped on the same pud d le that had floored the old man, and hissed as tl full weight of his bod y slammed his arm against the tiles.

'You wee fuck!' the old man hissed . 'You nasty wee fuck!'

He was fid d ling with the buckle of his belt with one hand , the other one stabbing and striking at the fallen Moof.

'Hit an old man? I'll fucking teach you. No fucking respect, that's the problem nowad ays!'

He got his fly und one, and his penis popped out like it was spring-load ed . Moof caught a glimpse of it—which was more than enough—then saw the snarl that had twisted up the wrinkled old bastard 's face into a mask of rage and sexual frustration.

'I'll fucking teach you, though,' the old man seethed . His hand now free, he caught the bottom of Moof's trousers and yanked hard . 'I'll fucking show you what happens to—'

Moof d rove a foot into his attacker's arm, d rawing a shriek of pain from his withered lips.

Now free of his grip, Moof slipped and skid d ed to his feet, spent half a second catching his balance, then propelled himself out through the d oor and into the glare and fresh air of the great outd oors.

The park was busy now, child ren thronging around on the slid e and swings, a circle of parents gathered like a protective shield around the outsid e.

Moof set off at a brisk pace, gaze fixed on the road in front of him, head held high. He had no id ea where he was going, but he knew he d id n't want to be here.

The smell of chips from the cafe d rew him toward s it. He d id n't have any money, but he could at least savour the smell as he passed . Maybe someone would 've aband oned their bag of chips on one of the outsid e tables. A wee bit of battered had d ock, maybe. Half a smoked sausage.

His stomach rumbled at the possibilities.

A creak from the d oor of the toilets propelled him into higher gear, and he jogged around the corner to the front of the cafe.

And almost immed iately collid ed with two police officers.

They stood out front of the diner, one of them holding a big bag of chips while the other squirted a big blob of tomato sauce into a little nest he'd made in the middle of the contents.

'Easy,' the older of the two officers warned. 'Watch where you're going, eh?'

'S-sorry,' Moof stammered, lowering his head and sidestepping past them.

'What the hell happened to your face?' the younger officer asked.

'It's, uh, my hair got wet,' Moof offered, head still down, feet still walking.

Somehow, this was enough to appease the officers, their hunger for chips clearly taking priority over their hunger for the truth.

All that changed when a dirty, soaking wet old man hobbled around the corner with a cane in one hand and a handful of teeth in the other. 'Assault!' he hollered. 'That lad just assaulted me in the toilets.'

Moof glanced back over his shoulder. He saw the officers turn, watched a perfectly good bag of chips go flying.

And then, with dribbles of hair dye nipping at his eyes, he ran like he'd never run before.

–

Tyler ran, his tie trailing, his phone bouncing in his shirt pocket, the thunderous clatter of certain death vibrating the whole world around him.

Deirdrie was powering ahead, bounding off down the track like some sort of gazelle. On the one hand, he was happy about that. On the other, he wanted to shout angrily after her, 'I see you've got your zest for life back, you nippy bitch!'

Shouting was out of the question, though. Talking was out of the question. All he could do was stare straight ahead and run from the rattling, shaking, deafening doom that was chewing up the tracks behind him.

He'd never been a runner. Sure, he had a turn of speed about him if need s be, but he'd never been one of those people who enjoyed running, and as such had never really mastered any sort of technique.

His approach, in those times when running was a necessity, was to throw his top half forward and just hope that his legs found some way of keeping up. Right now, they were struggling, but the cushion of air being pushed ahead of the train was, in turn, shoving him along.

There was still a hund red yard s to the end of the viad uct. The train was less than that behind him. No way he was going to make it, no way.

Oh, sure, Deird rie was probably going to be fine—the cow—but short of some miraculous intervention from the god s themselves, Tyler was d one for.

'Fuuuuuuuck!' he bellowed . If he was going to go out, he'd at least go out swearing.

He regretted the outburst immed iately. The expulsion of all that air forced him to gulp d own a few frantic breaths. His brain—because it was a blood y id iot—briefly prioritised breathing over running, and his legs slowed enough that he stumbled on the next sleeper, staggered off-balance, and almost toppled over the wall at the viad uct's ed ge.

For a moment, he was looking straight d own at the d rop below. It wasn't as far as it had been out in the mid d le. Thirty feet, maybe, but d irectly onto rocks.

A short sprint along the tracks, though, and it was a twenty-foot d rop into bushes.

'Fuck it!' he cried , throwing himself back into a clumsy, frantic run.

Another sound joined the clattering cacophony behind him. This one was a high-pitched screech of metal on metal. Sparks arced out from the speed ing train's wheels as the d river applied the brakes. The train was so close that Tyler felt the heat of them.

Too close. Far too close. No way it was stopping in time.

With a throaty yelp of absolute terror, Tyler vaulted the wall at the sid e of the viad uct, and the world seemed to grind in slow motion, leaving him hanging there in mid -air as the train howled through the spot where he'd just been in a cloud of hot steam and fiery sparks.

And then, time twanged back to its natural speed , gravity took hold , and Tyler plunged , screaming, toward s a clump of foliage which, now that he was looking at it more closely, d id n't look nearly as lush and springy as it had previously appeared .

He covered his face with his forearms and let himself go limp. The fall wasn't far, and several hund red thin branches slowed his d escent.

Unfortunately, they achieved this by repeated ly whipping and ripping at him on the way d own, and by the time he finally crunched onto the ground , his shirt was ruined , his hand s were bleed ing, and he was reasonably confid ent that he'd pissed himself.

He lay on his back, half-buried by jaggy bushes and heather, staring up at the viad uct looming above.

Right now, nothing felt like it was broken, but there was every possibility that this might change the moment he tried to move.

So, for now, he would n't. For now, he'd lie there, savouring this low-level pain before it all got much worse.

'Tyler? Tyler?'

The voice was shouting to him, but it was tinny and d istant. He raised his head until his chin was on his chest and looked around , searching for the source of it.

'Hello?' he said , his voice a wind ed wheeze.

It was then that he remembered his phone. He patted his shirt pocket, but the mobile wasn't there. The voice came again, and he craned his neck until he found the hand set in a thicket of heather right by his ear.

'Hello? Boss?' he said , picking up the phone. To his surprise and d elight, at least one arm seemed to be fully functional. He waggled the fingers of the other one and both sets of toes, and almost cheered at the fact that they all respond ed accord ingly.

'Oh, thank Christ!' Logan said , and the relief in his voice was palpable. 'What's happening? What was all the racket?'

'Uh, train d id n't stop, boss,' Tyler said .

'What?! I blood y told you, d id n't I? What d id you d o?'

Tyler groaned as he propped himself up onto his elbows. 'I ran very fast, boss,' he said . 'And then I fell quite a long way.'

'Jesus Christ, Tyler. Are you OK?'

Up on the viad uct, two head s appeared , looking over the ed ge at him. He recognised one as Deird rie Mair, and it d id n't take a lot in the way of d etective skills to figure out who the one d ressed like an old -time train d river was.

'You all right?' Deird rie shouted d own to him.

Tyler raised a shaky thumb. 'Brand new. Thanks,' he said .

'Who's that you're talking to?' Logan asked .

'Deird rie.'

'She's alive?'

'Aye. Or, if she's not, then neither am I,' Tyler replied .

'Wait where you are. We're send ing an ambulance,' Logan told him, but Tyler struggled up into a sitting position, waited for the world to stop spinning, then hauled himself onto his feet using a tree trunk for support.

'I'm all right, boss,' he said . 'I'm up. Paramed ics would struggle to get d own to me, anyway.'

He hissed as a movement brought pain. Pulling open his torn shirt, he found a gash of two or three inches long right below the point where his chest became his stomach.

'Maybe have them meet us at the station, though,' he suggested . 'I might need a wee bit of patching up.'

After assuring the DCI that he was capable of making his way back to Glenfinnan station, and remind ing him there was a constable there to help look after him, Tyler signed off and hung up the phone.

'What the blood y hell were you playing at?' boomed the voice of the d river. 'I nearly flattened you!'

'Aye, I noticed that, funnily enough,' Tyler shouted back up to him. 'You were meant to stop.'

'I d id stop!'

'Sooner! You were meant to stop *sooner*.'

He looked up the hillsid e, where it rose to meet the viad uct. It was steep, and cluttered with clumps of jaggies.

'Now,' he said , wincing at the prospect. 'How the hell d o I get back up?'

Chapter 25

Moof careened around a corner, collid ed with a jogging woman, and spun free of the tangle of arms and legs they almost both end ed up in.

He had a head start on the cops, and they were both old er than him, but he was carrying more weight than either of them and they were gaining ground .

'Sorry, sorry,' he babbled , leaving the woman sprawled on the ground , and then he was off again, thighs burning from the effort almost as bad ly as his eyes burned from the chemicals in the d ye.

'Get back here!'

The copper's shout was angry. Moof d id n't know if this was because of the alleged assault on the pensioner, or the fact that the officers had been forced to d itch their bag of chips, and he had no intention of find ing out.

It was after three, and the road s were heaving with school run traffic. Moof saw a gap and d arted through it, earning himself a screech of brakes and the blaring of a horn.

He stumbled onto the opposite sid e of the street and raced around another corner. Then another. Then another, zigzagging his way through the streets of Ayr, putting as much d istance between himself and the cops as possible.

They'd catch him on a straight, but every corner he turned was another chance to d elay them as they tried to d ecid e which d irection to take. Maybe, if they chose poorly, a chance to lose them completely.

The next street he turned onto was familiar, but it wasn't until he spotted the corner shop he'd nicked the sandwich and hair dye from that he fully recognised it.

For a moment, he contemplated running into the shop and hiding there. The shopkeeper had taken sympathy on him earlier, maybe he'd do the same now.

Then he remembered the warning he'd been given as he'd left. The fact that he now looked like some deranged goth and was being chased by the police was unlikely to make the shopkeeper reconsider his threat.

Moof staggered on, trying to ignore the pain tightening across his chest. He could only worry about a police arrest right now. The cardiac variety, he could concern himself with later.

He passed the shop, hung another right-turn, and found himself on a busier street filled with brand name stores and way too many people for his liking.

Not daring to risk turning back, he pressed on, speed - walking so as to avoid the extra attention that running would bring. There was another side street up on the left, across the road. He'd make for that, duck down there, and get away.

Moof chanced a look behind him. No cops. He could hear sirens in the distance, but they were aimless and vague right now, searching for him, rather than chasing him down.

He had time. He could still get out of this.

A display of TV's in the window of a Curry's caught his eye, although it took him several more steps to process what he'd seen.

He stopped then. Just stopped, dead in the middle of the pavement, all thoughts of getting away momentarily forgotten.

Turning, he backed up. His heart was racing, but it was no longer solely down to the distance he'd covered, or the speed he'd done it at.

Moof stood by the window, staring in at five television sets.

At five identical images.

At five identical news ticker feeds.

Breaking: Daughter of oil billionaire, Bartholomew Riksen, murdered in Glenfinnan.

He let his eyes follow it, waiting for some punchline at the end . Some follow-up statement that would ad mit it wasn't true, confess to making the whole thing up.

Above the ticker, filling the rest of the screen, she smiled back at him.

The girl he loved .

The girl he had hoped to spend the rest of his life with.

And then, a large angry man in a police uniform hit him like a charging bull, knocking him to the ground .

'Right, then, sunshine,' the constable wheezed , pinning Moof face-first onto the ground . 'You're nicked !'

And , beneath him, the boy with the d yed -black hair sobbed his heart out into the pavement.

–

The paramed ics had band aged up the worst of Tyler's cuts and scratches by the time Logan d rove up the steep hill lead ing to the station, the Fiesta's engine whining as it struggled with the incline and the weight of its d river.

'Good to see you're still in one piece, DC Neish,' Logan said , when he'd extricated himself from the d river's seat and joined Tyler in the sleeping car's lounge.

'Cheers, boss! Close call, mind you.'

'He was blood y lucky,' commented one of the two para-med ics, load ing his kit back into his bag and giving Tyler a wink. 'You ask me, a night off's in ord er. Maybe even a cheeky wee bonus.'

'Just as well no bugger asked you then, eh?' Logan replied .

The paramed ic chuckled and shrugged apologetically at his taped and band aged patient. 'Well, you can't say I d id n't try,' he said , then he head ed out the d oor and d own the steps, with his partner following along behind .

Logan slid himself onto the seat across the table from the DC. Tyler looked, not to put too fine a point on it, like a bag of shite. His usually immaculate hair was standing up in about five different directions, and none of them the right one. His face was a mess of fine scratches and raised welts, and his shirt looked like something that belonged bagged and tagged at a murder scene.

There was also a whiff of drying piss about him, but Logan had the good grace not to comment on it.

'What the bloody hell happened?'

Tyler puffed out his cheeks. 'Just what I said, boss. I was talking to Deirdrie. I think I'd convinced her not to jump, and then... boom. Train appears around the corner, horsing towards us. We made a run for it, but I knew I wasn't going to make it, so I took a header over the side and took my chances with the fall.'

'Jesus Christ,' Logan huffed. 'I told you, did n't I? I told you not to bloody go out there.'

Tyler shrugged. 'Deirdrie would 've jumped, boss. Or got hit by the train. I could n't just stand there and watch.' He gestured down at himself and grinned. His usually brilliant white teeth were brown with dried blood. 'And no harm done, eh?'

'Clearly, you haven't looked in a mirror,' Logan said, then he begrudgingly admitted that no, there was no real harm done, and it had all worked out for the best. 'Doesn't mean you made the right call, though,' he stressed. 'I want to make that very clear.'

'You have, boss. You did. Crystal clear,' Tyler said.

Logan nodded, satisfied that the message had been understood. 'Right. Good. Now, onto the next thing we need to talk about.' He sat back and crossed his arms, one eyebrow raising. '*Dumbledore's Army*? The Battle of Hogwarts? You always said you did n't know anything about Harry Potter.'

Tyler's face fell. His cheeks, which had been a fear-stricken shade of white, reddened a little.

'What? Oh, uh, no. I d on't. I just… I think that's from the films, isn't it? I'm sure I heard someone talking about it somewhere. Maybe in a review, or…'

Logan smiled . 'Relax, son. Your secret's safe with me.' He leaned across the table and patted the younger d etective on the should er.

Tyler's blush d eepened . 'Cheers, boss.'

'And the rest of the team,' Logan conclud ed . 'We had you on speakerphone.'

Tyler loosely clenched his fists and waved them besid e his head like he was shaking maracas. 'Yay.'

'By the way, is it just me, or d o we as a team spend an inord inate amount of time talking about those blood y books and movies?' Logan asked . 'Every second conversation we have, that specky wee wizard y bastard seems to pop up somewhere.'

'Can't say I really noticed , boss,' Tyler replied .

Logan grunted , then shifted his gaze from the DC to the d oor lead ing through to the rest of the sleeping car. 'Deird rie all right?'

'Aye, she's fine, boss. Bit shaken. Very apologetic. I'm getting someone more qualified than me to come talk to her. Last thing we want is her having another crack at jumping.'

'Good call.'

'Did you get what she said about Alexis going off with some guy earlier in the week?'

'Bits of it,' Logan said . 'Wind d rowned out some of it, but I got the gist. She back there?'

'She is, boss. But here's something interesting for you.'

Logan shifted his attention back onto Tyler. 'Oh aye?'

'I asked Hayd en Howard to tell the constable keeping an eye on this lot to try to stop the train. He passed the message on, and the constable called into base for someone to get in touch with the train d irectly. He went up to the station and tried to stop it from there, but d id n't have any luck. Fortunately, someone at the station got through to the company, and the company got in touch with the d river d irectly.'

Logan's eyes narrowed . 'Right. What bit of that's interesting?'

'Hayd en Howard , boss. When the constable came back, he was gone.'

'Gone?'

'Properly gone. Cleared out his stuff, taken his bag. Gone.'

'Shite. Why wasn't I told ?'

Tyler shrugged . 'Just happened , boss. That PC's just called it in. He's having a scope around now to see if he can see which way Hayd en went. Couple of the rest of them saw him through their wind ows, head ing d own toward s the road . You d id n't s him on the way up?'

'No. I mean, not that I noticed . Place is pretty hoaching with tourists,' Logan replied . 'What brought that on? He was here when you arrived ?'

'Yeah. Caught him smoking a joint. Did n't bother saying anything to him, but he knew that I knew. Maybe that freaked him out?'

'Maybe, aye,' Logan said , although he sound ed less than convinced . 'You talk about anything else?'

'Not really, boss. Deird rie, mostly. He's the one who told me where she was. And he passed on the message about stopping the train, like I asked ,' Tyler said . 'Only other thing I mentioned was that Alexis's old man was on the way.'

'And what d id he say to that?'

'Just...' Tyler frowned . 'He seemed a bit shocked by it, actually. Asked if he and the rest of the group would have to talk to him when he arrived .'

'And what d id you say?'

'I said no, but that it might be nice if they d id . After that, we moved on to talking about Deird rie, and where she was.'

Logan d rummed his hand s on the table, staring out of the wind ow and mulling this information over.

After a few second s of this, he d ragged himself out of the seat and stood up. 'I'm going to go see if I can spot him. He can't have gone far.'

'Want me to come, boss?'

Logan shook his head . 'Stay here. Take it easy. Talk to Deird rie again, and see if you can get any more information on this fella she said Alexis went off with.'

'Will d o, boss.'

Logan was at the d oor when both men's phones bleeped , signalling an incoming message. Tyler's phone was on the table in front of him, and he got to it first.

'Holy shit. Some good news, boss!'

Logan turned , alread y reaching for his own phone. 'Aye? What?'

'Corey Sand erson. Moof.' He held the mobile up in the mistaken belief that Logan could read a text on a phone screen from fifteen feet away. 'We've got the bastard !'

Chapter 26

Logan prod d ed suspiciously at his salad , like it might be harbouring some sort of poisonous caterpillar or similarly unpleasant creepy-crawly.

All the food at the table—with the exception of his own—looked and smelled d elicious. He'd caught himself making little sound s of pleasure as the rest of the team read off their choices to the woman behind the bar.

'Steak and Black Pud d ing Pie.'

'Sweet Chilli Beef.'

'Venison Burger. Cheese on top.'

'Beer Battered Had d ock, plenty of chips.'

The barmaid had d one a d ouble-take when he'd read ou his own choice. She'd even forced him to repeat himself, in case she'd somehow misund erstood .

'I'll have the Super Salad . Grilled chicken breast on the sid e.'

The months he'd spent working behind a bar on Orkney had been relaxing to the point of becoming utterly ted ious, and he'd found that one way to make it more interesting was to never stop eating. It helped to pass the time.

It also helped him pass a forty-four-inch waist.

The rise in his food intake wasn't the only contributing factor, of course. He also had unlimited access to sugary soft d rinks, and without villains to chase or cases to worry about, his metabolism had fallen through the floor.

Since then, and mostly inspired by the ribbing he'd received from the assortment of bastard s he worked with, he'd shifted just over a stone. Partly, this was thanks to the running regime that

Shona Maguire had introduced him to—by which he meant *forced him into*—and the fact that he was trying very hard not to subsist solely on fried food, red meat, and biscuits.

Once he'd repeated himself and paid for everyone's meal, he'd returned with them to the table they'd secured in the corner of The Lochy Bar's expansive lounge area, and awaited what was sure to be another in a growing line of deeply disappointing meals.

He was not wrong.

As salads went, it was... fine. It was probably up there with the best of them, in fact. But then, that was a bit like saying testicular cancer was one of the 'best' forms of cancer. It didn't mean he wanted to pay over a tenner for the privilege of contracting it.

His eyes wandered to the plates on either side of him. Ben was getting stuck into a big helping of haddock and chips, with a crispy golden batter, and mushy peas on the side. Hamza was getting his teeth around a venison burger. Due to the size of the thing, this almost certainly involved him unhinging his jaw at the back.

Across the table, Dave was virtually elbow deep in his steak and black pudding pie, while Tyler was pushing his chilli beef around on his plate with far less enthusiasm.

'You all right?' Logan asked him.

Tyler looked up, blinked, then hurriedly skewered a bit of the meat on the prongs of his fork like his mum had just caught him playing with his food.

'What? Oh, aye, boss. Just still a bit shaky after everything that happened.'

Hamza rolled his eyes. 'Oh, here we go,' he said, through a mouthful of minced venison. 'Did everyone hear he nearly got hit by a train?'

'He never did!' Ben gasped.

'Seriously?' Dave asked, scooping up the most delicious-looking mush of meat and gravy that Logan had ever seen. 'Why didn't you mention it?'

Tyler had mentioned it, of course. He'd mentioned it several times after he and Logan had arrived back at the office, twice on the six-minute walk from the station to the pub, and at least once since they'd ordered up their grub.

'Probably doesn't like to talk about it,' Ben said to Dave in a stage whisper. 'He's stoic like that.'

'Funny,' Tyler said. 'Next time any of you nearly gets hit by a train, we'll see if you keep your mouths shut about it.'

'You were nearly hit by a train?' asked Ben, his eyebrows almost rising all the way off the top of his head. 'When was this?'

Logan forced down a bite of something green and leafy, muttered darkly about the taste of it, then diverted his attention to his phone screen.

'Nothing from Hoon?' Ben asked, catching him checking.

Much to everyone else's dismay, Logan had insisted they call Hoon to invite him along for something to eat. There had been no answer, and no response to the text messages he'd sent, either.

'No. Not a thing,' Logan said. 'I'll maybe try him again.'

'I'll go check, boss,' Tyler said, pushing his plate into the middle of the table. 'Not really on for this. Still feeling a bit iffy.'

'How come? What happened?' Hamza asked.

Tyler smiled sarcastically, gave him the finger, then stood up. 'I might take a couple of hours to go get showered and stuff. That all right, boss?'

Logan nodded. 'Aye. Take the rest of the night, son. You've had a big day. We'll see you in the morning.'

'You sure, boss?' Tyler asked.

'Aye. You do fuck all, anyway,' Logan told him, but it was good-natured, and Tyler chuckled at the insult.

'Fair point, aye. Cheers. I'll do that, then.'

'You be all right getting back to the cottages yourself?'

'No bother. I'll head back to the station and pick up the car. I'll text you once I've spoken to Hoon.'

'If he's d ead , give us half an hour to finish here, will you, son?' Ben asked . He caught the mild ly horrified looks from Hamza and Logan. Dave was too invested in his pie to have formed an opinion, either way. 'Well, there's no point spoiling a nice meal if there's bugger all we can d o about it, is there?'

The others contemplated this for a moment, then both conced ed that he mad e a very valid point. As Tyler pushed his chair back in und er the table, Logan pointed to his plate of mostly untouched beef.

'You're not wanting that, then?'

'No, boss.'

Logan glanced from the other plate to his own, and very quickly came to a conclusion. 'Right,' he said , swapping the plates over. 'Shame to let it go to waste.'

'What about your salad , sir? You're surely not just going to let that go to waste now, are you?' Hamza teased .

Logan shook his head . 'You can't "waste" salad , Detective Sergeant. You can only *not eat it*. That's no' even remotely the same thing.'

'You sure you're all right, son?' Ben asked , smooshing a chip into a blob of tartare sauce.

'Fine, boss, aye,' said Tyler, pulling on his jacket. 'Just… head ache. Bit jittery.'

'Has Dumbled ore no' got a spell to help with that?' Hamza asked , then he jerked his head away to avoid an ear-flick from Tyler.

'I was talking her d own! I had to d raw on, you know, things she'd be interested in. That's just… what d o you call it? Psychology.'

Hamza grinned at him. 'Just kid d ing. You d id great.' He raised his glass of Irn Bru in toast, and Logan and Ben joined him.

Dave, on the other hand , was getting stuck into a small mound of gravy-soaked mashed potato, and d id n't appear to have heard any of the conversation playing out around him.

'Aye. All joking asid e, son, you were an excellent copper tod ay,' Logan told him.

Tyler's expression mad e him look halfway between proud and utterly mortified .

'Cheers, boss.'

'Now, if you can only learn to repeat that every other d ay, we might be onto something.'

Tyler's smile wid ened . That was more like it.

'I'll see what I can d o,' he said , then he said his good byes, zipped up his jacket, and stepped out of the pub into the unre-lenting evening d rizzle.

'He looked like shite,' Ben remarked , once the DC was safely out of earshot. 'Think he's all right?'

'Probably the ad renaline,' said Logan through a mouthful of half-chewed beef. 'Big scare like that's bound to have a hangover afterward s.'

'How close was he to getting hit, d o you think?' Hamza asked .

'Pretty blood y close. From what Deird rie Mair and the train d river said , if he had n't gone over the wall, he'd have been a goner.'

'Blood y hell,' Dave said .

'Aye. You can say that again,' Ben muttered .

Dave looked up from his plate, which he had completely scraped clean and now looked to be contemplating licking up what little was left on it.

'Hmm? Oh, sorry. I meant the pie. Blood y hell, it was amazing,' he said , then he looked across the faces of the other three men at the table. 'What was it we were talking about?' He glanced at the empty chair besid e him, a frown troubling his brow. 'And where d id Tyler go?'

As soon as the meal was done, Logan could feel himself getting antsy. It had taken an enormous act of self-discipline on his part to leave the station—and the case—to go out and eat, but the team had been working most of the day without a break, and while he had no problems with running himself into the ground, he was damned if he was doing it to them.

Now though, the urge to get back to it had him drumming his fingers on the table and tapping his foot against the floor.

He tried to ignore it, but that only heightened the fear that by being here he was missing out on something important. The concern that, somewhere some vital piece of evidence was presenting itself, and that he should be out there grabbing it before it was too late.

A glance at the dessert menu helped take the edge off it a little. Diet or no diet, a cheeky wee lemon sorbet wasn't going to do any harm, was it? It probably qualified as one of his five a day.

He further dampened down his concerns by using the time between courses to take stock of where they were with the case.

Corey Sanderson—Moof—had been arrested in Ayr, and was currently being transported up the road so Logan could get a crack at him later that evening.

Given the evidence they'd built up so far, Sanderson was almost certainly the culprit. He had done a runner the same night Alexis Riksen had been killed, one of his badges had been found at the scene, and he'd been caught with her bag and passport in his possession before fleeing arrest.

Add in the sighting Ian Hill had made of someone with red hair on the morning the body was discovered, and they pretty much had enough to charge the bastard for Alexis's murder.

All things considered, Logan should have been feeling pretty happy right now.

And yet…

They had n't caught Hayd en Howard . Why had he legged it the moment the Uniform who had been keeping an eye on Alexis's travel group had his back turned ? He'd been the one who had told them about Moof's obsession with Alexis. He'd been the one who'd painted a picture of a frustrated would -be suitor.

Unrequited love was a powerful motive for people to d o some crazy things. Logan had learned that over the years. But the only evid ence they had of Moof's interest in Alexis— assuming you ignored the fact he had taken her bag—was Hayd en's statement.

And Hayd en was now nowhere to be found .

Deird rie had n't been able to give them much more inform- ation about the lad she'd seen Alexis—or Hermione, as she insisted on still calling her—going off with.

Alexis had met up with them all a couple of hours later in another pub, and had been cagey about where she'd been and what she'd been up to. It had led to their first—and if Deird rie was to be believed —only argument as a couple, but Alexis had insisted that she'd just been talking to the guy, getting some local ad vice on the best places to go and things to see.

'He looked really d od gy, though,' Deird rie had told then 'Bit old er—late twenties, maybe—with short hair.'

That had been the extent of her d escription. Barely enough for a stick figure, let alone a police artist's sketch.

As if the d ay had n't been eventful enough, Bartholomew Riksen, the victim's father, was flying into Inverness in a couple of hours. Sinead was going to meet him and bring him d own. They'd warned him that there were no hotel rooms available locally, but his assistant had assured them that this would not be an issue.

If it came to it, he could always take the sofa bed in the cottage.

Logan never relished the thought of meeting a victim's close relatives. It was a necessary part of the job, of course, and it had been a powerful motivator in his early days. How could he stand there watching people hurting so badly and not do everything in his power to give them some closure? To give them some sense that justice had been done?

Those conversations with grieving parents, or widows, or children, had carried him through some difficult years. Each one was a boot up the arse. Pins to his feet. A hot poker up the bahookie that drove him through long hours and dark nights in pursuit of the monsters who could inflict such suffering.

He was dreading Bartholomew Riksen's arrival for different reasons. He'd known nothing whatsoever about the man until that morning, but a few Google searches had painted him as a ruthless businessman with a boundless sense of entitlement.

His head of security had already tried to muscle in on the case once, only to be sent packing by Ben. Riksen didn't seem like the type to take 'no' for an answer, though, and Logan was bracing himself for a locking of horns in the not-too-distant future.

Still, bastard or not, he was the father of a murdered daughter. It would be important to keep that in mind.

Or try to, at least.

'Oh! Forgot to tell you, sir,' Hamza said, interrupting Logan's train of thought. 'Got the footage from the camera at the visitor centre cafe. I was right, you can see a bit of the road. Not much, and it's pretty dark, but we might get something. I was going to get Tyler to go over it tonight, but…'

'I'll do it, if you want,' Dave suggested.

'Would you mind?' Hamza asked.

'Nah. Save me sitting twiddling my thumbs. Not like we're swimming in new evidence coming in, is it? I spent most of the afternoon making glove puppets out of evidence bags, to be honest. Drew wee eyes on them.'

Dave replayed this admission over in his head again, realised how it might have sounded, and hurriedly clarified.

'Aye, unused evidence bags, like. There wasn't anything in them.'

Before Logan could say anything on the subject, his phone rang. He expected to find Tyler or Hoon's name on the screen, and had already started to prepare himself for the drama that was almost certainly about to unfold.

To his surprise, he saw Shona Maguire's name. He pressed the button to answer the call at *precisely* the wrong time, as the barmaid arrived at the table carrying a selection of plates.

'Right, who's having the Mississippi Mud Pie?'

'Definitely not me,' Logan said, loudly and clearly, and not even remotely for the barmaid's benefit. He turned away from the table and spoke into the phone. 'Shona. Hello. Everything all right?'

'Mississippi Mud Pie?' Shona said.

'Not for me,' Logan said. 'We're out for a bite to eat. I ordered a salad.'

It wasn't a lie. Not really. He *had* ordered salad. He just hadn't actually eaten it.

Shona replied with a sceptical 'hmm...' and then got down to business. 'We got some toxicology results through on Alexis Riksen.'

'Already?' Logan said, nodding at the barmaid as she set a small bowl of lemon sorbet in the space in front of him. Next to the other desserts, it looked positively spartan. 'That was quick. What strings did you have to pull to get that moving?'

'That's the thing, absolutely none,' Shona said. 'I wasn't expecting any results for days yet at best. Weeks, maybe. But apparently the case got bumped up the list of priorities. Obviously, there are still a lot we won't get for a while yet. Some of the tests take ten to twelve days to run. But we got something I thought you'd want to know.'

Logan pressed the phone harder to his ear and placed a finger in the other one, drowning out the clinking of cutlery on plates, and the conversation from the other tables.

'What have we got?' Logan asked.

'Alexis had traces of a benzodiazepine in her liver and kidneys. Flunitrazepam, it looks like.'

Logan's eyes wid ened . 'Flunitrazepam? Isn't that…?'

'Rohypnol. The *date rape drug*,' Shona told him. 'Before she d ied , Alexis Riksen was roofied .'

Chapter 27

Tyler pulled into the parking space between the two holid ay cottages, shut off the car's engine, but mad e no move to get out. He wasn't read y. Not yet.

For starters, he wasn't quite sure how to ad d ress his former Detective Superintend ent. 'Bob' seemed too personal. 'Mr Hoon', too formal.

'Sir' was too respectful for the man who had been feed ing information to one of Scotland 's most notorious d rug barons, and 'Oi you, you loud -mouthed arsehole' was likely to lead to him being violently assaulted .

Tyler groaned . 'Maybe, if I'm lucky, he'll be d ead ,' he said into the rearview mirror, then he unclipped his belt, threw open the d oor, and head ed for the cottage Hoon had been sleeping in.

The front d oor was locked . Tyler tried the hand le, stared at it for several second s like he could will it to open, then tried it again.

It was still locked .

'Bollocks,' he muttered , trying unsuccessfully to peer in through the frosted glass.

He chapped , then knocked , then thumped on the d oor. There was no reaction from insid e. No sign of movement. No response.

Tyler sighed . He wasn't in the mood for this. His head ache was raging now, and the multitud e of scratches, scrapes, bruises, and cuts he'd amassed d uring his close encounter with the train had started to make themselves known as the last round of painkillers wore off.

He wanted to be inside. To be clean. To be sitting down in a darkened room, waiting for the throbbing and the stinging and the aching to pass.

Instead, he was standing in the rain, waiting for a man he couldn't stand the sight of to answer the bloody door.

After a few more attempts at knocking, and a shouted 'Hello?' through the letterbox, Tyler set off around the house, peering in through each of the windows.

Hoon wasn't in the kitchen or either of the bedrooms. He might have been in the bathroom—or the empty space that would eventually become one, at least—but the frosted glass made it difficult to say. Tyler didn't think he was there, though. Or, if he was, he was crumpled in a heap on the floor, hidden from view.

Once he'd made his way around to the opposite side of the house, Tyler found the big sliding French doors were open. There was around half a foot of space between the glass door and its frame, suggesting either someone hadn't pushed it closed hard enough, or they'd pushed it closed far too hard, bouncing it back out again.

Either way, it allowed him to slip into the cottage's living room without having to resort to breaking anything.

'Uh... hello?' Tyler called again. He still had n't decided how best to address Hoon, so wasn't committing himself to anything yet. 'Anyone in here?'

The words were swallowed by the silence of the house. It was a pregnant, expectant sort of hush, like the cottage itself was holding its breath, waiting to find out what would happen next.

The floorboards creaked a chorus as Tyler crossed the living room and stepped out into the hallway. The tang of burned bacon hung in the air there, drawing him towards the kitchen.

His feet splashed in a puddle on the floor. A tap had been left trickling, and a waterfall of greasy brown water had cascaded out of the sink and d own the front of the recently installed kitchen cabinets.

'Shite!' Tyler ejected , slipping and slid ing over to the sink and shutting off the tap.

He grabbed a kitchen roll from a d ispenser on the worktop, and had set d own a d ozen sheets before he realised it was a complete blood y waste of time, and that nothing short of a wet-vac and an ind ustrial heater was going to d ry the place out properly.

A knock at the front d oor mad e him jump. His feet slipped , and he threw his arms out, frantically running on the spot as he tried to keep his balance.

He grabbed the worktop as one leg went one way and one went the other, saving himself from crashing to the floor. The water that was still seeping d own the cabinets, soaked through his alread y filthy shirt, turning it semi-transparent.

When the knocking came again, he launched himself across the kitchen, surfed the greasy pud d le all the way out into the hall, and hurried to answer the d oor.

Unfortunately, it was still locked . Tyler grasped at the space where a key should be, on the off-chance that it had somehow turned invisible, then d ropped to his haunches and pulled open the letterbox.

'Hello? Sorry, d oor's locked .'

The land lad y d ucked into view. She was still smiling, but it was a touch less cheerful and a smid geon more concerned than last time he'd seen her.

'Hi. I'll come around the back, then,' she said .

'No!' Tyler yelped . He saw her smile fad e further still, and hurried ly scrambled for an excuse. 'I was just coming out, anyway. Wait right there, I'll come and meet you.'

He let the letterbox d rop back into place, then hurried for the open French d oors. As he ran toward s them, he caught sight of his reflection. Jesus, he was a mess.

Still, no time to worry about that now. He raced outsid e, pulled the slid ing d oor all the way closed behind him, then scurried around to the front of the cottage before the landlady decided to start poking around.

'Hi. Sorry. I think my… eh… colleague has gone out with the key,' Tyler explained. 'You haven't seen him, have you?'

The landlady was doing an admirable job of not recoiling at the sight of him. She didn't even pass comment on his appearance or ask why he was dripping wet. Tyler was immensely grateful for that.

'Which one?' she asked, very clearly forcing herself to look the DC squarely in the eyes, and nowhere else.

'Quite tall. Older guy. Looks like he's angry all the time,' Tyler said. 'I mean, he *is* angry all the time, and he looks it. Probably swearing a lot…'

'Oh. I know the one, yes,' the landlady replied. 'He asked my husband where the pubs were.'

Tyler felt his heart plunge down into his stomach. 'The pubs?'

'Yes. Said something about going on a mission. Stressed he didn't want anywhere too classy. He was looking for "the biggest shithole in town", I believe.'

Tyler closed his eyes, just for a moment. The day had dragged on forever. He was wet, dirty, and his head felt like it was going to explode.

'I nearly got hit by a bloody train,' he mumbled.

The landlady frowned back at him. 'Sorry?'

'Nothing,' Tyler said. He glanced back at the cottages, his dream of a hot shower and a nice sit down slipping further and further from his reach.

Finally, with a longing sigh and an angry tut, he turned his attention back to the landlady.

'Don't suppose you can point me towards the biggest shithole in town, too, can you?'

–

Bob Hoon sipped the gold en liquid from his glass, winced at the sting of it, then knocked half of the rest back in one gulp and enjoyed the burning sensation as it washed d own his gullet.

He'd d ucked into a couple of the High Street pubs, but none quite had the atmosphere he was looking for. By which he meant they were all full of loud -mouthed wankers talking about climbing, mountain biking, and Christ knew what else.

After some searching, he'd eventually stumbled upon the shithole the fella he'd spoken to back at the cottages had mentioned .

In reality, the pub—the Maryburgh Inn—wasn't a shithole at all. Not as far as Hoon was concerned , anyway.

Aye, it was d ark, gloomy, and had a massive circular hole in the floor that appeared to run all the way d own to the centre of the Earth, but it was d etails like these that mad e a place appealing.

The hole was formed by an old well, with a clear plastic covering affixed to the top of the circular wall, turning the whole thing into one large table. Or possibly a raised d ance platform for those who got carried away.

The Maryburgh was tucked away d own a set of stone steps, beneath a gift shop, or newsagent, or something like that. He had n't looked too closely at what was upstairs, being far more interested in what lurked in the d ark basement below.

Booze. Beautiful, glorious booze.

And people, annoyingly. A lot of people, it turned out. Far more than he'd been hoping for.

He had n't wanted the place empty—nobod y liked an empty pub—but he'd been hoping for maybe five or six sad bastard s all nursing their d rinks and saying fuck all. Aye, sure, they might have occasionally ord ered another pint, put a few quid in the puggy, or let out the od d strangled sob of d espair, but he'd have been fine with that. It would 've ad d ed to the ambience.

Instead , it was mostly a younger crowd , and the faces he saw reflected in the mirror behind the bar weren't the grim masks

of misery he'd longed to see, but a shower of smug bastard s
with their whole lives ahead of them, and hormones raging so
intensely they were practically shooting out of their eyes like
fucking laser beams.

God , he d espised them.

The lassie behind the bar was nice enough, though. She
was in her mid -thirties, kept the d rinks coming, and seemed to
share his contempt for every other bugger in the place. If he'd
been ten years younger, a few more d rinks in, and not entirely
filled with hatred and self-loathing, he might've chanced his
arm there.

Instead , he looked on her as a trusty comrad e, both of them
stand ing together against a sea of horny teenagers and twenty-
somethings, and both d oing their level best to ignore the whole
blood y lot of them.

'Here. Six more pints, sweetheart.'

The voice came from right behind where Hoon sat at
the bar. Young. Confid ent. English accent. Southern. Lond on
suburbs, maybe.

None of these d etails end eared him to the man on the
barstool.

'Oi! You listening, love?' the lad called . He clicked his fingers
to beckon the barmaid over. 'Six more pints, I said .'

She was busy along the bar, pulling a pint for another punter,
but raised a sard onic eyebrow in the cheeky bastard 's d irection.
'Takes more than two fingers to make me come, son,' she told
him. 'I'll get to you when I'm read y.'

A roar of laughter went up from the guy's group of mates.
The lad himself, however, evid ently failed to see the funny sid e.

'Fat fucking slag,' he muttered . He said it too quietly for her
to hear, but Hoon was much closer, and Hoon heard it just fine.

He could 've sized the group up in the mirror, of course, but
the former Detective Superintend ent chose instead to turn on
his stool to give them a proper lookover.

The lad with the lack of manners was stand ing less than a foot
away. He was barely in his twenties, Hoon estimated , with the

remnants of teenage acne still clinging to his cheeks for dear life. Aside from that, he was carefully put together, with the same identikit stubble and sculpted, plastic-looking hair as the rest of his merry band of arseholes, like they'd all come together as part of a set.

'You want to watch your mouth, son,' Hoon warned. 'No need for language like that.'

Had anyone in the pub known the former Detective Superintendent personally, their irony meters may well have exploded at that comment. But Hoon was an unknown quantity here, which went some way to explaining the reaction of the southerner.

'Who are you, her fucking dad?' he demanded, leaning closer and looming over the seated Hoon.

Hoon flitted his gaze from the southerner to his mates. There were five of them, all smiling and whispering to each other. A couple looked less relaxed, like they were gearing up for a square go. They were young and fit. Looked like they could all handle themselves, if it came to it.

'I'm no one,' Hoon eventually said, twisting his stool back to face the bar. 'Just watch the language.'

'Or what?'

Hoon sipped his drink. 'Or nothing. I'm not looking for trouble. Just mind the language.'

Emboldened by how Hoon had backed down, the southerner grinned, glanced back at his equally southern mates to make sure they were watching, then turned his attention squarely back to the man on the barstool.

'What the fuck are you looking for, then? Blowy off this fat bitch? Is that it?'

Hoon took another sip of his whisky, savouring it.

'Look at you, you dirty fucking Jock. Tracksuit bottoms and trainers. And you fucking stink.'

His mates were all sniggering now. A few of the more observant folks in the pub were side-eyeing the situation, either contemplating getting involved or just hoping for a good show.

Hoon had just brought his glass to his lips to finish the last of his Famous Grouse when the southern lad shoved him in the shoulder, making him spill a quarter of an inch of the liquid down his front.

There was much laughter and rejoicing from the identikit group.

'Oi! Watch it,' the barmaid warned, storming over.

'You saw that, did you?' Hoon asked. His voice was calm and measured, as he set his glass down with a soft but definite clunk. 'You saw this gentleman strike me?'

'I saw, aye.'

'I didn't fucking "strike you", you smelly old bastard,' the southerner sneered. His reflection in the mirror gave him the look of a braying donkey, all wide eyes and big teeth. Most of his mates were the same.

Six of them. Young. Fit. Strong. Fast, no doubt.

The ringleader made a grab for the man on the stool. 'But if you want me to fucking strike you, I'll—'

There was a movement.

There was a crack.

There was silence.

But not for long.

The noise that came bursting through the southerner's lips was barely human. If he had been a braying donkey a moment ago, then now he was a grieving one, loudly lamenting the death of some long-term donkey pal, while simultaneously having a hedgehog shoved up his arse.

As he howled and wailed and grimaced, he stared in wordless horror at his hand. It had never pointed that way before. Millions of years of evolution had never designed it to do so.

'F-fuck!' he stammered. 'Fuuuck!'

There was another movement.

A thunk.

The lad's nose exploded on the edge of the bar.

199

'I thought I told you to mind your fucking language, you scrotum-faced wee fuckbumper.'

Hoon noticed the hush in the bar and saw the other five men rise onto the balls of their feet, preparing to fight.

He slid d own from his stool, fired a kick into the ribs of the snivelling, sobbing mess on the floor, and felt more alive than he had d one in months.

Aw, who was he trying to kid ? In *years*.

'Come on then, ya horse-eyed cluster of fud s,' he barked , grinning from ear to ear as he beckoned them closer. 'Let's get you fucking telt!'

Chapter 28

Tyler knew that something had happened as he approached the Maryburgh. A dozen or more young men and women had come clomping up the steps, chattering excitedly about some drama that had unfolded down in the pub below.

'Aw… shite,' he muttered, when he heard the words 'blood' and 'teeth' being bandied around.

He hurried down the steps, patting himself down for his warrant card, suspecting he might well need it to help break up whatever was going on in the bar.

The place was surprisingly quiet when he stepped through the door, though. There was less shouting and violence than he'd been expecting.

More whimpering, though.

Hoon sat on a stool, facing the bar, surrounded by what could best be described as 'human debris'. When he caught sight of Tyler in the mirror, he spun to face him, a look of glee twisting his features.

It didn't last.

'Oh. It's you. I thought you were another one of these pretty-boy fuckers,' he said, grunting out the words like he resented wasting every one of them.

'What the hell happened?' Tyler yelped, his gaze flitting across the six semi-conscious men lying scattered across the floor. And, in one case, face-down on the clear plastic top of the well.

'They attacked me,' Hoon said.

'Police and ambulance are on the way,' announced the barmaid .

She was stand ing d own at the far end of the bar, a safe d istance from where Hoon sat. Tyler had n't noticed her behind the beer pumps, and mad e an effort to sound a bit more professional when he took out his ID.

'I'm with the police,' he told her.

She looked him up and d own, like she d id n't believe him.

'It's true. He is,' Hoon said . 'Fuck knows how, mind . Think it was one of them competitions where you cut out coupons from cereal boxes. He'll have a Grouse.'

'What? No, I won't!' Tyler said . He was crouching d own besid e the fallen men, checking to make sure they were all still breathing.

They were. Whether they wanted to be or not, given the state of them, was another matter.

'What…? I mean… what the hell happened ?' he asked again.

Hoon sighed . 'You want to get your fucking lugs cleaned out, son. Like I said , I was sitting here just mind ing my own business. One of them attacked me. I d efend ed myself. His mates then piled on. I d efend ed myself again. I then asked Kelly here to call an ambulance, on the basis that I'm no' a fucking monster, and then you walked in.'

He patted the stool besid e him. 'Now, come on. Park your arse. I'm about to make your fucking d ay.'

'What? No!'

'Trust me, Tyler,' Hoon said .

It was, DC Neish thought, the first time Hoon had ever ad d ressed him by his name. It mad e a refreshing change from 'that prick with the hair', and there was something about the way the former DSup said it that mad e Tyler's feet shuffle him closer.

Hoon caught the barmaid 's eye. 'He'll have that Grouse now.'

'I won't,' Tyler said . He felt Hoon's bead y gaze on him, then sighed . 'I'll have a Coke.'

'Fuck me pink,' Hoon muttered . 'Fine. Get him a Coke, Kelly, if you d on't mind ?'

Kelly looked about as far out of her d epth as Tyler felt. She hesitated for a moment, shot a glance at the d oor like she was consid ering making a run for it, then picked up the soft d rink d ispenser gun and skooshed a half-pint of the stuff into a tall glass.

'Sorry, d id you want ice?' she asked , as she placed the glass on the bar in front of Tyler.

'No, that's fine, thanks. What d o I owe you?'

'It's fine,' Kelly insisted , backing away again.

Tyler smiled reassuringly at her. 'Everything's OK. Honest. There's nothing to worry about.'

Hoon raised his whisky glass and held it there in the air between them. Tyler contemplated refusing, remembered the state of the six men scattered around them, then chinked his own glass against Hoon's.

'Cheers.'

'Attaboy,' Hoon said . He took a swig, swished it through his teeth a few times like mouthwash, then swallowed it d own. 'We never really got to know each other, d id we?'

Tyler ad mitted that no, they had n't. He left off the part about how he d id n't really want to start making up for that now.

'Still, this is nice, eh? A wee d rink after work,' Hoon said . 'How was your d ay?'

Tyler blinked . 'What?'

'Fuck's sake. Your d ay. How was it? That's what people ask, isn't it? That's the shite they say.'

The word s were out of Tyler before he could catch them. 'You really want to know? Shite. That's how my d ay was. I was nearly hit by a train, I wanted to go for a shower, and now I've end ed up here with you surround ed by...' He gestured around the mostly empty bar. '...all this. So, I'm not really in the mood for a bit of male bond ing.'

'Fuck's sake. I was only trying to be friend ly,' Hoon remarked .

203

'Aye, well, like I say, I'm not in the mood since—as I also mentioned —I was nearly hit by a blood y train.'

Hoon sipped his d rink. 'You know another way of saying "I was nearly hit by a train"?' he asked . He d id n't give Tyler any time to answer. 'I *wasn't* hit by a train.'

Tyler took a few second s to process this. It had , after all, been a long d ay. 'What?' he finally asked .

'It's about reframing things. That's what the shrink told me. "I nearly d ied ." "I d id n't d ie." "I started d rinking at noon" "I *didn't* start d rinking at nine."' He sniffed . It was a d eep, resonating belter of a sniff, with lots of burbling as fluid s moved around . 'I d id n't really buy into it, if I'm honest, but your train thing fits it to a fucking tee. You went to work and you*weren't* hit by a train.' He raised his glass in another toast. 'Sound s like a pretty fucking good d ay to me.'

'Aye. Well. You weren't there.' Tyler took a d rink of his Coke. 'Is that why you wanted me to sit d own? So you could give me life ad vice? No offence, but I'm not sure you're the best man for the job.'

Hoon's stare was piercing and intense, and almost knocked Tyler backward s off the stool. Then, to the DC's surprise, Hoon snorted out a laugh. 'You make a fair point, son. I'm hard ly one for word s of fucking wisd om. There's one bit of life ad vice I learned , though, that I will pass on, because I'm nice like that.'

He had another swig from his glass, then hissed and burped before d ispensing his wisd om.

'There are two types of people on this Earth,' he said , fixing Tyler with a look of absolute solemn sincerity. 'Avoid both.'

And with that, he turned to the woman behind the bar. 'Kelly, tell Thomas the Wank Engine here what you told me?'

'Thomas the…? Oh, the train,' Tyler said .

Hoon waved the remark away like it was a particularly irrit-ating moth.

'Shut your hole and listen,' he barked . 'Fire away, Kelly. Tell him what you told me.'

The barmaid shuffled from foot to foot, not quite sure what was being asked of her.

'What bit?'

'For f— the girl. The d ead lassie from the telly. Tell him what you told me.'

'Oh. Aye. Right. Sorry,' Kelly babbled , clearly now terrified of the man on the stool.

There was a creak from behind Tyler and Hoon.

'Did I say you could fucking move?' Hoon asked , not turning to look.

There followed a momentary pause, and then another creak that sound ed very much like the previous one in reverse.

None of the other injured men moved a muscle.

'Sorry, sweetheart. You were saying?' Hoon urged , shooting a smile across the bar.

'Uh… yeah. The girl on the telly, she was in here earlier in the week. With some friend s, I think.'

Tyler sat up straighter and set his glass d own on the bar. 'And ?'

'Well, go on then. Tell him what you told me,' Hoon said . He elbowed Tyler. 'Pin back your fucking earflaps and have a listen to this.'

'She, eh, she got talking to someone. A guy. She left with him.'

Tyler sagged a little. 'Oh. Right. We alread y knew that, actually.'

'Oh.' Kelly's gaze flitted between the two men. 'I see. Well, that's fine, then. So… I suppose you alread y know who he is?'

'No. Why, d o you?'

'Ha! "Do you?" he fucking says,' Hoon laughed . 'Tell him the good news.'

Kelly opened her mouth to reply, but Hoon jumped in first.

'Course she fucking knows who he is. And what's more, she knows where to find him.'

He knocked back his d rink, shud d ered , then slid off th
stool. This brought him close enough that Tyler's nostrils were
subjected to the full assault of his alcohol breath and bod y
od our.

'So, finish up your child 's d rink there, and what's say me and
you go nab the fucker?'

–

'Holy shit! Check this out.'

Hamza rolled his chair across to Dave's d esk, where the
constable's broad frame was hunched over a comparatively tiny
keyboard .

'What have you got?' the d etective sergeant asked , craning
his neck to see the computer screen.

'Right, so, I was looking through some of that footage,' Dave
said . 'You really can't see much of the road , and it's pretty d ark,
but there's a point when cars are about here…' He pointed to a
spot a couple of inches from the far left of the image, where the
road was only just visible. '…that their head lights reflect off the
glass enough to give you a look at them for, like, half a second .'

'OK…' Hamza said . None of this sound ed particularly
promising, and d efinitely not d eserving of a 'Holy shit!'

'Four cars passed in the hour before your bird watcher fella
shows up. Can barely see anything of them. One might be red ,
but it might be brown. The rest? White, or silver, or blue. It's
impossible to tell.'

Hamza could feel his d isappointment growing. None of this
was even remotely useful information. Still, he clung to that
'Holy shit!' like it was a life raft. All this was going somewhere.
It had to be.

'Your bird ie man said he turned up about half-five-ish,
right?' Dave asked .

'Thereabouts, aye.'

'And he saw someone head ing up the hill away from the
monument about then.'

'Aye. Why?'

'Check this.' Dave scrubbed back along the timeline of the video clip for a few seconds, then pointed to the numbers overlaid on the screen. 'Five forty-one. Observe.'

He hit play. The camera footage was dark and grainy, and nothing much appeared to be happening.

'What am I—' Hamza started to ask, but Dave held up a hand for silence.

'Wait for it...'

The road outside the cafe gradually grew brighter as head-lights approached. Dave leaned back a little, making room for Hamza to get closer to the screen.

A large vehicle passed. It was only visible for a fraction of a second, but it was enough for Hamza to recognise it. He'd seen that van a thousand times over the years. Everyone had.

He pointed to the screen, blinking in disbelief. 'Was that...?'

Dave nodded. 'Aye. I mean, it certainly bloody looks like it.'

'Was that *the Mystery Machine* out of *Scooby-Doo*?'

'Aye!' Dave confirmed. 'Which means, either Shaggy's the killer...' He pointed to the screen just as another vehicle passed, heading in the same direction. This one was smaller, darker, and didn't carry the garishly painted insignia of a gang of cartoon monster hunters, making it impossible to identify. '...or he might be able to tell us who is.'

Chapter 29

They led   Corey Sand erson in through the back d oor of the station, as far as possible from the pack of bastard s flashing their cameras and   record ers out front. It was well after nine, so there were fewer of them than earlier in the d ay, but Logan still wasn't taking any chances.

He was hand ed   over. Checked   in. Processed , by the book.

They offered   him a toilet break. A d rink. A wee bite to eat— a ham and   cheese sand wich from the Co-op, nothing fancy.

He was a vegetarian. They told   him to pick the ham out.

And   then they led   him through to an interview room, where one of the largest men he had   ever seen glad ly accepted   him into his custod y.

Exclud ing Moof himself, there were three other people in the room. The giant; a smaller, old er man sitting on one sid e of an interview table, nursing a cup of tea or coffee; and   a woman in her late forties d ressed   in a tweed   skirt suit.

She wore a pair of old -fashioned   half-moon glasses, and   had   her hair pinned   tightly in a bun, like she was worried   it might try to break free and   attack someone. Her look remind ed   Moof of the d owd y librarian trope from movies. All it would   take was for her to remove the glasses, shake out her hair, and   everyone would   gasp and   remark on how beautiful she was.

'Oi! Corey.'

The big d etective clicked   his fingers in Moof's face, d ragging his eyes away from what he guessed   must be his state-appointed lawyer.

'Did   you hear what I said ?'

Moof had not been aware that the d etective had even spoken. Since seeing the news head lines, there had been a veil over the world . He felt d etached from it. Removed . It was like some co-pilot he'd previously been unaware of had sid led into the main seat and taken over the controls. He could walk and talk, but everything else was a struggle.

'No. Sorry,' he said . 'What?'

The solicitor cleared her throat and stood up. 'Detective Chief Inspector. Detective Inspector,' she said , ad d ressing both men in turn. 'I need ten minutes alone with my client.'

'Why?' the much larger of the two men asked . He looked unhappy about this prospect. He looked unhappy in general, in fact, and Moof hoped the two of them were never left alone together. He'd heard what happened in police stations, and he was pretty sure this one had some steep flights of stairs.

'Because we haven't had a chance to so much as be intro-d uced ,' the solicitor said . She looked amused by the question, like they both knew the request wasn't up for d ebate. 'Please, we'd like the room. Thank you.'

The old er man at the table picked up a fold er that was sitting on the table in front of him, tucked it und er his arm, then stood up.

'Come on, DCI Logan,' he said , patting the towering d etective on the arm as he passed . 'Ten more minutes won't hurt.' He smiled thinly in Moof's d irection. 'This young man's no' going anywhere.'

–

Sinead stood by the Arrivals d oor at Inverness Airport, her arms crad led across her belly, her hand s tapping out an irregular beat on her elbows.

Her weight moved from hip to hip, unable to d ecid e which to stop on for any length of time. Her bottom lip was red and raw, the thin skin there having long-since been scraped off by her top teeth.

She had never, to her knowled ge, met a billionaire before. She had certainly never met one who had flown in on a private jet to d eal with the aftermath of his d aughter's brutal murd er. She reckoned she was probably in a pretty exclusive club on that front, in fact.

Was it too late to withd raw her application, she wond ered ? Hand in her membership card ? Pass this particular responsibility on to someone else?

Sad ly, yes. The jet had land ed a few minutes ago. Bartholomew Riksen was alread y on the ground . Any minute now, he'd be stepping through the d oors ahead of her, and she had no id ea what she was meant to say.

The fact that the airport was completely empty, asid e from a hand ful of resentful-looking staff who should 've been on the way home by now, d id nothing to ease her nerves. She could feel them all watching her, and the cavernous silence of the build ing would only amplify the awkward , nervous babbling that she was convinced was going to come tumbling out of her mouth.

She glanced around and smiled sheepishly at a baggage hand ler leaning on a hand rail thirty or forty feet away. He d id not smile back.

Sinead took a look through the small square wind ows in the d ouble d oors ahead of her, paced around in a tight circle, then checked again.

Still nothing.

She took a moment to have a word with herself. How many families had she spoken to while acting as a liaison officer? How many grieving parents, or partners, or child ren, or friend s had cried on her should er?

She'd known what to d o then. Somehow, she'd known exactly what to d o, probably because she'd been through all those same emotions herself and could still remember the rawness of the pain.

So, why was this time d ifferent? Because he was rich and powerful? What d ifference d id that make? First and foremost, he was a man who had lost his daughter. Everything else would come second to that.

Would n't it?

She paced another circle or two, checked for any sign of movement through the doors, then stole another glance at the baggage handler. He had clearly been waiting for her to look his way, and made a show of checking his watch.

'Sorry,' she said, and her voice sounded small and childish in the vast empty space. 'Should n't be long.'

'It had better bloody not be,' the man replied gruffly. 'I was meant to be out of here twenty minutes ago.'

Something about his tone drilled down through the anxiety until it struck a seam of pure Sinead buried below it.

'Aye, well, maybe you've seen the news? A teenage girl was murdered, and this is her father I'm waiting on. You want to be the one to tell him to shift his arse? Go ahead. Otherwise, sit there, shut up, and wait.'

She held his gaze until he looked away, then faced the door again, butterflies fluttering in her chest.

'Nicely done,' said a voice on her left.

Sinead turned to find Detective Superintendent Mitchell standing there, the whiteness of her shirt shining all the brighter between the black of her jacket and the brown of her skin.

'Uh, ma'am?'

'I hope you don't mind a bit of company, Detective Constable,' Mitchell said.

'What? No. No at all.' Sinead smiled. 'Worried I'd mess it up, ma'am?'

'On the contrary. You're one of the few I knew I could trust not to,' the DSup said, folding her hands behind her back. 'But it transpires that Mr Riksen has a lot of influence, even all the way over here. Got the orders from on high to join the welcome party half an hour ago.'

'Good timing,' said Sinead, straightening herself and pushing her shoulders back. She nodded in the direction of the door. 'I'm guessing this is him now.'

Mitchell's response came as a whisper from the sid e of her mouth. 'Really? What gave it away?'

Sinead bit back a laugh as the d oors swung open, revealing a tall, muscular man in an immaculately tailored white suit, cowboy boots, and a ten-gallon hat with a zebra-skin patterned band running around the crown.

His skin was the colour of antique bronze, from a lifetime of being outd oors in the Texas sunshine. He d ragged a single small suitcase with him. It looked large enough to hold clothing for a couple of d ays, a washbag, and maybe a laptop and an extra pair of shoes.

Or, to put it another way, one spare hat.

The case itself was patterned with large brown blobs against a tan-coloured background . It took Sinead a moment to recog-nise the d esign.

Giraffe.

'You with the police?' Riksen asked , aiming the question squarely at Sinead . Before giving her a chance to respond , he held his case out for Detective Superintend ent Mitchell to take, but mad e no effort to look at her. 'Here.'

Mitchell regard ed the offered hand le. It was only for a second or two, but to Sinead it felt like time had slowed to such a crawl that the moment was stretching on forever.

'Well?' Riksen d emand ed , finally shifting his gaze in the DSup's d irection. 'What are you waiting for?'

'I think there's been a misund erstand ing, Mr Riksen,' Mitchell said . Sinead d id n't know the senior officer well, but enough to know that the smile on her face was about as far from genuine as it could possibly be. 'I'm Detective Superintend ent Mitchell. This is Detective Constable Bell. I've been asked to greet you, and to pass on our d eepest sympathies for your loss. Detective Constable Bell will be escorting you to the mortuary, and then—'

'No need . I've alread y had a representative id entify the bod y this evening, and have travel arranged ,' Riksen said . 'And no need for sympathy, either. I d id my grieving on the plane. I'm just here to make sure you d on't screw the god d amn pooch on this.' He spotted the baggage hand ler leaning on the railing and whistled to him. 'You. Take this. Quickly now, boy, we ain't got all night.'

'Mr Riksen. Good to see you, sir.'

Sinead and Detective Superintend ent Mitchell both turned to see a man with a remarkable moustache come strid ing through one of the airport's front d oors.

There was nothing overly outland ish about the moustache— it was thick, mottled with flecks of grey, and a largely bog-stand ard affair—but the lack of anything else noteworthy about the man meant the facial hair was what really d rew the eye.

He was average height. Average build , or maybe slightly stockier. He wore a pair of d ark blue slacks and a heather-coloured blazer with a subtle brown check. Sinead thought he looked like the kind of man who should be wearing a tie, but the top button of his shirt was und one, and there was no neckwear to be seen.

Riksen gave the man a curt nod of acknowled gement. 'Dirk,' he said , then he d ismissed the approaching baggage hand ler with a wave and let the new arrival take his case. 'Car read y?'

'Right out front, Mr Riksen.'

Sinead and Detective Superintend ent Mitchell swapped confused looks.

'I'm sorry, who's this?' Mitchell asked .

'Dirk Sommercamp. I head up the investigative wing of Mr Riksen's security task force,' said the man with the moustache. He rattled it off like he had it memorised just for moments like these. 'Twenty years as a special agent with the Fed eral Bureau of Investigation,' he ad d ed , even though nobod y had asked .

'Dirk will be working alongsid e your officers,' Riksen said .

'Uh… no. I'm afraid that's not how—'

'I suggest you check your email, young lad y,' Riksen told her, d espite the fact they were both approximately the same age. 'Everything has alread y been arranged . We're going to get to the bottom of this here unpleasantness. I give you my word on that.'

And with those closing remarks, he swept out of the airport with Dirk Sommercamp strid ing along behind him, the hand le of the suitcase clutched in one hand .

'Uh, he was… interesting,' Sinead muttered , watching the d oor close behind the Americans. When she got no response, she turned to the Detective Superintend ent, who was staring in horror at her phone screen.

'Good grief.' Mitchell tutted , eyes fixed on the email she had brought up. '*Special consultant*? This is rid iculous. Just absolutely blood y rid iculous.'

'Ma'am?'

'The security chief. Sommercamp. The Chief Constable himself has appointed him as a special consultant on the case. He's to be given full access to everything. Statements, evid ence, access to witnesses. The whole lot.'

Sinead sucked air in through her teeth. 'DCI Logan's not going to be happy about that.'

'Yes. I mean, there's *that* silver lining, obviously, but still. Rid iculous. Utterly blood y rid iculous.' She shoved the phone back in her pocket, breathed some of her frustration out through her nose, then smoothed d own the front of her jacket. 'I shall complain, of course. Fat lot of good it'll d o, but may as well log my objection.'

The baggage hand ler appeared behind them, sid ling up with an impressive d isplay of stealth.

'Couple of quick questions,' he said . He was no longer full of the attitud e he'd d isplayed earlier, Sinead 's scold ing obvious having had some effect. 'One, d oes this mean I can finally go home now? And two…' He pointed in the d irection of the d oor. 'Was that suitcase mad e from real giraffe, d o we think?'

–

Sinead and Detective Superintendent Mitchell stepped outside the airport in time to see the security barrier drop back into place behind a black Mercedes-Benz SUV.

'One of us should probably warn DCI Logan,' Sinead said, watching the car speed across the round about, headed west toward s the city. 'Something tells me he's not going to like this guy.'

'Which one?'

'Both.'

Mitchell finished typing out an email, hit the button to send, then shoved the phone forcibly back in her bag like it had personally done something to get in her bad books.

'Yes. Well, he doesn't have to like them. He just has to work with them.'

'Him, ma'am.'

Mitchell frowned. 'Sorry?'

'You said it was just Sommercamp who had been appointed as an advisor, or consultant, or whatever. Did n't you?' Sinead said. 'DCI Logan might accept that—eventually—but he'll make a point of keeping Mr Riksen as far from the case as he can, even if only out of spite.'

Mitchell allowed herself a suggestion of a smile at that. 'I don't imagine "no" is a word Mr Riksen hears very often.'

Sinead shared the Detective Superintendent's amusement. 'And if he goes d own there with the same attitud e he had here, I'd imagine he'll hear a lot worse word s than that...'

Chapter 30

Tyler stood at the bottom of a dingy stairwell in a block of flats, floundering badly.

The barmaid had given them a name—Dean Stevens, known to his less imaginative friends as 'Deano'—and an address that was a short walk from the High Street, but up a very steep hill.

Given that every part of him currently ached, Tyler had suggested taking the car, but this only served to make Hoon question both his sexuality and gender, then set off marching like he was on a quest to conquer Everest, and had a plan to be back in time for breakfast.

Hoon shouldn't have even been there, of course, but Tyler's attempts to dissuade him had either been dismissed or ignored He'd tried to speak authoritatively—to 'use his polis voice' as Logan had once told him—but that had only earned a snort of derision from the former Detective Superintendent, and a barked order to 'fucking keep up.'

And now here they were, standing at the bottom of the stairs that led up to Dean Stevens's flat, Hoon already rolling up the sleeves of a shirt so large it could only have belonged to Logan.

'You shouldn't be coming up there, eh… Mr Hoon,' he said.

'Look, first thing's fucking first, son. Don't call me "Mr Hoon". All right?' He patted Tyler on the shoulder. 'Call me "sir".'

Tyler swallowed. 'But, eh, you're not my boss anymore.'

'Maybe no', but I'm older than you, am I not? Were your parents weird o hippie bastards, or something? Did they teach you fuck all? Bit of fucking respect for your eld ers goes a long way, son.'

'Right, but—'

'*Secondly*,' Hoon said , tramping all over the start of Tyler's sentence. 'I fucking am so going up there. I'm the one who found this prick, am I not?'

'But—'

'Yes or no? Did I find this prick?'

'Well, it's—'

'Yes or no?'

Tyler sighed . 'Yes. Technically.'

'See? Wasn't so fucking hard , was it?' Hoon said , then he started up the stone steps. 'I would n't touch the bannister. Fuck knows who's touched it, and you d on't know where they've been.'

'What are you d oing,*sir*?' Tyler asked , and the exasperation in his voice brought Hoon to a halt at the first land ing.

The flats were staggered on either sid e of the build ing. Five steps led up from the ground floor to where Hoon stood outsid e the first d oor. A turn to the right and another five steps would take him to the next floor. Two more turns from there would lead him d irectly to Dean Stevens's flat.

'The fuck d oes it look like I'm d oing?' Hoon asked . 'Going to nab this fucker.'

'But… it's not your job, sir. Not anymore. You should n't even be here.'

Hoon looked up the stairs to his right, then d own at the d etective constable leaning on the hand rail at the bottom.

'I thought I told you not to fucking touch that?' he said .

'You d id , aye,' Tyler ad mitted . 'But you d on't get to boss me around these d ays. And , in case you've forgotten, I was—'

'Don't start with the fucking train thing again,' Hoon warned him.

A silence filled the stairwell, and was eventually broken by a sigh from the old er of the two men. Hoon plonked himself d own on the floor, his feet on the next step d own.

'You're right,' he admitted . 'Stupid . I should n't be d oing this. I just… fuck's sake. Jack. I blame Jack. Something the d oughy-titted arse-nugget said back at the house. About me find ing a way to…'

He shook his head , letting the sentence tumble off into another burst of silence.

'Find a way to what?' Tyler asked .

'Fuck it. Forget it. Doesn't matter,' Hoon said . He shuffled sid eways until he was leaning against the wall, making room for Tyler to pass him. 'On you go, son. See if the trumpet-humping wee bawbag's home.'

Tyler almost stopped to question the 'trumpet-humping' thing, but d ecid ed it was probably in his best interests not to. Instead , he just gave his ex-boss a grateful nod , and hurried past him in case the mad bastard tried to bite his knees on the way by.

He d id n't. He d id n't d o much of anything, in fact, just sat there on the step with his head d own as Tyler's shoes scuffed their way up the next few flights of stairs and stopped outsid e Dean Stevens's d oor.

Tyler waited a few moments until his thighs had stopped burning and his breathing had stabilised , then raised a hand and came very close to knocking on the d oor before a boot slammed into it, smashing the frame and throwing it wid e open.

'What the fuck?!' Tyler yelped , jumping clear.

'Change of plan,' Hoon told him, his eyes ablaze with excite-ment. 'Got fed up waiting. Come on, let's go.'

'What? But—'

It was too late. Hoon was alread y marching into the flat like he was lead ing the world 's most reckless SWAT team.

'Deano? Where the fuck are you? I'm with the polis!'

Tyler hurried up behind him. 'No, you aren't!' he hissed .

'I am fucking so,' Hoon retorted . 'You're the polis, and I'm with you. What's the fucking problem?'

He threw open the first d oor they came to, revealing a messy bed room with a large TV fixed to the wall. A vid eo gam*Red*

Dead Redemption 2, unless Tyler was very much mistaken—was paused on-screen.

'Nope,' Hoon announced , spinning on his heels to face another d oor that was almost level with the first, but on the opposite sid e of the hallway.

There was no lock on this d oor, from what Tyler could gather, but Hoon brought his foot up anyway, and the DC barely had time to object before Hoon's foot buckled the flimsy wood and tore the d oor clean off its hinges.

'Stop fucking d oing that!' Tyler protested .

And then he locked eyes with the twenty-something in the kitchen.

The twenty-something who stood frozen behind a breakfast bar, mid way through sweeping a pile of two or three hund red pills into a clear plastic bag.

'Well, well, well, Deano,' Hoon said . He picked up one of the tablets, examined it, then set it back d own in the pile. 'It looks like someone's been a very naughty boy.' He pointed back over his should er to where DC Neish stood . 'And , for the benefit of this boggle-eyed sack of camel spunk, the "someone" I'm referring to in this instance is you.'

-

Hamza sprang out of his seat when Logan and Ben returned to the Incid ent Room. He had , until that moment, been staring at his computer screen, a slightly goofy smile on his face, and the fluttering in his stomach that always appeared when the ad renaline started to surge.

'That was quick,' Dave remarked , spotting the two d etect-ives. 'Confess to it all, d id he?'

'His brief wants a word with him,' Ben said , answering for Logan who looked far too annoyed to speak for himself without swearing. 'We've said they can have ten minutes.'

'Great! Good timing,' Hamza said . 'I was actually going to come get you. I've got something that you're d efinitely going to want to see.'

Logan and Ben followed the d etective sergeant to his d esk and stood behind him as he d ropped back onto his chair, one hand alread y reaching for the mouse.

'Remember we asked the local petrol stations for their CCTV footage?'

Ben frowned like this was news to him. 'Did we?'

'Uh, aye, sir,' Hamza said , his eyes flitting just briefly in Logan's d irection. 'In case we could find out who bought the oil that was poured over—'

'Oh. Aye. Of course,' Ben said . He fid d led id ly with the fine length of silver chain around his neck, making the weights on the end swing against his chest. 'The stuff poured over the victim. Aye. What about it?'

'We got a load through earlier tod ay. Dave and I were d ivvying up who was going to look through what, but there's a clip here from the little Gleaner station by the ind ustrial estate. The woman was bored , so she went through the footage herself and found six people buying oil in the last week.'

'Right...?' Logan said .

'And this is number four, sir.'

Hamza clicked the play button. The footage was taken from an outsid e camera. It was black and white, and showed a black car parked up at a petrol pump, and a man in a baseball cap filling the tank with his back to the camera.

Logan and Ben both bent d own to stud y the man, then switched their gazes to follow another man as he walked into frame and toward s the d oor at the bottom left of the image.

The footage then changed to show the insid e of the petrol station, now in full colour. The same man entered , and Hamza grinned triumphantly as his bright red hair was revealed in all its glory.

'Fuck me. Is that Sand erson?' Logan remarked .

'Certainly looks like him to me, sir,' Hamza said . 'And watch.'

Moof milled aimlessly around in the small shop for a while, then picked up a newspaper and a bottle of engine oil, and approached the counter.

The d etectives watched in a hushed silence, like they were worried they might scare him away, as Moof paid for the oil and the newspaper, stuffed them into the atom-thin plastic bag the cashier provid ed him with, and went scurrying out of the shop.

The footage changed again, this time showing a reverse of the first clip. The man in the baseball cap was still filling his car with petrol. He shot a momentary glance at Moof's back as the now grey-head ed youngster passed him, then returned to watching the numbers click up on the gauge.

'So... Corey Sand erson bought the oil,' Logan said .

'Surely we've got him?' Ben said . 'I mean, I thought we had him alread y, but this...?'

'Aye. It's going to be very blood y interesting hearing him trying to explain that away,' Logan agreed .

Ben checked his watch. 'Nine-forty,' he said . 'What's the bets we put this one to bed by half ten?'

Logan mad e a face that was d ecid ed ly non-committal. 'Aye,' he intoned . 'We'll see.'

The d oor to the Incid ent Room opened , and a some-what sheepish-looking Tyler popped his head insid e. 'Eh... all right, boss?' he asked , meeting Logan's eye just long enough to acknowled ge him, then quickly glancing away.

'Tyler? I thought you were going back to the cottage to... Christ. What's happened ? What's he d one?'

'Who, Hoon? Eh, well, funny you should ask, boss. He's at the cottage the now, but... well, he was in the pub. Got into a wee bit of a scrap.'

Logan squeezed the brid ge of his nose. 'Jesus. Is he all right?'

'Oh aye, he's grand , boss. The six lad s who he insists started it aren't in such great shape, mind you.'

'Six? Hard y!' Dave said , impressed .

'Ex-special forces,' Ben explained . 'And a psychopath, which also helps.'

'Anyway, the barmaid backs up that they started it, none of them want to press charges—although, I think they're too scared to, to be honest—and , well… he might actually have d one something useful.'

Logan's eyes narrowed in suspicion. 'Like what?'

'The lad Deird rie said she saw Alexis going off with? Hoon found out who he was. The barmaid in one of the pubs saw it happening. She was able to give us a name.'

'Seriously?' Logan asked . 'That's… that's actually good news. Give the name to Hamza, maybe we can pull up an ad d ress.'

'No need , boss. We got the ad d ress,' Tyler said . 'And we, eh, head ed up there.'

'We? What d o you mean "we head ed up there"? You d id n't bring Hoon, d id you?'

'I d id n't bring him, boss, no. He sort of brought himself. I tried to stop him, like, but… well, you know what he's like.'

Logan d id know what he was like. Hoon had never need ed a superior rank to get people to follow his ord ers, he just had that air about him that mad e it very clear that not following them wasn't in anyone's best interests, and especially not your own.

'Right, well that nugget of information d oesn't leave this room, all right?' Logan said , flitting his gaze across the faces of the other officers. 'Mitchell'll have my balls in a vice if she find s out Hoon's been getting involved in a case.'

'Secret's safe with us, Jack,' Ben said .

'Was he in?' Logan asked , turning back to Tyler. 'Your man. Was he home?'

'He was, boss,' Tyler said . He held up a large Ziploc bag bulging with the weight of several hund red pills. 'And , thankfully, we found him with this.'

'Why thankfully?' Hamza asked .

'Because now he's much less likely to complain about Hoon kicking his d oor d own,' Tyler said .

Logan muttered darkly below his breath, then took the bag from Tyler and studied the pills. There was an assortment of goodies in there. Much of it looked like prescription stuff—Viagra, Valium, that sort of thing—but there were a few dozen less legitimate-looking pills mixed in amongst them.

It had been a long time since Logan had worked a street-level drugs case, but this felt like a bloody impressive haul.

'Where is he?' he asked, passing the bag back.

'Stuck him in interview room two, boss,' Tyler said. 'Thought you'd want to talk to him.'

'Got my hands full with Corey Sanderson,' Logan said. He nodded from Tyler to Hamza. 'You two up to it?'

'Absolutely, sir,' Hamza replied. Tyler seemed a little more reluctant—he had, after all, almost been hit by a train that day—but he nodded to confirm he was in.

'Good stuff. Dave, you man this place. Hamza, Tyler, find out what you can from our new arrival about the night he went off with the victim. Use the drugs as leverage if you have to, but that's not our case. What happened between him and Alexis Riksen is all we're interested in, then we'll hand the rest over to CID.'

'Got it, sir,' Hamza said.

'Ben, I think we've given Mr Sanderson and his solicitor time enough to get acquainted, don't you?'

'Too bloody true, Jack. Let's get in there and nail the bugger,' Ben said. He cocked his head and narrowed his eyes for a moment, then held up a finger. 'I'll maybe just quickly nip to the toilet first.'

Chapter 31

Hamza pulled Tyler aside before they stepped into the interview room. He glanced both directions along the corridor, as if about to share some particularly juicy gossip, then did nothing of the sort.

'You really went with Hoon to arrest this guy?'

'Not quite, no,' Tyler replied . 'I wasn't going to arrest him, just to ask him a couple of questions, but that fucking head case put his door in before I could even knock, and we caught him trying to get rid of this lot.'

He held up the bag of pills. It bulged like a sack of pirate doubloons.

'Blood y Nora,' Hamza whispered . 'You could have land ed right in the shit.'

'Still might,' Tyler said . 'It wasn't exactly by the book. I d on't know if it's even *in* the book.' He shrugged . 'Maybe the earlier ed itions, but that sort of thing is pretty frowned on nowad ays.'

'Aye, you can say that again.'

'On the positive sid e, I *didn't* get hit by a train tod ay, so that's something.' He caught the furrowing of Hamza's brow before a question could emerge from the d etective sergeant's mouth. 'Reframing,' he explained . 'Don't ask.'

'Fair enough.' Hamza mad e a brief gesture toward s the d oor. 'You read y for this? You still look like shite.'

'Cheers for that, Sarge,' Tyler said .

He liked to use Hamza's rank whenever he wanted to wind him up. Being a step up the chain from his former fellow-DC d id n't yet sit comfortably with DS Khaled , and he practically flinched whenever Tyler mentioned it.

Hamza watched as Tyler licked his fingertips and ran his hand s through his hair a few times. He stood by, silently, while the DC flattened , and twisted , and teased , using his shad ow on the wall as a makeshift—if entirely ineffectual—mirror.

'Better?' Tyler asked , once he was d one.

'Worse. Much worse,' Hamza said . 'But maybe we can use it. I'll be Good Cop, you can be Jakey Homeless Cop who lives und er a bush.'

Tyler smiled , showing off his impressively white teeth. 'I like it. The bastard will never see that coming,' he said , then he put a hand on the d oor hand le and raised an eyebrow in DS Khaled 's d irection. 'Shall we, Sergeant?'

Hamza tutted , but then gave a slow, respectful nod , like he was a member of the aristocracy greeting some foreign king. 'We shall, Constable,' he confirmed . 'Lead the way.'

–

Corey Sand erson was sitting forward in his chair when Logan and Ben entered . His elbows were perched on the table, his legs bouncing up and d own so violently the d etectives could feel the vibration through the floor when they entered .

'You might want to invest in some better watches if you think that qualifies as ten minutes, gentlemen, but I suppose it'll d o,' the solicitor said , flipping open a notepad like she was impatient to get started .

Her name was Melissa Brid ge. Logan had never come across her before, and from his ad mitted ly limited experience, he d id n't much like the cut of her jib.

It wasn't that she was unprofessional in any way. Just the opposite. She seemed to be clued up, confid ent in her abilities, and not in the least bit afraid to state her case.

Basically, everything a client might d esire in a solicitor, and everything he d id not. Christ knew, his job was d ifficult enough without throwing informed , competent legal representation into the mix.

'Aye, well, you'll forgive our eagerness to get started ,' Logan said . 'Always get over-excited at the thought of getting a killer off the streets, d on't we, DI Ford e?'

'Gid d y,' Ben agreed . 'No feeling quite like it.'

The d etectives took their seats, Ben across from Corey, Logan face-to-face with the solicitor where he could keep an eye on her. He fixed his gaze very firmly on Corey, though. So firmly, in fact, that the lad leaned back in his chair, trying to escape the intensity of it.

Logan stud ied him while Ben ran through the formalities and started the record ing.

The red hair was… not gone, exactly. It was still there, but mostly masked by a black d ye that had n't quite taken. Not to the hair, anyway. It had taken to the forehead and cheeks well enough, staining the skin in uneven shad es of grey. Between the unnatural skin tone and his red , blood shot eyes, Corey Sand erson looked every inch the monster the d etectives were here to prove him to be.

Logan waited until Ben had finished giving the official spiel, then jumped straight in.

'It's the motive I d on't get,' he said , d rawing a puzzled look from Corey and a largely impassive one from Melissa Brid ge, who simultaneously scribbled something on her pad in short-hand . 'Which one to choose, I mean. You were a bit spoiled for choice. Unrequited lover, humiliated and embarrassed by her rejection of you, or proud environmental terrorist, striking a blow against the evil oil empire? I just d on't know which one to go with. How about you, DI Ford e?'

'I'm torn,' Ben said .

'You and me both,' Logan said . 'So, maybe you can help us out, son. Help square this away for us.' He prod d ed a finger against the tabletop, like he was pressing a button that would somehow force the suspect to answer. 'Why d id you kill Alexis Riksen?'

'I...' Moof quickly snapped his mouth shut and looked to the solicitor for guid ance.

'Go ahead .'

'No comment.'

'Why d id you kill her, Corey?'

Another glance at the woman besid e him. Another nod received .

'No comment.'

'Jesus Christ. I take it she put you up to this?' Logan barked , stabbing a finger in the solicitor's d irection.

'This won't help your case, Corey,' Ben said . 'It won't look good for you.'

'What won't look good , d etectives, is you d ragging him up here to question him in the mid d le of the night,' Brid ge bit back. 'He's a young man, currently homeless—and therefore vulnerable—and not only d o you have him carted all the way from Ayr to here, you then offer him nothing but a ham sand - wich. He's vegetarian!'

'He could 've taken the ham out,' Ben suggested .

'Why d id you kill Alexis, son?' Logan asked . 'Forget this clown, she's steering you full tilt toward s a blood y d ead end . It's no' her freed om that's on the line, it's yours. So, for your sake—'

'Ignore him, Corey.'

Logan banged his fist on the table, making everyone— Ben includ ed —jump in their seats. 'Why d id you kill Alexis Riksen?'

'I... I...'

'Corey,' the solicitor said , in the tone of a mother hen scold ing her young.

He stopped . Swallowed . 'No comment.'

'Come on, Corey. This isn't like you. You're meant to be full of the big talk. That's where the nickname came from, isn't it? *Moof*, because you never shut yours.'

'No comment.'

Logan buried his face in his hand s, let out a groan of exasperation, then sat back in the chair, all smiles.

'Fine. We'll play it that way. I'll tell you what I think happened , and you can sit there *commenting* your way to a life behind bars. How about that, son?'

Corey's gaze d arted furtively to his legal counsel, then back to Logan. 'N-no—'

'No comment. Aye. I think I've got the gist of it now,' Logan said . 'Fine. I'll spell out my version of events, and DI Ford e here will watch carefully for your reactions. He's got an eye for that sort of thing, so I hope you've got a d amn good poker face, Corey, that's all I can say.'

Pointing out that someone was going to be observing a suspect's reactions was always a surefire way to make them panic, and therefore make their reactions far more exaggerated than they might otherwise have been.

The trick was to look for the false, put-on reactions, and then assume the opposite. Suspect pulling a confused expression and scratching their head s? They knew fine blood y well what you were talking about. Looking overly relaxed and ind ifferent about a particular line of questioning? They were trying very hard not to shite themselves.

Read ing most people was easy, and Corey Sand erson was shaping up to be easier than most.

'Right, are we all sitting comfortably?' Logan asked .

'Primed and read y, Detective Chief Inspector,' Ben said , his gaze locked on Corey like a tractor beam.

Logan sat forward , still smiling, like he was having the time of his life. Or about to have. 'Good ,' he said , looking Moof straight in the eye. 'Then we'll begin.'

–

To both Tyler and Hamza's d elight, Dean Stevens had d eclined the offer of a solicitor. It was a small town, people talked , and he d id n't want his mum find ing out about his arrest.

Neither d etective chose to point out that, given the size of the stash he'd been caught with, his mum find ing out was likely to be the least of his immed iate problems, and Hamza had him state for the record that he had been offered legal counsel, but had turned it d own.

'I can explain,' Dean said , when Tyler d eposited the bag of pills on the table between them.

'Great! That'll make life easier,' Hamza said .

'Want me to write the explanation d own, Sarge?' Tyler asked , making a show of taking out his notebook and pencil.

'Aye. Good thinking, DC Neish. Might as well get it in writing, and get it all squared away.'

Tyler licked the point of his pencil and positioned it on his pad , then locked eyes with the man across the table.

Dean was roughly the same age as Tyler, and a little younger than Hamza. His hair was lank and greasy, and at that length where it was impossible to d etermine if it was being grown into a longer style, or was just long overd ue a cut.

He had n't shaved in some time, but his stubble was putting in a poor showing. The d arkest areas were on his neck, while his chin and cheeks were comparatively sparse. Any attempts to grow a beard would result in a patchy, uneven mess of a thing.

Not that it would make him look much worse.

He was a textbook example of what Tyler's mum had always referred to as 'a half-shut knife'. His eyelid s were heavy, his clothes were a crumpled mess, and d espite the high-pressure situation he had found himself in, he had an air about him that suggested he'd just woken up from an afternoon nap.

'Right then, Dean. So, we entered your flat, and we found you with a great big stash of d rugs. What part of that are you going to explain?'

'They're not mine,' Dean said . 'I've never seen them d rugs before.'

'Aye you have,' Tyler said .

Dean sagged . 'All right, aye, I have. But they're not mine. I'm just hold ing onto them for a mate.'

'Right. Fair enough,' Tyler said . He wrote something in his pad , then flipped it closed . 'Reckon he can go now then, eh, Sarge?'

'Aye, that about wraps it up,' Hamza agreed .

Dean looked between them, his half-closed eyes wid ening so they were almost three-quarters of the way open. 'What, seriously? I can go?'

'No, ya fud d ,' Tyler said , leaning forward . 'Of course you can't. We caught you with a massive bag of d rugs.'

'Aye, but… they're not mine! I told you. They're my mate's.'

'What's your mate's name?' Hamza asked . 'Quickly.'

They practically heard Dean's brain spluttering into life. 'Jim.'

'Jim? Jim what?' Tyler pressed .

'Jim… Jim.'

Dean winced .

'Jim Jim?' Hamza said . 'Well, he should n't be too hard to find .'

'No, it's not Jim Jim,' Dean replied , scratching his head .

'You just said it was,' Tyler remind ed him.

'It's Jim… I d on't know his second name,' Dean said , then inspiration seemed to strike him from nowhere. 'Ball. Ball…ton. Bolton. Jim Bolton.'

Both d etectives clasped their hand s on the table in front of them and waited .

It took six second s for Dean to cave in to the pressure.

'Right, fine. They're mine. But they're for personal consumption.'

'Fuck me, are you d ying?' Tyler asked , hold ing up the bulging bag. 'I've been in hospitals that carry less d rugs than that.'

'I've, eh, I've got a cond ition.'

'You've got more than one cond ition if you're taking all of these,' Hamza said . He thumbed at the pills through the bag, picking out a few he recognised . 'From what I can tell, either you're an impotent schizophrenic with HIV, Dean, or you're spilling us a load of old shite. I'm sure a quick call to your mum will tell us, one way or another.'

'Don't. Naw, d on't,' Dean plead ed . 'She'll be raging.'

'Then tell us the blood y truth,' Hamza barked . 'Are these, or are these not, your d rugs?'

Dean shunted himself from sid e to sid e in his chair, then wrapped his arms across his chest like he was ad opting some sort of brace position. 'Aye.'

'And were you, or were you not, planning to punt them?'

Another shift. More bracing. 'Fine. Aye. I was. But most of them aren't even illegal.'

'No, but unless you're playing your registered GP and qual-ified pharmacist card s very close to your chest, I reckon it probably *is* illegal for you to be d ishing them out, eh?' Tyler said . 'Would you agree, DS Khaled ?'

'I think your assessment of the situation is spot on, DC Neish,' Hamza confirmed .

'And how long, would you say, would someone be facing in jail for an offence of this nature?'

'For possession with intent to supply Class B narcotics?' Hamza said . 'Oof. Fourteen years. Give or take.'

Across the table, the seriousness of the situation hit Dean like a sucker punch to the gut. 'Fourteen years?! Why?'

'What d o you mean "why"?' Tyler snapped . 'Big bag of d rugs, Dean. Remember? You just told us you were going to supply them.'

'I d id n't know I could go to jail for it, but! The guy d id n't say anything about that!'

Hamza and Tyler both hesitated . The point of the interview was to get the scoop on what had happened between Dean and Alexis, but another opportunity was presenting itself and their polis instincts were urging them to explore it.

It was Hamza who eventually asked the question. 'Who?'

Dean's reply was lightning-fast, like he'd realised his mistake and had been bracing himself for the follow-up question.

'I can't say.'

The two detectives both shrugged. 'Fine,' Hamza said.

'He was some foreign guy,' Dean offered. 'Skinhead. Polish, or something. Tracksuit. Angry-looking. I don't know his name.'

'Aye you do,' Tyler said.

Dean shook his head emphatically. 'No, honest. I don't. I swear! I meet him in Inverness once every couple of months. He gives me a stash, I hand over the cash, and that's it.'

'Right. Well, here's what's going to happen, Dean,' Hamza said. 'Tomorrow morning, you're going to speak to a couple of our colleagues in CID. You're going to tell them what you told us—they'll already have the recording, so they'll know if you're lying to them—and you're going to do whatever they ask you to do. Otherwise, you're looking at spending the whole of your thirties in the nick.'

'Imagine what your mum'll say,' Tyler added. He sucked air in through his teeth. 'It'll break her bloody heart.'

'Now, here's the thing, Dean. Our colleagues? They aren't as nice as us. No' as friendly, ken? But us... me and him? We can make sure they treat you fairly. Would you like that?'

Dean nodded enthusiastically. 'Yes. Please.'

'All we ask is that you help us out with another matter,' Hamza said.

Taking his cue, Tyler slid a slightly grainy photograph of Alexis Riksen across the table. It was taken from her Facebook profile, and was the same image the media had been splashing around everywhere all day.

'Tell me, Dean,' Tyler said. 'What do you know about this young woman?'

Chapter 32

Corey Sand erson had sat squirming as Logan started to go through his version of events. The DCI had only just begun to d iscuss his theories as to why Moof had murd ered Alexis when it all got too much for the young man across the table, and he broke his 'no comment' programming.

'I d id n't kill her!'

'Corey, remember what I said about—' the brief began, but he cut her off.

'I need to tell them I d id n't kill her! I would n't. Never d o that. *I'd* never d o that,' he said , tripping over the word s in his rush to get them out. 'I loved her.'

'We know you d id , Corey,' Logan said , shooting the solicitor a look of victory. 'It's a shame she d id n't feel the same about you, eh? That must've stung.'

'No! She d id ! She d id   feel the same way!'

'Funny, that's not what her girlfriend tells us.'

'Deird rie? That was… I d on't… that wasn't the same. She d id n't feel the same way about Deird rie as she d id   about me!'

'No, she actually *liked* Deird rie,' Logan said . 'Did   that make you jealous, Corey?'

'Powerful motivator, jealousy,' Ben remarked .

'Aye, you can say that again,' Logan agreed . 'It's making me lean toward s the unrequited love motive, I have to say. You?'

Ben gave a non-committal sort of shrug. 'I'm hed ging my bets.'

'Probably wise,' Logan said , and Ben slid his fold er in front of the DCI without saying a word . 'You're big into the environmental stuff, aren't you, Corey?'

Moof's eyes d arted across all three other faces, like he was sensing a trap. 'I... uh... yes.'

'Greenpeace. Save the whales. What's her name? The wee lassie who d oes the speeches?'

'Greta Thingyberg,' said Ben, getting surprisingly close to the right answer.

'Aye. Something like that. You're big on her, Corey, going by your social med ia presence,' Logan said .

'I just... it's an important message, I just—'

'What d oes this have to d o with anything?' asked the solicitor. 'I wasn't aware that caring for the environment was a criminal matter these d ays.'

Logan smiled at her. It was not a friend ly smile. It was barely a smile at all, in fact. 'Just establishing the facts, Mrs Brid ge. Setting the scene, so to speak. Because, you see, your client's commend able commitment to environmental issues is important context for the oil.'

The solicitor scribbled something on her pad , then followed up with a question. 'What oil?'

'On the bod y. Poured over Alexis Riksen as she lay d ying, we reckon. At first, I thought maybe she'd been forced to d rink it. But no. She was just strangled . Old school, but effective.' Logan leaned forward and rested his forearms on the table. 'Mind showing me your hand s there, Corey?'

Brid ge gave him an almost imperceptible shake of the head , but Moof ignored it and d id as he was asked , bringing up both arms until they were in the classic surrend er position. They were shaking uncontrollably, like he was in the ad vanced stages of some d egenerative brain-wasting d isease.

'My my, Mr Sand erson,' Logan said . 'What big hand s you have. All the better for throttling lassies with, eh?'

Moof shook his head , tears springing to his eyes. 'No. N-no, I d id n't!'

'You found out, d id n't you, Corey? You found out who "Hermione Grey" really was. Heiress to an oil fortune. Dad d y who's out there d rilling and pumping and polluting the atmosphere twenty-four hours a d ay, seven d ays a week. The enemy of everything you stand for. She'd strung you along, d rip-fed you just enough encouragement to keep you keen.'

'No.'

'She probably got a kick out of reeling you in like that. Knowing your beliefs, and knowing what she was. Probably loved every minute of it. Her family getting richer and richer from raping the planet, and you, big proud environmental campaigner, trotting around after her like a lost puppy.'

'No!'

'I can't imagine the shock when you found out. Christ, you must've felt like a blood y id iot.'

'No! It wasn't like that! It wasn't like that!'

Both d etectives fell silent for a moment, waiting for Sand erson to say more.

When he d id n't, it was Ben who offered some gentle prompting.

'Then tell us what it was like, son,' he said . His voice was low. Soft. Calming. A hypnotist send ing an anxious client into their first-ever trance. 'Talk us through what happened . Get it off your chest.' He smiled . It was warm and caring, and brought tears to Sand erson's eyes. 'Tell us everything, and maybe we can help.'

-

Dave was 'resting his eyes' at his d esk when the d oor of the Incid ent Room opened , and Sinead leaned in.

'Hello?' she said , snapping Dave into an upright position in his wheelchair.

'What? Oh. Hello,' he said , stifling a yawn.

'We in here, are we?' Sinead asked .

Dave looked around , as if trying to work out where 'here' was. 'Um... Aye. I think...' He checked his watch, seemed momentarily taken aback by what it told him, then nod d ed . 'Yeah. Everyone's in d oing interviews. I was just, eh... med it- ating.'

Sinead stepped fully into the room, a half-smile playing across her lips. 'Med itating? You?'

'Oh aye. I'm very sensitive, me. I'm right into...' Dave waved a hand , searching for the correct terminology. '...all that shite.'

'You're full of surprises,' Sinead told him, slipping off her jacket. 'How's it all going?'

Dave gave up on trying to hold back his yawn and finally set it free. He rubbed his watery eyes on his sleeve, then nod d ed . 'Good , I think. They've got the fella they think d id it.'

The d oor opened again, much more forcefully this time. Logan stormed in, with Ben hurrying along behind him.

'He d id n't d o it,' Logan announced for the benefit of anyone within earshot.

'We d on't know that for sure,' Ben protested . 'It still mostly fits.'

The DCI wheeled around . 'Come off it, Ben. We both knew from the moment we clapped eyes on the bugger that it wasn't him. You saw the size of him. How d id he get up those stairs and out of the hatch at the top? Hmm?'

'Maybe he just, you know, squeezed through.'

'Squeezed through? Have you seen that staircase? What d id he d o, turn himself into a gas?' He spun around to face Sinead , ad d ressing her d irectly for the first time since she'd arrived . 'Where is he, then?'

'Hi, sir. Who, Riksen? He, eh, he d id n't come d own with me.'

'Why not?'

'He had someone meet him at the airport. Dirk Sommer- camp.'

'FBI,' ad d ed Ben, with suitable d ramatic emphasis.

'Aye, that's him, sir. You know him?'

'Spoke to him,' Ben said . 'Cheeky bastard wanted access to the case files, would you believe? Told him to sling his hook.'

Sinead rocked from one foot to the other. 'Uh, yeah. About that. Detective Superintend ent Mitchell came out to meet him with me. And , well, it turns out that Mr Riksen has been using some political influence—money, probably—to get Sommer-camp appointed as a special consultant on the case.'

Logan's 'WHAT?' was so loud that Dean Stevens almost jumped out of his skin in Interview Room Two. 'What d o you mean "special consultant"?' the DCI d emand ed .

Sinead took a shuffled step backward s. It wasn't that she expected Logan to lash out at her in any way, but jud ging by the colour of him there was every chance he might explod e, and she d id n't much fancy being in the blast rad ius.

'I think Mitchell's going to send you an email about it, sir,' she said , trying to make it very clear that she was in no way responsible for any of this. 'He's to be given access to all files, evid ence, statements, and supervised access to witnesses, in case he wants to question them further.'

'Well, they can fucking forget that!' Logan cried . *Special consultant*. What are they giving us next? A crime fighting blood y d og?' He clicked his fingers and turned to Dave David son. 'That remind s me. Any joy tracking d own Scooby-Doo?'

Sinead sid led up to Ben. 'I feel like I must've missed some-thing…' she said .

Ben gave a chuckle. 'I'll catch you up in a minute.'

'Narrowed it d own a bit, aye,' Dave said , clicking across to a spread sheet that Hamza had set up for him to fill in. It was neatly arranged , with d ifferent colours for each of the columns, but Dave would 've preferred to just scribble everything d own in his notepad and try to d ecipher it later.

'There are three camper van rental companies in Scot-land who let you hire out Mystery Machines. One's in the

Bord ers. One's just outsid e Ed inburgh. And the other one is in Aviemore, so that's probably our safest bet.'

'You contacted them yet?' Logan asked .

'Tried to. Left messages. They're all shut for the night.'

'We should be packing up soon, too, Jack,' Ben said . 'Come back fresh tomorrow and go over what we've got.'

The d oor opened for a third time before Logan could get out a reply. Hamza led the way into the Incid ent Room, with Tyler shuffling along behind . The DC's face lit up at the sight of Sinead , and he hurried over to hug her.

'Eh… hiya,' Sinead said , blushing at the overt show of affection.

Tyler squeezed her for several long second s, then released his grip and brushed his fingertips lightly across her cheek, pushing back a stray strand of hair.

'Hey,' he said . He realised everyone else was watching him, d ropped his hand , and smiled a little too broad ly. When h spoke, there was just a suggestion of a crack in his voice. 'Glad you could make it.'

'How'd you get on with your man?' Logan asked Hamza.

The DS had a look about him like the cat who'd got the cream. And , it turned out, for good reason.

'Alexis Riksen d id come and talk to him. Mond ay night, he reckons. She then went with him back to his flat.'

'For sex?' Ben asked .

'No, sir. For d rugs. One specific d rug, actually. He d id n't have any with him, hence him taking her back to his place.'

'And ?' Logan d emand ed . 'What was it?'

'Rohypnol, boss,' Tyler said . 'The roofies in the victim's system? She bought them herself.'

There was a momentary pause as they all gave this some thought.

'Why the hell would she buy them herself? That makes no sense,' Ben said , voicing what most of them were thinking.

'Rohypnol's a sleeping pill, isn't it?' said Sinead. 'That's what it's designed for, I mean. Maybe she just had trouble sleeping?'

Judging by his expression, Logan wasn't buying that, but he conceded that it might be a possibility. 'Someone get hold of Deirdrie Mair first thing in the morning. See if she's aware of Alexis taking anything to help her sleep.'

'I'll get on that first thing, boss,' Tyler said.

'Aye. Best coming from you.'

'How did things go with Corey Sanderson, sir?' asked Hamza.

Logan tutted and shook his head. 'Not great. He told us… well, a lot, and nothing. Solicitor stepped in to call a halt to it for the night, so we're keeping him in the cells overnight and are going to pick up where we left off in the morning.'

'You'll have company, sir,' Sinead reminded him. 'Dirk Sommercamp.'

'FBI,' Ben added again.

'Shite. Aye. Are they coming here tonight?'

'As far as I know, sir.'

Logan checked his watch. 'Right, well, it's getting late. You should all call it a day. I'll hang off here for them arriving.'

There were sighs of relief all round, not least of all from Dave, who hadn't quite woken up again after his head-on-desk snooze. Only Tyler seemed reluctant to shoot straight off.

'What's, eh… what's the sleeping situation, boss?' he asked.

'How do you mean?'

'Well, I mean…' Tyler tried to think of a better way to phrase the question, but failed to find one. 'Who's sleeping where tonight?'

'Just… basically as it was,' Logan said, then he caught the way Tyler's eyes flitted to Sinead, and realised he hadn't factored her into the equation. 'Oh. Aye. Well… who's where now?'

Tyler started to count on his fingers. 'Hoon was in one of the singles in the first cottage…'

'Second cottage,' Ben corrected.

'Sorry, boss?'

'Second cottage. The one I'm in is the first.'

'How d o you work that out?' Logan asked .

'It's the first one you come to as you head into the street,' Ben said .

'Well, aye, I suppose that's true, right enough,' Tyler ad mitted . 'I just thought that, trad itionally you'd go left to right. Ours is on the left, yours is on the right. One, two.'

'That's no' how I'd work it,' Ben said . 'First one you come to is one—mine. Next one is—'

Logan tutted . 'Let's call them Bathroom Cottage and Kitchen Cottage.'

'Which is which?' Ben asked .

Logan glowered at him. 'The one with the bathroom is…' he began, then he realised the DI was taking the piss.

'Right. So,' Tyler said , steering them back to the main crux of the d iscussion. 'Hoon's in one of the single bed s in Kitchen Cottage. Dave's in the d ouble. You were on the sofa bed in the living room, boss, and I was next d oor.'

'In the Bathroom Cottage,' Ben said . 'Sharing with Hamza.'

'Aye. That's right. So…' Tyler looked across the faces of the others. 'Who's going where?'

'You could bunk in with Hoon, Jack,' Ben suggested .

'Fuck off!' Logan objected . 'Why d on't you bunk in with Hoon?'

'Because I need to be near the bathroom. And he's a blood y head case.'

'I d on't mind where I go,' Sinead said .

'You're not going in with Hoon!' Tyler told her.

'Well… no. Id eally not,' Sinead agreed .

'And , sorry, call me old fashioned if you like, but we're no' having you two in a d ouble bed ,' Ben said , eyeballing Sinead and Tyler. 'Not on the job.'

Sinead nod d ed her agreement, even as Tyler tried unsuccessfully to mask his d isappointment. 'I agree, sir. Be unprofessional that.'

'Also, I've been sitting next to him in a wind owless room for the last half an hour,' Hamza said . 'He's pretty ripe.'

'I was nearly hit by a train!' Tyler protested .

Logan, who had been rubbing his temples for the past thirty second s, became sud d enly animated by agitation. 'How is this blood y d ifficult?' he asked . 'How many of us are there? Six?'

'Seven,' Ben said . 'Hoon.'

'Right. Seven. And we've got… what? Seven bed s? So, where's the problem?'

'It's a bit like that thing with the chicken and the fox and the grain,' Ben explained . 'We know what we're d ealing with, and what need s to happen, but it's the getting there that's the tricky bit, isn't it?'

He sat d own.

'Why are you sitting d own?' Logan d emand ed .

'I just thought it might take us a few minutes to work it all out.'

'It won't! We're blood y d etectives. On your feet.'

Ben stood up again.

'You could swap with Tyler, sir,' Hamza suggested to Logan. 'Share with me, Sinead could then have the sofa bed in the first cottage.'

'Second cottage,' Ben corrected .

'Kitchen cottage,' Dave further corrected .

'Right, aye. That one,' Hamza said .

Logan gave a reluctant shake of his head . 'No. Best if I'm in the same house as Hoon. I want to be able to keep an eye on him.'

'Anyway, where would I go in that scenario?' Tyler asked .

Hamza stared blankly at him, like he had n't consid ered that bit. 'In with Hoon.'

'No chance! You go in with the mad bastard ! Me and Sinead will take the room you're in.'

'There'll be no blood y hanky panky!' Ben warned them.

'I'm not going in with Hoon!' Hamza said . 'He's probably sleep-racist.'

'Hold on, hold on,' Logan said , raising his hand s for quiet. 'Why's that bastard getting a proper bed , anyway?'

There was some general consensus that this was unfair.

'He can have the sofa bed ,' Logan announced . 'Hamza, me and you can share the twin room in the Kitchen Cottage. Tyler and Sinead can share the other twin room in the Bathroom Cottage, and Ben and Dave stay where they are.'

The next few moments passed in silence as everyone went over the plan, hunting for a flaw in it. To Logan's immense relief, they d id n't find one.

'Aye. I think that actually works, boss.'

'Well d one, Jack,' Ben said , giving the DCI a congratulatory pat on the back.

It was then that they noticed the d oor was open behind them. Two men stood there—one sporting a white linen suit and oversized Stetson, and the other almost entirely unremark-able asid e from an impressively full moustache.

Christ. How long had they been stand ing there?

'I'm Bartholomew Riksen,' the man in the hat said , his voice a sard onic Texas d rawl. He looked the group up and d own, his lips d rawing back into the beginnings of a sneer. 'And I must say how reassuring it is to see that my d aughter's murd er investigation is in such capable hand s.'

Chapter 33

With Logan staying at the station to talk to Riksen and Sommercamp, it was left to DI Forde to break the news to Hoon that he was going to be shifting beds. Ben was less than overjoyed about this, but accepted the responsibility with a heavy heart.

The others waited out front while Ben ventured into the Kitchen Cottage. The three detectives stood huddled together behind Dave's chair while they waited for the fireworks to begin.

It wasn't that Hoon would particularly care about what bed he was in, they knew. It was just that he didn't like to be told what to do in general. While he might well have no issue whatsoever with shifting to the sofa bed, he almost certainly would take objection to anyone suggesting it to him.

That was why Ben had entered the cottage so cautiously a moment ago, and why Tyler, Hamza, and Sinead were essentially using Dave as a human shield.

'Maybe one of us should 've gone in with him,' Sinead said.

'Be my guest,' Hamza said.

Sinead made no move to enter. Nor, for that matter, did anyone else.

The blanket of night had been drawn fully over the sky now, but the glow from the street light across from the cottages bathed them in a pool of weak orange light.

There had been no lights on in either house when they'd arrived. Since entering the Kitchen Cottage, Ben had turned on almost all of them, making his way from room to room.

Dave hummed quietly below his breath as they waited . A light breeze was d rifting along the cul-d e-sac, bringing a slight chill to the air. On the upsid e, it was keeping the mid ges away, so they were grateful for it.

'You think Hoon's killed him?' Tyler asked , after a protracted period of silence from within the house.

None of them believed that. Not really. But the fact that nobod y laughed the notion off spoke volumes about their opinion of their former boss, and there was a palpable sense of relief when DI Ford e appeared in the hallway again.

'You all right, boss?' Tyler asked , once Ben had emerged from within the cottage. He was hold ing a piece of A4 paper in one hand that looked like it had been ripped out of a notebook.

'Hmm? Oh, aye. Fine. Fine,' Ben said . 'It's Hoon. He left a note. He's… gone.'

'Shit. What?' said Tyler.

'Like… gone gone?' Hamza asked .

'God . I should 've stayed with him!' Tyler groaned . 'But I had to take Dean Stevens in for questioning. How was I to know he'd … God .' His eyes went to the cottage d oor. 'Is he… is he in there?'

'What? No. What are you…?' Ben frowned at them, then d own at the note in his hand . The penny d ropped . 'No, he's gone back to Inverness. Back home. He's no' killed himself.'

Dave let out a long, loud sigh of relief. 'Oh, thank God for that!' he said . 'You had me worried there.'

Ben peered over his glasses at him, eyebrows rising in surprise. 'I d id n't know you were such a fan of his.'

'Oh, no. Could n't really give a shit,' Dave replied , wheeling himself forward . 'Just knew if he'd topped himself in there none of us would be getting to bed for hours yet, and I'm blood y knackered .'

'What d oes it say, boss?' Tyler asked .

'It was actually ad d ressed to Jack,' Ben said . 'But curiosity got the better of me. It just says: "Jack. How's that for making a fucking d ifference? Suck ma banger, ya tubby-titted muff-huffer. I'm going to fuck off home. Hoon out".'

'He's got such a way with word s,' Sinead remarked , shaking her head in d isapproval.

'And then, at the bottom, it says, "PS. You were right about the prick with the hair gel".'

'Who's the—' Tyler began, then he touched himself on the head . 'Wait. Me? Am I the prick with the hair gel?'

Sinead tried very hard not to laugh, and came within spitting d istance of succeed ing.

'Not necessarily,' Hamza said . 'I'm sure there are other pricks using hair gel out there. Maybe he was talking about one of them.'

'What was the boss saying about me to him?' Tyler wond ered , having now accepted that he was the hair gel prick the note referred to.

'Damned if I know, son,' Ben said , fold ing the note in half. 'Best ask him yourself. For now, I'm head ing insid e and head ing to bed . And remember, you two—' He pointed with the corner of the note, first at Sinead and then at Tyler. 'No blood y shenanigans!'

They both vowed that the cottages would remain a shenanigans-free zone, then said their good nights to Dave and Hamza.

There was no ramp at the front of the cottages, and Tyler and Sinead spent an enjoyable few second s listening to the PC and the DC bickering as Hamza tried to heave Dave's chair up the steps and into the house.

Once everyone else was insid e and out of the way, Sinead turned and planted a kiss firmly on Tyler's lips. They stood there, pressed together in the pool of light, savouring their private reunion.

A full minute or more later, Sinead started to pull away, but Tyler put his arms around her and pulled her in more firmly, like he was hold ing her in a bear hug.

She laughed at first, but then she felt him shake. It started slowly—a subtle shuddering of his shoulders, a trembling of the hands on her back—but in moments, his whole body was heaving, his breath choking him on its way in and out.

'Hey. Hey, what is it? What's wrong?' she asked, tightening her own grip on him.

He tried to speak, but his voice betrayed him, and all that emerged was a strangled croak, sandwiched between two big sobs.

'Shh. Shh, it's all right,' Sinead soothed, rubbing his back.

'I thought... I thought I was going to die,' he whispered, his head buried in against her neck. 'The train. I thought... I thought it was going to hit me. I was *sure* it was going to hit me, and that would be it. And I was never going to see you again.'

'It did n't. You're all right,' Sinead said. 'I'm right here.'

He tightened his grip on her further, then let her go and stepped back, looking away to hide his tears and his shame.

'Sorry. I'm being stupid.'

Sinead reached for his hands. He tried to keep them to himself at first, then relented and let her take them.

'You're not being stupid. You're not. Anyone would be upset. You were nearly hit by a train.'

'Aye, but I wasn't,' Tyler pointed out. 'I'm fine.'

'You're not fine. You should n't be fine. Just because it did n't hit you, d oesn't mean it did n't affect you,' Sinead told him. 'It must've been terrifying.'

'I was fine. I was hold ing it together.' Tyler's face crumpled. 'And then, I saw you, and ... I remembered. I realised.' He hugged her again. 'God, Sinead, I thought I'd lost you.'

'Well, you did n't. I'm here. I'm right here,' she assured him. 'I'm not going anywhere, and neither are you.'

Tyler stepped back. This time, it was he who interlocked their fingers. He who squeezed her hands. He who sniffed back his tears and locked his eyes on hers, his face a marble carving of absolute sincerity.

Sinead 's stomach flipped .
Oh God.
Oh God .
He wasn't.
'Sinead … will you marry me?'
Oh God.
He was.

Chapter 34

Logan had nothing against rich people in particular. Sure, he d id n't trust them as far as he could throw them, and he'd id eall never spend any time whatsoever in their company, but then he could say that about most folk.

He was never particularly comfortable around grieving parents. Given all the practice he'd had at it, you'd have thought he'd be a d ab hand by this point in his career, but he'd never quite found a way to d eal with it. He'd never been able to d o what so many other senior officers had learned to d o, and treat it like just any other part of the job.

He consoled himself with that thought, sometimes. Used it to remind himself that he wasn't yet too far gone.

His worry about being stuck in a room with a grieving billionaire was unfound ed , though. There were no tears being shed for Alexis Riksen by her father. Hurt had been switched out for efficiency. Where pain should have been there was merely an impatience to get all this over with so he could return to the more important business of... well, his business.

Riksen had d emand ed to be brought up-to-d ate there and then. He wanted full d etails of how the case was progressing, copies of statements, a list of material evid ence collected (with photographs), and the contact d etails for everyone who had mad e any sort of statement regard ing the case thus far.

'No,' Logan had said .

That was it. No apology. No explanation. No attempt to appease. Just 'no.' Plain and simple.

But clearly not simple enough.

'Excuse me?' Riksen replied , practically snorting the word s out through his flared nostrils. 'What d id you say?'

'I said , "no", Mr Riksen,' Logan replied . 'I'm afraid I can't hand over that sort of information. Truth be told , you're not even supposed to be in here.'

'Oh, I think you'll find I can go pretty much anywhere I want,' Riksen said . 'We have clearance.'

Logan gestured to his screen. He'd mad e both men stand by his d esk waiting while he'd checked his email. Sure enough, to his d ismay and utter d isbelief, the ord er was lying in wait there in his inbox, like a d og turd lurking in a pile of leaves.

'No, Mr Sommercamp has clearance. Somehow,' Logan said . 'You d on't.'

'The hell I d on't,' Riksen hissed . It was his first d isplay of emotion since arriving—beyond 'utter contempt,' anyway— and it reassured Logan that there might be a human being buried und er the bronze skin and muscles, after all. 'I'm Bartholomew Riksen, son. I can go wherever I please.'

'Maybe in Texas, Mr Riksen,' Logan said . 'But here, we d o things d ifferently.'

With his hooked nose and bead y, glaring eyes, Riksen resembled some sort of bird . Not the majestic eagle he'd prob- ably hope to be compared to, but some sort of buzzard . Or a vulture, maybe, circling the carrion below, waiting to swoop d own and tuck in.

Either way, it wasn't a good look.

'Does staring at folk like that usually work, Mr Riksen?' Logan asked , unmoved by the power play. 'Because it'll get you halfway to nowhere with me.'

'You will give me access, or I will have you fired , son,' the billionaire said .

Logan yawned , jabbed the button on the front of his monitor to turn it off, then stood up. 'Is that a promise?' he asked .

'I mean it. I will see to it that you never work in law enforcement again!'

'Aw, that's music to my ears, Mr Riksen,' Logan said , reaching for his coat. 'Do you mind if I hold you to that?'

'Is this some sort of *joke* to you?'

'No. Not remotely,' Logan said . 'I'm very sorry for your loss, Mr Riksen. I'm also sorry that your... security guard here is being allowed access to a live case, and I'll be strenuously voicing my objections to those responsible for that d ecision.'

He finished pulling on his coat and ad justed the collar, using his reflection in the wind ow to check everything was straight.

'But let me assure you, I'm taking your d aughter's d eath very seriously. We're build ing a strong case, and I'm confid ent we can get everything wrapped up in the next forty-eight hours. I am not your enemy here, Mr Riksen.'

Dirk Sommercamp interjected before his employer could respond . 'And nor are we yours, Detective Chief Inspector,' he said . 'We're all pulling toward s the same goal here. Mr Riksen and I believe I have experience and expertise that will prove invaluable to the investigation, and your superiors agree. I'm here to help, not to get in your way. You have my word on that.'

Logan regard ed the ex-FBI agent in silence for a few second s, getting the measure of him. He was shorter and less packed than his boss, but he had an air of quiet authority that Logan would almost have found impressive, had it not been for that blood y rid iculous moustache, which took the ed ge right off it.

'Well, unfortunately, there d oesn't seem to be anything I can d o about your involvement, Mr Sommercamp.'

'Call me Dirk, please.'

'*Dirk*,' Logan said , trying the name out.

He d id n't think he'd ever had cause to say the word out loud before, other than to refer to the short-blad ed d agger that bams had occasionally tried to chib him with over the years.

'Fine. No offence, *Dirk*, but I find your presence here a total fucking imposition, and while I'm sure you're a lovely fella and very good at your job, I think it's fund amentally wrong for you to be given access to a single scrap of information regard ing Alexis's murd er.'

'But you d on't have a choice,' Sommercamp remind ed him.

'But I d on't have a choice,' Logan sighed . 'So, since that's the case, meet me here at eight-thirty tomorrow morning, and we'll go over everything together. I'm afraid you, Mr Riksen, will not be allowed in. If you insist on coming to the station, we can find a room for you to wait in, but I suspect it'll be less comfortable than you're used to.'

'I'd prefer to take away the case notes now,' Sommercamp said . 'I'd like to get started this evening.'

'I'm sure you would , Dirk,' Logan said . He gestured to his d arkened monitor. 'But would you look at that? My computer's all switched off.' He marched past the men, and over to the Big Board . 'There is something you might be able to help me with now, though.'

'And what might that be?' Riksen asked .

Logan yanked on one of the pictures, tearing a notch out of the top where the pin had been. He held it up, showing both men a slightly out of focus head shot of the missing Hayd en Howard .

'Either of you recognise this man?' he asked .

'No,' Riksen said , without a moment's hesitation.

'You sure? You d on't want to take a minute to look at him first?' Logan asked .

'No need . I've never seen him before in my life.'

Sommercamp took the photograph and gave it some consid - eration while Logan continued to press Riksen.

'How can you be so sure? You must see a lot of people.'

'I d o. And I remember all of them,' Riksen said . 'Him, I d on't remember, therefore I've never met him. This should n't be d ifficult to grasp, son. It's not a hard concept.'

Logan bit his lip, and turned his attention to Sommercamp. 'You? Any id eas?'

Dirk shook his head and passed the photograph back. 'Can't say I recognise him, no. Why d o you ask?'

Logan turned and pinned the photograph to the board . 'I'll explain tomorrow morning.' He smiled thinly, and gestured for both men to lead the way to the d oor. 'Eight-thirty.'

Sommercamp looked to Riksen. It was the same look that Corey Sand erson had given his solicitor back in the interview room. The seeking of permission.

'Very good . Eight-thirty,' Sommercamp said , once Riksen had given the go-ahead with a single blink. 'I'll look forward to it.'

'Aye, well,' said Logan, flicking off the lights as he followed the other men out into the corrid or. 'That'll make one of us.'

-

Sinead lay in the small single bed , eyes pointed to the ceiling, listening to the sound of Tyler not sleeping in the bed on the opposite sid e of the room.

The streets were empty now, the traffic crossing the brid ge over the river red uced to the occasional late-night lorry d river, or prowling polis patrol car. Outsid e, the river itself babbled quietly, still going about its business, but d oing its best not to d isturb anyone.

Tyler was curled up with his back to her, facing the wall. The room was large. Even if they'd both reached their hand s out, there would still have been a gulf between them.

'I just... I d on't think you're in the right frame of mind ,' she said .

Again.

'Yeah. Yeah, you're probably right,' he replied .

Again.

He wasn't angry, she knew. Disappointed , yes. Mortified ? Almost certainly. He'd laughed it all off, pinned his smile in place and nod d ed as she'd given her reasoning. He had n't been listening, though. Not really. Not all the way.

She rolled onto her sid e, supporting her head on one arm. 'I mean, I'm not saying... it's not that I d on't...' She sighed , annoyed at her inability to find the right word s. 'I just d on't want you regretting it in the cold light of d ay. And I d on't want to d oubt your motives, you know? Like, if I'd said yes, would I always be thinking you only asked because of your... you know... heightened emotional state? Would I always be worried you regretted it?'

'Aye. No. It make sense, right enough,' Tyler said . 'You're right. It was stupid .'

'I'm not saying that.'

'You d on't have to,' Tyler replied . 'It was.'

They lay there in silence, the space between them wid er than it had ever been.

'Well, good night,' he said .

Sinead lowered her head onto her pillow.

'Yeah. Night,' she said . 'Let's talk tomorrow, OK?'

The only answer was a soft snore from the other bed .

Sinead rolled onto her back, fixed her eyes on the ceiling, and listened to the sound of Tyler pretend ing to be asleep.

Chapter 35

Dirk Sommercamp was d ue to arrive at the station at eight-thirty, Logan explained , hence him d ragging the team out of their bed s and into the Incid ent Room for seven.

'I want us to go over everything before that Yank bastard shows up,' Logan told them, hurrying Hamza and Dave out the d oor at half-six.

He'd alread y gone knocking on the Bathroom Cottage d oor, rousing Ben, Tyler, and Sinead , and bellowing through the letterbox for them to get a blood y move on.

Sommercamp was stand ing outsid e the d oor of the Incid ent Room when they all stumbled , half-asleep, around the corner. He stood with his hand s behind his back, like a sold ier at ease, his shirt, blazer, and matching cream slacks all neatly pressed , and every strand of his moustache carefully arranged for maximum bushiness.

'Ah, good . You're early,' Sommercamp remarked . 'I hoped you might be.'

'I said half-eight,' Logan remind ed him.

'You d id . Yet, here we all are,' Sommercamp replied . He placed the flat of a hand on the Incid ent Room d oor and held it open. 'After you, gentlemen. Ma'am.'

Logan hung back, letting the rest of the team go through before him. Once they were all insid e, he motioned for Sommercamp to follow. 'After you.'

'No, please. After you.'

'I insist,' Logan said .

Sommercamp almost continued the back-and -forth, then relented with a nod and stepped into the Incid ent Room. Logan took a moment to savour the resentment bubbling away in his gut, then followed the former FBI agent into the room, and tossed his coat onto the closest available chair.

'Right. Kettle on,' he announced , rubbing his hand s together. 'Tyler. Teas and coffees, if you please.'

Tyler nod d ed . 'Sure, boss,' he said , flatly.

'Want me to come help?' Sinead asked .

He shook his head , just once. 'I'm fine, thanks,' he told her, turning to the others. 'Who's on tea, and who's on coffee?'

'I'll take a soy latte,' Sommercamp said , before any of the others could place their ord ers.

Ben snorted . 'Aye, no' here you won't, son. Your coffee choices are Nescafe with milk, or Nescafe without milk. And there's no saying how long the milk's been knocking about for.'

'Black, then. Thank you.'

Tyler took all the other requests—there were more coffees than teas tod ay, although given the time of d ay it was, this was no great surprise—then left the room without another word .

'Everything OK?' Ben asked , noticing the way Sinead watched him go.

'Oh. Yeah. Fine, sir,' she replied . She pointed to an empty d esk. 'OK if I sit here?'

'Aye, that's grand ,' Ben told her.

After placing his ord er, Dirk Sommercamp had strolled over to the Big Board . He bent forward at the waist, stud ying every photograph and Post-It Note. Across the room, Dave rolled his chair over to Hamza's d esk, and ind icated the newcomer with some not-so-subtle pointing.

'Who's this fanny?' he whispered .

'That's right. Most of us d id n't get properly introd uced ,' Sommercamp said , turning his back on the board . He smiled below his 'tache and threw a thumb back over his should er. 'Cute, by the way. Very retro.'

He cleared his throat, giving everyone the opportunity to settle d own, listen up, and prepare themselves for whatever pearls of wisd om he planned spilling from his mouth.

Logan d id n't give him the chance.

'This is Dirk Sommercamp. And yes, before you ask, Dirk's his actual name,' he said . 'He's a glorified security guard for Bartholomew Riksen, the victim's father, who has presumably paid someone somewhere a lot of money so that Dirk here can temporarily take his nose out of the crack of Mr Riksen's arse, and start poking it around in our case. I'd say that's about the size of it, Dirk, would n't you?'

Sommercamp crossed his hand s in front of himself, as if about to lead the room in a minute's silence. 'Well, I d on't much care for the tone, and some of the terminology, but the broad strokes of that are correct,' he confirmed . 'I am not here to get in anyone's way. I bring a wealth of FBI experience. I knew Alexis personally. Through Mr Riksen, I have access to near unlimited resources. We've alread y had the toxin report fast-tracked through your systems. I believe that Alexis had been d rugged the night she d ied ?'

'That was you?' Logan asked . 'You got the toxicology report sped through?'

'Yes, Detective Chief Inspector, that was me,' Sommercamp said . 'We are all pushing toward s the same goal here. We're all on the same team. We all want justice for Alexis. Work with me, and this will be the smoothest, easiest case any of you have ever been involved in.'

The smile that had been tickling the bottom of his mous-tache fell away as if at the touch of a button. 'Work against me—against Mr Riksen—and it will be the last case that any of you are ever involved in.'

'Now, wait a blood y minute—' Ben began.

Sommercamp raised his hand s in a surrend er pose. 'That is not a threat. I d o not make threats. But I know Mr Riksen and , for better or worse, I know how passionate he is about us all working together on this. Resist, and there will be consequences. For all of us.' He looked across their faces and stopped on Logan's, apparently unperturbed by the rage written there. 'Is that clear?'

Logan took several slow, ponderous steps closer. He had a good eight or nine inches height advantage on the other man, and used it to its full effect.

'You know something, Dirk?' he growled. 'I've a good mind to pick you up and throw you out the bloody window.'

'I wouldn't recommend it,' Sommercamp replied. 'I've trained in six different methods of unarmed combat, studying under teachers from all over the world.'

'Nice!' said Dave, suddenly interested. 'What ones?'

'Krav Maga, Shotokan Karate, Shaolin Kung Fu—'

'All right, all right,' Logan grunted, cutting the list short. 'We're all very impressed. But I don't care if you're Bruce bloody Lee, pal, you don't come in here and threaten my team.'

'As I told you, Detective Chief Inspector, and had you been listening you'd have heard —I make no threats. I just report the facts,' Sommercamp replied. 'And the big takeaway fact on this occasion is that my employer, Mr Riksen, will stop at nothing to get justice for his daughter's murder. Anyone who is an obstruction to that—you, me, anyone—will be dealt with. Hence why it is in all our best interests to collaborate and co-operate.'

The door opened and Tyler returned, balancing seven mismatched mugs on a small tray. He stopped when he saw Logan and Sommercamp almost nose to nose by the Big Board, and everyone else staring at them in silence.

'Um… teas and coffees are here,' he announced.

The sentence hung there for several seconds, suspended in the uneasy silence.

'Good,' Logan said, after an uncomfortably long period of time. 'Then we'd better get started.'

As well as his various black belts, Sommercamp could also ad d 'speed -read ing' to his list of skills—a list which Logan had previously assumed was limited to his ability to grow unflattering facial hair.

He had accepted his coffee from Tyler, taken a single sip, then returned it to the tray with a 'no' and a curt shake of his head .

He'd then burned through the reports in less than ten minutes, his eyes moving d own the page, but not apparently left or right.

'The trick is to use your peripheral vision,' he'd explained , catching the others watching him as he turned his third page in less than forty second s. 'Start five word s from the beginning of a line, stop five word s from the end . Repeat.'

Ben had given it a bash with the notes he'd mad e the d ay before, but as he had to squint to see the spid ery hand writing, and could barely make out a word of what it said , he fell some way short of mastering the technique.

Once he'd finished read ing, he stood by and listened whil Logan went over those events of the previous d ay that had not yet been typed up.

'Right. So. First things first. How d id you two get on with Dean Stevens?' he asked , d irecting the question at Tyler and Hamza, who sat sid e by sid e behind their ad joining d esks.

'Just like we said last night, sir,' Hamza replied . 'He insists Alexis bought the roofies off him herself.'

'Roofies?' Sommercamp interjected .

'Rohypnol,' Logan explained .

'Why would she buy it herself?'

'You tell us, Dirk. You're the blood y expert on her, so you say.'

Sinead tried to cut through the tension. 'I wond ered if maybe she had any issues with sleeping?'

'Not that I'm aware of,' Sommercamp said . His phone had appeared in his hand from nowhere, and his thumbs tapped away at the on-screen keyboard as he spoke. 'I'll check.'

'Right, well, if you d on't mind …?' Logan scowled . 'I'd like to continue and —'

Sommercamp glanced d own at his phone screen. 'She suffered from occasional insomnia. Infrequent, but she'd taken med ication before, back in the US,' he said , returning the phone to the insid e pocket of his blazer. 'Apologies, DCI Logan.' He turned his gaze on Hamza. 'Continue.'

'Here, I'm the one who tells him to continue,' Logan objected .

Sommercamp crossed his arms. 'Sorry. I d id n't realise it was so important to you. Please, go ahead .'

Logan felt backed into a corner now. He almost d id n't want to tell Hamza to continue, simply out of spite.

'Carry on, Hamza,' he urged , d eliberately avoid ing using the same word as the ex-FBI man had . It was petty, of course, but Sommercamp's patronising smugness brought it out in him.

'Eh… right. I mean, there's not a lot else to say, sir,' Hamza replied . 'She bought three roofies off him, paid him sixty quid —'

'Sixty quid ? That's steep, isn't it?' said Sinead .

'He reckoned she had more money than sense,' Hamza said , then he shot Sommercamp an uncomfortable look. 'His word s, not mine. He said she seemed to know exactly what she was after, but kept asking him questions about how much to use to put someone und er for a few hours.'

Dave frowned . 'Doesn't sound to me like she planned using them on herself,' he said . 'I mean, d on't take my word for it, obviously, I just put stuff in bags, but sound s to me like she was planning on d rugging someone else.'

'Funny you should say that.' Logan picked up the photograph he'd pulled d own from the Big Board the night before, and held it up for the others to see. 'Hayd en Howard . Travelling with

Alexis's group. As most of you know, he's d one a runner, and we've had no sign of him since yesterd ay.'

'He's a witness, yes?' Sommercamp asked . 'Then how was he allowed to just leave? Weren't you watching him?'

'We were, but he snuck away,' Logan said . 'We haven't got eyes in the backs of our head s.'

'But you d o have them in front, yes?' Sommercamp asked . 'So, maybe have people watching in that d irection.'

'We were. He *was* being watched "in that d irection", Dirk, but one of our colleagues was in d anger, and he used that as an opportunity to leg it.'

'No offence to your colleague,' Sommercamp retorted , 'but I'd wager that this is the most significant murd er case of any of your careers. Alexis is the most important victim you'll ever d eal with. You can't afford to be making slip-ups.'

Logan glowered at him, hatred practically humming through the air between them.

'They're all important,' he said . 'Every last blood y one of them.'

'Oh. Sure. Yeah. I und erstand . Absolutely,' Sommercamp said , in a way that was clearly meant to humour the d etective. *We both know better*, the word s secretly said *We both know I'm right.*

Logan rose above it.

This time.

'My point is, before his solicitor called a halt to everything last night, Corey Sand erson had suggested that Alexis was scared of this man. Of Hayd en Howard . She believed he was working for her father. Keeping an eye on her for him. Reporting back.'

He angled the photograph in Sommercamp's d irection. 'You sure you d on't recognise this man, Dirk?'

Sommercamp scrutinised the image, one hand slid ing into his jacket pocket. 'No. I d on't know him. Hold it stead y, please.'

He snapped a photo on his phone's camera, cropped out the background image, then sent it off into the electronic ether.

'Time difference could hold up processing,' he said. 'But we'll know within the next ninety minutes if he's on Mr Riksen's payroll.'

'Right. Well...' Logan began, looking for a reason to be annoyed by this. Disappointingly, he couldn't find one. 'Good. Hamza, Tyler, I want you focusing on finding his whereabouts. Does he have a phone with him? Has he made any calls? Can the network help narrow down the search? The usual.'

'Isn't that a waste of resources?' Sommercamp asked. 'We have Corey Sanderson in custody, correct? Going by the reports, he's almost certainly the killer. I count at least two motives. We have him on camera buying the oil that was poured over Alexis, and he was caught with her bag, passport, and other personal items.'

'He denies any involvement in her death.'

'Oh, *does he*? Sorry, I did n't realise. Oh, then I guess he *must* be innocent. My mistake.' Sommercamp uncrossed his arms, his movements becoming more agitated. 'See, the thing is, where I'm from—the cases I work—criminals have been known to lie. I know, right? Selfish assholes. Makes our job that much more difficult, but what are you going to do?'

'There are other factors that make us question Corey's guilt,' Ben said.

Sommercamp picked up the report again and leafed through it. 'Where? I don't see any. What makes you think he did n't do it?'

'Well, he's a big fat lad, for one,' Ben said.

The look Sommercamp gave him could 've peeled paint. 'Fat people can't commit murder?'

'I'm sure they can, but they can't fit through an eighteen-inch wide hatch,' Logan countered.

'Eighteen inches? I don't think so. More like two feet,' Sommercamp argued. 'You have officers there? Have one take measurements. Even if it is eighteen inches, you'd be surprised by the lengths a killer will go to in order to carry out their task, Detective Chief Inspector.'

'Oh, believe me, I would n't,' Logan told him. 'Hayd en Howard told us that Alexis had no interest in Corey. He's the one that said they went away somewhere just before she d ied , and that Corey seemed angry and withd rawn afterward s.'

'Right. She shot him d own,' Sommercamp said .

'But how can we trust a word Hayd en says if he ups and pisses off on us the first chance he gets?'

'Deird rie Mair confirmed nothing was going on between Alexis and Sand erson. Correct?' Sommercamp said , ind icating the report on the d esk besid e him.

'No. She had no knowled ge of anything going on between them. That's no' the same thing.'

'Can I give you some ad vice, Detective Chief Inspector?' the former FBI man asked .

'Can I stop you?'

'The correct solution is often the simplest. Sure, we'd like to think it wasn't. Make it more of a challenge, like in the movies. Shock killer. Big twist, that in hind sight we should 've all seen coming. But the reality is, it isn't like that. Our first instinct? It's usually correct.'

Logan wasn't going to argue on that. He'd hated this arsehole on sight, and it appeared that instinct had been bang on the money.

'Corey Sand erson had motive. He's a spurned suitor. He's an environmentalist who somehow found out the object of his d esires was the d aughter of a man he could , in his warped mind , conceivably see as some arch-nemesis,' Sommercamp continued .

He was speaking slowly, d ishing out the eye contact to everyone in the room, making sure they were following along.

Dave was heavily invested in picking his nose when Dirk looked his way, and froze like a rabbit in head lights until the gaze swept on past him again.

'He marked her up as a "planet rapist". He poured oil over her. This was as much an attack on Mr Riksen's company as it was on Mr Riksen's baby girl.'

He d id another sweep of the room. Having guessed this might happen, Dave now sat with his arms fold ed , his head nod d ing, and his nostrils untroubled by wand ering d igits.

'Just based on motive alone, he should be our number one suspect. Throw in the fact that we have him buying the oil, going on the run, and taking her personal belongings. Well, I'd say that's all we need . Hell, one of his bad ges was even found at the d amn scene!'

Logan blinked . Hesitated . It wasn't much, but it went on long enough for Ben to step in.

'So, why d id Hayd en Howard pull a d isappearing act?' the DI asked .

'Why d o young men d o anything?' Sommercamp asked . 'Generally, because of some primal d esire. Lust. Rage. Or, in this case, fear.'

He picked up the report and passed it across to Ben. Ben accepted it with an unstead y hand and a look of mild confusion.

'Top of page nine,' Sommercamp said . 'Statement from Detective Constable Neish. He caught the young man smoking a cannabis joint. Illegal in this country, and in Hayd en's native New Zealand . The guy was likely terrified .'

He stood up, walked past Logan, and jabbed a finger into the photograph of Corey Sand erson's forehead . 'This is the killer. Right here. I'd stake my career on it.'

Sommercamp wheeled around on his heels until he was facing Logan.

'So, are we going to go get ourselves a confession, or are we going to stand around here all d ay with our fingers up our asses?' He glanced at Dave. There was a thump as the PC hurried ly clasped his hand s on the d esk in front of him. 'Or noses, in his case.'

Logan and Sommercamp had barely taken their seats in the interview room when the DCI stood up again.

'Actually, I'd better run to the toilet first. This could take a while.'

Sommercamp clicked his tongue against the back of his teeth in irritation, checked his watch, then nod d ed . The seats across from him were currently empty, but Logan had assured him that Corey and his solicitor were on the way.

'Very well. But I'd like to get this cleared away before noon. Mr Riksen has a lot to attend to back home, and he'd like to fly out later tod ay.'

'Christ. His d aughter's been murd ered . Can he no' take a few d ays off?'

'No, Detective Chief Inspector, unfortunately, he cannot. Mr Riksen's company employs over six hund red thousand people around the globe. His sharehold ers require constant personal attention. The oil ind ustry is a precarious one, and his business is a d elicately balanced machine. It's a testament to his strength of feeling on this matter that he was able to attend at all.'

His strength of feeling *on this matter.*

Jesus Christ.

'You're very loyal to Mr Riksen, Dirk. Been with him long?'

'Long enough,' Sommercamp replied . 'Everyone in Mr Riksen's close circle of high-level employees is equally as invested in the success of the company. Now, if you could hurry along the bathroom break? I'm keen to get started .'

Logan patted the seated man on the should er as he passed . 'Aye. No bother. I'll only be a couple of minutes.'

From the interview room, Logan hung a right, then entered the next d oor along. Ben and Hamza sat there in the d ark, watching Sommercamp through the one-way mirror.

'That's you told , Jack,' Ben said .

'Knew I'd find you in here, you nosy old bastard .'

'That's my blood y seat he's in,' Ben pointed out. 'If I can't be co-pilot, I'm at least being a backseat d river.'

'That why you brought Hamza in? To moan at how you'd d o it better?' Logan asked .

'Too blood y true,' Ben said . 'If a genius d etective inspector has been brilliant in an empty room, and there's no one around to hear it, has he even been brilliant at all?'

'Plus, he wanted me to write stuff d own, sir,' Hamza ad d ed .

'Aye, and that. Murd er trying to see anything in this blood y light,' Ben said . 'My eyes aren't what they used to be.'

'None of you's what it used to be,' Logan pointed out.

'Thanks a bunch! Did you just pop through here to slag me off, or was there another reason for your visit?'

'I'm not interviewing Corey Sand erson,' Logan said .

Ben and Hamza swapped looks of confusion. 'Why not?'

'No, I mean, he'll be in the room. I'll be asking him questions.'

'Right… so… you *are* interviewing him, then?' Ben pressed .

'No. It'll look and sound like I am, but I'm not. I'm interviewing that bastard ,' Logan said , pointing through the glass to where Sommercamp sat staring d ead ahead , like some sort of robot.

'Dirk Sommercamp, ex-FBI?'

'Aye.'

'Why are you interviewing him?'

'Because nowhere in the report d oes it connect the bad ge found at the scene with Corey Sand erson, and yet he d id . He knew. And , given that he's never supposed to have been there, how d id he know—'

'The size of the hatch at the monument?' Hamza said . 'Aye, I noticed that, too.'

'We alread y know he's got connections, though,' Ben reasoned . 'He could 've found all this out relatively easily. Are you sure you're not grasping at straws because you d on't like him?'

'What makes you think I d on't like him?' Logan asked .

Ben mad e a vague up and d own gesture, ind icating the entirety of Logan's bod y. 'The way you talk to him. The word s you say. The way you look at him. Your face. Your bod y language—'

'All right, all right. Aye. Fine. I d on't like him. He's an arse-hole. But let's face it, Benjamin, I'm surround ed by arseholes on a d aily basis. I d on't think they're all murd erers.' Logan turned to Hamza. 'Get the rest of them d igging. I want to know if the Scooby gang can tell us anything about the car that was d riving behind them around the time the victim d ied . Sinead said Sommercamp picked Riksen up at the airport. Where was he before that? I want his movements. Hayd en Howard 's, too. He d id n't vanish into thin air. Get his phone record s.'

'You think Corey was telling the truth last night?'

'Truth?' Hamza asked . 'About what?'

'You'll see soon enough,' Logan said , about-turning and head ing for the exit just as the d oor to the interview room was opened on the other sid e of the glass, and a Uniform led Moof and his solicitor insid e. 'Get on all that, and anything else you can think of. I want to know who this bastard really is, where he's been, and what he's been d oing. Anything flags up, you come get me, all right?'

'Right, sir,' Hamza said .

'Well, hurry up then,' Logan barked , ushering him out the d oor. 'He wants this wrapped up by lunchtime. Let's make him careful what he blood y wishes for in future.'

266

The introd uctions were mad e. Melissa Brid ge, Corey's solicitor, voiced her objections to Sommercamp's presence, but while Logan offered his full sympathies and total agreement, it was his sad d uty to inform her that there was hee-haw either of them could d o about it.

Corey had n't slept a wink. That much was obvious just by looking at him. His responses were slower than they'd been the night before, like he was listening and respond ing from behind a veil that masked just enough of the sound that he had to take a few second s putting what he'd heard together before he could reply.

They'd given him a thin, and yet simultaneously lumpy, porrid ge for breakfast. He'd poked around at it, struggled through a few spoonfuls, then had settled for d rinking the mug of weak tea that had come along with it.

Now, fully d ressed and half-asleep, he sat listening as Logan went over most of what had been d iscussed the night before, for the benefit of the intense man with the moustache besid e him.

Dirk Sommercamp sat unmoving through the rapid recap, his gaze d rilling slowly into the red -and -black-haired younger man hunched in his chair on the other sid e of the table. It was the sort of stare Moof had been on the receiving end of once or twice before, usually from nutters in pubs, although those rarely had the same level of fiery intensity as this one had .

'So, you were obsessed with Alexis Riksen. You came onto her. She led you away somewhere private so as not to embarrass you when she told you she wasn't interested . She revealed who she was—who she really was—maybe in an attempt to put you off, knowing your environmental concerns, and then you snapped . You lured her out on the pretence of need ing to talk to her about something, then you d rugged her, strangled her, d ressed her in that t-shirt, poured oil on her, somehow contorted your bod y through a gap consid erably too small for it to physically pass through…'

Moof blinked . The solicitor frowned .

'Then you lowered a rope d own, passed through the same impossibly small gap again to tie the noose around her neck, then squeezed through two more times, once before and once after you hoisted her up the sid e of the monument.'

Logan sat back in his chair. He could feel Sommercamp's gaze shifting to him, but ignored it.

'Does that sound likely to you, son?' Logan asked .

Moof waited for the word s to be processed through the invisible veil of exhaustion, then shook his head . 'No.'

'No. Me neither,' Logan said . 'Can you pick locks, son?'

'What?'

'Can you pick locks?' Logan asked again.

'No.'

'No. Did n't think so. It's a rare skill in this d ay and age. Your average burglar will just put in a wind ow. It's not something officially taught by the polis, of course, but a few of us have picked it up over the years.' He turned to Sommercamp. 'What about the FBI? Training there cover lock picking?'

'How is that relevant?'

Logan stud ied his face for a moment, then d irected his attention across the table.

'Would you mind telling Mr Sommercamp here what you told Detective Inspector Ford e and I last night? About Hayd en Howard .'

Sommercamp quietly but firmly cleared his throat. 'Detective Chief Inspector Logan. A word .'

Logan held a hand up for silence, then pointed to Moof. 'Corey. Hayd en Howard . Please. Why was Alexis concerned about him?'

Moof's gaze flitted briefly from Logan to the man with the moustache. Last night, the DCI had been the scary one, and the other d etective with him had been much nicer. Now, though, the roles had changed , and the more familiar of the two men sitting across from him now felt like his only chance at safe harbour.

'She thought he was working for her d ad .'

'Bartholomew Riksen?' Logan prompted , earning a nod from Moof.

'She thought he was following her. Reporting back to her d ad about where she'd been and what she was d oing.'

'He was a spy, you mean?' Logan asked .

'Something like that, yeah.'

'This is lud icrous,' Sommercamp sighed . 'Even if she d id believe such a thing, how would you even know? Alexis had been keeping her id entity secret.'

'Not from me,' Moof protested . 'I knew for ages. She told me who she was after we first…'

The end of the sentence was left hanging. Logan finished for him.

'Slept together.'

Another nod .

'This is bullshit. He's lying,' Sommercamp snapped . 'You're lying.'

'I'm not! I'm not lying! It's why we got together. I mean, I think it's why. She hated what he was d oing. Her d ad , I mean. She d id n't hid e her id entity because she wanted to fool people, she d id it because she was ashamed of who she was. Of who is. Of what he's d one to the planet. To the Native Americans whose land he's d ug up for his pipes, and —'

'I'm not prepared to listen to this,' Sommercamp said , losing just a little more of his cool. 'These accusations are sland erous and without merit. You killed Alexis. We know you d id . She treated you with respect, and you repaid her by taking her life.'

'No! I d id n't!'

'Why d id you have her bag? Her passport? Her personal belongings?'

'Because she gave them to me!' Moof yelped . 'She was meant to come and   meet me. We were going to take a stand   together.'

Logan got a question in before Sommercamp had   a chance to blow his lid .

'A stand ? About what?'

'About her d ad 's company, how it's been covering up the environmental d amage it's been causing. Millions of acres of land   mad e sterile. Rivers so toxic nothing can survive. Child cancer rates skyrocketing in communities around   three of his sites.'

'This is nonsense,' Sommercamp barked . 'This is the same god d amn leftist propagand a we're combating back home. It's lies, all lies.'

'It's not! It's true! She had   all the information. We were going to tell the world ! Me and   her, together.'

Sommercamp shook his head , incred ulous. 'This is clearly a perverse fantasy of some kind . Some d elusional, hormonal teenage—'

'Why d id   she stay behind ?' Logan asked   Moof, turning a d eaf ear to the former FBI agent's protests. 'Why not go with you?'

'She...' Moof shifted   uncomfortably and   stole a look at his solicitor. She tipped   him the nod , her 'no comment' strategy having long-since gone out the wind ow. 'She was worried Hayd en was going to follow us. She had   a plan to stop him. Not permanently! She wasn't going to kill him, she just... she was going to expose him. Leave him for everyone to see. Send a message to her d ad , and   to the whole world , before Hayd en could   report in.'

'He wasn't reporting in to anyone!' Sommercamp insisted .

'We were going to say I'd   gone home. Hayd en had   seen us talking, and   we thought he was getting suspicious, so if everyone thought I'd   gone home, we thought it might take the heat off a bit,' Moof explained . 'She was going to give it a d ay, and   then...'

Again, the sentence fell away. Again, Logan stepped in to finish it.

'She was going to drug him and sneak away before he woke up.'

Moof nodded. 'And pour oil on him. Leave a note. Like… like a statement to her dad. We knew it would get us into trouble, but we didn't care if it struck a blow against her dad. But… Hayden must've found out, somehow. Must've…' Corey shifted, the thought of it turning his stomach and making his skin flush hot. '…stopped her.'

There was a knock at the door. Logan got up and opened it, briefly revealing DC Neish standing out in the corridor.

'Excuse me for a moment,' he said to the other occupants of the room, then he stepped outside and closed the door behind him.

Sommercamp used the time to glower at Moof across the table, his arms folded crisply across his chest, one foot tapping out a slow, steady rhythm on the floor.

The door opened again, but Logan didn't step inside. 'I'm sorry, Mr Sommercamp and I are going to have to step out. Detective Sergeant Khaled and Detective Inspector Forde will continue the interview.'

'I'm sorry?' Sommercamp said, turning in his chair. 'We're in the middle of—'

'Trust me, Mr Sommercamp,' Logan said, meeting the other man's gaze. 'You're going to want to see this.'

Chapter 37

It had n't been d ifficult to find Hayd en Howard in the end . H
was hid ing in plain sight.

A d og walker had spotted him. Well, technically the d og had
sniffed him out, and the walker had gone over to find out what
all the barking and fuss was about.

He lay between two bushes in the shad ow of the Glenfinnan
Viad uct, his legs twisted and mangled , his face an unrecognis-
able mush of sinew and flesh. A feast for the flies.

Logan, gloved and booted , squatted by the bod y, grateful that
it was lying in the great outd oors, and not in some confined ,
wind owless space with limited airflow.

Officially, he d id n't know for sure that this was Hayd en
Howard . With his face all but gone, how could he?

Unofficially, though, he had no d oubts about the bod y's
id entity. It just fit. It was the only thing that mad e sense.

Cause of d eath? Some extreme blunt force trauma seemed
like a pretty safe bet, given the state of him. Shona Maguire
was alread y on the way d own, though, and would be able to
tell him with more certainty.

He'd have Geoff Palmer's company to look forward to, too.
As if the violent murd er of a young man wasn't enough bad
news for one d ay.

A few feet away, Dirk Sommercamp was rifling carefully
through the spilled contents of a rucksack that had been split
wid e open at the bottom. The shad e cast by the viad uct, and the
early hour of the d ay, meant visibility was limited , but he held a
small pocket torch in his mouth, and d irected that into the bag

as he squatted to examine the clothing, sleeping bag, and other assorted items that had been strewn across the heather.

'Detective Chief Inspector,' he said , after just a few second s of searching.

Logan turned on his haunches to find Sommercamp now hold ing his torch in one hand , pointing with it at an item that was half-hid d en beneath the prickly branches of a gorse bush.

It was a beanie style hat. Bright red .

'Your witness. Mr Hill? He d escribed someone with red hair or a red hat walking near the scene of the crime, correct?'

'He d id ,' Logan confirmed .

Sommercamp crouched d own by the backpack itself. Taking a pen from his pocket, he lifted the torn flap of fabric, allowing him to shine his torch insid e.

'Uh-huh.'

'Something else?'

'I'd say so, yes.'

The former FBI man stepped asid e, still hold ing the flap open with his pen. Logan carefully picked his way across the d amp ground and peered into the opening.

'Look familiar?' Sommercamp asked .

It d id . Very much so.

It was a coil of rope, cut at one end . A perfect match, Logan had no d oubt, for the one that had been used to string Alexis up.

'Looks like I owe you an apology, Detective Chief Inspector,' Sommercamp said .

Logan sighed heavily. 'It's not me you owe the apology to, Dirk.'

Sommercamp nod d ed . 'Mr Sand erson. Yes. Him, too. I may have been a little… forceful.' He looked up at the viad uct looming far overhead . 'My hypothesis? He grabbed his bag and tried to follow your officer along the train line to spy on them. Unlike your officer and the young lad y he was talking with, however, Hayd en d id n't make it off the brid ge in time. The train collid ed   with him up there, knocking him over the ed ge, causing him to hit the ground   here.'

'Aye,   that   fits   perfectly,' Logan   agreed . 'Very   neat. Although… why would   he have been following them? You were so insistent he wasn't a spy earlier.'

'I said   he wasn't a spy *for us*. He may have been working for a competitor, perhaps. Alexis was a bright girl. If she thought he was watching her, then it's very probable that he was. All I can say for certain is that he wasn't und er Mr Riksen's employ.'

'And   you'd   testify to that, would   you?'

Sommercamp smiled   thinly. 'Of course. Whatever I can d o to help clear this whole mess up.'

Logan's phone buzzed   in his pocket. He checked   the screen, asked   Sommercamp to excuse him for a moment, then walked far enough back d own the hill to be out of the other man's earshot.

'Tyler. What have we got?'

He stood   and   listened , gazing out past the flapping cord on tape and   the row of parked   polis cars to where the Glen-finnan Monument stood   proud ly on the shore, and   beyond   that to where a d ozen or more black-throated   bird s skimmed   the choppy surface of Loch Shiel.

DC Neish had   quite a lot to report, as it happened . Between him, Sinead , and   Dave, they'd   had   a very prod uctive morning, and   it was still barely nine o'clock.

'Two d ays of solid   polis work in a row, son. Are you sure you're feeling all right?' Logan asked , once Tyler had   finished listing off their find ings. Then he d ished   out a couple of ord ers, asked   for the information to be texted   to him, and   hung up the phone.

That d one, he turned   and   looked   back up the hill to where Dirk Sommercamp stood   over the bod y of Hayd en Howard .

'Right, then,' Logan muttered , and   he set off on the climb with the breeze at his back, pushing him on.

'Everything all right?' Sommercamp asked , once Logan had huffed   and   puffed   his way back to the bod y.

'Half and half,' Logan replied . He looked back over his shoulder. The curve of the hill and the height of the bracken made it impossible to see the cordon, or the officers standing guard just beyond it.

The wind would mask a lot of the sound , too. Even if he shouted , it would be almost impossible for them to hear him.

It was risky doing this here. No support. No immediate backup.

Still, maybe he'd go quietly.

Aye, right.

'I'm afraid there was a bit of a flaw in your plan, Dirk,' he said .

Sommercamp raised a greying eyebrow. 'Plan?'

'Sorry, your *hypothesis*,' Logan corrected . 'Turns out, Hayden could n't possibly have been hit by that train.'

'Oh?'

'He made a phone call a few minutes after it passed . So, unless he tried to call for help as he lay there with no face and a shattered skeleton, I'm thinking he was alive and unhurt. Particularly given that we haven't seen his phone lying around here anywhere.'

'Yes, that does change things,' Sommercamp admitted . 'Another train, then? Perhaps he hid until later, tried to make his escape across the bridge, and —'

'See, I'd have asked who he called ,' Logan said , cutting him off.

Sommercamp's features subtly shifted . Logan could n't pinpoint what about them had changed exactly, but something about their arrangement had fractionally altered .

'Excuse me?' the American asked .

'If I was you, standing there, and someone told me that the prime suspect in my "hypothesis" made a call before he died , my first thought would be, "who to?" In fact, that was my very first question a moment ago to my colleague on the phone.'

Sommercamp's response was a half-second too slow, his voice a semi-tone higher than it should have been. 'Of course. That

275

would have been my next question.' His tongue flitted across his lips. 'And ?'

Logan prod uced his mobile. 'And he texted me through the number,' he said . 'Turns out Hayd en called this number regularly. Every two or three d ays, often very late at night. Over a d ozen times on the d ay Alexis's bod y was d iscovered . Suspicious that, eh?'

He and Sommercamp stood facing each other, a d ozen feet between them, should ers square and eyes locked like Old West d uelists about to d raw.

'Will we call it and see what happens?'

Sommercamp's eyes shifted to the phone in Logan's hand , then returned to meet the d etective's gaze. 'If you think it'll achieve anything,' he said . 'By all means, go ahead .'

'We'll soon find out,' Logan said , then he tapped the number in the text Tyler had sent him, and pressed the phone to his ear.

For a long moment, nothing happened , and then the ringing tone began to burr through the speaker. Logan's gaze flitted to roughly where Sommercamp's insid e jacket pocket would be, hoping to hear a correspond ing ringing coming from there.

He d id n't. Instead , the sound in his ear changed after a single ring, and a robotic voice informed him that the number he was calling was unable to take his call.

'No luck?' Sommercamp asked , seeing the d isappointment on Logan's face.

'Not yet,' Logan ad mitted . He tapped the screen again, listened until the ringing stopped again, then lowered the phone to his sid e. 'But we'll find out who owns the number.'

'I d oubt that very much,' Sommercamp said . 'I mean, if it were me… if I was somehow mixed up in all this, I'd have used a burner number and d isposed of it alread y.' Below his moustache, his lips curved upward s into a suggestion of a smile. 'Would n't you, Detective Chief Inspector?'

Logan was forced to conced e that yes, he would , and that, on balance, the phone number would probably turn out to be a d ead end .

'Shame,' Sommercamp said . 'I bet you really thought you were onto something.'

'I d id ,' Logan ad mitted . 'Still, one d oor closes, another opens, as they say.'

There it was again, that slight change to Sommercamp's expression. That fluctuation between *brazenly confident* and *momentarily concerned*.

'Meaning?'

'Meaning, other avenues of inquiry have opened up. You told DI Ford e on the phone that you and Mr Riksen were flying in, d id n't you, Dirk?' Logan said . 'Except, you d id n't fly in. You were alread y here when Mr Riksen's plane arrived . In fact, accord ing to what my colleagues back at the station were told by our friend s at the Home Office a few minutes ago, you've been in the country for some time, Dirk. Going on two months now.'

'Mr Riksen has been consid ering setting up a new base of operations here in the UK, and growing his investments in North Sea oil. He asked me to help with the research.'

'Not to spy on his d aughter, then?'

'Absolutely not,' Sommercamp replied . He stood his ground , feet planted , hand s relaxed by his sid es.

On the count of three, pardner...

'You want to hear my *hypothesis*, Dirk?' Logan asked .

The American gave a nod . 'Why not? I expect I'll find it highly entertaining.'

'I think Hayd en was reporting d irectly to you. I think he found out that Alexis and Corey were planning their big exposé, and you d ecid ed to put a stop to it. You found a way to d rug Alexis, killed her, and then tried to frame it as some act of environmental terrorism to help your boss out with all that— what d id you call it? "Leftist propagand a" he's d ealing with back home. After all, how can these tree-hugging nutters be the good guys if they'd string up an innocent lassie like that? Riksen would be a man in mourning, und er siege by the same

277

lunatic hippie fringe mob who murdered his daughter. Public support for him would shoot up. And, I mean, I don't know much about the stock market, but I'm betting all those good vibes wouldn't hurt the share price, either.'

Sommercamp laughed drily. 'That's very creative.'

'I'm not finished.' Logan gestured down at Hayden's remains. 'He was a loose end. Either he knew what you'd done, or he suspected. Whatever. First chance he got, he grabbed his stuff, and he called you. Was he asking for you to pick him up, or telling you he was out?'

Sommercamp smiled and shrugged. 'This is your story, Detective Chief Inspector. You tell me.'

'Either way, doesn't matter,' Logan said. 'You knew that him doing a runner was going to draw suspicion. You couldn't have him mouthing off, so you took care of him, planted evidence on him, and staged his death to look like an accident. Maybe you'd put out a press release later saying he was working for a competitor, like you tried to tell me, or maybe you'd try to pin him as part of the outraged environmentalist lobby.'

'That would be sensible,' Sommercamp said. 'Were it not so absurd.'

'I don't think it's absurd, Dirk. I think it's probably pretty bang-on the money.'

'I'm sure you do. But let me give you some friendly advice. Professional to professional. Hell, man to man,' Sommercamp said. The wind swirled around them, making the heather dance at their feet. 'If you are seriously going to suggest that I had something to do with Alexis's murder, then I would say this: tread lightly, Mr Logan. Were you seriously to propose your ludicrous theory, I would not take such a hurtful and upsetting accusation lightly. And —lest I need remind you—I am an extremely capable adversary.'

He took a step closer. The breeze bowed the bracken, until it lowered its head in deference.

'Whoever you've dealt with before—whatever you've faced, Mr Logan—it has *nothing* on me. And none of it had the resources that I have at my disposal.'

'Aye, maybe. But would you still have all those resources if your boss thought you'd murdered his wee girl, though?' Logan asked. 'That's the question.'

'Then allow me to furnish you with the answer to that question. Mr Riksen demands the utmost loyalty from his employees, and he grants us the same in return. You have no evidence to connect me to Alexis's death. None. Mr Riksen would support me in refuting any and all baseless allegations you might foolishly choose to make against me.'

Logan nodded slowly. 'Maybe. Aye. I suppose that would make life difficult, right enough,' he said. 'Except... you're wrong.'

'I highly doubt that,' Sommercamp said, but that flicker was there again on his face, eroding the look of smug self-satisfaction that had been there a split-second before. He couldn't help but ask the question. 'Wrong about what?'

'About us having no evidence,' Logan said. He smiled. It was cheerful and relaxed, and designed to be as irritating as possible. 'We do.'

Sommercamp snorted, but there was just a suggestion of uncertainty to it. 'I highly doubt that, also.'

Logan shrugged. 'Doubt what you like. We have two eyewitnesses who can place you near the scene around the time that Alexis was murdered.'

The FBI man shifted his weight from one foot to the other. 'Impossible.'

'You probably remember passing them, actually. Big van, painted like the one out of Scooby-Doo. Hard to miss it, even at that time in the morning,' Logan said. 'Turns out they had a dashcam fitted. Good one, too. Caught your car registration in full-colour HD when you went barrelling past them on the lochside.'

'That's not true,' Sommercamp said .

'Overtaking—d rawing attention to yourself like that? Bold move, given what you'd just d one,' Logan said . 'They told DC Neish they were d oing about sixty when you came flying past them. Eighty, they reckoned , given by how quickly you pulled away.'

'They're lying. That wasn't me.'

'Aye, it was,' Logan told him.

'No, it—'

'The bad ge was the thing that gave you away, in case you were wond ering.'

Sommercamp frowned , confused by this sud d en change in d irection. 'Bad ge?'

'Before the interview. You said that we'd found Corey's bad ge at the scene. You could n't possibly have known that.'

'It was in the report.' Sommercamp was starting to sound exasperated now, his cool exterior sud d enly plagued by jerky arm movements and twitches.

'The bad ge was, aye. The fact that it belonged to Corey wasn't. Because, well, frankly we d id n't know. We still d on't. And yet somehow you d id know, Dirk. And the only way you could 've known that is if you planted it there.'

'This is—'

'Right before you went speed ing off, and were caught on the d ashboard camera of some early morning campers head ing home to beat the rush.'

'I alread y told you, that wasn't me!' Sommercamp insisted , spitting the word s out like they were poison in his throat.

'Yes, it was!' Logan said , raising his voice and jabbing across the gap at him with a finger. 'We know it was you. We've got your number plate, Dirk!'

'That's impossible!' Sommercamp yelled back.

'It's right there on camera!'

'It can't be! *I wasn't driving my own car!*'

Logan saw the moment, near the end of the sentence, when Sommercamp tried to stop himself. It was too late by then, though. There was no stopping the word s in time.

When Logan spoke, his voice was calmer. Less antagonistic. There was no need for the shouting now. He'd got what he need ed .

'There,' he said . 'Doesn't that feel better?'

Sommercamp said nothing. He just stood there, his lips pressed together like he was worried about what else might come tumbling out between them.

'You used a hire car from a local company. Took it out und er a fake name, using forged d ocuments.'

Sommercamp looked d own at his feet. His should ers heaved .

'No point crying over spilt milk, Dirk,' Logan told him.

'I'm not crying, you id iot,' Dirk replied . He raised his head to show the laughter lines creasing his face. 'We're in the mid d le of nowhere. Just me and you. You still d on't have any evid ence. Sure, you can try the rental company, but I assure you, they will not be able to link me to the transaction, and you won't find any DNA evid ence in the vehicle. The *hypothesis* you're proposing comes d own to my word against yours, and that won't stand up in a court of law. Not with the lawyers we can afford .'

Logan consid ered the FBI man's remarks for a moment. 'I mean… I can probably…' he said , grasping at straws.

Sommercamp laughed . 'It's a shame, really. You came so close. I'm almost impressed . But… you knew from before the bad ge, d id n't you?'

Logan nod d ed to confirm that he d id .

'The hatch?' Sommercamp guessed .

'The hatch. Aye. You corrected me when I mentioned the size of it,' Logan told him. 'That set alarm bells ringing.'

'Good spot,' Sommercamp said . 'I realised right away that I'd said too much. Wasn't sure anyone had picked up on it, though.'

'Aye, well, we're smarter than we look,' Logan said . 'Some of us, anyway.'

Sommercamp approached him, patted him on the should er, then started to make his way d own the hill. 'Just not quite smart enough, I guess.'

Logan waited until the other man was a few feet away, then raised the phone to his ear again. 'You get all that, Detective Constable Neish?'

Sommercamp stopped .

'Got it, boss. Had you on speakerphone, just like you said ,' came the reply in Logan's ear.

'Good for you, son. We'll see you shortly. Get a cell read y, eh? I'll be bringing a guest.'

'On it, boss,' Tyler replied , then Logan terminated the call and slipped the phone into his pocket.

'Like I said . We're smarter than we look.'

Sommercamp had n't moved . Had n't turned . When he spoke, his voice was like d ry autumn leaves. 'So, what happens now?'

'Now, I place you und er arrest. I've alread y got my team bringing Mr Riksen into the station. They'll all be waiting for us.'

'He wasn't involved . Not d irectly. He wanted me to look out for Alexis. Make sure she wasn't hanging out with the wrong crowd . That's all. He d id n't even know about...' Sommercamp gestured behind him to the remains of Hayd en Howard . 'He was employed by me personally. Mr Riksen had no involvement with him, and played no part in Alexis's d eath. I want to make that crystal clear.'

Logan nod d ed to say he und erstood . 'You weren't kid d in about the loyalty thing, eh?' he said .

'My fate is inconsequential. The company is all that matters,' Sommercamp proclaimed , d rawing himself up to his full height.

'Jesus, is it a company or a cult?' Logan asked . He took a few steps d own the hill until he was within grabbing d istance of Sommercamp. 'Now, are you going to walk nicely, Dirk, or am I going to have to—?'

Something hit him. A fist. An elbow. A brick. He wasn't sure, it all happened so quickly, and the impact was so jarring that his brain was unable to fully process it.

Logan stumbled back, blood gushing from his nose, eyes streaming with tears.

'Rear horizontal elbow strike, Krav Maga. Learned it in Israel,' Dirk said, turning to face the semi-blinded DCI.

Logan was dimly aware of another flurry of movement, and brought his hands up to defend himself. Too late. A knee was driven into his stomach, and all the air left him in a single bloody cough.

'Hiza Geri. Japan,' Sommercamp said, as Logan sunk to one knee, his lungs cramping and his head going light.

BAM! Another strike caught him out of nowhere, spinning him onto his front in the bracken.

'Wang Phek Choui. Tibet.'

The world spun as Logan heaved himself over onto his back. He wiped away the blood and the tears in time to see Sommercamp bending over him, his hands reaching for the detective's throat.

'I warned you to tread lightly, Detective Chief Inspector. I didn't want this to happen. I didn't want any of this. Now I'm going to have to kill you. Then I'll slip away, step into one of the many identities I have prepared for such a scenario, and jump on the first plane to—'

Logan threw himself upwards, driving his forehead into Sommercamp's nose. Blood erupted, and Sommercamp howled, grabbing at the injury with both hands.

'Kiss. Glasgow,' Logan wheezed, then he brought up a foot and slammed it into the smaller man's groin with enough force to lift him off his feet. 'Boot to the bollocks. Primary School.'

He tried to get up, but the world was spinning too far and too fast, and he flopped down onto his back.

Sommercamp was down, too, the explosive force of Logan's foot having lodged his testes somewhere around his upper abd omen. The bastard would be up and about soon, though, and so Logan gritted his teeth, raised himself up onto his elbows, then let out a strangled sob of relief when he saw three Uniforms coming barrelling up the hill toward s them.

'Oh. Thank fuck for that,' he muttered , then he let his head flop back, closed his eyes, and let the world spiral in circles around him.

Chapter 38

Logan led Sommercamp through the front door of the station in handcuffs, right through the pack of media jackals gathered in the car park.

There were very few questions when they first emerged from the marked polis car, the journalists too stunned by the state of them to speak.

It didn't last, of course, and Logan pointedly ignored every question as he placed a hand on the back of Sommercamp's neck and physically steered him towards the station entrance.

Moira Corson peered over her glasses at Logan and his prisoner as they entered, her face fixed in a mask of disapproval. Logan stopped in front of the main desk, his own face a mask of shiny wet blood, crispy dried blood, and grim satisfaction.

The prisoner whose neck was almost entirely encircled by the detective's hand was slightly less blood-soaked, but appeared to be having more difficulty walking.

'All right, Moira?' Logan asked. 'Any chance you could sign us in? I'm all...' He held up his hands to reveal they were equally as bloodied as his face. 'Wouldn't want to make a mess of your nice book.'

Moira hurriedly waved them both out of her sight and pressed the button that buzzed open the door. Logan smiled his appreciation, showing his red teeth, then he manhandled Sommercamp in the direction of the door and marched him through it.

The thought of the stairs was a d aunting one, but Logan knew Sommercamp—still suffering the effects of Logan's groin-kick—would enjoy it even less, so they bypassed the lift and huffed and panted up the steps until they reached the first floor, where they were met by Tyler, Sinead , and —behind them— Bartholomew Riksen.

'Jesus Christ, boss. What happened ?' Tyler gasped . 'Did you crash the car on the way here or something?'

'Mr Sommercamp got a bit frisky,' Logan said .

'What with, a sled gehammer, sir?' Sinead asked .

The interview room d oor opened a little further along the corrid or, and Ben stepped out. 'Blood y hell, Jack. Were you in a car crash?' he asked , when he clapped eyes on the two blood - soaked men.

'That's what I said , boss,' Tyler told him.

Riksen tutted impatiently and shoved his way past Tyler and Sinead . Behind him, Corey Sand erson and his solicitor joined Ben in the corrid or, with Hamza poking his head out to see what was going on.

'Dirk. What they've said … the things they've told me…' Riksen began. His voice faltered . It was the first note of real emotion Logan had heard from the billionaire since his arrival. 'Is it true?'

Sommercamp kept his head d own, his gaze averted .

'I asked you a question,' Riksen said , his tone becoming sterner. 'Is it true what they told me? Did you kill Alexis?'

The whole corrid or seemed to hold its breath, until the silence became so heavy and oppressive that Sommercamp was forced to break it.

'I d id it for the company, Mr Riksen,' he whispered . 'I d id it to protect your business.'

Riksen's face fell. Not into sad ness, or grief, but into some-thing blank and d etached . Something removed from the here and now, from this place and this time. Something not quite all the way human.

'Wait. *He* killed Hermione?' said Corey.

Riksen stepped back, reached behind him, and sud d enly a snub-nosed revolver was there in the space in front of him, barrel pointed squarely at the centre of Sommercamp's chest.

'Shite. Gun!' Tyler warned with a yelp.

Logan managed to keep his voice somewhat stead ier than the d etective constable's. 'Aye, we can all see that, son,' he said . 'Mr Riksen, I und erstand why you think you want to d o this, but believe me, you d on't. Not really.'

Riksen's gaze was firmly locked on his target, who was regard ing the gun with a sort of casual d isinterest. If the billionaire even heard Logan's word s, he d id n't show it.

The DCI continued , regard less.

'We've got him. Fair and square. He's going to go to jail for what he's d one, Mr Riksen. He's going to be punished .'

Riksen's finger twitched on the trigger. With the gun in his hand and the Stetson on his head , he looked every inch the cowboy.

Logan saw Sinead shuffle closer, and gave just the briefest shake of his head , warning her not to try anything stupid .

'I've got a d aughter, Mr Riksen. Old er than Alexis, but not by much. Someone tried to… hurt her recently. They were going to kill her.'

'But they d id n't?' Riksen said through his gritted , immaculately white teeth.

'No. No, they d id n't.'

'Then shut your d amn mouth. You have no id ea what I'm going through.'

Logan shrugged . 'Fine. Then shoot him, if you like,' he said . 'In your shoes, I might be tempted myself. Hell, in *my* shoes, I'm tempted myself. But here's the thing. That's it, then. He becomes the victim, and you become the killer. You're the one arrested . You're the one in jail.'

'So be it,' Riksen said . His gaze still had n't moved from Sommercamp. The hand hold ing the gun had n't trembled . Not once.

'Your daughter's body will be flown home without you. She'll be buried without you. Her grave will be tended by people who didn't know her. People who didn't really love her. Not like you knew her. Not the way you loved her.'

There was no immediate response to that from the man with the gun.

'We've got him, Mr Riksen. We did this much. Let us do the rest,' Logan urged. 'Let us put him away for what he did.'

And there it was—a tremble. A shaking of the hand that made the gun sway just a fraction.

'She was my baby girl,' Riksen said, his voice breaking. 'She was my sweet, innocent, baby girl.'

Sommercamp shook his head. Impressive, considering Logan was still holding him by the back of the neck.

'N-no, sir. She was working against you. Against the company. She was going to betray you. I had to do it. I had to.'

'Shut up!' Riksen hissed, eyes so wide they threatened to pop right out of their sockets.

'I'd do what he says, Dirk,' Logan urged.

The gun trembled. 'She was a *child*! What could she have done?'

'No! No, not a child, Mr Riksen, not a child,' Sommercamp babbled, gaze flitting between his boss's face and the dark hollow at the end of the gun. 'Alexis was... she was pregnant! She was pregnant! It was in the report!'

'What?' The question came from further along the corridor. Moof sagged against the wall, and had to raise a hand to stop himself falling the rest of the way. 'What did he say?'

'Pregnant?' Riksen muttered, frowning like he didn't understand the word's meaning. 'How could she be...? But she was just...'

'She wasn't who you thought she was, Mr Riksen,' Sommer-camp insisted. 'She was going to bring everything you built crashing down around you. She was going to destroy everything

288

you'd worked for. I had to stop her. God knows, I didn't want to, sir, but it was the only way to protect you. To protect the company.'

'Let's discuss his fucked-up motives later, will we, Mr Riksen?' Logan suggested. 'For now, how about you just put down the gun?'

The weapon shook again. Riksen's tanned face crumpled like old leather, and Logan braced himself for the shot.

It didn't come. With a sob, Riksen let his arm drop to his side, and the corridor itself seemed to heave a sigh of relief.

'Thank you, sir,' Sommercamp whispered, a tear of relief rolling down his cheek. 'Thank you.'

There was a flurry of movement from behind Tyler and Sinead. Logan saw Ben throw himself forward, arm grasping too late for Moof, as he went thundering along the corridor.

'No!' Logan bellowed, as the world wound down into agonising slow motion.

Moof knocked Tyler aside, sending him crashing into Sinead.

He grabbed the gun, wrenched it from Riksen's fingers.

His arm came up. His finger twitched.

The noise was overwhelming in the narrow confines of the corridor. Logan could only close his eyes and brace himself as Sommercamp slammed backwards into him, the burnt-match stench of sulphur dioxide swirling in the air.

The former FBI agent stumbled and fell, breath burbling through the hole in his chest, his eyes already glassing over.

The gun hit the floor with a thunk. Corey Sanderson stood there, his hand still outstretched, tears cutting tracks down his cheeks.

'He killed her,' Moof croaked. 'He killed her, and … and my baby.'

He fell, then, his legs giving away beneath him.

A pair of strong arms caught him and pulled him into a hug. 'It's OK, boy,' Riksen told him. 'It's OK. I've got you. I've got you.'

Chapter 39

The rest of the d ay was spent tid ying up the loose end s, putting the case to the Procurator Fiscal, and d ealing with the fallout of the shooting.

Riksen was being charged for bringing an illegal firearm into the country, but it was d ecid ed not to try pressing any further charges, given the man's emotional state and , frankly, the size of his legal team. CID was hand ling the case, and Logan was relieved to be rid of it.

Corey Sand erson wasn't so fortunate. He was charged with the murd er of Dirk Sommercamp, and given that it had been witnessed by five police officers, one solicitor, and an ind e-pend ent eyewitness, the case was pretty watertight.

Logan would push for the extenuating circumstances to be taken into account, of course, but ultimately, it was out of his hand s. Riksen was going to pay for his lawyer, though, so Moof might not end up spend ing the rest of his life behind bars, only the best years of it.

He'd gone up to meet Shona Maguire at the site where Hayd en Howard 's bod y had been found , and hung aroun d own by the road sid e while she'd d one her thing.

While waiting, he'd invented a fun way to pass the time, which largely involved shouting at tourists who'd parked their cars in stupid places until they got back in them and d rove away again. It was incred ibly cathartic, and he mad e a mental note to come back and d o it again whenever he was feeling stressed .

After Shona had finished , they'd grabbed a bite to eat at J.J.'s—two bacon rolls and a big slab of Maltesers cake between them—and he'd filled her in on what he could of the case. She'd almost cried when he'd told her about Moof. He'd almost felt like joining her.

'By the way, been meaning to say,' Shona said , eyeing up the last chunk of the d ense, chocolatey cake on the plate between them. 'You know your face is all mashed up, aye?'

'Aye, I'd noticed that, right enough,' Logan said , d aubing at the butterfly stitches that were hold ing his nose together. 'No' sure what happened there.'

'You be all right d riving up the road ?' Shona asked .

'Aye. Fine. Be head ing up soon, actually. The others are just sorting out the cottages. Trying to leave them looking presentable. No' easy when Hoon's spent time in them.'

'I've only met him once or twice,' Shona said . She rolled her fork between finger and thumb, the prongs pointing at the cake. 'He sound s like a blood y nightmare, though.'

'He is. Still, he has his moments,' Logan ad mitted . 'You can eat that, by the way. Some of us are watching our figure.'

'I've been watching your figure,' Shona said , then she replayed the word s in her head and gasped just as she shoved the piece of cake in her mouth, almost sucking it straight into her wind pipe. 'I mean… your weight loss,' she said , after several second s of coughing and two big back-slaps from the DCI. 'I've been noticing how well you're d oing. All that running's paying off.'

'You think?' Logan looked d own at himself. 'I was, eh, I was thinking of going for a wee jog tomorrow, actually. I hear the beach at Nairn is nice.'

Shona smiled . 'I've heard similar things. Mind if I join you?'

'If you think you can keep up.'

'Well, I was planning using both legs, so I'd imagine I'll be fine.'

Logan laughed . 'You're on,' he said , then they both turned as a portly red -faced man got up from a neighbouring table, slammed his d irty d ishes onto his tray, then stormed past them.

'You off, Geoff?' Shona asked .

Geoff Palmer thunked his tray d own on the counter, sniffed loud ly, and turned . 'Yes, actually. I need to get d one sharp, so I can get back up the road to meet a lad y friend , if you must know.' He had n't yet looked at Logan, and showed absolutely no intentions of d oing so. 'Do you want a lift back home, Shona? Plenty of room.'

Shona sid e-eyed the DCI across the table. 'Well, I mean, I d rove d own myself, so it would mean leaving my car here...'

'Which would n't really make sense,' Logan ad d ed .

'No. It would n't really make sense,' Shona agreed . She smiled at the Scene of Crime investigator and raised her half-finished cup of tea. 'Cheers for the offer,' she said , then she slid her hand across the table, and to Logan's d elight and surprise, interlocked her fingers with his own. 'But I'm fine.'

–

'So, eh, sorry.'

Sinead finished tying a knot in the top of the black bag, then looked over at the kitchen d oorway. 'For what?'

'You know what,' Tyler said .

Sinead pulled an exaggerated look of confusion and shook her head . 'No.'

Tyler sighed . She was actually going to make him say it. 'For being an arse. For asking you to marry me when—like you said —I clearly wasn't in the best frame of mind .'

'Oh.' Sinead pulled the bag out of the plastic bin. 'That.'

'Aye, that,' Tyler said . He held a hand out and she thrust the neck of the bag into it. 'I d id n't mean to go in the huff.'

'You totally went in the huff,' Sinead teased .

'Yes, that's what I'm saying,' Tyler said . 'But I d id n't mean to.'

'Buuuut you d id .' She jabbed him in the ribs with a finger, making him jump. 'But I'll let you off. I mean, being shot d own in flames like that... ouch. I'd have been mortified .'

'You'd think. But it's only, like, the fourth most embarrassing thing that's happened to me in the last year,' Tyler replied. 'At least you weren't physically sick on me.'

Sinead smiled. 'Give it time.'

There was a moment of uncomfortable laughter that eventually fell away into an equally uncomfortable silence.

'What the hell's that supposed to mean?' Tyler asked.

Sinead shook her head, visibly cringing. 'I have no id ea. It was just out of me before I knew what I was saying,' she ad mitted.

Tyler grinned. 'Tell you what, I won't mention that again, if you d on't mention my blubbering mess of a proposal. All right?'

'Deal,' Sinead said, hold ing her hand out for him to shake. Instead, he passed her the black bag back.

'Nice one. Now, I d on't know what you hand ed me that for. I d on't d o rubbish. Smell makes me gag.'

Sinead laughed, shook her head, then leaned over and kissed him, the bin bag crinkling as it was squashed between them.

'I thought I told you two,' came Ben's voice from out in the cottage's hallway. 'No blood y funny business!'

-

After the cleanup, they all assembled outsid e the cottages, just as Logan returned.

'Funny that, you showing up after all the hard work's d one, Jack,' Ben remarked.

'Oh, are you finished?' Logan asked, with an impressive d isplay of innocence. 'I d id n't know. I was on my way back to give you a hand.'

'My arse,' Dave said, and there was a general murmuring of agreement over this well-mad e point.

'We all fit, then?' Logan asked, ind icating the line of cars parked outsid e. There were four of them—Ben's, Sinead 's, and Tyler's, with Logan's car plonked at the back. Logan looked over at Dave and Hamza. 'Either of you coming with me?'

Both men shifted their gaze from Logan's small Fiesta to Ben's big Volvo.

'Definitely not, sir, no,' Hamza said , after just a moment's consid eration.

'See if I care, ya bastard s,' Logan replied with a scowl. 'You'll no' get there any quicker in that thing, you know?'

'No, but we won't have our chins resting on our knees the whole way, either,' Dave pointed out.

After some good byes, and an instruction from Logan for them to take the evening off, d rivers and passengers got into their respective vehicles. Logan watched them all pull away, took a final glance at the holid ay cottages to make sure Hoon had n't smeared any obscenities in excrement over the exterior walls when no one was looking, and then wrestled the Fiesta's fid d ly gearstick into first and joined the convoy of his colleagues on the long, wind ing road going north.

Chapter 40

Hoon d id n't answer the d oor when Logan arrived at his house that evening. The lights were on, and he could hear some 80s rock ballad playing from somewhere, but the front d oor was locked .

Logan walked around the front of the d etached house, cupped his hand s at a couple of wind ows and peered insid e. The living room was a mess of d irty plates and strewn clothing, but the takeaway tubs and beer cans had been tid ied away, and some vague attempt had been mad e to at least stack the crockery into a couple of uneven, teetering piles in the centre of the coffee table.

Following the music, Logan continued around the sid e of the house. The wind ows there were in d arkness, the curtains d rawn.

He carried on, led by the glam-rock stylings *Skid Row,* or the *Scorpions,* or *Europe,* or whoever the hell it was being blared out.

As he d rew closer to the back of the house, Logan heard a series of fast, powerful thwacks and the hissing of several quick breaths.

He stopped at the corner, and peered around into the back-yard area of Hoon's house. A security spotlight shone d own on a wood en frame with a heavy punchbag hanging from it. Hoon stood before it, feet planted , d ucking and weaving and throwing jabs with hand s bound by strips of band age.

Each high punch he threw sent the heavy bag spinning on its chain. Every low blow buckled the bag's mid d le, making it flop erratically back and forth, and forcing him to block it with a hand or a knee.

'You just going to fucking stand there?' Hoon asked, without turning. 'Or are you going to come and hold this bastarding thing?'

There was no reply. Hoon steadied the bag and turned to where he expected to find Logan watching him. Instead, there was only empty darkness.

Hoon gave a low grunt, then he cranked up his stereo, blasted 80s metal into the night, and went right back to throwing punches.

-

The following morning, Tyler was waiting for Sinead outside the station entrance. He waved to her as she pulled into the car park, clicked his fingers and pointed finger guns at her as she got out of the car, then waited awkwardly while she made the thirty-second walk to the front door.

'Everything all right?' she asked. 'There's not another case already, is there?'

'No. No, nothing like that. I just...' Tyler took a deep breath. 'I wanted to say sorry. Before we went in. I wanted to apologise.'

Sinead smiled at him. 'It's fine. You apologised. Nothing to be sorry for.'

Tyler turned and led her in through the station's front door. 'Aye, I'm not apologising for the other night,' he said. He swallowed, and let out a tiny puff of the breath he'd been holding in. 'I'm saying sorry in advance. For this.'

They stopped just inside the reception area. The whole team was there. Logan, dressed in shorts and t-shirt, with two black eyes and a nose so swollen he was barely recognisable as human, let alone as himself. Beside him were Ben, Hamza, and Dave, all assembled in a line. Even Detective Superintendent Mitchell was there, although to be fair, she did look quite confused as to why.

'What's going on?' Sinead began to ask, then from the corner of her eye she saw Tyler lower himself d own onto one knee.

'I wanted them all here to back me up,' he said . 'So you'd know I wasn't mental, or having a breakd own, or d oing something I'd later regret. Because they're always the first to tell me if I'm being an id iot.'

'We just take it as read that you usually are, son,' Logan remarked .

'Especially him,' Tyler said , jabbing a thumb back over his should er. 'But they all agree that this… what I'm d oing now… this isn't me being an id iot. Far from it.'

'Tyler…'

'I d on't care if you say no,' Tyler said , cutting her short. 'Well, I mean, I d o obviously. But I won't mind . Because I have to tell you. I have to put it out there for you, and all these other bastard s to hear… which seemed like a good id ea at the time, but now I think about it…'

'Just get on with it, son,' Ben told him. 'The lassie's no' got all blood y d ay.'

'Shut up, I was nearly hit by a train!' Tyler shot back over his should er.

'Aye, no' nearly enough,' Hamza remarked .

'I love you, Sinead ,' Tyler said . 'More than anything. I want us to spend the rest of our lives together. Me, you. Harris.'

Tears sprang to Sinead 's eyes so sud d enly she snorted out a laugh. 'Just until he's old enough to piss off.'

Tyler smiled . 'Aye. Just until he's old enough to piss off. Don't really want him und er our feet when he's fifty, like.'

'Id eally not, no!'

Logan leaned closer to Ben. 'Do these things usually take so blood y long?' he asked in a stage whisper.

'Be quiet, Detective Chief Inspector,' Mitchell told him. 'That's an ord er.' She met Sinead 's eye, gave her a smile and the briefest of nod s, then stood back to watch the show.

'I'm not shell-shocked . I'm not suffering PTSD. I'm not bawling my eyes out,' Tyler said . 'I'm just me. Here. In front of all these arseholes. Asking you if you'll make me the happiest man in the world and marry me?'

Sinead sniffed, ran a hand d own her face, then shrugged. 'Ah, what the hell?' she said . 'Go on, then.'

A cheer went up. Tyler sprang to his feet. There were hugs, tears, laughter, and the od d 'I thought he was never going to get to the blood y point' type remark from the assembled aud ience.

'Right, then, let's see the ring,' said Mitchell, after the congratulatory back-slapping and hugging had subsid ed .

Tyler's face fell. 'Ring? Shite. Aye.'

'Jesus Christ, Tyler. You d id n't bring a ring?' Logan said .

'I d id n't know if she was going to say yes!' Tyler protested . He shot Sinead a sid eways look. 'We can go ring shopping later. Can't we? Then you can pick something that...'

'Here.'

Tyler stopped talking. A hush fell over the reception as DI Ford e unhooked a thin silver chain from around his neck and held it out to DC Neish. Two rings hung from the chain—a simple gold wed d ing band , and an engagement ring with a brilliant blue stone.

'Oh, boss, I can't—'

'Aye, you can, son,' Ben told him. 'Alice would want you to. *I* want you to.'

'But, sir—' Sinead began.

'Neither of you knew Alice well,' Ben said , cutting her off. 'But Jack will tell you, she wasn't a woman to take "no" for an answer.'

'You can say that again,' Logan remarked .

'And nor am I,' said Ben. 'I mean... obviously, I'm no' a woman... I'm not saying... you know what I mean. Just take the blood y engagement ring.'

Tyler accepted the chain, removed the engagement ring, and then passed the rest of the jewellery back to Ben. He kept his hand held on top of the old er d etective's for a moment, and they shared a nod of und erstand ing.

Then he turned , took hold of Sinead 's offered hand , and slipped the ring on her finger.

It immed iately slipped off again.

'Aye, she was a bigger lass, Alice,' Ben remarked , as Tyler caught the ring and tried again. 'You can probably get it ad justed …'

Soon, they all head ed upstairs to get stuck into 'the wee spread ' that Hamza's wife had prepared after Tyler had phoned him to tell him the plan the night before. Everyone got stuck in, with the exception of Logan, who had a running d ate, and Ben, who wasn't a big fan of anything too spicy, and settled for half a packet of chocolate d igestives, instead .

Half an hour later, when many embarrassing stories had been shared at Tyler's expense, Logan said his good byes, d ished out two big bear hugs, and left.

He mad e it to the corrid or before Detective Superintend ent Mitchell appeared behind him.

'Jack? A quick word ?'

Logan groaned inward ly, glanced pointed ly at his watch, then turned to face his superior officer. 'Ma'am?'

'Good work again. You know, apart from your main suspect being shot d ead .'

'Aye, that wasn't id eal,' Logan ad mitted . 'But thank you. Team effort, though, as always.'

Mitchell looked out of the corrid or wind ow at the car park. 'I've been thinking. How's the Fiesta treating you?'

'About as bad ly as you'd expect, thanks for asking,' Logan told her.

'Interested in an upgrad e?' the Detective Superintend ent asked .

Logan's ears pricked up. 'An upgrad e? Aye. Definitely.'

'Excellent. Glad to hear it,' Mitchell said . From behind her back, she prod uced a small hanging air freshener shaped like a tree. 'There. You've earned it.'

Logan stared impassively at the air freshener for a moment, then chuckled . 'You spoil me, ma'am,' he said , accepting the offered gift. 'You really d o.'

Then, with the smell of young love and forest pine d rifting through the air around him, DCI Jack Logan head ed d own the stairs, and out into the blustery city beyond .

Penguin Random House LLC
1745 Broadway
US-NY, 10019
US
https://www.penguinrandomhouse.com
1-800-733-3000

The authorized representative in the EU for product safety and compliance is

Penguin Random House Ireland
Morrison Chambers, 32 Nassau Street
D02 YH68
IE
https://eu-contact.penguin.ie

ISBN: 9798217261277
Release ID: 154078558